Her Only Desire

Her Only Desire

Gaelen Foley

W F HOWES LTD

This large print edition published in 2008 by
W F Howes Ltd
Unit 4, Rearsby Business Park, Gaddesby Lane,
Rearsby, Leicester LE7 4YH

1 3 5 7 9 10 8 6 4 2

First published in the United Kingdom in 2007
by Piatkus Books Ltd.

ISBN 978 1 40741 223 8

Typeset by Palimpsest Book Production Limited,
Grangemouth, Stirlingshire
Printed and bound in Great Britain
by Antony Rowe Ltd, Chippenham, Wilts.

ACKNOWLEDGMENTS

I owe a lot of people thanks for helping me to shape this book into what it needed to be, most of all my insightful editor, Charlotte Herscher, who always seems to know what's needed, and my eagle-eyed agent, Nancy Yost, for her excellent suggestions on a few story points, as well. I would also like to thank author Meredith Bond for her gracious and unstinting help with my research on India, my dear friends and fellow authors Marjorie Allen and 'Angel' Kihlstrom, and my favorite military historian, Bill Haggert, for providing me with some hard-to-find details on the Regulars in India during this period. Any mistakes that may arise are entirely my own.

CHAPTER 1

India, 1817

Beneath a bold sky of peacock blue, the sun-baked city of Calcutta unfurled along a palm-lined meander of the Hooghly River like a living tapestry, or a rich silk shawl that billowed on a spice-laden breeze.

Flocks of birds swirled around the curving spires of ancient Hindu temples, under whose profusely carven gateways worshipers in flower-bright robes bathed on the stone steps leading down to the water. The noisy bazaar also hugged the misty riverside, a tumult of haggling, jumbled stalls and tents offering everything from Afghan carpets to aphrodisiacs made of rhinoceros horn.

Farther away from the crowded banks, the river bustled with all the teeming commercial activity of the British capital of India. Monopolies long held by the East India Company had just been lifted; there were fortunes to be made, and now it was anyone's game. Merchants and traders all along the docks loaded square-rigged vessels with their goods, bound for distant worlds.

Amid all of this chaos and exuberance, a low-slung schooner docked quietly.

A tall, formidable Englishman stood leaning at the rails with his hands planted wide, his chiseled jaw taut. His imposing size, hawk-eyed stillness, and the gentlemanly reserve of his London attire distinguished him from the commotion as the grubby, barefoot sailors raced around behind him at their tasks, dropping anchor, taking in sails.

Dark-haired, with stern, patrician features, his gray-green eyes gleamed with intelligence as he searched the quay-side panorama in guarded watchfulness, taking it all in, and brooding on his mission . . .

Each year, by the end of September, when the torrential rains of monsoon tapered off and the skies cleared, and the churning floodwaters receded, then came the season of blood: the season of war. Even now, the drums beat; many miles away, the armies gathered.

October had come. The drying ground would soon harden enough for caisson wheels and cavalry charges. Soon the killing would start.

Unless he could stop it.

Looking slowly over one broad shoulder, Ian Prescott, the Marquess of Griffith, scanned the riverboats nearby, well aware that he was being followed.

Well, nothing new in that. He had not yet glimpsed his pursuer, but in his line of work, a man developed a sixth sense about such things or

2

he didn't last long. No matter. He was harder to kill than the average courtier, a fact that assassins in several foreign courts had learned, to their woe.

Concealed inside his impeccably tailored clothes he carried a discreet arsenal of weapons; besides, the rival colonial powers in the region could not assassinate a diplomat of his rank without causing an international incident.

Still, it would be nice to know who was tailing him.

French? he mused. Likeliest suspects, as ever, though he could not rule out the Dutch, much aggrieved by the recent loss of Ceylon to the British. The Portuguese maintained a strong presence at Goa. No doubt all three had agents out trying to learn what the British were up to.

If the spy had been sent by the Maharajah of Janpur, well, that was another matter, and made for a slightly more unpredictable affair. But whoever it was, if they meant to kill him, he thought, they would have tried by now.

He'd simply have to watch his back and take it as it came.

As the gangplank banged down onto the stone ghats leading up from the water, Ian beckoned to his trio of Indian servants, stole one last, casual glance over his shoulder, and then went ashore.

His black boots struck the gangplank hard with his every brisk stride, small spring-bolted blades hidden inside the leather soles. His silver-handled walking stick contained a sword, and strapped beneath his muted olive morning coat he wore a loaded pistol snug against his ribs.

He climbed the ghats with his servants in tow, but paused for a second at the top of the stairs. Facing the thronged, seething cauldron of the bazaar, he wished he'd had more time to prepare, to educate himself in depth on the country as he normally would on his assignments, but they had needed him right away.

Though he was a recognized expert in conducting the sort of delicate negotiations soon to take place, Ian had never been to India before. He had been on holiday in Ceylon when he had been summoned, stretched out on a white-powder beach and trying very hard to escape a few private demons of his own. Trying to reason his way through or perhaps around the emptiness that had grown so deep over the past few years, leaving him in this inward state of isolation, hollow and numb.

But with no more success than before in resolving his carefully concealed pain, he had been all too happy to volunteer his services to help sort out the unpleasantness with the Maratha Empire. Until he got his bearings, however, developed more of a feel for this place and its people, he knew he would have to tread with extreme care and meet all who crossed his path with meticulous courtesy. The worst thing any diplomat could do was to unwittingly give offense.

Fortunately, he had a general grasp of the rules

and a little of the two main languages he'd need for the mission, Bengali and Marathi, thanks to his trusty guide and interpreter, Ravi Bhim. For now, the bazaar loomed ahead. There was no way to go but through it; he moved on.

The moment Ian stepped into the main aisle designated as the spice market, a wall of scent washed over him, pungent and intoxicating. His eyes smarted at the sharp flavors hanging thickly in the humid air: black pepper and cloves, turmeric and mustard seed, all sold atop wide, woven platters by robed men willing to haggle. Ian waved his hand, declining their bargains, and pressed on. There were sacks of cardamom, saffron, and mace; fine nutmeg by the pound, coriander, sultry cinnamon.

He glanced behind him again and saw one of his servants dawdling. The wide-eyed coolie, balancing one of Ian's traveling trunks on his bare back, had stopped to watch a snake charmer coaxing a deadly spectacled cobra from its basket, enchanting the serpent with the winding melody from his reedy pipe. Another turbaned man played a pair of deep-voiced drums. Their song competed with the Muslim call to prayer now echoing down from the minarets of all the mosques across the city.

The coolie saw Ian's raised eyebrow and blanched, hurrying after him. Soon they were in the thick of it – close heat, body odors, a clamor of polyglot voices, the motion of the place whirling around him like a dervish dance. His earnest attempt to absorb everything dissolved into a dizzying overload of sight and smell and sound.

His senses throbbed as he walked down a narrow aisle lined with a delirious array of Eastern treasures. Kanchipuram silk so fine it would have made his fashionable mistress back in London moan with pleasure. Gold and silver-thread brocade; printed cotton light as feathers; gorgeous intricate carpets; bright beads and terra-cotta animals; leather sandals; dyes and powder paints; rare cypress furniture, and gilded figurines of multi-armed goddesses and blue-skinned gods.

Moving through the market, Ian and his servants were carelessly jostled by people who were as varied as the goods they had gathered to buy and sell. Hindu ladies, rainbow-dressed and silken-scarved, bantered back and forth, their smiles beaming, the married ones marked by the distinctive red dot, or *bindi*, on their foreheads.

English officers in uniform rode past the perimeter astride prancing horses worthy of Tattersall's. Buddhist monks in saffron robes strolled by with shaved heads, almond-shaped eyes, and radiant smiles as though they hadn't a care in the world.

Certainly the peace-loving monks had no idea that another war was brewing.

A small group of Muslim ladies covered in black from head to toe had stopped to browse at a jeweler's stall, and one was leading her child by

6

the hand, a small boy. The tot was eating a mango, and Ian smiled faintly, for the youngster looked about five years old, the same age as his son.

Ignoring a vague pang in the region of his heart, he looked around to find a trinket for his heir before his mission got underway in earnest. This was a ritual he always observed no matter where in the world his work took him. There might not be time later. He chose an elephant of carved teakwood and approached the artisan.

'*Koto?*' Though he was never one to haggle unless the fate of nations hung in the balance, *not* to protest the first stated price would have been an insult to the trader.

And so Ian haggled to show his respect.

Ravi looked on in amusement. With the purchase finally made and good-natured laughter all around at the English lord's attempt to speak Bengali, Ian handed off the toy to his servant, gave the trader a farewell *namaste*, and then led his small band onward through the market.

At last they emerged on the other side, where he sent Ravi off to find a carriage to take him to the Akbar Grand Hotel, which Governor General Lord Hastings had recommended in his friendly letter accompanying the communiqué explaining Ian's assignment.

He dispatched one of the coolies to Government House to let Lord Hastings know he had arrived and would call on him as soon as he had procured lodgings. From there he would be briefed, and would finally get to meet the two distinguished cavalry officers whom he had specifically requested for his diplomatic detail – Gabriel and Derek Knight.

Though he had not yet met this transplanted branch of the Knight clan, ties between their two powerful families ran deep. Back in London, Ian's closest friend since boyhood and strongest political ally was the head of that clan – Robert Knight, the Duke of Hawkscliffe, or 'Hawk' to him.

Gabriel and Derek were Hawk's first cousins; quality was in the blood. Born and raised in India, moreover, the brothers knew the ground and the people better than he did. Ian's show of preferment by selecting them for this mission, in turn, would help to advance their already stellar military careers. For his part, if he had to go into a hostile foreign court, he wanted men around him he could trust.

Feeling eyes upon him again, and increasingly certain that someone was watching his every move, Ian glanced casually behind him, hoping to spot the spy, but instead he went motionless at the awesome sight of a great Bengal tiger being carried through the market in a cage.

Suspended on long poles, the cage rested on the sun-browned shoulders of no less than eight porters. The creature must have weighed five hundred pounds. As they carried it toward the river to be shipped, no doubt, to some European nobleman's menagerie, the beast let out a roar, terrifying its crowd of turbaned handlers and trying to slash at them through the wooden bars of its cage.

The coolies cried out and nearly dropped the cage in their rush to clear the area. But when their overseer verified that the wooden cage would indeed hold and waved them back to work, the men let out nervous laughter and returned with all due caution, warily lifting the poles onto their shoulders again.

Ian watched, riveted by the wild animal, and somehow wounded by its fate. Of course, if it were free, it would have destroyed everything in its path. Some beasts were better off caged.

Didn't he know it, too.

'Sahib!'

He turned as Ravi came hurrying back, bringing another Indian fellow with him – a footman of the aristocracy, in white wig and lavender livery. Ravi gestured to a luxurious black coach with four snow-white horses waiting across the street. A groom in matching livery held the leader's head.

'Sahib, this man says he was given orders to pick you up when you arrived.'

Ian eyed the footman cautiously. 'You are the Governor's man?'

'No, my lord.' He bowed. 'I was sent from the home of Lord Arthur Knight.'

'Lord Arthur?' Ian exclaimed. Derek and Gabriel's father.

'Yes, sir. I have been ordered here every day for

a fortnight to greet you. I was told to give you this.' Reaching into his showy waistcoat, the footman withdrew a folded piece of creamy linen paper, which he presented to Ian.

It seemed that Ian's suspicious reaction had already been anticipated, for the note had been sealed with a red wax wafer firmly stamped with the family crest of the house of the Dukes of Hawkscliffe. The moment he saw the authentic Hawkscliffe insignia, he nearly grinned. He knew this coat of arms as well as he knew his own. He might be a stranger in a strange land here, but the familiar sight went a long way toward making him feel at home.

Lord Arthur was Hawk's uncle, younger brother to the previous Duke. A bit of a carousing rake in his youth, as younger sons of the nobility tended to be, Lord Arthur had been a great favorite with all the lads before he had set out some thirty years ago to make his fortune with the East India Company.

Ian had promised to deliver salutations from the London branch of the Knight family to the scion that had taken root here, but he had not expected to make a social call until he had gotten settled in at the hotel and had taken care of preparations for his mission.

In any case, short of Lord Arthur coming to greet him in person, the authentic Hawkscliffe crest was the best proof he could ask for to ensure that the footman's story was genuine and not the cunning trap of some enemy agent. With that, he cracked the seal and read.

> *Dear Lord Griffith,*
> *Welcome to India! The finest hotel in Calcutta cannot rival the hospitality of a good friend's home, and as I hear that you are all but a member of the family back in England, you must hasten here and be our guest. We shall endeavor to see to your every comfort.*
> *Very truly yrs,*
> *Georgiana Knight.*

Well, well, well, he mused. *Georgiana.* Lord Arthur's daughter. He had been trying hard not to think about her.

It wasn't easy, considering he had been hearing intriguing stories about the young lady from as far away as the Bay of Bengal – not just of her beauty, but of her good deeds. Though she was a leading belle of British society in Calcutta, with innumerable friends and more suitors than she could count, the bulk of her considerable energy, it seemed, went into her charitable work for the good of the Indian people.

Rumors of an orphanage Georgiana had endowed with the proceeds of her father's East India Company fortune were only the beginning. There was also an almshouse for old ladies, an animal hospital in the Jain tradition, a shrine she had prevented from being destroyed to make way for a new British road, and she was a major patroness of the Orientalist Society, funding the livelihoods of scholars who were dedicated to the study of ancient Sanskrit texts and all branches of Eastern thought and art.

The villagers a hundred miles away had spoken Georgiana's name in a reverent hush, as though invoking some divine or sainted being. But having known all about the shocking exploits of the first Georgiana, Hawk's mother, for whom she had been named, Ian had his doubts.

Knight women were pure trouble, born and bred for scandal.

And yet somehow he could hardly wait to have a look at her.

There had been talk for generations, after all, of a desire to unite their two powerful clans, the Hawkscliffe dukes and the Griffith marquesses. But it did not signify. His interest was academic only; the grand alliance would have to wait for a new generation. Perhaps one day his boy, Matthew, could marry Hawk and Bel's new baby daughter. Himself, his married days were over.

He had been married once. Once had been enough.

The footman looked at him expectantly, but Ian hesitated. If he was being watched by foreign powers, he did not want to bring danger to his friends.

On the other hand, with two military officers in the house besides himself – Gabriel and Derek, waiting to join him on his mission – any spy would think twice about coming too close. Besides, old Lord Arthur might have something useful to tell him about the renowned Maharajah of Janpur.

His mind made up, Ian tucked the note into his breast pocket, nodding to the footman. 'Thank you. I will come.'

'This way, my lord.' But as the servant began to show him over to the carriage, a slight shift in the wind suddenly carried the strong scent of smoke to his nostrils.

Something was burning.

He turned to look and saw a change in the crowd's shifting currents; the people in the market were surging toward the west.

'What's happened?' he asked quickly, worried a fire had broken out somewhere in the cluttered bazaar. His instant reaction was to begin looking for a way to stop pandemonium from breaking out, fearing people would get trampled if there was not a swift and orderly evacuation of the old tinder box of a market.

Ravi halted a passerby and asked what was happening, then turned back to Ian in relief. 'It is only a funeral, sahib. Some local dignitary has died and is being cremated. His ashes will be scattered on the river.'

'Ah.' Relief washed through him, and he gave his servant a cautious nod. 'Very well, then. Let us be on our—' His words broke off abruptly, for at that moment, without warning, a rider came barreling into the market.

Astride a magnificent white Arabian mare, she came tearing through the bazaar, careening nimbly through the crowded zigzag aisles and leaving a tenfold chaos in her wake. Chickens went flying, vendors cursed, a tower of handwoven baskets crashed down, knocking over a fruit stand, and people flung themselves out of her way.

Ian stared.

In a cloud of weightless silk swathed exotically around her lithe figure, the woman leaned low to murmur in her horse's ear. Above the diaphanous veil that concealed the lower half of her face, her cobalt eyes were fierce.

Blue.

Blue eyes?

As he watched in disbelief, she leaped her white horse over a passing oxcart – and then she was gone, racing off in the direction of the fire.

Ravi and Ian exchanged a baffled look.

He and Ravi and both coolies, along with the Knight family's footman, stared after the girl for a moment, dumbfounded.

There was only one sort of woman he knew who could cause that much chaos that quickly.

Aye, in an instant, somehow, deep in his bones, Ian knew exactly who she was.

The footman had turned pale and now started forward in recognition, but Ian stopped him with a sardonic murmur.

14

'I'll handle this.' With a cautionary nod at Ravi, he walked away from the servants, and followed irresistibly in the direction the young hellion had gone.

Georgiana Knight urged her fleet-footed mare onward, dodging rickshaws, pedestrians, and sacred cows that loitered in the road until, at last, she reached the riverside, where a gathering of some fifty people surrounded the funeral pyre.

Towering flames licked at the azure sky.

The sickening, charred-meat smell made her stomach turn, but she would not be deterred. A young woman's life depended on this rescue – more than that, a dear friend.

The relatives of old, dead Balaram now noticed Georgie's approach. Most of them still milled about the funeral pyre, sending up all the spectacle of mourning for the respected town elder, wailing and waving their hands, but a few watched her uneasily as she arrived at the edge of the crowd. They knew the British detested this holy rite, and she quite expected that at least a few of them would try to stop her.

The self-immolation of a virtuous and beautiful widow not only pleased the gods, but brought great honor to her family and that of her husband. Burning herself alive in a ritual suicide just to honor her husband's name!

There could be no more perfect illustration, Georgie thought, of *everything* that was wrong with the whole institution of marriage – in both their cultures. It gave all the power to the man. And, good heavens, the way females were treated in the East was enough to put any sane woman off marriage entirely!

A cheeky aphorism from the writings of her famous aunt, Georgiana Knight, the Duchess of Hawkscliffe, trailed through her mind: *Wedlock is a padlock.* Well, today, she would not allow it to become a death sentence, too.

Then she spotted dear, gentle Lakshmi standing before the blaze in her red silk wedding robes, heavily encrusted with gold and pearls. The raven-haired beauty was staring at the fire as though contemplating what agony she would know before oblivion. Absorbed in her thoughts and no doubt lightly drugged with betel, the dead man's bride was not yet aware of her British friend's arrival.

Angered by the smoke, the white mare reared up a bit on her hind legs as Georgie pulled her mount to a halt at the fringe of the funeral crowd; she gave her horse a firm command to stay and leaped down from the saddle.

Murmurs rippled around her as she stalked through the gathering, her sandals landing firmly in the dust with each long, limber stride. The tiny silver bells on her anklet tinkled eerily in the hush.

Everyone knew the two girls had played together since childhood, and that Georgie was far more Indianized than most British folk, so perhaps the relatives thought she had merely come to say her last good-byes. Lakshmi's family were wealthy Hindus of the Brahmin caste, on a par with the aristocratic rank of Georgie's clan in their respective cultures.

They let her pass.

Behind her, she now heard Adley's rather noisy arrival at the edge of the crowd, tumbling along after her, as always, but Balaram's relatives did not let the foppish young nabob any closer. She could hear him sputtering with indignation.

'I say! This will not do! Miss Knight! I am here – should you need me!'

Fixed on her purpose, she did not look back, surveying the dire scene before her.

The massive bonfire had already turned old Balaram's bones to dust when Lakshmi looked up from the inferno and saw Georgie marching toward her. She faltered slightly at Georgie's infuriated stare.

Reaching Lakshmi's side, Georgie gripped her shoulders with a no-nonsense look and turned her friend away from the flames. 'You are out of your mind if you think I'm going to let you go through with this – ridiculous superstition!' she scolded in a hushed tone. 'It's savage and cruel!'

'What choice do I have?' Lakshmi's delicate voice quavered. 'I cannot dishonor my family.'

'You most certainly can! It was bad enough they made you *marry* the old goat, but to die for him, as well? It is obscene!' she whispered furiously.

'But it isn't dying, really,' Lakshmi insisted half-heartedly. 'I'll go straight to heaven, and w-when the people pray to me, I'll grant their wishes.'

'Oh, Lakshmi. What have they done to you?' Had the three years her friend had spent living in the strict marital seclusion of purdah robbed her of all common sense? 'I know you know better than this!'

'Oh, Georgie – my life will be too awful if I live!' she choked out, her big brown eyes filling with tears. 'You know how it is for widows. I'll be an outcast! People will flee me and say I'm bad luck! I'll be a burden on my family, a-and I'll have to shave off all my hair,' she added woefully, for Lakshmi's night-black hair was her crowning glory, hanging all the way to her waist. 'What's the point?' she said in utter misery. 'My life is over. It's forbidden that I should ever remarry. All my childhood happiness came to an end the day of my wedding, and it will not return, so I might as well be dead.'

'You don't know that. No one knows the future. My dear, you mustn't give up.' Georgie hugged her for a moment, with angry tears in her eyes. 'Look,' she resumed in as soothing a tone as possible, 'don't try to think about the whole rest of your life right now. Just think about this moment, and the next.'

Georgie coughed a little from the smoke, but willed away the pain that flared up in her chest and ignored the fear as the smoke began snaking through her lungs, agitating her old ailment.

'Think of all the reasons left to live,' she continued, 'all the fun we have. Throwing powder paints on people at the Holi festival? Playing pranks on Adley? If you die, who will finish teaching me the Odissi dances? If you die, oh, my dearest, you can never dance again.'

Lakshmi let out a strangled sob, barely audible above the fire's roar.

'Now, you listen to me,' Georgie ordered softly. 'You won't be a burden on your family, because—' A painful spasm in her lungs halted her words all of a sudden. She clutched her chest, alarmed. She hadn't felt that harsh constriction in her lungs since she was a child. It was worsening. She cleared her throat but it was no use; she had begun to wheeze.

'What's wrong?' Lakshmi searched her face.

'Nothing,' she lied impatiently, determined to save her friend or die trying. 'You won't be a burden on your family,' she repeated, refusing to yield to panic, 'because you will come and live at *my* house. Papa won't mind. He's never home anyway, and as for my brothers, well, Gabriel and Derek will never forgive you if you go through with this – and they'll never forgive *me* if I fail to stop you.'

When she coughed again and then muttered a curse, Lakshmi realized for certain what was wrong. 'It's your asthma, isn't it?'

'Don't worry about me!' Georgie retorted, but concern for her was now rousing Lakshmi out of her trance of despair.

'Gigi, you can hardly breathe,' she insisted, using her childhood nickname. 'You have to get away from this fire!'

Georgie fixed her with a meaningful stare. 'So do you,' she replied in an urgent whisper. 'Be brave, my dear. Be brave enough to stand up to them, and *live*.'

'Miss Knight, you must let her go now,' Lakshmi's father interrupted. 'It is time. Hurry, Lakshmi, while the fire is still hot enough.'

A shower of sparks popped violently and flew toward Lakshmi in a plume, as though old Balaram himself were reaching out from the depths of the fire, trying to grab the poor girl and drag her down with him to her doom. Lakshmi glanced from her sire back to Georgie, sudden panic in her eyes. 'Help me,' she whispered.

'Put more wood on the fire!' one of the kinsmen ordered a nearby servant.

Georgie's heart pounded. 'Of course I will. That's why I'm here. Come. Link arms with me. Let's get you out of here.' *Before your relatives make you go through with it whether you want to or not.* Pressuring her to the brink of this ritual suicide was one thing, but would they resort to murder, throwing her into the fire against her will?

She glanced around warily, knowing this danger was certainly possible. 'Everything's going to be all right, I promise. Come, now. Let's go.' Holding onto her friend protectively, Georgie drew her away from the inferno.

At once, the dead man's relatives sent up a clamor of protest all around them, yelling at the girls; in an instant, they were surrounded by a sea of angry brown faces.

A few seized the girls' arms, trying to separate them.

'Leave her alone!' Georgie shouted, shoving them away, but in their eyes, this was completely unacceptable.

The brother of the dead man came over and gripped Lakshmi's other arm, rebuking her in Bengali, reminding her of her sacred duty and trying to drag her back toward the fire, as though he would throw them both forcibly into the blaze before he would see the late family patriarch dishonored.

'Let go of her!' Georgie pushed the man away with one arm and held fast to Lakshmi with the other. 'Stay back! I'm not going to let you murder her!'

'Ungrateful daughter! Do not give in to this foreigner's meddling! How dare you shame our family?'

'Father, please!' Lakshmi wailed, struggling against her kin, jarred this way and that in the tug of war over her, but when the men began steadily pulling both girls back toward the fire, terror came into her large brown eyes. Now instinct took over, and the girl fought for her life.

Georgie was having trouble drawing a simple breath, but she held onto her friend with both arms, sparing only a glance over her shoulder. '*Adley!*'

'I am here, Miss Knight! Hold on, hold on!'

It was only a minute or two, but it felt like an eternity before her faithful, flaxen-haired suitor came barging into their midst astride his fine chestnut gelding, leading Georgie's white mare by the reins.

The tall stamping horses helped stave off the mob. Georgie pushed Lakshmi up into the saddle behind Adley.

To her family's fury, the Indian girl wrapped her arms around the Englishman's slim waist.

'Take her to my house! Go!' Georgie urged them, but Adley hesitated, eyeing the hostile crowd in doubt. 'I'll be right behind you!' She slapped the gelding on the rump to get them moving before the situation turned any uglier.

In the next moment, Georgie sprang up onto her horse's back. The white mare tossed her head, but one of Lakshmi's kinsmen grabbed the bridle and would not let go, excoriating Georgie as a meddler, a pagan, and a few even less savory epithets. Well, the world had called her famous aunt worse – the defiant duchess had been dubbed 'the Hawkscliffe Harlot' for her many scandals. Georgie was not about to be intimidated. 'Let go of my horse!'

They were closing in, rioting around her, and as her fear climbed, her difficulty breathing increased.

'Would you like to go into the fire in her place?' the infuriated brother-in-law yelled.

'Don't – touch me!' As she fought them, she could hear her heartbeat thundering in her ears, her breath rasping in her throat, and in a flash, it brought back the long-forgotten, inward sound of panic.

She had come to know it well as a child. Unable to gulp enough air into her lungs, a wave of light-headedness washed over her, terrifying her with the fear of passing out and falling from her horse into the irate crowd.

Suddenly, a towering Englishman exploded into their midst, driving the dead man's relatives back.

'Stand down!' he roared, thrusting one arm out to hold the men at bay and blocking the others from getting at her with nothing more than a walking stick.

Georgie's eyes widened.

The mob fell back before his furious commands for order, backing away from him as though a tiger had gotten loose in the market.

As she regained her balance in the saddle, Georgie's stunned gaze flashed over the magnificent interloper – all six-feet-plus of him – lingering briefly on the sweeping breadth of his shoulders and the lean cut of his waist.

Moving into their midst with athletic elegance, a simmering cauldron of intensity, polished to a high sheen, he was crisp and formidable – lordly – from his sleek short haircut to his gleaming black boots. In terms of solid, unsmiling mass, the man was two of Adley, with none of his foppish flamboyance.

In her heart, Georgie knew him at once – not because of his fine London clothes, nor even because she had been expecting his arrival any day now at the nearby docks. She knew he was Lord Griffith because he did not draw a weapon on these unarmed people.

A man like him didn't have to. The famed marquess wielded more force with his aura and his eyes than other men commanded with a pistol.

She watched him in awe. It seemed her illustrious guest had finally arrived, and from the first second, Georgie was more impressed than she liked to admit.

Somehow, in short order, Lord Griffith began single-handedly bringing the riot under control. Deliberately creating a distraction, he drew the crowd's fury away from her to himself, so that, at last, she could take a few seconds to try to breathe. But she knew they had to get out of here – both of them. At any moment, the whole thing could erupt in violence.

When he threw her a piercing glance full of question – *Are you all right?* – she suddenly forgot to exhale, never mind the asthma.

Good heavens, he was easy on the eyes!

Having proudly doted on her two darling brothers all her life, a handsome face did not usually impress her. But in the midst of the fray, the diplomat's striking good looks made her blink.

Some of the local men now recovered their courage and moved toward the marquess again, yelling at him in various dialects with renewed pugnacity and wagging their fingers in his face. At any second now, it was sure to come to blows.

His glower tamed them briefly when he looked back at them in warning, but the angry Hindus were doing their best to shout down his ever-so-reasonable-toned commands for calm.

Steadying her horse, Georgie finally managed to take a decent breath, though it burned all the way down into her chest.

She edged her mare closer toward him. 'Lord Griffith, I presume?' she greeted him in a tone that strove for at least a show of levity.

He looked over at her with a strange mix of surprise and exasperation, but then he watched the crowd again distrustfully. Rather in spite of himself, the stern line of his mouth crooked in a saturnine half smile. 'Miss Georgiana Knight.'

She coughed. 'In the flesh.'

'I got your note.'

'Care to make a timely egress?'

'Delighted.'

He turned his back on the mob just for a moment and swung up behind her like a born horseman. Large, lordly hands encased in tan kid gloves reached past her waist. 'Better let me take the reins.'

She snorted. Men! 'It's my horse, and you don't know the way. Hold on.' Shoving away one of Lakshmi's in-laws, Georgie finally managed to wheel her mare around.

At last, her powerful horse broke free of the crowd, and, with her newfound ally riding behind her like a hard wall of warm, male muscle at her back, they went racing homeward.

CHAPTER 2

Hellfire, what had the mad chit gotten him into? He had come here to stop a bloody war, not to start one.

But the Marquess of Griffith was not a man who lost his temper. Ever.

Displays of emotion were for peasants.

Tapping into his formidable reserves of steadfast patience, Ian clenched his jaw and refused to say a word.

For now.

A true gentleman, not to mention a diplomat up to his eyeballs in protocol, habitually treated ladies with a degree of courtesy that placed them on shining pedestals; as a female member of the Knight family, this was doubly true of the consideration he felt compelled to show Georgiana.

But it was not easy.

Not when he had half a mind to wring her pretty neck for putting herself – and his mission – in danger.

He couldn't believe she had dragged him into disrupting the solemnities of a damn funeral and could only pray that those people back there did not include anyone he'd have to work with on his assignment. As for her, what on earth did she think she was doing, dashing around the streets of Calcutta in this wild fashion?

He definitely meant to speak to her father about this.

Yes, he thought sternly, not to the girl, but to her menfolk would he address his displeasure. Somehow he doubted Lord Arthur knew what mischief his beautiful daughter had gotten into this day, but that was no excuse. The chit had nearly gotten herself roasted alive.

It was shocking that her father and brothers were not keeping a better watch over her than this. Did they not know that as the niece of the Hawkscliffe Harlot, she would in all likelihood require even *more* supervision than the typical impulsive young female? This branch of the Knight family was flirting with disaster by giving *their* Georgiana such free rein.

Of course, in all fairness – both training and native inclination tended to make Ian look at everything from both sides of a situation – having witnessed her display of courage back at the fire, having seen for himself that her rescue truly had been a matter of life and death, he could hardly fault her.

The girl had just saved someone's life. He had never seen a woman risk herself for another that way. In truth, his previous cynicism about the new Georgiana had thinned considerably.

Too, he was only a guest. It was not his place to lecture her or her father on propriety, much as he might have enjoyed doing so; and in light of the fact that riding tandem with the delectable creature had driven his own thoughts into the most lascivious territory, he really had no room to talk. *Merciful heaven.* Her warm hips rocked snug against his groin, while his hands molded her slender waist. His awareness of her had turned to ferocious want within the first furlong.

Her long legs brushed against his thighs, teasing him; he could feel each subtle flex of her calves as she directed her horse. It was enough to drive a man insane.

He tried to ignore it: Lusting after his host's virginal daughter was surely the height of bad form.

Then she coughed – a short sound, harsh and dry – and his protective instincts surged instantly to the fore once again.

Furrowing his brow, Ian suddenly realized the girl was experiencing some difficulty with her respiration. Listening more closely, he could hear it in each painful breath she drew, could feel it in the clenched tightness of all the muscles down her back. His face turned grim.

Disapproval and lust both thrown aside, he steadied her with a firmer hold on her waist. 'The smoke has distressed your lungs.'

'No – I am well – truly.' She tried to stifle another cough, and he cursed himself for his lechery.

'My dear, you are a very poor liar. Tell me what is wrong,' he ordered in a clipped tone.

'It's just a – touch of asthma. I've had it since childhood. Usually it gives me no trouble, but the smoke—'

'Do you require a doctor?'

'No. Thank you.' She sent him a grateful glance over her shoulder, then hesitated. 'When I get home, there are things I've learned to do that help.'

'Good, then let's get you there quickly.' He murmured to her not to try to talk; took the reins gently, brooking no further argument; and let her point the way, his entire focus fixed on getting her to safety, where she could receive the appropriate care.

Relief and gratitude had been Georgie's main reactions since the moment Lord Griffith had appeared, and she had been savoring with covert pleasure the way his magnificent body enfolded her so safely as they rode together on her horse.

But when he forced her to surrender the reins, her triumph over rescuing Lakshmi turned to a sense of unease. Though she did not argue with him this time, his smooth usurpation of control jarred her memory back to her true and original stance about the man, the one she had formed before he had exploded onto the scene and performed so valiantly back there at the fire – in short, a healthy skepticism.

Oh, yes, she knew that all the world considered the Marquess of Griffith some sort of paragon, a man of justice and sterling integrity. Ever since she had received his letter to Papa informing them of his imminent arrival, she had been asking around about him in Society, trying to gather whatever information – or gossip – she could about their renowned London guest.

A top diplomat and expert negotiator with the Foreign Office, indeed, a personal friend of the Foreign Secretary, Lord Castlereagh, Lord Griffith had averted wars, brokered cease-fires, procured treaties, parlayed for the release of hostages, and stared down power-crazed potentates with, she'd heard, unflinching cool and steely self-control. Whenever there was an explosive conflict brewing somewhere in the world, Lord Griffith was the one the Foreign Office sent in to defuse the most potentially explosive situations.

As a woman who embraced India's centuries-old Jainist philosophy of nonviolence and social equality, Georgie could not help but respect a man whose driving mission in life was to stop human beings from killing each other.

Still, she had her doubts.

Nobody was that good. The Eastern mystics taught that for every light within a man there was an equal darkness. Besides, she had grown cynical after seeing every new diplomat, politician, and administrator sent from London to help rule India arrive with an ulterior motive – *gold*. They no sooner stepped off the boat than they began scrambling to line their own pockets with the wealth of the East, usually by exploiting the Indian people. Only the rarest of Englishmen ever cared about *them*. But Georgie cared intensely.

From the time of her childhood, she had come to think of the Indian people as her second family. After her mother's death, she had been virtually raised by her kindhearted Indian servants. They had welcomed her, a lonely little orphan girl, into their world – their joyful, dancing, parti-colored, mysterious, paradoxical world.

And it had shaped her.

She used her place in British society to try to protect them from the worst ravages of Western avarice, but women had little power beyond what charm and wits and beauty God gave them. Despite her family's ducal connections, her father's rank as a now retired member of the East India Company elite, her brothers' posts as wildly popular officers with the Regular Army, and her own status as a relatively highborn English debutante, her efforts to aid the Indian people often seemed a losing battle.

And now the power brokers in London had sent Lord Griffith, the heavy cannon in their arsenal.

It did not bode well.

Something big must be happening, and she intended to find out what it was. She had heard rumors of another war against the Maratha Empire, but she prayed to God it was not so, not with two brothers who couldn't bear to stay away from a battlefield. And then there was that disturbing letter from Meena . . .

Not long ago, another of her highborn Indian friends from childhood, dear, lovely Meena, had wed King Johar, the mighty Maharajah of Janpur. Handsome and brave, both a warrior and a poet, King Johar ruled one of the most formidable Hindu kingdoms of north-central India. His royal ancestors had been founding members of the Maratha Empire, an alliance of six powerful rajahs with territories around Bombay and the rugged forests of the Deccan Plateau.

Bound by an age-old treaty of mutual defense, which promised that if any one of their kingdoms was attacked, all the others must go to its aid, the Maratha kings of the warrior caste had first united hundreds of years ago to fend off the Mughal invaders who had come storming down from Afghanistan to conquer India.

To this day, they continued to protect their sovereignty by holding off the British. There had already been two wars between the English and the Marathas over the past fifty years, but for more than a decade now, thankfully, an uneasy peace had reigned. Many felt, however, that it was only a matter of time before war broke out again.

Georgie worried so. She detested violence and hated the thought of a just ruler like King Johar being brought low. So many proud Indian kingdoms had already fallen to British machinations, some quelled by wars, others by humiliating treaties: Hyderabad, Mysore, even the warlike Rajputs in the north. Only the Marathas remained completely free and independent.

But maybe not for long.

If war broke out and the warrior king were slain in battle, then all thirty of Johar's wives, including her dear Meena, not to mention his hundreds of concubines, all would burn on his funeral pyre in an act of suttee, just like Lakshmi had nearly done today.

Georgie shuddered at the hideous thought, at which Lord Griffith held her a little closer.

'Are you all right?' he murmured.

What a tender touch he had. His gentleness arrested her attention. She managed a nod. 'Yes, thanks,' she forced out, reminded anew that, whatever intrigues were afoot, this man was mixed up in the middle of it all.

She intended to find out through her guest what was going on – though, of course, she could not do so directly. After all, she was 'only a woman.' Lord Griffith would never tell her government secrets, and she had no right to ask. Best, therefore, not to arouse his suspicions in the first place, she decided. If she used her woman's tools, kept her eyes and ears open, charmed him, soothed his guard down, then she'd soon have all the information she required.

She intended to watch him like a hawk.

As much as she longed to believe in Lord

Griffith's brilliant reputation, she wasn't that naive. She saw little reason to hope that the supposedly wonderful marquess was in truth any different than all the other greedy Europeans who had come to plunder India for centuries.

If his motives were pure – if he really was here to stop a war from breaking out and could be trusted as a human being, then she would do all she could to help him.

But if it turned out that he was just like all the rest, corrupt and callous, and that his true purpose boiled down to greed – his own, the Company's, and the Crown's – then she would stand with her Maratha friends and find a way to work against him.

Having him stay at her house as her guest would help her keep an eye on him; thus, she had sent him that note opening her home to him in hospitality. His visit should give her plenty of time to observe him, get to know him, and judge his true nature for herself.

Presently, they turned onto the broad, elegant avenue known as the Chowringee, Calcutta's answer to Park Lane. As they rode past the row of stately mansions where the richest English families lived in splendor, Georgie ducked her head, having donned the veil and Eastern clothing to help conceal her identity from her nosy neighbors.

Most of them were probably still sleeping, for there had been a grand ball last night, but she wasn't taking any chances. She did not want to end up as mired in scandal as her late, great aunt, for she couldn't be of help to anyone if she was ruined.

No, she embraced the duchess's ideals, but not her methods.

When they approached her house, she signaled to Lord Griffith to rein in. 'Here we are.'

Ian pulled the horse to a halt before the most whimsical home on the stretch. Glancing up at it, he beheld a snow-white Oriental fantasy, an exotic confection topped by a turquoise onion dome with four quaint little towers like minarets rising from the corners. It almost seemed to float before him like that mad poet's dream of Kubla Khan, a shimmering illusion, gleaming white against the azure sky.

He blinked, half expecting it to vanish.

It remained.

But as he gazed at it, once again, as in the spice market, he had the oddest sensation of being slowly bewitched, overcome, perhaps *seduced* by this strange land, as though he had caught the subtle whiff of opium fumes.

Jumping down off the horse's back, he turned automatically to assist Georgiana. As she set her hands on his shoulders and he clasped her waist, setting her down gently on her sandaled feet, they stared at each other for a fleeting instant. Above the translucent veil that draped the lower half of her face, her deep sapphire eyes lured him with

36

hypnotic power. In contrast to those dark violet-blue eyes, she had skin like pure ivory, and midnight hair gathered back tightly in a smooth chignon.

Ian stared. Desire hit him like a fireball shot from a catapult, slamming through the outer wall of all his white-towered chivalry.

'Thank you,' she whispered a tad hoarsely.

Suddenly remembering his annoyance at her, Ian gestured to the front path without a word. She stiffened and dropped her gaze, alerted to his displeasure.

When a liveried Indian groom dashed out, she ordered the man to walk the mare for a while to ensure that she was cool before putting her back into her stall.

The groom bowed. 'Yes, memsahib.'

She cast Ian another wary glance full of guarded allure. 'Come,' she murmured, then strode ahead of him to the front door, her gait willowy-limbed, gliding. She lifted the hem of her fluid silk sari as she walked with a magical tinkling of bells.

Ian watched her through narrowed eyes, feeling a bit like Odysseus, far from home, being lured into Circe's den.

Most ancient bards agreed that lusting after a sorceress was imprudent in the extreme. It would probably serve him right if she turned him into a newt.

He followed anyway.

Tracking her to the entrance, he stole one last,

vigilant glance over his shoulder. With any luck, his hasty exit from the marketplace may have shaken off anyone following him. Narrowing his eyes against the sun, Ian scanned the broad, green park across the street, then the parade ground that wrapped around Fort William.

A haze of humidity softened the hard angles of the looming, octangular stronghold. Imprinting his surroundings on his memory, he saw no one who looked suspicious. So far, thankfully, it appeared they had not been pursued by the dead man's relatives, either.

Then he followed Georgiana over the threshold.

Inside, her household was in an uproar with the arrival moments ago of the Indian lady, delivered by the young gentleman whom Ian had also seen riding away from the fire. He gathered that the lad had carried the woman upstairs to recuperate from her ordeal.

Meanwhile, a score of Indian servants of all shapes and sizes were running to and fro in panicked disorder, alarmed and scandalized, it seemed, by this turn of events. They clustered around their mistress the moment she walked in the door, and all began talking at once. The lightning-fast dialogue in Bengali was too rapid for Ian to understand.

He waited for a moment or two, but neither her father nor brothers appeared; so, while Georgiana attempted to answer all their questions and soothe their fears, answering them in their own language and calmly giving them their instructions, Ian took matters into his own hands, making sure that the house was secure in case that angry mob came after them.

He locked the front door behind him and then prowled from room to room throughout the first floor, closing windows and doors. Along the way, he was bemused to find that the decor inside the house was similar to that of any wealthy home in London, for all its exterior whimsy. The only real difference was a profusion of lush tropical palms that flourished in huge stone urns here and there.

When all the windows and doors were locked, and he had glanced out from various positions around the house to make sure no one was coming, Ian returned to the entrance hall, satisfied that at least these basic precautions had been taken. Georgiana finished dealing with her anxious staff.

She turned and looked at him in mild surprise, as though she had been wondering where he'd gone.

Scanning her face, Ian marched to her side and took her elbow, gently steering her toward the nearest chair. 'How are your lungs?'

'Much better now – thank you.'

'You are pale. Please sit down. Let me send for a doctor—'

'No – truly, my lord, I will be fine,' she interrupted. 'The worst has passed now. Besides, I have – other medicine.'

He frowned, folding his arms across his chest. 'Very well, then. Go on and take it. I will wait.'

Goodness, he was an imperious fellow, giving orders mere moments after stepping through her door! Admittedly, he meant well, she thought. Still, she was uneager to share with him the full extent of her eccentricity. Best to keep it vague. 'It's, ah, not exactly a potion or pill.'

His eyebrow lifted in skeptical fashion.

Reading his stern countenance, polite but all business, Georgie recognized the piercing stare of a male in full protective mode and sighed. If he was anything like her domineering brothers, that stare meant that he had no intention of leaving the subject alone. 'Very well. If you must know, there are breathing exercises I was taught when I was small – to help address the problem. Stretches, too, which benefit the lungs.'

'I see.' His stare intensified. He did not look entirely convinced.

'It's called yoga,' she mumbled. 'It's the only thing that helps.'

'Ah, I have heard of this.' He nodded slowly, studying her in wary interest. 'An ancient art, is it not?'

'Indeed. More importantly, it works,' she replied, surprised that he showed no sign of condemnation. Outside of her family, she did not like to admit to any of her British acquaintances that she

40

practiced yoga, for most of them would have considered it over the line.

Many in local Society already thought she had 'gone native,' but all that the British doctors had ever been able to do for her was to bleed her with horrid leeches and to give her doses of laudanum, liquid opium, that had made the paintings in her bedroom come alive and the ceiling squirm. If she had stayed on that path, she'd have become an addict and an invalid by now.

Fortunately, years ago, her beloved ayah, or Indian nurse, Purnima, had reached her wit's end with her young charge's ailment, and had sent for her kinsman, a yogi mystic, who had instructed Georgie in all the asanas to relax her chest and back and open up her lungs again.

It had also been wise old Purnima who had pointed out that Georgie's attacks seemed to have something to do with her loved ones leaving her. The ailment had become serious only after her mother's death, striking hardest whenever Papa had to go away on business again, or when her brothers had to leave once more for boarding school.

As a little girl, crying inconsolably with the panic of being left alone, she would sob until her grief impaired her breathing, turning from a fit of wild, wailing temper into a gasping, choking struggle for air. Whenever her loved ones left her behind, she had always felt like she was dying.

41

Thus the importance of her friends. She had learned to cope with her loneliness by surrounding herself with so many companions that no matter who left her, there were always a dozen others on hand to take their place. British or brown-skinned, female or male, all friends had always been welcome in her life.

By now, she knew nearly everyone in both Calcutta and Bombay, where her family had a second home – but she had never met the likes of Lord Griffith before.

What a mysterious man he was, his impenetrable visage betraying no sign of his thoughts. His gray-green eyes were full of secrets, though she detected perhaps a fleeting shimmer of haunted pain in their depths.

As he stood there watching her, his powerful arms folded across his chest, she indulged in a fleeting study of his proud, patrician face. Its rectangular shape and chiseled features bespoke dignified strength and authority: He had rather a high fore-head, angular cheekbones, a fine, assertive sort of nose, and a square jaw. A wavy lock of his dark brown hair had tumbled forward over his left eyebrow in the fray, but perhaps her stare made him a bit self-conscious, for he tossed it out of his face with a boyish motion at odds with his com-manding presence. His firm, sensuous mouth, bracketed by the manly grooves in his cheeks, still showed little sign of a smile.

More intrigued than she liked to admit, Georgie

looked away, slowly pulling the silken scarf off from around her neck, but she continued to survey him from the corner of her eye. She couldn't seem to help herself.

Nankeen breeches hugged his muscled things. A morning coat of muted green broadcloth, subtle-toned like forest shadows, molded the sweeping expanse of his shoulders; the shade accented the complex celadon hue of his eyes.

But there was something else about him, a restless, hungry magnetism. A smoldering slow burn beneath his polished surface. It summoned up wayward thoughts in her mind of the erotic pleasures so vividly depicted in the temple carvings she had seen, or the curious illustrations from that wicked little book she had found once beneath her brother's bed. She had been searching for her pet mongoose, fearing he had escaped the house. Instead, she had found the *Kama Sutra*.

She wondered if Lord Griffith had ever read it.

Well! This was hardly the time to ponder her secret obsession with sex.

Shaking off her momentary daze, Georgie turned away, irked to realize she was blushing. 'Would you care for a drink, my lord? I should check on Lakshmi soon – and Adley.'

Poor poppet, the servants said her lovable bumbler had walked through the doorway and fainted the instant he'd gotten Lakshmi to safety.

'No, thank you,' Lord Griffith said with only a

slight easing of his terse, formal manner. He clasped his hands behind his back. 'I should be happy to pay my respects to your father at his earliest convenience.'

'Oh, Papa's not here,' she said with a studied air of blithe unconcern, even as she braced herself for his reaction. *Here we go.*

'Oh,' he said in surprise. 'When do you expect him back?'

'Haven't the foggiest.'

'Pardon?'

'Oh, he's sailed off halfway 'round the world again on some new venture with our cousin Jack,' she informed him with a dismissive wave. 'He probably won't be back until next year.'

'I see,' he murmured, a distracted frown settling over his chiseled face. 'I was not aware of this.'

'Yes, I am sorry about that,' she answered in a soothing tone. 'I had no way of getting word to you since you were already en route. But I did forward your letter on to my father at sea,' she added. 'Jack's merchant ships will often carry our letters for us, and Papa had asked me before he left to open his mail for him, and to send on anything of importance.'

'Well, I am very sorry to have missed him,' he said, absorbing the news. 'Your father was a great favorite with all of us when we were boys, back in the days when he still lived in England. Will you give him my regards?'

'Happily, and I'm sure he sends you his own.

44

Now then, come in, for heaven's sake!' she chided, crossing the entrance hall to take his arm. 'Don't just stand there by the door, my dear guest! You must make yourself at home. Something to drink? Brandy? Lemonade?' She smiled up at him as she steered him toward the adjoining parlor.

'The latter sounds good,' he admitted, eyeing her with a cautious smile.

She flashed a grin. 'I agree!'

Ian feared he enjoyed having the lively beauty on his arm a bit too much. When she had shown him into the parlor, Georgiana released her hold on him gracefully and went to the mahogany cabinet in the corner, where she poured out their drinks from a pitcher.

He watched her every move, still mesmerized in spite of himself. In short order, she carried two goblets back over and handed him one. He accepted the lemonade with a nod of thanks, then she lifted her glass in a toast to him.

'Welcome to India, Lord Griffith. And, ah, thanks for saving my life.'

He bowed to her in wry nonchalance.

She laughed at his modest reaction, then clinked her glass against his. They drank.

'Well, I may have missed your father, but at least I got a chance to meet you,' he murmured, studying his hostess with a narrow smile. The slight blush that rose in her cheeks surprised him. She did not seem the blushing type.

'La, sir, the honor is mine,' she shot back in an airy tone. 'You're the famous one.'

'Nonsense. Shall I wait here while you check on your friends?' he asked, gesturing toward the nearby couch.

'They'll be all right for another moment or two without me. My servants are with them.'

'Good.' He nodded, and then dropped his gaze as a decidedly awkward silence descended, one, he feared, fraught with her full knowledge that she captivated him. He was certainly not the sort of man who gawked and lost his tongue in the presence of a beautiful woman, but . . . there was something about her.

He cast about for a change of subject and cleared his throat. 'So, when do you expect your brothers home, then?' He assumed that Gabriel and Derek Knight were at the garrison, or perhaps waiting for him at Government House. He hoped, as an after-thought, they did not mind his brief, unchaperoned visit with their sister. But why should they mind? He was a trusted friend of the family, honorable to a fault, if he dared say so himself, and it was not as though anything naughty was going to happen.

Pity, that. Those lovely, rose-hued lips wanted kissing, but it wasn't worth the risk. She was no worldly widow, no high-priced courtesan, but a marriageable young lady. Trifling with her would get him the one thing in the world that he least wanted: another wife.

Yet when Georgiana skimmed her lips with the tip of her tongue after her sip of lemonade, Ian fought off a violent shudder. Such forbidden urges would not do. She had inherited her scandalous aunt's famed appeal. That was all. He looked away. 'Your brothers?'

She, too, seemed to have lost track of the question. 'Oh – um, they're not here, either. Sorry.' She favored him with a sudden, breathtaking smile. 'You'll have to make do with me, I'm afraid.'

He stared again. 'What a shame,' he murmured softly, trying not to think about all the things that he could do to her before her brothers showed up from their day's work. He looked down at his glass. 'Perhaps you should send for them to come home and meet me here, instead of over at Government House. That way, we'll all be on hand in case that mob comes back.'

'Oh, don't worry about Balaram's relatives,' she said. 'They'd never dare trifle with my family. Besides, I've got the garrison across the street, and most of the officers over there have promised my brothers they'd look out for me.'

He looked at her in question.

'Derek and Gabriel aren't at Government House,' she admitted.

'No?'

'No.' She shook her head slowly, holding his gaze. Then she squared her delicate shoulders. 'My brothers are two hundred miles north of here, with their regiment.'

'*What?*'

'Shall I show you to your room? My servants have prepared a very pleasant bedchamber for your stay. I am sure you will be very comfortable there. If you'd like to relax for a—'

'Wait! Just – wait one moment.' He set his glass of lemonade aside and then rested his hands on his waist. 'Are you telling me, Miss Knight, that your father's not here, and your brothers aren't here; that, in short, you're here alone?'

'Well, I wouldn't say *that*. I have Purnima, of course, and Gita, and all my other servants—'

His noisy exhalation cut her off as he turned away and raked his hand through his hair, striving for patience. *Damn and blast.* He should have known.

It was lucky for her that he was not a man who lost his temper. He scratched his eyebrow for a second, took a deep breath, and said: 'Very well, what are we going to do to rectify this situation?' Perhaps Lady Hastings would have a few suggestions.

'What do you mean?' Georgiana asked, furrowing her pretty brow. 'There is nothing to rectify.'

He scoffed none too tactfully. 'You cannot stay here by yourself! What on earth your family was thinking, I do not know, but I will not hear of it. Especially now.'

'I already told you Balaram's clan is not a threat, and besides, I'm not alone. *You're* here!' she said with a cheerful but rather forced smile.

At least she was beginning to look nervous, he thought dryly, shaking his head at her. That meant at least she had some vague clue that what she was suggesting, his staying the night with her – alone – was beyond inappropriate.

It was scandalous.

Ah, but what else did he expect of the niece of the Hawkscliffe Harlot? He'd be a fool to trust this woman. For a moment, he even wondered if this was some devious trick to snare him in marriage. God knew it happened every time he set foot in London! Fortunately, he had become as wily as a Berkshire fox over the years in escaping the huntresses of the town, from the tuft-chasing debutantes to their matchmaking mamas.

Maybe she thought she'd be doing her family a favor, snaring him for the long-awaited alliance, but Ian was having none of it.

He wanted a wife like he wanted a hole in his head.

He folded his arms across his chest and fixed her with an exacting glare. 'I did not come here to ruin a young lady, Miss Knight. Nor to play chaperon to one. I came to try to stop a war, if it's quite all right with you. I cannot possibly stay here with you alone, as I'm sure you know quite well.' *And as much as I might relish the idea.* Good Lord, the temptation might be more than he could stand. 'I realize we've only just met, so forgive me if I sound a bit unmannerly, but what in blazes are you up to?'

'What? Whatever do you mean?'

He arched a brow at her feigned innocence, some of his vexation giving way to intrigued amusement quite in spite of himself. 'You're playing games with me,' he said softly, 'and I don't recommend you continue.' He narrowed his eyes, watching her. 'What's going on?'

'I have no idea what you're talking about,' she replied, all big blue eyes and a hurt little pout. 'On the contrary, sir, as you are my father's friend, I am doing my best to make everything simple and convenient for you!'

'Really?'

She nodded. Such an earnest picture, the little hellion! 'I sent my carriage to wait for you every day for a fortnight. Now that you're here, I have a lovely day planned out for us. Once you've settled in, we'll spend the afternoon relaxing in the garden, and you can make your preparations for your mission. Then we'll have a good supper and a nice long chat – get to know each other better, won't that be nice?' Certain portions of his body throbbed with agreement, but she forged on. 'And finally, after a good night's sleep, we'll set out bright and early for Janpur.'

Ian's eyes flared, and then he clenched his jaw. 'Janpur,' he echoed in a strangled tone, barely knowing where to begin.

He turned away and began to pace.

If Miss Knight had known him better, she would have recognized this as a cause for worry.

'Janpur,' he said again, taking his now simmering vexation firmly in hand.

She nodded. 'Yes, I hear it's very beautiful this time of year.'

'Miss Knight, your brothers were not at leave to reveal to you our destination. Which part of 'confidential mission' don't they understand? Good God!'

'No, no, no, my dear Lord Griffith, you misunderstand!' she soothed, hastily coming toward him in a swirl of silk. 'Do not trouble yourself, I pray you! It wasn't my brothers who told me you're going to Janpur. The security of your task has not been compromised, I swear.'

'Ah, that is a relief. Did it run in the newspapers, then?' he inquired sharply.

'Now, now, there's no need to grow testy, my lord. Of course it wasn't in the papers. I found out through a private letter from my friend Meena, who happens to be married to the Maharajah of Janpur.'

He eyed her in distrust. 'Really.'

'Yes, really. We played together from the time we were children, along with Lakshmi, the girl from the fire.'

Ian clamped his jaw shut and scanned her face, trying to detect a lie, but she appeared to be speaking the truth.

'Meena – rather, Princess Meena now – is not just *married* to King Johar, but happens to be the royal favorite at the moment. She is the youngest and the fairest of all the maharajah's thirty wives.

Everyone says he dotes on her and calls her his pearl. Isn't that sweet?'

Ian gave the chit a warning glower. 'Go on.'

'When Meena wrote to me that my brothers would be coming to Janpur leading the military escort for a British diplomatic party soon to pay a call on her husband, I knew it had to be you she was referring to, since you had just written us that letter, telling us you were on your way. Honestly, it was a simple matter of putting two and two together. Don't worry, I'm the only one who knows where you're going, and I'm not going to tell anyone. I haven't and I won't. You can trust me,' she added a bit too earnestly.

'Hmm.' The single syllable rolled out of him like a low growl.

'Don't you believe me?'

He flicked a wary glance over her, but did not answer, and then she scowled a bit.

'Meena has been wanting me to visit her at her new home ever since she got married. I'm afraid she's rather unhappy there, as well she should be, with twenty-nine other wives in the palace jealous of her. I'm sure they make her life unpleasant.'

He snorted, rather pitying the maharajah. Thirty wives? The man must be insane.

'Meena knew my brothers' presence at Janpur would be a lure I couldn't resist. Poor thing, she's lonely up there, so far from home.' She paused, looking troubled by her musings on her friend. Of course, Ian had already seen the lengths to which she was willing to go to save someone she cared about. Then Georgiana shrugged. 'Meena thought it would be fun for me to surprise my brothers up at Janpur. If you don't believe me, I can get the letter—'

'That won't be necessary.' He paused and scratched his eyebrow once more, collecting his thoughts. 'Miss Knight, I cannot adequately stress to you the importance of discretion in this matter. You must understand that many, many thousands of lives are at stake, including your brothers' – and mine. You must not discuss this with anyone, or you could jeopardize the entire mission. I'm here to secure the peace between ourselves and Janpur, and there are many powers in India who would like to see me fail.'

'I would *never* jeopardize the cause of peace, Lord Griffith. As I've already told you, I will not and haven't told a soul.'

'Good. See that you don't.'

Heavens, for a diplomat, the man was awfully rude! Georgie thought. Just then, the sound of a carriage rolling up outside drew their attention. She glanced out the window and saw that her footman had arrived with Lord Griffith's servants and his luggage.

Brushing off her frustration, she turned back to her guest with her most winning smile. 'Ah! Your things have arrived. Let me show you up to your room. Now that we've got all that sorted out, you might as well stay and make yourself comfortable—'

He interrupted her with exasperated laughter. 'Your persistence is to be admired, my dear young lady, but I cannot possibly stay. It would be entirely improper, as you well know.'

'But Purnima's here—'

'Do you really think your ayah's presence is enough to satisfy the local gossips?' he cut her off. 'My dear, I do not ruin young ladies.'

'You're not going to ruin me!' She scoffed. 'Oh, why must we stand on ceremony? We're practically family.'

'But we're not,' he replied in a pointed murmur. 'We are definitely . . . not.'

Her heart skipped a beat at the potent innuendo beneath the surface of his words. 'Perhaps not,' she admitted, inching closer. 'But, Lord Griffith . . . I trust you.' She lowered her head and peeked up at him from under her lashes. 'Everyone knows you have the most sterling reputation.'

He snorted. 'It's your reputation I'm worried about.'

'Nobody has to know,' she coaxed him. 'Besides, it's only one night – and then we're off for Janpur.'

'No!' He pulled away. 'You are not coming with me, Georgiana!'

She lifted her eyebrows at his use of her first name; he even seemed to have startled himself with how easily it had rolled off his tongue. Well, maybe he didn't have quite so much starch in his cravat as he pretended, she thought with a faint, mischievous smile.

'Pardon – Miss Knight,' he corrected himself in a clipped tone, reverting to formal mode once more. 'The point is, this is no time for a social call. Besides, it's much too dangerous. Speaking of which, will you please send for the constable now? They're waiting for me at Government House, but I will stay with you until the constable sends men to guard the house in case that mob comes back. Frankly, I am shocked that your brothers would leave you here unprotected—'

'Oh, please. They would never do that.' Georgie raised her hands and loudly clapped twice.

At once, a dozen armed sepoys in turbans, red coats, black breeches, and riding boots came jogging into the entrance hall and halted in formation, swords gleaming. They dropped the butts of their bayoneted muskets to the floor with a loud bang in unison.

When their captain saluted her, she nodded to him, then glanced proudly at Lord Griffith and couldn't help gloating a wee bit. 'Aren't they smart?'

Her brother Gabriel, one of the most feared men in India, had trained them himself.

The marquess regarded her bodyguards dryly. 'May I inquire why you did not see fit to bring these chaps with you to the, er, bonfire, Miss Knight?'

'Certainly. If Lakshmi's kin had seen me coming with all my bodyguards in tow, they'd have known at once what I intended, and would not have let me close enough to save her.'

'Ah. Well!' he concluded, his tone edged with irony. 'Since you seem to have everything under control here, I shall bid you adieu.'

'Oh, don't go—' she pleaded, but he ignored her and shook his head.

'Miss Knight.' He bowed to her, pivoted, and strode out.

Georgie felt a twinge in her lungs at his stubborn exit and stifled a vexed growl. Blast!

Ah, but he did not know her very well if he thought he was getting away that easily. She clenched her fists by her sides and marched out after him. 'Lord Griffith!'

He was a few feet ahead of her down the front path, waving his three servants back up onto the roof of the carriage and telling the footman he wouldn't be staying.

'Lord Griffith!' Georgie called again, incensed at being ignored. She felt the burn rise anew in her lungs, but she refused to be bothered by that right now. She stopped and planted her hands indignantly on her waist. 'I wasn't asking your permission!'

He froze halfway down the path, and then, slowly, looked over his shoulder at her, his glance dark and ominous.

With a small gulp at the brooding look he sent her, Georgie lifted her chin. 'I was invited by my friend to go and visit her at her new home. You can't stop me. I am going to—' she stopped herself from announcing their destination publicly. 'I'm going *there*,' she amended, 'with or without you. So it seems to me that we might as well travel together. It's safer that way for us both.'

He looked at her but said not a word.

Georgie gulped. She held her ground, however, with a fine view of the magnificent man as he turned around and stalked back up the path toward her.

Her heart beat faster.

Tall as he was, when Lord Griffith stopped just a few inches in front of her, she had to tilt her head back a bit to keep holding his icy stare, but she refused to let him intimidate her with his silence or his size.

'Meena needs me,' she informed him, 'and if there's going to be another stupid war, I want to see my brothers before they go charging off to fight on the front lines. They could be killed, you know. Besides—' She squared her shoulders, standing up to him. 'You have no right to tell me what to do.'

For a long moment he just stared at her impassively, sizing her up.

The silence stretched her nerves thin.

And then, at last, he nodded, conceding. 'Very well,' he answered in a mild tone, his eyes like mirrors, shutting her out. 'If that's how you feel. Wait here. I'll be in touch.'

'But—'

'I have to go and meet with my contacts,' he interrupted her succinctly. 'You will hear from me soon.'

'Oh – good, all right,' she forced out, quickly hiding her shock that she had managed to gain his compliance without too much additional arm-twisting.

Finally, a reasonable male!

'Well, um, carry on, then,' she instructed.

'Thank you,' he replied with etched-glass courtesy. 'Now, my dear – *princess* – do you mind if I borrow your coach to take me over to the hotel?'

'Please – be my guest. Why did you call me a – never mind.' She bit her tongue at his dark, warning look. 'You will be back?' she persisted with great delicacy, but he still glared.

'You will hear from me soon,' he repeated emphatically.

Georgie pressed her lips shut, folded her arms, and nodded agreeably, not daring to press her luck one inch further. As she watched him step up into her carriage, she almost called out another question for him, but deemed it wiser to hold her tongue. When the coach pulled away, she finally exhaled.

Well, that was interesting. She hadn't had much of a chance to interview him in order to learn his nature and gather information, as she had planned. Indeed, she was dismayed that he had rejected her offer of hospitality, but there would still be plenty of time to figure him and his mission out while they were on the road to Janpur. The journey would take several days.

That reminded her – she had to pack! But first, she realized, she had better check on Lakshmi.

After learning from a servant that her friend had come downstairs, Georgie went through the pair of dainty French doors at the end of the main corridor and walked out onto the breezy colonnade that girded the sun-splashed garden, around which the courtyard-style house was built.

This lush sanctuary was her favorite part of the house: a paradise garden in the Mughal style, divided into four quarters by little trickling waterways with a fountain in the center. The colonnade surrounding it was paved with smooth gray flagstones, and adorned with statues and hanging flower baskets here and there. Overhead, latticed arches spanned the slim white columns, continuing the house's fanciful theme of an exotic pavilion.

A balmy breeze whispered through the tamarind tree and wafted down the shady covered walkway, making the flower tendrils dance and blossoms nod. Sure enough, here she found her friend seated at the white wrought-iron garden table, weeping into an oversized handkerchief.

She winced at Lakshmi's sorrow and joined her at the table. 'Oh, my dear, don't cry.' Laying a comforting hand on her shoulder, Georgie bent down and gazed earnestly into her face, casting about for some words to bring her out of this weeping fit. 'Why are you crying? You should rejoice – you're free!'

Lakshmi blew her nose, then looked at her in doubt with red-rimmed eyes.

'Don't you see what a splendid opportunity you have before you?' Georgie continued, moving into the chair opposite Lakshmi and trying again to spark some enthusiasm in the girl for her altered station in life. 'You can do whatever you want now. You can change your name, create a whole new identity for yourself—'

'Oh, Gigi, you were always such a heretic.'

'What's wrong with that?' she countered, flashing a smile. 'If I obeyed every little rule, you and I could never have become friends. Here. This may help renew your courage. It always does for me.' Reaching into her pocket with an almost secretive motion, Georgie took out her most prized possession, the slim volume that she carried with her everywhere, like a talisman. Merely running her finger across the faded gold letters engraved upon the worn doeskin cover gave her strength: *Essays on the Natural Rights of the Fair Sex, by Georgiana Knight, the eighth Duchess of Hawskcliffe.* The complete collection of her scandalous aunt's writings.

She offered it to Lakshmi. 'Here. Go on. Take it. It may give you a . . . a new perspective on things.'

Lakshmi made no move to accept the book, only eyeing it warily.

Georgie waited, aware that it had been three years since Lakshmi had touched a book, ever since her marriage to Balaram, in keeping with the unofficial rules of purdah. The most traditional Indians had a superstition that if any married woman touched a book, her husband would die. Then, of course, the wife would have to join him by means of suttee. Georgie could only wonder what Aunt Georgiana would have said about that, but to the best of her knowledge, the duchess had never visited a land where wives were cloistered away in harems like a rich man's private collection of jewels. Indeed, from what she had heard about her aunt, the duchess probably wouldn't have minded having a harem of men.

For her part, Georgie saw the rule against books in purdah as an obvious tool to keep women in convenient ignorance. A naive woman was so much easier to control. The angry thought doubled her resolve to guard her heart and never fall in love, lest she, too, end up under some man's ruthless power.

Slowly, carefully, Lakshmi took the book from her hand. 'Well . . . it's not as if I can kill him now,' she said with a timid smile.

Georgie smiled back at her, more proud of her friend than she could express.

On the other hand, if any book *could* kill a husband, it would probably be this one, for it had nearly given Aunt Georgiana's husband, the previous Duke of Hawkscliffe, a fit of apoplexy when it had first appeared in Society. Papa had told her all about the scandal. As the late duke's younger brother, he had been there to witness all of it.

The duchess had spent her pin money to have one hundred copies of her essays printed and bound, and these she had distributed to her aristocratic lady friends in London. This, in turn, had nearly caused a riot in the House of Lords as the crazed husbands tried to figure out what had suddenly gone so wrong with their rebelling wives. When Hawkscliffe had found out about it, and realized that the source of all the commotion was his own headstrong lady, he hunted down every copy of her book that he could find and burned them. Lord Arthur Knight, Georgie's father, younger brother to the duke, had been sympathetic to the duchess's heartbreak at her works' destruction, and had managed to save a few copies for posterity.

At any rate, Lakshmi had begun to take an interest, and was now riffling cautiously through the dangerous pages. 'You know,' she said, 'sometimes I think you really might be the reincarnation of your aunt.'

'Oh, I don't think so. I'm only named after her. But . . . I do know one thing. If I *am* her reincarnated, I don't intend to make her same mistakes.'

Lakshmi flicked her a curious glance. 'Like what?'

'Like marrying a man she didn't love – and loving a man she wasn't married to. Like you, my poor aunt was bullied into marriage by her parents.'

Lakshmi sighed.

'But enough of all that,' Georgie said, brightening. 'I have news that I know is going to make you very happy.'

'What is it?' she asked woefully. 'I could use some cheerful tidings.'

Georgie gave her hand a squeeze. 'You and I are going to visit Meena!'

CHAPTER 3

What a completely impossible woman! Staring straight ahead, Ian rode in the carriage, arms folded across his chest, in a state of intense annoyance, not to mention hot and bothered by her kittenish invitation to spend the night at her house. Absurd creature. He was so, so very glad that Georgiana Knight was not his problem.

He did not know what unfortunate trait it was in him that attracted women who liked playing games – but at the same time, he couldn't help wondering how far she might be willing to go to get her way. *No. Don't even think about it.* He quivered, trying to thrust from his mind the wicked fantasy of letting her try to persuade him, also rejecting as best he could the tantalizing memory of her body rocking against his while they had ridden together on her horse. The scent of her exotic perfume lingered in the carriage, and it was not helping matters.

Damn, if he were not a gentleman . . .

But, of course, alas, he was, and would not lay a finger on her. Which meant the lovely little demon knew full well that he was safely chained by his honor, leaving her free to torment him with her beauty as she willed.

Well, it wasn't going to work! he thought staunchly. Even at eighteen, he had been too disciplined, too responsible, too intelligent, and too well-bred to let females lead him around by his cock. He was careful.

Always careful.

And he saw he would have to be doubly careful with Georgiana, for she was no fool. If only she were, he thought in begrudging admiration, fighting a smile at her little games. Most unmarried young women turned into helpless pools of goo when he attempted to have a conversation with them, but not Miss Knight.

Hardly. Instead, the girl had dared to play a round of verbal chess with him. He nearly laughed aloud to think of it. Not even Metternich liked arguing against him. And all the while, she had been doing her best to try to twist him around her finger with her very considerable charm.

Well, he mused, savoring the memory of her saucy allure, charm only went so far.

Her family might take an indulgent stance toward her, but he knew the folly of that, and was not about to let a bona-fide troublemaker impinge upon his mission. *She thinks she's going to Janpur? Well, princess, you had better think again.*

Her little social call on her royal friend would have to wait until the larger crisis had passed. This was no time for a ladies' holiday. He wished she had not made it necessary, but if he had to take stronger steps to rein her in, then so be it. No one else appeared inclined to do it.

Arriving at the Akbar Grand Hotel, Ian got out and headed up the wide front steps of the elegant establishment. Striding toward the entrance with its pair of large stone lions, he stole a glance over his shoulder to see if there was any sign of the watcher he had sensed back at the bazaar. A quick scan of the sunny avenue brought his attention to a group of robed men loitering on the corner several yards away, a motley assortment of what appeared to be locals milling about idly. None wore Western garb, but that meant nothing. The French or Dutch could have hired an Indian to spy on him, or a European agent easily could have donned a disguise.

Movement.

A flash of furtive motion at the back of the group caught Ian's eye. A fleeting glimpse was all he got before the swarthy, black-robed man disappeared around the corner. *So, there you are.*

His lips thinned as he considered going after the spy, but then again it could be useful to let the fellow believe he had not yet been spotted. At least now Ian had an idea of whom to watch for.

Turning away before anyone else noticed his stare – he had paused for no more than a few seconds – he continued smoothly toward the entrance, jogging up the few front steps.

He breezed into the hotel lobby with Ravi, the coolies, and his luggage in tow. When Ian walked in, they were already expecting him, and all was in order.

Now, this was more like it.

A fresh-faced adjutant who appeared all of eighteen greeted him with a brisk salute. 'Sir!'

The smartly uniformed junior officer announced himself as Lieutenant Daniel DeWitt, assigned by the governor himself to make sure Ian had all he needed.

Then the hotel's concierge showed Ian up to his apartments with the pup DeWitt following at his heels. 'We heard your boat got in a while ago, my lord—'

'I was delayed,' he said vaguely. 'News from Hastings?'

'Yes, sir—'

Ian tipped the concierge while Ravi shepherded the coolies into the adjoining bedchamber, where they deposited Ian's several portmanteaux.

'Lord Hastings has left the city,' the boy told him once the door was closed. 'He is already on the march against the Marathas. He's amassing an army at Cawnpore even now,' he added, clearly envious of the troops who'd been chosen to go. 'He bade me give you this.' DeWitt presented him with a leather-bound folio containing more details on the Janpur situation.

Ian thumbed through it. 'What of the men I asked for?'

'Yes, sir. The Knight brothers were already in the north when they were sent their orders. They will be riding down to meet you at Varanasi, on the road to Janpur.'

The little hellion had been right about that. Irksome thought.

'For now,' the lad continued, 'Major MacDonald will be in charge of finalizing all aspects of your transport and supplies.'

'MacDonald, eh? Highlander?'

'Oh, yes, sir, quite.' DeWitt grinned, and Ian nodded. He had some Highland blood himself.

'How soon can the major have his men ready?'

'By daybreak, sir. With Lord Hastings already mobilizing the army, he thought you'd probably want to go as soon as possible.'

'Excellent.' Ian nodded, folding his arms across his chest.

'Is there anything else that you require, sir?'

'Actually, Lieutenant, I do have a request.'

'Sir?'

'There is a young lady here in town – you probably are acquainted with her. The sister of Gabriel and Derek Knight, Georgiana.'

The lad's eyes widened, and an awestruck, slightly dreamy expression passed over his countenance. 'Oh, *yes*, sir.'

'I am concerned that her brothers' involvement in my mission could make her a target—'

DeWitt gasped aloud. 'Er, sorry.'

Ian raised a brow. 'I would like a few of your

68

most trustworthy men posted around her house to ensure her safety. They are to watch over her at all times, make sure she does not leave Calcutta, and accompany her when she goes out.'

'*Yes, sir*, I will see to it personally!' The boy saluted as though Ian had just knighted him. 'And now, my lord, I shall leave you to settle in. I'm sure you must have had a tiresome journey.'

'Thank you, Lieutenant. You've been most helpful,' he said dryly.

Somehow Ian gathered there would be no shortage of volunteers.

Well, that should keep her busy.

He would love to have seen the look on her face when the chosen soldiers showed up at her house to guard her, but with the spy lingering outside, he could not risk drawing further attention to Georgiana by visiting her again.

Meanwhile, DeWitt bowed and marched out.

Left alone for the time being, Ian spent a few minutes reading the first part of Lord Hastings' notes on Janpur and reviewing the maps of the rocky, rugged territory.

Loosening his cravat in the midday heat, he put the report aside for the moment and opened one of his orderly traveling trunks.

As always, the first thing he did upon arriving at any new destination was to take out the thin, round silver case no bigger than a fob watch that he carried with him everywhere. He opened it and started to place it on the table next to the bed, but instead of setting it aside, he paused and gazed for a long moment at the round-faced little boy who stared out from the miniature portrait with such big, serious eyes.

Matthew.

When the familiar pang of fatherly guilt besieged him, he told himself for the hundred-thousandth time that there was never any need to worry for Matthew. He had the best care money could buy. Besides his nanny, tutor, governess, and a small army of maids, the boy was being watched over by the London Knights themselves.

His son and Robert's were best friends, just as *they* had been at the same age, and their fathers before them. Robert and Bel treated Matthew as if he was their own.

And he might as well have been, at that. Matthew adored his Aunt Bel and Uncle Hawk, but as for his own papa, hell, Ian thought, the kid didn't even like him.

Stripped down to the black *pyjama* leggings and snug *choli* undershirt that she had worn beneath her sari, Georgie was in the garden, gliding through the motions of a few sun salutations to help erase the effects of her earlier bout with asthma. Stretching her arms high over her head until her fingertips touched, she then folded forward from the waist until her nose gently bumped her shin. From there, she jumped back lightly into plank pose, flexed her body into upward-facing dog pose, and cycled through her *vinyasa* in smooth, unhurried motion.

With each repetition, she felt the clenched muscles deep in her chest further relax. Thankfully, it no longer hurt to breathe.

Lakshmi was upstairs looking through Georgie's wardrobe for things that she could wear. Adley had long since left. Georgie's servants had packed her belongings for her jaunt to the interior, and now she was merely waiting in keen anticipation for word from Lord Griffith to find out what came next. He had said he would be in touch with her soon.

Pressing her heel down for a good stretch in her calf, she was wondering if he intended for them to leave for Janpur tomorrow morning, as she had suggested, when her maid, Gita, came hurrying out to the garden carrying a note.

'Memsahib, this just came for you by messenger.'

'From Lord Griffith?'

'Yes, Miss.'

'I will take it here,' she answered quickly. She folded her legs and sat in lotus position. '*Dhonnobad*, Gita,' she murmured, accepting the note with a nod of thanks. Her heart skipped a beat as she cracked the seal and read:

Dear Miss Knight,
  I have, alas, too many preparations to attend to before I leave Calcutta, so this missive comes to you in my place. You will soon note that I've

taken the liberty of ordering a few additional measures to ensure your safety, just in case there's any sign of trouble from the people at the funeral today. I will give your brothers your best regards when I see them. Will call on you when I return.

Yr servant,
Griffith

Georgie furrowed her brow and frowned, thinking she must have missed the part about the two of them traveling together to Janpur.

She read it again as the truth dawned. *He means to go without me!* A spasm immediately racked her lungs in protest of his intention to abandon her, but Georgie was suddenly livid and paid it little mind. Jumping to her feet, she pulled on her tunic and dashed upstairs to change her clothes, seething. *I don't believe it. That traitor! Blackguard! Double-crossing knave!* Well, she was not going to stand for this. She would drive right over to the Akbar Grand Hotel and straighten that man out!

When she arrived at her silk-hung bedchamber, Lakshmi was standing before the mirror holding Georgie's blue sari up against her, considering it on herself. 'What's wrong?' she asked abruptly at Georgie's wrathful expression.

'I need something to wear,' she muttered. 'Fast.'

'This?' She held out the blue sari, but Georgie waved it off impatiently.

'English. Day-dress.' She strode over to the tall

mahogany wardrobe and whisked through the hanging gowns that weren't packed.

'Gigi, what's the matter?'

'That verminous Londoner – lied to me!' she exclaimed as she wrenched off her yoga clothes and fought her way into the first decent walking dress that her hand seized. She pulled it on over her head. 'Well, maybe not lied,' she amended, angrily fluffing the ruffled skirts, 'but he certainly didn't tell me the truth. He told me what I wanted to hear – so he could get rid of me. Very tricky, Marquess. Very tricky!' she railed at the air. 'What additional measures was he talking about, anyway?' she asked rhetorically, eager to get to the hotel to make him explain the cryptic statement.

She did not like the sound of that one bit.

'Um, Gigi, are you decent? I – I think you had better come and see this,' Lakshmi called uneasily. She had drifted over to the window and now pointed downward, sending Georgie an anxious glance over her shoulder.

'What is it? Has he come?' she demanded, adjusting the neckline of her gown to a more respectable situation. 'Oh, I hope he's found the nerve to show his face. There are so many things I'd love to say to him right now!'

'No, it's not the marquess. Look,' Lakshmi said, as Georgie marched over and joined her by the window. 'There are soldiers posted all around your house!'

Her jaw dropped. It was true.

'Gigi?'

She heard Lakshmi's worried inquiry as though it traveled to her through a great, watery distance. Her heart was pounding in her ears.

'I don't believe it,' she said faintly. 'He's put me under house arrest!' She straightened up, her mind reeling.

He had taken additional measures, all right, but not to protect her – to prevent her from following him to Janpur! With that, all of her worst suspicions about his true nature came rushing back.

'That *snake!*' she cried as a furious flush filled her cheeks. Suddenly animated out of her daze, she rushed off to peer out through various other windows around her house. Sure enough, soldiers from Fort William were stationed at each of the four corners. Lakshmi hurried to keep up with Georgie as she went to check out the back.

'How dare he? Does he think I'm a child? A pet to be kept in a cage?' *Wedlock is a padlock* – but they weren't even married!

'Dearest, perhaps you had better calm down—'

'Calm down?' Georgie shouted. 'I'm not going to stand for this! Who does he think he is? He has no right to confine me here against my will! He's made me a prisoner in my own home!'

'He's put you in purdah,' Lakshmi agreed barely audibly.

Georgie turned to her, wide-eyed, sobered. 'You're right.'

Over my dead body.

Horrid man!

'What are we going to do?' Lakshmi asked in distress. 'Now we won't be able to see Meena.'

'Oh, yes, we will,' Georgie vowed. 'That man has no power over me, and never will.'

'But how will we escape?'

'Well – I haven't quite figured that out yet,' she admitted, staring out the window that overlooked her home's northwest corner. 'But don't worry, Lakshmi. I'll think of something.'

Just then, the soldier on duty below strolled into view, glancing right and left as he prowled around patrolling with a dead-serious expression. But as Georgie squinted for a closer study of the clean-shaven face beneath the shadowed brim of his shako, a smile spread across her lips; she recognized him as one of her admirers.

Tommy Gray.

Perhaps the young sergeant sensed her gaze, for he glanced up at the window where she stood. Georgie summoned up all her feminine wiles and lifted her hand languidly, wriggling her fingers at Tommy with a coquettish wave.

He swept off his shako and waved it in a wide arc, back and forth, grinning up at her from ear to ear.

Sweet boy.

Fool. Just like all silly, power-mongering males. What good were they, anyway?

'Don't you worry, Lakshmi,' she assured her

friend, holding her sweet smile as she set her chin on her palm and pretended to admire Tommy from the window. 'You think I'm going to let some arrogant marquess stand in my way? I promise you, my father raised me better than that.'

Late that night, Ameer Firoz Khilji slipped off his shoes and walked with a stealthy, gliding gait into the torch-lit Kali temple. It had rained softly throughout the evening, the lingering remnants of the monsoon leaving the darkness damp and full of whispering secrets.

Satisfied that the Englishman would remain in his hotel room for the rest of the night, Firoz had taken this fleeting opportunity to come and pay homage to the goddess he revered. With his stare fixed on her towering image at the end of the soaring, shadowed space, he moved deeper into the temple. The animal sacrifices had been over since twilight, but although he had missed the rites, he gave the priest who greeted him a weighty purse full of gold, the proceeds of his labors in her name. Firoz bowed his head as the old man touched his brow and gave him a blessing.

When the priest left to put his large donation in a safe place, Firoz prostrated himself before the massive idol, down on his knees and bowing low. But he peered upward slowly from below his lashes and searched her vicious form with a creeping horror that still raised the hairs on the back of his neck, even after all these years.

Monstrous.

Kali, the goddess of destruction.

She was absolute night, the Dark Mother, the end of time – nightmare. Death, fear, and pain. And to serve her, he had made himself into all of those things. To be worthy of worshiping her.

It was a hard and lonely path, but he was one of the few who grasped its importance. After all, without the horror of her and all she stood for, everything good and light in the world would be meaningless.

Kali's naked body was painted black, her long ebony hair wildly disheveled from her dance of death. She wore a necklace of human skulls and a skirt made from the severed arms of men. Her eyes bulged with bloodlust; her gold tongue thrust from her mouth, as though to devour the world. In her four arms, she held a bloody sword, a decapitated head, the power to vanquish fear, and the secret of bliss.

Firoz wondered how many more he'd have to kill before that secret was given to him.

It was true that he was favored by the goddess. Even his brethren in the Thuggee cult were jealous of him. Jealous and afraid. But none of them served her as ruthlessly or as skillfully as he.

So much did he enjoy her protection that the British authorities could not catch him, and though he had killed in the hundreds, he remained immune to Hindu law. She protected him by sending him constant communication through many signs and omens, and tonight, the cawing of the crow had signaled to him that it was time to go to her to pray at her great temple.

He crouched low as he praised her by her many names in a fervent whisper: Devi, Bhavani, and of course, Mother Kali, for whom Calcutta had been named.

Shiva's wild consort.

She was all he had, all he had known ever since the night long ago that his own parents were slain in her name. They, too, had been travelers on the road, overcome by a band of Thugs. He had been a small boy then, and the brotherhood refused to kill children, so he had been spared.

After his parents had been placed in the earth, the men who had sacrificed them took him in and raised him, and initiated him into her secret ways.

Through years of training, Firoz had risen to become the most revered killer in all the brotherhood. First he had served as a scout, mastering the skills of planning missions and gathering information without drawing attention to himself.

Next, he had been designated as one of the gravediggers, disbursing the required rituals over their victims and learning how to dispose of the bodies so they would never be found. Dismemberment was grisly work, but even as a lad of barely sixteen, Firoz had never flinched.

Thus he had gained the approval of his guru, and had been promoted to *shumseea*. His job then was to lull and charm the wealthy travelers he met along the road and soothe away their fears so they suspected nothing, becoming easy prey for the highest rank within their organization: the stranglers.

Firoz had achieved the level of *bhurtote*, ritual killer, some ten years ago. Each month since then, unfailingly, he had sacrificed four lives to the goddess, one to place in each of her hands. He was as efficient as he was remorseless. Why mourn? Their souls lived on through reincarnation, and their deaths helped to maintain the balance of the universe, which the Dark Mother represented in her terrible dance. If there was life, there must be death; if there was light there must be darkness.

Her dance whirled now in his brain as he prayed. Sometimes in his mind, the two mysterious female powers that he served blurred into one, the terrible goddess and the dark queen.

For all he knew, the earthly lady behind her heavy veil might be an incarnation of the goddess herself, testing him, as the gods were wont to do with their favorites; therefore, the tasks *she* gave him carried an extraordinary weight. He did Her Majesty's bidding with an urgency no king or priest could ever have inspired in him.

Killing for the goddess was his dharma, but serving Queen Sujana of Janpur had long been his occupation: spy, assassin, whatever she required. He drew upon the same skills in both secret lines of endeavor.

On her orders, he had followed the English

diplomat for many miles, ever since the Maharani had first heard through her palace spies that Lord Griffith was coming to Janpur.

This nocturnal prayer time was for Kali, but soon, he knew, he should report back to his worldly duty.

A short while later, Firoz rose from his prayers and walked closer, his stealth-trained footfalls silent in the temple's gloom. He lit some incense at the giant feet of her statue, and waved the smoke up gently to her.

Like Kali, he was terrible; like every victim he had slain, he was alone.

Sunlight streamed through the scalloped arches, illuminating colorful mosaics and bright gilding everywhere. A humid breeze smelling faintly of sandalwood rustled through the potted palms, but with their two empires on the brink of war, the air nearly crackled with distrust as Ian rose to address the royal court.

A week had passed, and Ian was now knee-deep in negotiations in the Maharajah of Janpur's sumptuous Throne Room.

Exuding calm power and cool determination, he swept the gathering with a steely glance. Not for an instant did he forget that countless lives hung in the balance.

They always did, in his line of work.

Well aware that this was his final chance to avert the looming war – or at least to curtail it before the first shot was fired – he chose his words with meticulous care.

'Loyalty.' His firm, cultured voice echoed under the ceiling dome. 'This, Your Majesty, is what lies at the heart of the controversy.'

The robed and turbaned viziers stopped their murmurings to heed him. Though interpreters stood at the ready, the British had been in India long enough by now that most of the nobles spoke English.

Ahead, meanwhile, seated on his cushioned stool-throne, the formidable Hindu king, Johar, Maharajah of Janpur, sat stroking his black beard and listening intently.

Dressed in Eastern splendor, the maharajah wore a loose, sleeveless, knee-length coat of rich brocade over a white, belted tunic with long sleeves, and leggings of white silk. A sapphire the size of an egg secured his turban, which was also adorned with an aigrette of peacock feathers – a royal prerogative.

Behind him, various dark-clad attendants and fierce palace guards were arrayed in crescent formation, one holding the fringed *chatri*, or ceremonial umbrella, while others slowly waved huge peacock-feather fans to keep His Majesty cool.

By his side, his son, Crown Prince Shahu, lounged on his lesser throne, looking bored and malcontent, as if he'd rather be out hunting in the dense surrounding forests with his royal falcons and his entourage of toadies.

'For hundreds of years,' Ian said, walking out from behind the long teakwood table where the hand-picked members of his delegation were seated, 'the six royal houses of the Maratha Empire have held off invaders by your sacred blood-oath of mutual defense. Far and wide it is known that if any one of your kingdoms is attacked, all the others shall rouse their armies and come to the besieged one's aid. It is enviable in this world to have such stalwart friends.'

He had brought friends of his own to this fight. Gabriel and Derek Knight sat at the table with the other members of his team, the big braw Scotsman, Major MacDonald, and the old battle-ax, Colonel Montrose, the ranking military member of his party. All four men watched Ian pace slowly across the white marble floor as his speech now took a new twist.

'But what if one of your brother-kings abuses the great loyalty of the Marathas?' he posed the question. 'Makes a grievous error in judgment? Picks a fight where none is warranted, for reasons known only to himself? Is it fair for him to prevail on all of you to come to his rescue, when he alone has acted irresponsibly?'

Halting at one end of the space, he pivoted and looked at the whole court matter-of-factly. 'Are your people to suffer the privations of war, your soldiers to bleed, all for the vain delusions of your great ally, Baji Rao?'

'Delusions?' The crown prince leaped to his feet.

'How dare you speak of my uncle with such disrespect, you English—'

'Sit down!' Johar barked at his son. The king fairly rolled his eyes with impatience at his son's impassioned outburst. 'We crave your patience with our son, Lord Griffith. He has much to learn of statecraft.'

Ian bowed, far from ruffled, in truth, hiding a smile of worldly amusement. Through diplomatic eyes, such temper was a sign of weakness.

Prince Shahu clamped his mouth shut and obeyed his father with a simmering look. His long, gold earrings flashing, he swept his garish robe around him and prowled back to his seat in his curl-toed shoes, the Oriental version of a London dandy.

'Perhaps His Highness wishes me to specify the exact nature of our dispute with Baji Rao,' Ian offered with frosty aplomb.

'Indeed!' the young man snapped.

'I shall be happy to explain.' He walked back to the long table, where Derek Knight handed him the map. 'Hiding themselves in the mountains of your kinsman's territory, a colony of criminals has taken root. They are known as the Pindari Horde, and a greater trash heap of human riffraff was never assembled. Murderers, rapists, thieves. Each year, the Pindari come thundering down from their mountain strongholds to carry out raids on the surrounding lands, burning whatever they cannot steal. Last year alone, they destroyed four hundred villages, British and Hindu alike. This map records the path they took. The villages marked with the X's no longer exist.'

Unrolling the map, he carried it to the pair of thrones.

'When their plundering urges have been satisfied, the Pindari simply ride back up into their mountain hideaways – until the next raid. Our intelligence officers report that in this easy and comfortable existence the outlaws enjoy inside the safe haven that Baji Rao has granted them, their numbers have swelled to fifty . . . thousand strong.'

A shocked murmur rippled through the durbar hall at hearing the enormous number.

'Thirty thousand cavalry, twenty thousand foot – and they continue to acquire heavy artillery. Sounds like an army, doesn't it? An army of barbarians, who are not beholden to any code of conduct, and respect no rules of war. Your Majesty, Your Highness, gentlemen of the court, by all that is honorable, this cannot be allowed to continue.'

When nods and vague murmurs signaled that everyone seemed to be with him so far, Ian clasped his hands behind his back and forged on. 'Governor Lord Hastings has repeatedly asked Baji Rao to gather his army and hunt these killers in their mountain hideaways until the problem is eradicated. But he will not. For reasons known only to himself, your fellow king has chosen to protect these outlaws – one cannot help but

84

wonder why. Does Baji Rao fear the Pindari too much to move against them? Or does he perhaps find them . . . useful?'

The sinister possibility hung upon the silence.

Ian shrugged. 'It is not given to us to see inside another's mind. All we can know for certain is our own, and our view of the matter is clear. If your kinsman refuses to stop the Pindari – to stamp out this evil – then the British will.'

'But Baji Rao will not permit your troops to cross his borders in pursuit of the Pindari,' the maharajah spoke up.

'Yes, Your Majesty. You are quite right. Baji Rao has proclaimed that if even one British soldier sets foot on his territory, he will consider it an act of war. As I understand it, he has already sent out his clarion call to you and all the other Maratha kings, laying claim to the old alliance.'

'It is so,' King Johar admitted. 'We have received Baji Rao's request for military support against what he describes as the threat of a British invasion.'

'And I am here, Sire, to assure you that no invasion was ever intended. Our only concern is eradicating the Pindari bandits. We cannot permit them to continue slaughtering innocent people. If Baji Rao wishes to call up his army and summon his allies to stand in our way, we will fight the Marathas, too, if we must. But in reality, it is completely unnecessary. The Pindari are a threat to all of our people. *They* are the enemy.

We should not be fighting each other, but should work together to destroy *them*.'

'So, what do the British want from us?' King Johar asked.

'Nothing but your continued friendship, Sire,' he answered smoothly. 'The British have no quarrel with Janpur. Indeed, over the past decade, our two peoples have enjoyed a prosperous co-operation. Your Majesty has graciously allowed British merchants to cross peacefully through Janpur transporting their goods back and forth between Calcutta and Bombay. In return, your kingdom has increased its coffers many times over by the tolls and taxes collected on this trade.'

'Indeed,' Johar said with a slight smile of pride. 'But, in terms of friendship, well, perhaps you could be more specific.'

Ian nodded, lowering his gaze. Twelve years in the diplomatic service had taught him all too well that the universal sign of loyalty was gold.

He also realized that, as proud members of the Kshatriya, or warrior caste, the Marathas were bound to find his answer shocking. He braced himself for the reaction. 'We would like to enter into a treaty of neutrality with Janpur,' he said. 'In light of how much in the wrong Baji Rao is, we ask you to forsake the old alliance in this case and leave your kinsman to his own devices. Without your support, he may come to his senses and stand down, and this whole war can be avoided!' His final words were shouted, for the court had already erupted at his proposition, barely hearing his conclusion.

The viziers had burst into argument. The scowling palace guards gripped their giant spears and looked to their ruler for orders, but King Johar was silent.

The same could not be said for his hotheaded son.

'Neutrality?' Prince Shahu cried, shooting up out of his seat again. 'By the sword of Shivaji, we will not betray our kinsman! We know the real reason you come here to sue for peace – because you are afraid of us, as well you should be! But if the British are too cowardly to stand against the full Maratha force, then you should go back and tell Lord Hastings—'

A blaring trumpet fanfare suddenly sailed in on the breeze, cutting off the prince's tirade. Everyone turned to look.

The bold, brassy notes sounded the herald a second time, echoing up from the castle's winding approaches.

Ian frowned, irked at the interruption. *Sounds like His Majesty's got visitors.*

At once, the gaggle of advisers seized the reprieve to whisper among themselves.

King Johar sent his son out to investigate, along with a muttered order to get hold of his temper while he was gone. 'Another such outburst from you, and you will not be invited back,' Johar growled at him.

'Yes, Father. I apologize,' he said quietly, though he still seemed to simmer with resentment. Scowling, but no doubt glad of the excuse to escape the odious presence of Englishmen, the heir of Janpur bowed to his father, then exited under the arches of the arcade, which led out onto the sentry's walk atop the windy ramparts of the fortress.

Ian glanced at the maharajah, a little uncertain of the status of their meeting given the interruption. He knew King Johar would need time to think and that the advisers, too, would want to debate their response to the British proposition, but between Shahu's outburst and the trumpets' hail, everyone except for him seemed to have lost focus.

The whole court had turned into hubbub. Even King Johar had beckoned a minister over and now they were conferring in low tones, using the interruption to discuss the idea of neutrality.

Ian curbed his annoyance with the disruption and, leaving them to their murmurings, exchanged stoic glances with the Knight brothers as he returned to the table to take a quick swallow of water. The men needed no words to communicate their displeasure with the unexpected halt in these highly delicate proceedings.

Suddenly, Prince Shahu came rushing back in. 'Father, a caravan's coming – it looks like a royal entourage! There are twenty soldiers on horseback, and servants, and musicians, and many camels laden with gifts – and a princess, riding on an elephant!'

'A princess?' King Johar rose, frowning as the young man dashed back out again.

Ian's first thought made him blink.

No – it couldn't be! He shook it off. *Impossible.* 'Was Your Majesty expecting visitors?' he inquired with studied calm, on his guard.

'No.' The maharajah's rugged face darkened with mistrust. He looked at Ian, and Ian looked skeptically at him.

'Most irregular,' Ian opined, narrowing his eyes in suspicion. He would not have been at all surprised if it were some sort of ruse from the court of Baji Rao.

'Hm,' Johar murmured, almost as though he in turn suspected that the British might have had something to do with it.

Irked with the interruption and unsure what mischief was afoot, Ian frowned. Perhaps the royal advisers had some devilry up their sleeves. 'With your leave, Sire, I should like a moment to appraise the situation.'

Johar waved his hand, inviting him do as he pleased.

Eyeing his hosts warily, Ian bowed to the maharajah and then left his post, striding out onto the windy ramparts to see this 'royal princess' for himself.

Though he had not yet laid eyes on her, he had half a mind to wring the woman's neck. Ah, but it took a female to muck things up properly – a principle as unfailing in his experience as Newton's laws of motion.

The rushing breeze tousled his hair as he strode out onto the lofty battlements. Beneath an endless azure sky, Janpur Palace sat atop a sun-baked precipice, its mighty ramparts and soaring outer walls carved from the mountain's lustrous ocher sandstone. Fantastical rounded bastions topped with airy cupolas guarded the approaches, each tower adorned with bands of glazed tiles made of brilliant lapis lazuli.

From its craggy peak, the ancient stronghold dominated the surrounding rugged vastness – tiger country – hills clad in teakwood forest and bamboo, swift rivers swollen with the end of monsoon, rushing waterfalls crashing through ravines.

As Ian rested his hands on the rough, sun-warmed stone and leaned forward, peering over the crenellated battlements, his vantage point directly overlooked the steep stone road that came winding up the mountainside in tight meanders, doubling back on itself, snakelike, as it approached the ominous main gate.

Prince Shahu had painted an accurate picture.

Ian counted twenty armed sepoys on horseback flanking the caravan. There were camels, too, a full dozen, their humped backs laden with glittering treasures. Six musicians in an ox-cart were already playing as their resplendent party approached, beating drums, playing ecstatic ragas on the sitar, accompanied by a reedy pipe.

But the centerpiece of this extravagant party wending its way slowly, musically, joyously up the road had to be the painted elephant. The creature's gray face and trunk had been decorated with bright pink and yellow and green designs; the covered howdah on its massive back was festooned with colorful streamers that waved on the breeze.

Shading his eyes from the sun with one hand, he made out four figures riding in the howdah, but despite the gaiety of their parade, he bristled with suspicion.

What Trojan horse is this?

The music ended abruptly as the long procession reached the towering iron gates. The contrast of sudden silence was dramatic. There was only the blowing of the wind as the whole caravan came to a halt.

The mahout let out a curt order, and the great elephant hunkered down gently to let her passengers out of the whimsical conveyance. Then a dainty set of steps tumbled out, folding into place, and two ladies-in-waiting dressed in pastel veils and saris minced down the little stairs and assembled in a line, side by side, facing the castle.

Ian suddenly gasped. *Oh, God.*

He recognized the footman – from the marketplace!

The footman in showy lavender livery skipped

forward and assisted a stout, black-clad matron of more advanced years down the little steps. Her ayah.

Last of all, the veiled 'princess' herself glided down gracefully from the howdah.

He hadn't really believed it until he saw her, but then she appeared, and the lightest breeze could have knocked him off the wall. Oh, to be certain, it was she – unmistakable Georgiana, with her flowing, liquid stride so full of self-assurance and the sleek lines of her feminine curves as elegant as the silhouette of a calla lily.

A silk sari dyed in bright pinks and vibrant rose hues draped her lithe figure, and Ian held his breath, unsure if he had heard or merely imagined the tinkling, ever so faintly, of those tiny silver bells around her ankle.

He stared, incredulous at her audacity, and once more irresistibly, almost magically drawn to her. The little enchantress mesmerized him. He didn't even blink, watching her in guarded fascination.

A few feet away, Prince Shahu seemed to be suffering the same effects. 'Ah, she is an *apsara*,' he breathed. *Celestial maiden*. The young warrior-prince was practically salivating.

Shahu's obvious lust jarred Ian out of his stupor. He glanced at the prince uneasily.

Below, Georgiana's liveried footman hurried after her, trying to keep a parasol positioned over her head to protect her from the sun, but instead, she handed him a small piece of paper and sent him forward to the gate with a graceful twirl of her hand, like that of a temple dancer. Her ladies, including the old one, gathered behind her.

Ian saw the footman run the piece of paper up to the iron gates, where he handed it through the outer portcullis to a guard.

While the little paper – Ian could only guess it was her calling card – began its rapid journey up through the fortress, relayed by sprinting pages, Georgiana lifted her gaze, as though she had felt them watching her.

When she looked up, the dramatic kohl lining around her eyes startled Ian. She had decorated her eyes in the Indian ladies' style. Accented by the rich sable of her hair, the kohl heightened her sultry, exotic appeal. A translucent scarf was thrown carelessly over her head, with the long end flowing back to one side of her neck; it billowed languidly on the breeze.

Ian looked at her and in that moment wanted her more intensely than he had ever wanted any woman before. But her cool gaze dismissed him.

Searching the battlements, she spotted the maharajah, who had just now come out to see for himself what was the matter. Johar stared at her in recognition with a smile full of warm, male pleasure at the sight of a beautiful woman coming over his rugged face.

She pressed her fingertips together and bowed her head, greeting His Majesty with a graceful *namaste*. Johar was known as a bit of a ladies' man – no great surprise, from a man with thirty wives and a hundred concubines – but Ian was startled by an inward jolt of some violent, inexplicable reaction as the king returned her gesture of greeting in kind.

In a deep voice full of amusement, he murmured an order to his servant: 'Bring me my pearl.'

Then he gestured to the nearest guardsman. 'Let her in!' Without further ado, His Majesty strode back inside.

Ian looked over the wall at Georgiana again, his jaw clenched. This did not bode well. The prince wanted her. The king wanted her. He wanted her. And no doubt, so would the Pindaris.

Bloody hell! How in blazes had she gotten away from her guards?

'What's going on?' Derek and Gabriel Knight came out just then to see what was happening.

Ian swept a sardonic wave in their visitor's direction.

The Knight brothers looked down at her, and suddenly exploded with shocked expletives.

'I don't believe it! Georgie!' Derek lifted his fingers to his mouth and gave a piercing whistle while Gabriel waved.

'Georgiana! Griff, we must go to her! Do you mind?'

'Yes, will you pardon us for a moment?' Derek turned to him, his face beaming. 'The meeting does seem to have broken up, after all.'

'Yes, mysteriously so,' he drawled.

'May we go and see her?'

'By all means.'

Ian had told her brothers he had met her in Calcutta, though he had spared them the details of the trouble she had gotten into. He had figured the particulars of the suttee rescue could wait until after their mission. He had hoped, apparently in vain, that they could all stay focused on the task at hand.

So much for that silly notion.

'Don't worry, we'll make sure she stays out of trouble,' Gabriel promised.

Ian smiled blandly. 'Right.'

The brothers dashed off to greet her as the great gates of Janpur slowly began creaking open.

Only now, having first paid her respects to the maharajah, and then waving eagerly to her brothers, did Georgiana deign to meet Ian's gaze. Her glance was sharp, lightning-bright, full of angry challenge.

Oh, this girl was trouble.

Glowering at her, Ian planted his hands atop the wall and shook his head slowly at her with a stare that promised the lovely young hellion his wrath.

CHAPTER 4

*S*afe *at last.* Behind her veil, Georgie's small sigh of relief puffed the light gauze silk that floated against her lips.

Two days into their journey, they had heard rumors from other travelers on the road that some of the Pindari Horde had been spotted in the area. But thankfully, they had made it to Janpur without incident.

As the towering gates slowly creaked open before them, she could feel her servants' lingering uneasiness – indeed, she shared it – but she waited with a serene stare ahead and an outward show of tranquility until the Maratha guards waved them in.

With a nod to her trusty footman, who, in turn, signaled the whole caravan back into motion, they moved on. Rather than getting back up on her hired elephant, Georgie continued on foot up the castle's processional road.

Still open to the sky, the long, narrow corridor rose on a slight grade, its smooth floor and austere, soaring walls built from huge blocks of stone. The processional way was lined with colossal statues set about every ten yards. There were massive deities,

96

rampant desert lions with teeth bared and claws unsheathed, but most imposing of all were the giant pairs of stone war elephants. Their raised trunks formed arches under which visitors had to pass. The ceremonial walk was meant to awe all those who entered, and Georgie was beginning to feel quite small, but leading her party into the Maratha stronghold, her footsteps did not falter. She might have a little fear coursing through her veins, but she did not intend to let Lord Griffith see it.

Passing under a triumphal arch held up by more sandstone elephants, each holding a lotus in its trunk, the corridor ended in a huge central plaza that buzzed with activity.

Here, the maharajah's household staff took charge.

Georgie's animals and their keepers were escorted away in one direction, lumbering off to the elephant stables and those for camels and horses. Except for her maid and her ayah, all of her other servants, footmen and coolies, sepoys and musicians, were led off in the other direction to their accommodations, past the pyramidal Shiva temple and the huge wrought-iron cage full of shady trees that was home to the maharajah's tigers.

A member of King Johar's household staff led Georgie and her ladies straight ahead to the other end of the plaza, through another massive gate, and into a large enclosed courtyard with a fountain in the center. They were now in the palace proper; her heart beat swiftly. She and Lakshmi exchanged a bolstering glance, both certain that they'd feel much more at ease once they had been reunited with Meena.

Enormous columns supported the two-storied galleries that surrounded the large rectangle of the courtyard, which itself lay open to the cloudless blue sky. A few palm trees thrived here and there. The shade was pleasant, but Georgie felt a bit unsettled to notice the palace guards posted everywhere, like more stone statues, staring straight ahead as they gripped their tall, gleaming battle-axes.

The palace guards were uniformed in black, belted tunics with black leggings and appeared almost identical, each one bearded, their long hair gathered into twin queues over their shoulders, neatly bound with red twine. They were fearsome beings, with black-sheathed swords and silver daggers strapped about their waists.

One of them swiveled his head, alerted, as her two favorite warriors in the world suddenly came racing into the courtyard, their shiny black boots clattering on the flagstones.

'Georgie!'

She let out a joyous shriek at the sight of her handsome brothers. 'Hallo!' She threw back her veil and ran to greet them.

Hearty embraces enfolded her at their reunion, Gabriel lifting her off her feet with a bearlike squeeze, Derek hugging her fondly and planting a loud kiss on her cheek.

'Good Lord! I can't believe my eyes! Is it really you?'

'You hoyden! What are you doing here?'

'I had to come. I had to *see* you. Oh, my darling brothers, how are you both?' She touched each hard, handsome face fondly, having assumed the role of mother to some degree since their own had died, despite the fact that she was younger than they. 'You're looking well enough. Are they feeding you properly?'

They laughed at her making a fuss over them, but her heart could have burst with pride over the dazzling pair of rogues. She loved seeing them like this, looking all smart and heroic in their dark-blue cavalry uniforms, with gold epaulets glimmering on their broad shoulders, cream-colored riding breeches, and gleaming knee-boots. Why, she could not blame all the ladies who fell in love with them practically at first sight. With such excellent brothers for comparison, no wonder she had such impossibly high standards in men.

Both of her brothers had black hair, but Derek's hung to his shoulders, while Gabriel's was cropped short. Gabriel's eyes were a deep, dark sapphire, soulful in their expression; Derek's eyes were paler, sky-blue, like Papa's, and usually twinkling with roguery. Both men were darkly sun-tanned from their years of riding across the plains with their squadrons.

'How did you know we were here?' Derek demanded.

'Meena told me! She wrote to me weeks ago. Have you seen her?'

''Course not, we're not allowed,' Gabriel murmured. The stern eldest shook his head, slung his arm around her shoulders, and tugged her closer, pressing a fond kiss to her temple. Then he sighed 'It was mad of you to come.'

'Oh, you're not angry, are you?'

'How could I be? We haven't seen our little sister in over a year.'

'Just don't get us into trouble with Lord Griffith,' Derek warned in a low tone. 'Good man, but he prefers things to go by the book, if you know what I mean.'

'Tell me about it,' Georgie muttered.

'You'd better promise us that you'll behave,' Gabriel said, eyeing her askance.

Georgie snorted. 'I shall do nothing of the kind.'

Derek laughed and tugged a lock of her hair. 'You haven't changed.'

'Well, I see the identity of our "princess" is finally revealed,' a deep, droll voice remarked from a few yards away. The sound of crisp, slow footfalls rang out across the flagstones.

Georgie froze. Although her back was to him, she recognized the voice, and it took no great skill to detect the irritation underlying his sardonic tone.

Griffith.

'Ah, sorry, sir.' Gabriel cleared his throat and sent Georgie a warning glance that told her to mind her manners. 'We were just finishing up here.'

'Not at all, gentlemen,' he replied, his tone as mild as a spring day. An ominous sign. 'Take your time, by all means. Negotiations have been adjourned for the day. Curious, that,' he added. 'It's only . . . one o'clock.'

Bracing herself to confront him, Georgie turned around just as the marquess finished glancing at his fob watch. He closed it with a reproachful snick. His eyes gleamed, and the moment their gazes collided, she felt the impact with a thrill that ran all the way down to her toes.

Oo, I can't stand him, she told herself, but was irked to know she was not immune to his worldly magnetism.

He looked like a dream.

Suave and polished as ever, he wore a dark chocolate tailcoat, flawless white cravat, and fawn trousers. Fixing his cool, dissecting stare on her, he tucked his fob watch back into his burgundy-striped waistcoat. Georgie noted the taut set of his jaw and wondered if she might be safer out there with the Pindaris.

Nevertheless, the marquess appeared resigned to their reunion. *Good.* For she wasn't leaving. In truth, she could barely wait to get him alone so she could give him a piece of her mind.

This imperious London grandee needed a lesson or two in how to treat a lady, starting with the fundamentals: namely, that he could not simply lock her up like some pampered prisoner for the sake of his own convenience.

It was unfair of him to judge her entire character on the basis of one incident, that unfortunate business near old Balaram's funeral pyre. Most importantly, he needed to learn that he had no authority over her. How that must drive him mad, now that he saw the evidence of it – her standing here! She would make her own decisions, thank you very much.

'You, ah, already met our sister, my lord,' Gabriel reminded him cautiously, breaking the awkward silence.

'Oh, yes. I most certainly did.' The marquess angled his head toward her with courteous precision. 'Miss Knight,' he said in a voice as smooth as glass. 'How very charming to see you again.'

'Likewise, my lord.' She gave him a queenly nod.

They stared at each other, and Georgie decided not to tell her brothers yet that the beast had tried to put her under house arrest. No, far wiser to hold that threat over his head in case she needed to wrest a few concessions from him.

Besides, there were one or two things she'd rather he not tell her brothers, either. Like her rescue of Lakshmi and the calamity that had nearly resulted.

Derek cleared his throat. 'The, er, king's advisers probably needed time to digest your proposal,' he offered, making a valiant attempt to deflect Lord Griffith's displeasure, which, though restrained, was palpable.

'Indeed.' He clasped his hands behind his back in gentlemanly fashion. 'Curious time for a family visit,' he remarked in an ever-so-civilized tone, at which both of her brothers immediately started trying to make excuses for her, but he cut them off with a practiced smile and an idle wave of his hand. 'I wonder if I might have a private word with the three of you?'

'Yes, of course,' Gabriel murmured at once, dutiful as ever, and Derek nodded, stepping forward, too, but Georgie stopped them.

'That won't be necessary,' she announced, turning to Lord Griffith. If it was a fight he wanted, it was a fight he'd get.

He arched a brow.

'You boys stay out here,' she ordered, barely glancing at her brothers. 'I'm the one who's earned His Lordship's wrath. We might as well have this out between us two.'

'Are you sure about this?' he asked softly, a glint of intrigued amusement at her challenge shining in his eye like a star.

She lifted her chin. 'I can fight my own battles.'

'As you desire.' He swept a formal gesture toward one of the private side rooms off the main courtyard, inviting her to go ahead of him.

As she lifted the hem of her sari and started toward the nearest parlor, her ayah protested at the impropriety, while Lakshmi fretted in alarm. Georgie told them in Bengali that she would only be a moment. Besides, the man had that blasted saintly reputation.

Derek and Gabriel were frowning, but when she shook her head at them with a firm look that told them not to worry – she knew what she was doing – they seemed to accept her move.

After all, she had gotten herself into this and could jolly well get herself out. Gabriel put his hands in his pockets and leaned against one of the sturdy palm trees to wait for her, while Derek turned and greeted their old nurse with knavish affection. Purnima, for her part, was not happy about any of this.

Georgie walked toward the room he had indicated, acutely aware of Lord Griffith's riveting presence behind her, but she was very glad her brothers had chosen not to countermand her decision.

This was between her and Lord Griffith, and she did not want them involved. She could not risk the marquess taking out his anger at her on *them*, for if he wanted to, he could easily use his high position to give her brothers poor marks in his report following their assignment. One ill word from a man of his influence could cast a shadow over their brilliant military careers, and Georgie knew full well that for Gabriel and Derek both, the army was their life.

She might not like their dangerous profession any more than she had liked Papa working for the horrid East India Company, but knowing how much soldiering meant to them, she would never do anything to jeopardize their careers.

At any rate, the fact that Derek and Gabriel had worked with Lord Griffith for nearly a week now, getting to know him and having ample opportunity to size him up for themselves, along with his sterling reputation, no doubt helped to ease their misgivings as their sister marched ahead of him into the private salon.

He held the door for her, and she ignored a frisson of awareness as she brushed past him into the room.

He followed her in, closed the door behind him, and turned to face her, folding his arms across his broad chest. 'Well, well, Miss Georgiana. Here we are again,' he said in an ironic tone, but she held up a finger, silencing him while she scanned the room for any sign of a peephole or listening grate.

In these lavish palaces, the very walls had ears.

A painted mural wrapped around the walls depicted the story of the descent of the Ganges, with flying goddesses and stylized heavenly guardians on horseback. A jewel-toned carpet of intricate weave covered the cool flagstone floor. Overhead, an iron chandelier hung from the beamed ceiling, at midday its candles unlit. The only other objects of note in the room were a low-slung couch with red cushions, a long, heavy table with spiral-carved legs, and, flanking the single window, a pair of small mango trees in clay pots.

She went over and glanced out the window to

make sure there was no place for anyone outside to overhear their conversation. One couldn't be too careful. 'Good,' she murmured, seeing that the window was set high above one corner of the bustling square. 'Now we can speak freely.' Or, more to the point, now she could tell the brute exactly what she thought of him.

'What are you doing here?' he asked, watching her with a dark, brooding stare, while his long, tapered fingers slowly began to tap upon his thick biceps.

'I'll ask the questions, you snake!' She swung around to confront him head-on. 'You know what you are? You're a despot, a tyrant—'

He laughed softly. 'A tyrant?'

'You heard me!' She had been waiting days to give free rein to her outrage. Now she let him have it. 'Who do you think you are to tell me what I can and can't do? To lock me up under guard, like a prisoner in my home? You had no right to do that to me! How *dare* you! And—' she interrupted when he tried to speak. 'You lied to me!'

He cocked an eyebrow at this accusation, but perhaps now he began to grasp there was a bigger fight brewing than he had anticipated.

'You let me believe like a fool that you were going to include me in your journey, but instead, you locked me up as though I were in purdah and rode away without me! That was low. Altogether low! But as you can see, my dear marquess, you have no control over me.' She held out her hands, presenting herself with a flourish, propping her fists on her waist and lifting her chin. 'I'm here, and there's nothing you can do about it! Your little plan to cage me didn't work.'

He studied her coolly for a long moment, but the tension around his hard mouth hinted that he was not so unaffected as he seemed. *Good!* She hoped she made him every bit as furious as he had made her. If she got him angry enough, it might stymie his ability to work his smooth manipulations on her again.

'I asked you repeatedly to stay home, Miss Knight,' he said in a consummately reasonable tone. 'To stay out of trouble and to behave yourself. This was for your own protection, as well as the security of my assignment.' He paused and shrugged. 'I knew you weren't going to listen. That's why I asked DeWitt to send his men. You gave me no other choice.'

'Rubbish!'

'On the contrary, my dear. You forget, I had already seen the kind of chaos you're capable of, and the situation here is precarious enough as it is. It did not need you barging in like a damned bull in a china shop,' he finished in a sharper tone.

'Bull in a china shop?' she echoed with an indignant gasp. 'Well, I never!'

'You had no business coming here.' He started toward her, looming tall, his mask of aloof indifference dissolving to reveal a thunderous scowl. 'How dare you completely defy me!'

She laughed. 'You're not used to that, are you? Well, I don't grovel for anyone.'

'Obviously, it was too much to hope that my saving your life would count for something—'

'I could've handled those people myself.'

He stopped and looked at her in utter shock. 'Ha!'

Georgie pursed her lips and refused to take back her probably overconfident claim.

Staring at her incredulously for a second, the marquess shook his head as though he feared she ought to be locked up with the lunatics. Then he narrowed his eyes and pointed a finger in her face. 'You know what your problem is? You're spoiled.'

'I am not!' she huffed as his words struck a nerve. 'You don't know me!'

'Let's look at the facts! *You* had to see *your* friend, the princess; *you* wanted to see *your* brothers – and to blazes with everything and everybody else!' he said angrily, the volume of his deep voice climbing. 'Do you have any idea what's at stake here? Why can't you blasted women ever learn to use your heads?'

Georgie clamped her jaw shut and looked away, striving for patience. She took a deep breath, steadied herself, and regrouped. 'All right, let's just calm down here—'

'I *am* calm!' he bellowed.

She ignored him. 'I see now why you fail to understand me. That much is my fault. You judge me spoiled, but that's only because I have not been entirely . . . forthcoming with you about my real concerns. But, as it seems you're too *thick* for the subtle approach—'

'The subtle approach?' he exclaimed with a bark of laughter. 'Where was that, pray tell? I must have missed it.'

She shot him a warning look. 'Instead, I must be frank.'

'Please do. Oh, this should be most enlightening.' He propped his foot on the stool nearby and leaned down, resting his elbow on his bent knee. He waited with an expectant gaze, taunting amusement written all over his handsome face.

'I am not the vapid debutante you think I am,' she said. 'Do you really believe I'd come all this way for a social call?'

The question appeared to take him off guard. He studied her warily for a second, then shrugged. 'Very well, I'll bite. If not for a social call, then why *did* you come, Georgiana?'

She held him in a piercing stare. 'Because of you.'

'Me?' Again, he appeared startled by her answer, a flicker of confused, adorable modesty flaring in his eyes, but then he was back on his guard again, and let out a cynical scoff. 'Right. I'm very flattered, but—'

'Don't be. It's not your well-turned calves that interest me, Lord Griffith, but the substance of your mission here at Janpur.' She paused and pinned him in a no-nonsense stare. 'I want you to tell me, right now, what is going on here.'

He went very still, then lowered his foot from the stool and turned to her. 'Why should I do that?'

She gave a demure shrug and clasped her hands behind her back. 'Because I have influence here, Lord Griffith. I have the ear of the king's favorite, and am privy to information that you have no way of obtaining. All this means I can either help or hinder your progress, depending on your aims, so I suggest you start with the truth.'

His green eyes narrowed like those of an angry tiger.

She forged on. 'I want to know what you're here to try to accomplish. If you refuse to tell me, then I must assume the worst. Which means I'm going straight to Meena and telling her to warn her husband not to trust you.'

There.

He had thought her idle and indulged, but now he would begin to see that she was deadly serious.

He said nothing; though his eyes glittered angrily, he looked stunned down to his lordly fingertips. What, had he never met a woman with brains before?

Reveling in his new understanding of her nature, Georgie lifted her chin. 'In Calcutta, you told me you had been sent to stop a war. If that is true, then we are in accord. Naturally, I would much rather work with you than against you. Yet, somehow, after what you did to me, I have trouble believing your motives are so pure.'

He looked away in fury and pretended to

study the mural. 'You are a fascinating woman, Georgiana.'

'Thank you,' she replied. 'So, which is it? Is peace your true goal, or are your dealings here just another devious trick aimed at expanding the East India Company's grasp?'

He slanted her a brooding glance and seemed to grow larger as he took offense. 'Do I look like some merchant's errand boy to you?'

'Not at all. But that doesn't answer my question.'

He looked away again with a silent curse on his lips and began to scowl.

Georgie watched him, intrigued. 'You are offended. Well, that is why I tried to find out nicely first,' she explained with a shrug. 'If you had accepted my hospitality in Calcutta and talked with me a while, I could have found the answer for myself without perturbing you.'

'I doubt it,' he growled.

She lowered her head. 'You haven't lived in India, my lord. You haven't seen how the Company ruins all it touches, like cursed King Midas, destroying everything it tries to turn to gold. The Indian people have borne the brunt of this curse. They've watched the Company armies defeat one ancient kingdom after another, and always some corrupt, indifferent Englishman is put in charge.' She checked the note of anguish that had crept into her voice. 'The Company's administrators don't give a fig about this land or its people. All they care about is lining their own pockets by whatever means they can devise.'

111

He eyed her warily.

'This cannot be allowed to happen to King Johar. He is a good ruler and a just man, and his people need him. And if I have to fight you to help save his reign,' she added in a harder tone, 'I will.'

'Aha.' He pinched the bridge of his patrician nose for a second, clearly striving for patience, then he let out a low, cynical sigh and his hand fell back down to his side. 'So, this is the direct approach?'

She just looked at him.

'Why didn't you tell me any of this before? You should have told me in Calcutta what was really on your mind.'

'I didn't know if I could trust you.'

'Thus the need for subtlety . . .' He let out another musing sigh. 'Well, perhaps we both have hidden from each other too much of what we are.'

'I have been honest with you now.' Her expectant pause invited him to do the same.

'Very well, since this obviously means a great deal to you, let me first assure you that I am not the Company's lackey, nor the Crown's.' His tone turned steely, for, after all, she had insulted his pride. 'I have no interest in "lining my pockets" with the wealth of the East. I did not come to India seeking profit. In fact, I was on holiday in Ceylon, minding my own business, when they called me in to deal with this. I gave up my holiday to help, and if you still don't believe that I did not come here seeking Indian treasures, then you'll pardon the vulgarity of my informing you that I already happen to be extremely rich. Born with the silver spoon in my mouth, if you must know, and if I lived like a profligate for the rest of my life, I would still die with more gold in my coffers than most men could spend in three lifetimes.'

Georgie absorbed his terse chastisement with a downcast gaze. 'Oh.'

'Furthermore, if I thought our aims in this matter were unjust, I would have refused the mission.'

She could feel him staring at her.

'In short, I don't do this job for the pay, Georgiana. I am here for the good of my country, in the hopes of saving lives. If there is any meaning to my life, I've dedicated everything to trying to make the world at least a slightly more civilized place, so I really don't appreciate your insinuations about my character.'

She wilted further and kept her gaze down, her cheeks turning scarlet as she began once more to recall all the admirable things that people in Society had told her he had done. Averting wars, negotiating truces . . . she hadn't believed a word of it, in her general prejudice against men, learned from the pages of her aunt's book and the injustice toward women she so often saw around her.

Even now, that prejudice hung on like a terrier with its teeth in her ankle. 'You still haven't told me what your business is in Janpur,' she mumbled with a slight tremble. Her head down, she glanced at him warily from under her lashes.

He laughed and shook his head. 'You're not going to let this go, are you?'

'I cannot. These people are my friends.'

'Well, you are loyal. I'll give you that.' He snorted to himself and sauntered off toward the window.

Holding her ground, she said nothing, but found the strength to lift her head again and meet his gaze.

He rested his arm along the window sill, studying her; then he looked outside, squinting against the brilliance of the light. 'Once again, you leave me little choice.' He shrugged. 'On the other hand, I've been in this business long enough to know that you women have . . . your ways. So, whatever mysterious back channels you are privy to, Miss Knight, if you want to see this maharajah keep his throne, then let him be persuaded to take the deal we're offering.' Lord Griffith paused, then continued in a lower tone. 'It's not Johar who is slated for destruction, but his brother-in-law, Baji Rao. Have you heard of him?'

She nodded, and her heart leaped with hope that he was finally going to take her into his confidence. 'Baji Rao is the Peshwa, head of the Maratha Empire,' she answered, eager to display for him her familiarity with the region.

'Well, the man has become quite a thorn in our side.'

She leaned her hip against the sofa's arm,

considering this. 'I cannot say I am surprised. Baji Rao is no Johar. He has a reputation as a coward and a bully with a cruel streak. Even his own people hate him.'

'He does seem to have a talent for making enemies.' The afternoon sunlight haloed his dark hair as he nodded. 'Governor Lord Hastings has ordered the destruction of the Pindari Horde, but now Baji Rao has gone and granted them safe haven. This puts us in a position of having to invade his kingdom in order eradicate them.'

'He won't co-operate?'

'Not in the least.'

'I guess he doesn't trust you,' she remarked, concealing her jubilance at having wrung a proper measure of respect out of the imperious marquess at last.

'From what I hear, the Peshwa doesn't trust anybody.' He left the window and came closer, leaning against the table across from her. 'Hard to say what he hopes to gain from all this, but he'd rather use the dispute over the Pindaris as an excuse to go to war with us. He's been trying to summon all his usual allies. I'm here to convince King Johar to stay out of it. We've sent another team to Gwalior for the same purpose,' he added in a confidential tone. 'Ideally, both Janpur and Gwalior will sign a treaty of neutrality with the British.'

'Well, they *are* the two strongest members of the Maratha alliance,' she mused.

'Precisely. And without them, Baji Rao and the rest of his allies will lose. It's as simple as that.' He sighed and drummed his fingers on the edge of the table for a moment in thought. 'Of course, both Johar and Gwalior are at liberty to refuse our proposal, join Baji Rao, and be destroyed along with the rest of the Marathas. But, if they go along with our wishes and sit this war out, then we expect to defeat Baji Rao in short order, and the territories stripped from him will be split between Janpur and Gwalior to rule.'

'At least you're making it worth their while to abandon their old treaty.'

'First principle of diplomacy, my dear. You've got to give if you want to get,' he agreed with a wry half smile.

They stared at each other for a moment too long.

She dropped her gaze. 'Still, I doubt Johar will go for it. Loyalty and honor are everything to the Marathas.'

'I've noticed,' he said ruefully, looking away, as though, he, too, were disconcerted by this strange alchemy between them. 'That Prince Shahu is a fine example of that. Damned fireball, all made up of overweening pride. Be careful of him, by the way,' he warned. 'You really caught his eye.'

She shrugged it off. 'So, that's the extent of your mission? I mean, isn't there a catch? There's always a catch.'

He gazed at her for a moment. 'No more Maratha Empire.'

Georgie winced. 'I knew it. This was what I'd feared.'

'It's not our doing, Georgiana. The fault lies with Baji Rao. He's the head of their alliance and he won't give an inch. He wants every last white person out of India – or dead. *We* did not want another war with the Marathas. Things were stable until Baji Rao came to power. This whole situation is unfortunate for us, too, you know,' he pointed out. 'The Marathas have long been a buffer between ourselves and the Ottomans to the north. But this is the best solution for now, and I'm trying to usher it in with as little bloodshed as possible. When it's all said and done, the Maratha people will be ruled by these two wiser maharajahs who value peace with their neighbors – men who can be trusted. Baji Rao will be dealt with, and the Pindari Horde will be gone.'

'That does sound safer for everyone,' she admitted.

'So, you see?' he teased very gently, leaning toward her. 'I am no great snake, come to swallow Janpur.'

'Well, maybe not.' She smiled cautiously at him. 'Sorry I called you a reptile. No hard feelings, I hope? Friends?'

'Of course we are.' He offered her his hand.

She rose and went to him, clasping it.

'I shouldn't have said you were spoiled,' he murmured as he held her hand between his own. 'The loyalty you bear your friends is an admirable trait.' He lifted her hand to his lips and pressed an affectionate kiss to her knuckles, watching her. 'I hope some of that loyalty may pertain to me now that I've put my mission in your hands, and that you will not take lightly the trust I've placed in you. One wrong word in the right ear, Georgiana, and it could result in disaster.'

'I won't let you down,' she said quietly, looking into his eyes.

He nodded. 'All right.'

When Lord Griffith released her hand from his light hold, she dropped it to his chest and playfully tugged at one of the buttons on his waistcoat, giving him an impish smile. 'There, now, you see? It wasn't so bad, was it? Trusting me?'

'Don't make me sorry for it.'

'You won't be. I'll keep my eyes and ears open in the harem for you. If I find out anything useful, I will let you know.'

His soft gaze turned sober. 'Be careful.'

'Relax,' she whispered with a smile. 'You worry too much.'

'With good reason. I mean it, Georgiana. If you start causing trouble again, I'm sending you back to Calcutta—'

'I'll be good,' she hushed him, and with a mischievous glance, suddenly unfastened the top button of his waistcoat. Before he could protest, she stepped past him and headed for the door.

'Trying to undress me?' he called in a soft murmur as he buttoned it again.

She glanced over her shoulder and sent him a naughty half smile. 'I can't say it hasn't crossed my mind.'

Mine, too, Ian thought ardently, fighting a hearty smile as he stared at her walking away. Entranced by the play of light over the lustrous silk that swathed her lithe curves, his hungry gaze slid down to contemplate her hips. At the same time, he hoped it had not been a fatal error to trust her with his information. On the other hand, she had left him little choice.

Quickly concealing his persistent lust for the young siren, he followed her back to the court-yard, where they rejoined her brothers and her ladies.

A female servant of the maharajah's household was already waiting to escort Georgiana and the other women into the zenana, the harem quarters, while a captain of the royal bodyguards had come to treat Ian and the majors to a display of traditional Indian weaponry for their entertainment.

They parted ways.

Georgiana bade her brothers adieu and then sent Ian a wary glance of farewell from beneath her lashes. The look she gave him could have melted the iced-over Thames in a Frost Fair. He drew in his breath silently, but she had already dropped her gaze with neat discretion and turned away, following the chatelaine out of the courtyard.

He stared as she was led off through a grandiose, gilded doorway that opened into some other region of the palace.

'I hope she wasn't too much trouble in there,' Gabriel said rather sheepishly, turning to him with a worried look. 'I'm afraid our sister can be a handful.'

'One of these years we've got to get that girl married off,' Derek muttered. 'If only she weren't so damned picky.'

'No matter,' Ian said. 'I think we understand each other now.' Fearing they might notice his preoccupation with their sister, he dropped his gaze and cleared his throat, then turned to the Maratha captain waiting to take them to the Hall of Arms. 'Shall we?'

'After you, sir,' Derek said politely.

Ian nodded and walked away.

Behind him, Derek and Gabriel exchanged an intrigued and rather sly glance, but said nothing, and strode after him.

CHAPTER 5

Meanwhile, Georgie and her ladies followed the chatelaine through the palace until they came to the great *deodhi*, the harem's entrance, framed by giant pillars. Towering eunuchs with shaved heads stood guard on either side, blocking the giant gilded doors with their crossed spears. When the women approached, however, the husky guards uncrossed their spears and opened the doors for them.

Down another long corridor they proceeded, until at last they came to the harem's marble atrium and were greeted by an anxiously waiting Meena. With exclamations of joy and exuberant hugs, the three childhood friends were reunited.

Meena was stunned to see Lakshmi. 'Oh, by the tusk of Ganesha, this is a treat twice over!' The royal bride was positively glowing, and all three girls immediately began talking at once.

While Purnima and Gita were shown away to get them all settled in for their visit, Meena proposed to show Georgie and Lakshmi the private zenana that was being built for her in another wing of the palace.

'It's still under construction, but at least over there we can talk without a hundred people eavesdropping,' the princess murmured.

They agreed.

Through a labyrinth of winding hallways, cramped passages, odd-shaped rooms, hidden galleries, and twining spiral stairs, they were able to move through the palace, unseen by male eyes.

The women's invisible realm formed a palace within a palace; while the men conducted their worldly business, the women were forever cloistered. Everywhere there were listening grates, peepholes, and intricately carved screens through which women were at least allowed to observe the world of men. Some rooms, however, were off-limits to the female audience.

At last they reached the wing of the palace where the new zenana was under construction, but because of purdah, all of the workmen had to be dismissed while the princess showed her friends around.

'My husband is extremely generous,' Meena declared as they picked their way through the various half-built rooms. 'But do you know what the best part is?'

'What's that?' Georgie asked, smiling.

'Queen Sujana has to live with knowing she gave Johar the idea.' Meena giggled. 'She told him she can't stand the sight of me, so this was his response! Look, this will be our bedchamber,' she informed them with a risqué smile, leading them into a soaring, vaulted room. 'Ah, my sisters,' she said with a dreamy sigh, 'when a man has thirty wives and a hundred concubines, I will say one thing – practice makes perfect.'

Georgie burst out laughing at Meena's scandalous words, but Lakshmi let out a glum sigh. The young widow's misery about all she had missed out on by being married to an old man stopped Georgie from asking Meena a dozen questions about that subject that so frequently preoccupied her thoughts. Later, she thought, after poor Lakshmi had gone to bed, she would ask Meena what it was really like to lie with a man skilled in lovemaking . . . how it felt to be seduced. She could barely wait to hear what her ex-virgin friend had to say on the matter, but she kept her questions to herself for now.

When their tour ended, they retraced their steps through the maze of corridors, but this time, the Hall of Arms rang out with a skilled demonstration by some palace guards of the ancient Indian style of wrestling, along with some traditional Maratha weapons.

Georgie spotted her brothers and Lord Griffith among the men watching the warriors' display of prowess. Others were examining Maratha spears, lances, and javelins, and admiring jeweled swords and colorful round shields. One of the guards was showing Gabriel and Derek the collection of razor-sharp *chakras*, or 'wheels,' deadly, jagged, blade-edged weapons meant to be thrown at an attacker. Behind the carved wooden screen, the girls stifled laughter and hushed each other, lingering to spy on them.

Georgie paid her brothers little mind, focusing all her attention on Lord Griffith. Hands in pockets, casual as a schoolboy, the marquess sauntered over to study the display of huge plates of shiny armor and intricate chain mail made to protect the maharajah's war elephant in battle. Watching him in secret filled her with a strange sort of pleasure. She bit her lip, smiling a little when he thumped the elephant armor with his knuckle and asked a guard a question about it.

She had to admit some small corner of her heart danced at the sight of him.

His noble words about serving his country and saving lives still haunted her. It troubled Georgie to consider the number of wrong assumptions she had made about him. *Perhaps I was too hard on him.* Maybe she should have given him the benefit of the doubt, especially since he had saved her from Balaram's kin.

She found herself wanting to know this man better.

As the girls continued watching from behind the screen, the captain of the palace guards invited the Englishmen to participate in their exhibition.

Gabriel declined with a cool smile. 'I crave your pardon, gentlemen. I don't pick up a weapon unless I really mean it.'

'I will!' Derek volunteered cheerfully, always game for a challenge.

The girls exchanged private grins as a Maratha warrior tossed a long lance to Derek. He caught it nimbly in both hands and twirled it into position like they had done, much to the Marathas' hearty approval.

They asked Lord Griffith if he would participate, but he waved them off with a self-deprecating laugh. 'I wouldn't dream of making a fool of myself next to you fellows,' he said smoothly. 'I'm just a diplomat. I'll leave the feats of arms to the warriors.'

His modest answer pleased her Jainist inclinations, but Georgie wondered if his words were quite sincere.

From behind the safety of the screen, she let her gaze travel over the marquess slowly, enjoying the sleek, elegant architecture of his tall, manly form. After her tour of Meena's chamber under construction, Georgie couldn't help wondering what Lord Griffith was like when he took a woman to his bed.

She remembered the silken strength in his touch when he had held her hand, the smooth caress of his lips when he had kissed her knuckles . . . the safety she had felt with his big, warm body enfolding hers as he had ridden behind her on her horse.

As her leisurely perusal of him wandered all the way down to his spotless black shoes and back up his fawn-colored trousers, climbing the muscled length of his thighs, he turned oh-so-casually, with a piercing stare straight at the wooden screen – almost as though he could feel her inspecting him!

Georgie jolted backward in guilty surprise. Her sudden motion drew her friends' notice.

'What's wrong?' Lakshmi asked.

Her face radiated such fiery heat, she was sure her cheeks must be beet-red, as if she had just eaten a spicy green chili.

'Are you all right?' Meena inquired with a puzzled look.

'I'm – fine. It's a – a little – hot in here. Maybe we should go,' she mumbled.

'Yes, come, let us go and have refreshments. Your journey has been long.' Meena linked arms with her, and Georgie did the same with Lakshmi, vowing to put the marquess out of her mind as best she could.

Continuing on their way, the girls passed the vast, sparkling banqueting hall. Here, an army of servants hurried about, busily polishing ornate candelabra and readying a sea of dining tables.

'There's to be a feast tonight in honor of the English delegation,' Meena informed them; then she nudged Georgie's shoulder fondly. 'You should go, *shona*. It would give you a chance to visit with your brothers. Lakshmi and I won't be invited, of course, but there's no reason you can't attend. You're a foreigner and a guest. It's not as if you're keeping purdah.'

'Would either of you mind?' Georgie asked hopefully, refusing to acknowledge that sparring with

Lord Griffith again held even greater appeal than catching up with her brothers.

'Not at all,' Meena said, and Lakshmi nodded in earnest agreement. 'Though I will warn you, you may cause a bit of a stir—'

'She's used to that,' Lakshmi chimed in.

'The only women the men are used to seeing in the banqueting hall are the dancing girls. But certainly you should visit with your brothers while you can,' Meena said. 'We're not sure how long their party will be staying – only until the nego- tiations are concluded, I should think, and who knows how soon that might be?'

'Yes, who knows . . . ?' Georgie echoed, wondering how much Meena had been told about the substance of her husband's current wranglings with the British on one hand and Baji Rao on the other. Probably very little.

Then she followed her friends into the main harem, a place of wonder.

From its sunken gardens to its lotus-shaped pools strewn with water lilies, from its whimsical pavilions to its arched colonnades, the royal harem was an airy space dedicated to leisure, luxury, and relaxation.

There were rooms devoted to art and music, painting and dance, and courtyards for horseback riding, archery, and a lively ball game similar to tennis. There was a serene ladies' temple, small but beautiful, dedicated to Parvati, and elaborate nurseries filled with happy children. There was even a large durbar hall, where the maharani heard cases brought by the female residents of her kingdom.

There also were countless pets – little monkeys, tame deer, brightly colored parrots in cages. The birds had been taught by the ladies to perform all manner of silly tricks, but Georgie found it difficult to smile at their antics.

However beautiful it was, however peaceful and safe, this place was still a cage.

She said nothing of her thoughts, however, determined to remember that this was only her British view. It was clear that Meena was radiantly happy, and Lakshmi looked overwhelmed by the grace of this Elysian haven. No doubt it was paradise compared to the tiny prison of her marriage to strict old Balaram.

The girls were still watching some of the concubines making the parrots perform their tricks when, suddenly, across the green, a tall, slim woman of about forty emerged from the temple, a cluster of attendants and ladies-in-waiting following at her heels.

'Oh, no,' Meena whispered, paling. 'It's Queen Sujana.'

'Is it?' Georgie murmured with great interest, following her gaze.

The maharani's elegantly thin frame was wrapped in a dark sari of indigo silk shot through with silver and gold thread, like a starry night sky. She was a beautiful woman, with a jeweled *bindi* gleaming on her forehead. She had sleek, jet-black hair, distinctly pale skin, and brooding kohl-lined eyes. The moment she appeared, however, a pall dropped over the gaiety of the entire harem.

Everyone in view stopped what they were doing, leaving their games, dancing, and artistic pursuits to bow down low in her presence, almost as if they were cowering before her. The music halted. Even the children stopped playing as she crossed the gardens with swift, driven strides.

'Blast, she's seen us,' Meena said under her breath as Queen Sujana paused in her arrow-like forward motion. Her dark-eyed stare homed in on them. 'I'm afraid, my dears, that Her Majesty will expect a greeting in the old style.'

'Oh, bother,' Georgie muttered. But as certain diplomats had accused her of causing trouble, she was determined not to do so, especially for her friend. No, it was easier to go along with the custom of the *mujira* rather than offend Her Majesty with a simple British curtsy.

'But I'm not touching her feet,' Georgie added under her breath.

'Down we go,' Lakshmi urged them in a quiet tone.

Beside her friends, Georgie sank down onto her knees as the maharani approached, and for Meena's sake, dutifully performed the traditional bow to royalty, which required one to bend until one's forehead nearly touched the ground.

'Meena, who are these ladies?' Queen Sujana

inquired as she stopped in front of them. Her crisp tone admitted a small degree of mollification by their homage.

'Your Majesty, these are my friends from Calcutta,' Meena said timidly.

'I was not consulted on this visit.'

'H-his Majesty gave me permission.'

'Have you no breeding whatsoever? It does not matter what Johar says. First you must ask me. That is our protocol here.'

'Y-yes, my queen.'

Georgie scowled into the grass, but didn't dare look up just yet. She could feel the queen seething.

Poor Meena. Georgie pitied her. *She* would not want Queen Sujana for an enemy. At length, Lakshmi and she were ordered to rise. Georgie could not help but notice the maharani's venomous glance at the beautiful young rival who had replaced her in her husband's affections. Though Georgie could all but see Meena shaking in her sandals, the girl stood her ground and told the queen their names.

The maharani studied them with cool interest, unconcerned by Lakshmi, but looking not at all pleased to find an Englishwoman inside her harem. 'Well, if my husband wills it, I can do naught but obey,' she said in a voice like a poisoned dagger.

Disregarding them without a backward glance, she glided on.

Meena exhaled slowly as the queen retreated out of earshot.

'Is she always like that?' Lakshmi asked with a wince.

'That was nothing,' Meena whispered, still quaking a little. 'Usually, she's ten times worse! She thinks she's practically divinity, just because she's the sister of Baji Rao!'

Georgie's ears pricked up.

'They're such an arrogant family,' Meena added.

'Where is she going now?' Georgie asked, watching the queen march toward a pair of heavy wooden doors beneath a pointy stone archway.

'Probably to her private audience box. No one's allowed in there without her, and only her eunuch guards and her highest-ranked lady-in-waiting are ever permitted to attend her when she goes in there. She accuses me of being spoiled, but Johar lets her receive visitors from the outside world as long as she stays behind the screen.'

'Like him?' Georgie asked in surprise, nodding toward the young man who had just opened the thick wooden door of the queen's audience chamber, and poked his nose into the harem, though he came no further than the threshold.

'Oh, what is *he* doing here again?' Meena remarked in a sudden tone of annoyance.

'Who is that?'

'Her *precious* son, Prince Shahu. He's the *Yuvraj*, the crown prince. And he is – what is your English word – coxcomb?'

'Oh, yes,' Georgie murmured. 'I can see that.'

Flamboyantly dressed in patterned silk drapery,

with curly-toed shoes and showy gold earrings in both ears, the turbaned prince appeared in his early twenties and was clearly very pleased with himself. Exuding cockiness, he sent Georgie a bold smile, but he was so ridiculously dressed that she had to look away, pressing her fingertips to her lips to stop herself from laughing.

'Look at him ogling you! Ugh, what a preening fool he is!' Meena scowled at the prince. 'He's too old to be in here anymore, but he still comes every day to see his mother. Ah, well, at least he doesn't stay long. He's not allowed to come any farther than the doorway of the queen's audience chamber.'

'Why does he visit so often?'

'They're very close, he and Queen Sujana. He was raised in the harem, of course, like all the other children, and now he just can't seem to get it through his head that he's supposed to be a man. He'd rather cling to his mother's skirts like a spoiled little boy. To think that someday he'll be the one to rule Janpur!' She shook her head in dismay.

Georgiana was still trying to make sense of Prince Shahu when Lakshmi spoke up in a strange and faraway tone. 'Meena? Gigi?'

They turned to her.

'What is it, dear?' Meena asked her.

Lakshmi had crouched down gracefully beside the lotus pool. She had lifted one of the blooms from the water and was staring down into its delicate cup. 'I have come to a decision.'

'Lakshmi?' Georgie furrowed her brow as worry flared in her heart. 'What's wrong?'

'Yes, what decision do you mean, *shona*?'

'I've been thinking about it ever since my husband's death.' She looked up at them with great, somber eyes. 'I've decided to go through with all the proper duties of a surviving widow.'

Georgie started to protest, but Meena laid a hand on her shoulder, halting her, as Lakshmi cupped the flower.

'I'd like your help,' she said softly.

'Of course we'll help you,' Meena murmured, crossing to Lakshmi and slipping a motherly arm around her shoulders. 'You needn't worry, my sister. If you wish to keep purdah, you can stay here with me. I would so love to have you nearby. You can serve as my lady-in-waiting in my new zenana. That is an appropriate role for a widow. One day, you can help me take care of my children.'

Georgie stood there startled into a dismayed silence by Lakshmi's announcement, not knowing what to say.

'Yes,' Lakshmi said softly. 'I think that would be for the best. Thank you, Meena.' She kissed her cheek, then turned to Georgie with a look of regret. 'You've been as kind to me as a sister, Gigi, but I don't belong in your world.'

No more than you belong in ours, her unspoken words seemed to say.

Georgie felt a lump rise in her throat. She

squeezed her hand. 'Whatever you feel will be best for you,' she said. 'I only want you to be happy.'

'I cannot be happy if I shirk my duty,' she replied with a sober gaze. 'I refused the fire, and I must face the consequences of that choice.'

Georgie couldn't – perhaps refused to – understand, but a firm look from Meena advised her to hold her tongue. This was a part of their world that she could not grasp, but if it made sense to them, then who was she to argue?

Lakshmi changed into a white sari, the color of death. This was the only color she would wear from now on – no more vibrant yellows, no more cobalt blues, and certainly no more reds, the color of Indian wedding gowns.

Then Meena and Georgie went with her into one of the private chambers in the harem, where she sat before a mirror, slowly rubbed off the red *bindi* that was the married woman's badge of honor, and lastly, picked up the scissors.

Tears rose in Georgie's eyes as Lakshmi held out a three-foot-long section of her gorgeous ebony hair and, with an unflinching glance into the mirror, cut it off, half an inch from her scalp. Georgie wanted to turn away but forced herself to watch, fighting tears as her friend succumbed to her society's heartless code of womanly honor. Lakshmi had done exactly what her family asked of her, and this was what she got for it. At last, the girl could have been free, but instead she had chosen this quiet annihilation.

Meena looked on, her face a mask of compassionate resolve, as if she, in Lakshmi's place, would have done the exact same thing.'

Well, such stoic enduring was not in Georgie's blood. With her scandalous aunt's book fairly burning a hole in her pocket, she vowed that, by God, she'd go to that feast tonight and show all those men that there were some women whose light could not be ground out under their cruel, ruthless heels.

For her part, they'd have to kill her before she'd ever let them put her in a cage.

'You sent for me, my queen?'

Firoz stood motionless on the outside of the wooden screen that bisected Her Majesty's audience chamber.

In the dim mysterious region behind the lattice of the teakwood screen, she paced back and forth like a caged tigress.

Sometimes he longed to let her out – he had the strength to free her if she wished – but he was a realist, and honestly, what would he do with a queen? Sujana belonged to Johar. He knew his place.

Today she was alone.

She usually came alone to their meetings. She had already sent her foolish son away with a few gold coins and a pat on his cheek.

Only Firoz knew the full extent of the control Sujana wielded over Shahu. They were more than just mother and son, they were puppet-master and puppet. Through the boy, one day, Sujana would rule Janpur.

Shahu was the key to all her plans.

'Soon I will have another message for you to take to my brother. He grows impatient,' she added in contempt, still pacing. The shadows from the screen's carved whorls rippled over her sleek figure. She pivoted at one end and strode back again. Firoz watched her, mesmerized. 'For now, I want you to find out more about this Georgiana woman if you can. I don't like her being here, not one jot. It's bad enough to have these Englishmen crawling through the palace, but even here, in the very harem? To think of what I have to bear! Oh, that rotten little harlot, Meena, bringing her here. I wish she was dead!'

Firoz looked at her inquiringly.

From behind the screen, Sujana paused and let out a low laugh, delicious and sinister. 'My friend, for now, at least, I was speaking rhetorically,' she chided him in amusement. 'All in good time.'

Firoz nearly smiled, but he hid his pleasure and bowed his head, then went out silently to do his queen's bidding.

Bagpipes had never before been heard beneath the domed roofs of Janpur Palace, but as the throng of Maratha courtiers milled about waiting for the feast to begin, Major MacDonald had gathered a few of his Highlanders to treat their hosts to a martial display of their proud regiment's Highland sword dance.

In full Highland regalia of kilts and tam-o'-shanters, the braw Scots warriors performed their vigorous jig over pairs of crossed swords arranged on the floor. While the pipes wailed and the Highland drums pounded, they showed off their strength and agility with a grueling series of light jumps back and forth around the blades, each man with one hand above his head, the other planted on his hip.

'It was originally intended to help the men limber up before battle,' Ian told the cluster of Maratha courtiers nearby, with Ravi dutifully translating. 'Have you tried the whisky, gentlemen?' he added with an urbane wave of his glass in the direction of the table where a servant was pouring shots of the fine Scotch whisky they had brought in by the barrel. 'It is a favorite libation amongst men of our land.'

Fortunately, they had also brought the maharajah's court a gift of five hundred bottles of Champagne, for some of the Marathas sipped the dry, bitter whisky and nearly spat it out. Ravi had translated one man's muttered reaction as 'drinking liquid dirt' on account of the mellow undertones of peat smoke. Some of them looked as though they wondered if this 'gift' was actually an insult, but thank God, the Champagne had found favor.

Scanning the banqueting hall on full alert behind his amiable demeanor, Ian took a sip of whisky, ignoring the homesick pang that it inspired – his ancestral pile in the North of England was a stone's throw from the Scottish border. Hooking his thumb in the small slit-pocket of his white silk waistcoat, he surveyed the dazzling display of colorful Indian tunics and turbans and resplendent military uniforms throughout the hall, and, despite being dressed with an impeccable black-and-white formality worthy of Almack's itself, he was beginning to feel a tad under-dressed.

There was no help for it. Gaudiness was not in his nature.

His watchful gaze traveled on over the crowd until it came to the Knight brothers. They had been an excellent choice for his diplomatic detail. Fine men. Their ability to win the respect and goodwill of the Maratha court had impressed him – then again, charm ran in the family. Even now, he could hear the brothers conversing with their hosts on some of the pleasures of cavalry life: The Marathas were also known as superior cavalrymen.

Gabriel was the quieter and more serious of the pair, and Ian sensed brooding depths in the man that he probably would not have time to try to decipher, but Derek had a larking, accessible manner, and soon he had the group of courtiers and royal bodyguards laughing at some off-color story.

As the Scots dance grew toward its grand crescendo, nearing the end, Ian's gaze traveled on, homing in on a solitary figure lurking by the wall – a dark-robed, dark-bearded man who seemed to be keeping an eye on him. All of a sudden, he was fairly sure he recognized him as the spy he had glimpsed outside the Akbar Hotel in Calcutta. As before, the man whirled away in a swirl of black fabric and vanished out the nearest doorway.

Ian snorted once he had gone.

So, that's who had sent the spy – Johar. Well, at least now that mystery had been laid to rest.

He considered going after the maharajah's agent and confronting him, but the king was due to arrive any moment now for the feast, and in the end, it didn't really matter. Now that Ian had established a foundation of understanding and mutual respect between himself and King Johar, why risk dissent over a little prudent spying? Such things were to be expected in these situations.

At that moment, the music ended with a flourish. The thronged hall burst into applause for the Highlanders, but Ian noticed that men were turning to look toward the pillared entrance. Shocked murmurs spread.

Ian followed the direction of their craning stares and froze to find Georgiana Knight standing in the grand doorway.

The sight of her hit him like a kick in the chest.

The glistening light from the chandeliers played over her fresh, flawless face and danced in fiery spangles through her soft shadow-black hair, all pinned up with saucy ringlets falling here and there. No trifling chit in innocent pastels, she wore an open robe-style gown of midnight blue, the split skirts pinned back with red satin roses to reveal a fancy white petticoat beneath, all ruffles and lace.

Atop her white elbow gloves, a ruby bracelet glistened on her wrist, but what most drew his stare was the breathtaking sweep of milky-white skin that her gown's tiny bodice revealed with its low, heart-shaped neckline and off-the-shoulder sleeves.

The effect left him speechless.

He, who had argued before kings and earned a reputation for eloquence in the House of Lords, could do naught but stare.

Hesitating in the doorway for a moment, she had also thrown the Marathas into something of an uproar. He did not require any great mastery of their tongue to interpret the general reaction: a mix of surprise, uncertain affront at her bold intrusion, and simple male bedazzlement at her lavish beauty.

The Marathas knew that Englishwomen did not keep purdah, but Ian gathered by their reaction that they had never seen anything quite like Georgiana Knight before.

For that matter, neither had London. Not since her aunt, anyway.

Ian wasn't sure if he was exasperated or amused. What on earth was she doing here? Did nothing scare the girl?

Though she must have sensed their scandalized reaction, the intrepid Miss Knight was clearly not about to be deterred. She was glancing around the banqueting hall as though she had every right to be there, searching for someone she knew.

Subtle signs of uneasiness in her movements and posture drew Ian's chivalry again as he realized she was not as brazenly sure of herself as she wished to appear. It looked as if his little hellion-damsel was in need of another timely rescue.

With a polite nod, he took leave of the gentlemen he had been talking to and went to collect her, determined this time to take in stride whatever mischief the minx tried to throw his way.

Heading toward her, he downed his last swallow of fiery Scotch whisky.

He was probably going to need it.

CHAPTER 6

Georgie hesitated in the doorway, looking out upon a glittering sea of bold colors and shocked brown faces, but she refused to back out. She had invited herself to the feast in order to make a statement: She was here because the other women couldn't be.

Still, it was a bit intimidating, and behind her outward show of total poise she was terrified, pulse pounding, mouth dry. The Maratha courtiers' hostile stares, and even the scowl from Colonel Montrose and a few of the Highlanders, underscored the point that nobody felt she belonged here. It pained her, for at the back of her mind, she was still upset by the reminder from Lakshmi and Meena that she didn't quite belong in their world, either, as much as she liked to pretend.

Georgie wasn't sure she belonged anywhere.

But she bunched up her white-gloved hands into fists by her sides, lifted her chin a notch, and scanned the crowd, desperately seeking her brothers. Surely, they would not turn her away.

Instead, it was Lord Griffith who emerged from the crowd, his stare clamped on her – though it was impossible to tell by his guarded expression if he was coming to browbeat or to rescue her. Either way, her heart soared at the sight of him, dazzling in his formal evening wear, all black-and-white lordly magnificence. The tails of his ebony coat swung with the vigor of his long strides as he marched toward her.

Wondering if he'd order her to leave, she braced herself, ready to fight him again if need be, but when he reached her, he completely upended her expectations with his greeting.

'Miss Knight.' He took her hand and bowed over it with polished aplomb. 'You look lovely.'

She gazed at him in perplexity.

Her brothers arrived a step behind him, hurrying to intercept her. Derek greeted her with a tense smile, but Gabriel drew Lord Griffith aside and spoke to him in a low tone.

'My lord, I'm so sorry about this. I didn't know she was coming. I'll tell her she has to return to the harem—'

'Nonsense, they've already seen her,' he answered in a murmur, glancing from Gabriel to Georgie again. 'If we try to hide her away now, we'll look weak. We'll all lose face. She must stay. She'll sit at the king's table with us.'

'Are you sure, sir?' Gabriel murmured.

'It'll be fine,' the marquess replied. 'Let her come with me. That way, they can't get rid of her without insulting the whole delegation.'

Gabriel nodded. 'Very well, then.'

Lord Griffith turned to her with a suave smile. 'Won't you join us, Miss Knight?' When he calmly offered her his arm, she passed a searching glance over his face.

His expression was a perfect mask of gentlemanly courtesy, but there was a great deal more going on behind his eyes. He really was the most intriguing man. 'Why, thank you, Lord Griffith,' she replied with a formal courtesy to match his own. Then she took his arm.

She saw the shrewd glance her brothers exchanged but decided to ignore it.

Nothing could spoil the sudden lilt in her stride as she walked through the banqueting hall on the marquess's arm. He'd probably subject her to another lecture later over this, but for now, it was just as well that he had chosen to take her under his wing, she thought. For at that moment, she noticed Prince Shahu staring at her again from across the room.

Georgie had developed a wide range of skills for keeping amorous males at bay, but they were usually British nabobs raised on Western chivalry. Not Kshatriya royalty accustomed to taking what they wanted.

Soon King Johar made his entrance, and the palace's army of servants hopped to the work of serving the great banquet.

Waiting for the meal to officially begin, everyone lounged in their seats – or rather, on the array of square cushions and large cylindrical pillows arranged for the guests around each long, low table, Ian found it an extremely intimate way to take a meal, especially when one had a charming and beautiful woman by one's side.

Removing her gloves for the meal, Miss Knight sat between Gabriel and Ian, while barefoot servants cooled them all, slowly waving long-handled peacock fans.

Large silver platters bearing a dizzying selection of exotic foods were soon presented between each pair of guests. Next, stacks of disc-shaped breads, both leavened and unleavened, were brought out. Soft and steaming, the fresh bread circles came in a variety of textures and flavors, which Georgiana explained to him: wheat bread, mint bread, corn flour bread, a dark bread made from the flour of water chestnuts, another from ground lentils. These were used instead of cutlery to scoop the food into one's mouth.

The platters offered a broad array of Indian delicacies as well as staples like rice. There were grilled kebabs with alternating vegetables and bite-sized pieces of chicken and lamb, all skewered on miniature swords. The collection of bowls nesting within the platters' indented compartments offered things like lentil puree and *biryani*, a slow-cooked chicken stew rich with colorful vegetables and full of aromatic flavors: cinnamon, saffron, and cardamom. Ian felt like he was back in the spice market, where he had first laid eyes on Georgiana.

He investigated another interesting dish that she described as the Indian version of mutton stew in a white cream base, mildly flavored with almonds. He asked her if she'd try it, too, but she informed him she did not eat meat. He raised an eyebrow at this, but while she helped herself to the curried potatoes and the more curious vegetables, crispy lotus root and bitter gourd, he asked her to explain the condiments: mint chutney, pickled mangoes with ginger, tamarind sauce, and a whipped yogurt sauce to counteract the hotter spices – their plates were garnished with little green chili peppers.

Raised on bland English fare, in the sit-up-straight school of aristocratic manners, Ian knew it was time to be adventurous in his palate. He only hoped that in this lounging position, he did not end up wearing the lentil puree on its precarious journey from the table to his mouth atop the scoopy bread. Georgiana watched him in amusement, laughing at his occasional self-deprecating remarks, such as his grumbling jest that, of all nights, he had chosen this to don a white waistcoat.

'My dear Lord Griffith, didn't your interpreter mention the Indians' view of the colors black and white?' she murmured, leaning closer.

'No, why?'

'Because in India, white is the color of death and black is bad luck,' she whispered.

'Are you joking?' he exclaimed, sitting up straighter.

She shook her head and daintily licked a little

stray sauce off her finger. 'Personally, I think you look very handsome, but if you want to charm our hosts, try red or green or blue. Yellow's a fine choice. Pink is also acceptable.'

'Pink? My dear lady, no descendent of a Norman warlord ever wore pink.'

'You could start a new fashion, then. Adley would do it,' she added with a merry wink.

He laughed aloud.

All the while, the maharaja's troupe of musicians played. The winding *veena* music accompanied by an expressive flute, together with the slow, complex rhythm of the drums, proved quite relaxing.

The meal passed in pleasant conversation.

Pleasant, except for Prince Shahu's efforts to get Georgiana's attention. No doubt the young coxcomb found her a novelty, but her gracious indifference seemed to leave him completely confounded. The more she politely ignored him, the louder and more insistent grew his boasts. His two royal bodyguards were left the unenviable task of having to continually affirm the royal whelp's claims of his own prowess in a variety of areas, from his hunting triumphs to the excellence of his horses, to his own much-vaunted skill at swordplay.

King Johar looked like he wanted to slap him.

So did Gabriel.

Sensing the exasperation building within his serious-minded friend, Ian took it upon himself to allay their mutual irritation with a welcome change of subject. 'So, how is your father, Major?'

'We haven't seen him in months, since he headed out to sea to meet up with our cousin Jack,' Gabriel said, 'but I imagine he's in fine health.'

Down the long table, Derek leaned forward to meet his gaze. 'Did you know Jack owns a shipping company?'

'I had heard that.'

'Warehouses all over the world. The moment the East India Company's monopoly was lifted here, he expanded into the Indian market. He's got offices now in Madras, Calcutta, and Bombay.'

'Good for him,' Ian murmured, impressed at how the village troublemaker when they were lads had turned his life around so drastically.

Georgiana nudged Ian gently with her elbow. 'I understand you knew our father when he was a young man? What was he like?'

'Oh, we loved him,' he declared with all sincerity. 'Back in those days – God, we were mere cubs, ten, eleven – Lord Arthur was the only adult who would ever tell us the truth about anything. We were desolate when he left. Especially Jack,' he added.

'It's a shame how the two branches of our family grew apart,' Derek remarked.

'I understand Father had quite a falling-out with his elder brother, the previous Duke of Hawkscliffe,' Gabriel said.

'Yes, I have heard that, too,' Ian answered. 'But I do not know the substance of what happened.'

'I'm not sure it matters anymore,' Derek said.

By now, the meal had drawn to a close.

Dishes were whisked away by an army of efficient servants and a sweet course of the most luxurious order was served. The desserts were cooling in contrast to the vibrant spiciness of the meal. There was fruit-flavored sherbet and air-light pistachio-and-saffron ice cream. Magnificent fruit trays arrived mounded with sliced melon, mangoes, apricots, and huge lush plumes of grapes. There was *tilgul*, made of cinnamon and molasses, and sweet biscuits ornately decorated with icing like little works of art, lavishly trimmed with paper-thin threads of real silver. Scattered among the *paan* were silver-coated cloves to aid the digestion and sweeten the breath.

'Lord Griffith?' Georgiana asked.

Ian washed down a biscuit with a swallow of Champagne. 'Yes, my dear?'

'Did you ever meet our aunt, the Duchess of Hawkscliffe?' she asked almost shyly.

'Er, yes. On several occasions.' His dutiful smile betrayed none of his real opinions on that topic. He steered the subject elsewhere. 'I also knew your uncle. He was my godfather.'

'Really?' she exclaimed.

He nodded. 'Our families have always been great allies. You should visit London sometime. I'm sure your cousins would love to meet you.' He noticed the flicker of tension behind her cobalt eyes after his suggestion. His gaze sharpened and he studied her with a narrow smile. 'What is it?'

She tried to wave away her fleeting response.

'Oh, I'm sure a visit to England would be very nice. But . . . I don't expect I ever will go there.'

'Why not? Surely you don't share that native superstition Ravi told me about, that "crossing the great water" leaves one cursed?'

'No! I just have . . . no desire to,' she said with an evasive shrug.

'Why?'

A pink tint crept into her cheeks. 'I'd really rather not say.'

He lifted one eyebrow.

'I don't wish to be rude.'

He laughed softly. 'Now you have to tell me. Come, I'm too intrigued.'

'Well, it's just that people from London don't seem very agreeable.'

'Really?' he exclaimed in surprise.

'Yes! I am sorry, but whenever they come to India, all they do is complain and criticize everything. The weather, the people, both Indian and British – they treat us like backwater provincials. If my cousins are like that, I'd just as soon admire them from afar. Thankfully, you're nothing like that,' she added with great sincerity.

Her attempt to reassure him of his quality greatly amused Ian. 'I thank you, Miss Knight, but if I may say so, you have nothing to fear in that vein. Your cousins are all that is good, and kind, and honorable.'

'Well, that may be true for you, but they haven't been very nice to their brother Jack.'

Fiercely loyal, this one.

'I realize Jack may be the black sheep of the family, but around here, he is our favorite cousin. He taught me how to use a slingshot when I was ten years old,' she informed him. 'And how to pick a lock.'

'Well, that's a useful skill for a small child,' he said dryly.

She grinned. 'More than you know.'

'I'm glad he's kept in touch with you,' Ian said to them. 'His brothers back in London haven't heard from him in years, but I believe his sister, Jacinda, corresponds with him.'

'I should like to meet my cousin Jacinda,' Georgiana remarked. 'I wonder what it would be like to grow up as the daughter of such a great lady.'

'Your mother *was* a great lady,' Gabriel murmured, giving her a look of mild reproach.

'I'd hardly know.' She dropped her gaze.

Derek cleared his throat. 'Our mother died when we were all quite young,' he told Ian. Then he slung his arm affectionately around his brother's neck. 'That's why we get along so well. We had to, you see. All we had was each other – Father and us.'

Ian saw the way Georgiana looked at her brothers, both adoring and sad, and he realized that in some degree she felt left out of their soldierly male bond; and yet it was written all over her face that these brothers of hers meant everything to her. Her blue eyes seemed to say that they were all she had.

He turned away from her poignant smile at Derek and Gabriel, and peered into his drink for a moment with an unsettled feeling, as though he has seen too much, too deeply into the core of her. A naked vulnerability that tugged at the very heart of him.

Just then, a friendly shout broke the awkward silence that had descended. He looked up and saw some of Janpur's colorfully garbed courtiers a few tables away waving Gabriel and Derek over to come and smoke with them now that they had finished their desserts.

The brothers looked to Ian for direction, seeking his opinion on whether they should accept the invitation or decline. He nodded, impressed with the good-will they had helped to foster between their delegation and their Maratha hosts.

'Just watch what you say, and, er, mind there's nothing stronger than tobacco in that pipe,' he warned quietly.

They nodded and went to join their new acquaintances.

When her brothers had gone, Ian wondered how best to use the opportunity to speak to Georgiana alone. Truth be told, there was so much more he wanted to know about her.

'How is your friend holding up?' he asked softly. 'The young lady from the fire?'

'Lakshmi? Oh, well enough under the circum-stances, I suppose. It's kind of you to ask.' She smiled at him. 'Lakshmi has decided to stay here with Meena. It's been arranged.'

'You sound disappointed,' he murmured, studying her ambivalent expression.

Georgiana shrugged, shaking her head. 'She's choosing purdah. I can't believe it. She cut off all her hair.'

'Really? Hm.' He took a thoughtful sip of wine. 'I can't say I'm surprised.'

She turned to him. 'You're not? You don't even know her. I do, and I'm in shock.'

'Everything's set against her. You can't make a fish swim upstream.' He leaned closer and lowered his voice. 'Most people don't have the courage to go against the mold, Miss Knight, let alone the fortitude to stand up to public censure. You know that.'

She frowned at him and looked away. 'I just find it hard to understand. I gave my friend the most splendid chance at freedom – for the first time in her life! But she refused it.'

'Freedom scares some people, believe me. You can't force anyone to take a gift they aren't ready to receive.'

'Well, it doesn't scare me,' she declared.

'Yes, I can see that,' he murmured with a fond half smile, gazing at her. Then he decided to venture out on a limb. 'Is that the reason you're not married? Jealously guarding your freedom?'

She looked at him warily and then gave way to an uncertain laugh. 'You have me all figured out, don't you?'

153

'Not in the least,' he said, 'but I'm trying.'

'In that case, allow me to explain.'

He gestured to her to proceed.

She took a swallow of wine and licked her lips daintily. 'As you probably gathered from our earlier discussion, living under any man's control does not sound to me like a very pleasant manner of existence. I shall never be any man's chattel.'

'Well, naturally, but what exactly makes you think that is the nature of marriage, Miss Knight? I mean, I'm not so much in favor of the whole messy business myself, but must it necessarily be some sort of domestic battle for power?'

'Isn't it?'

'Maybe, though, in theory, I don't see why it should have to be.'

'Theory and practice are two different matters, my dear Lord Griffith. Under law, marriage gives men all the power. Women are defenseless by compare, at their husband's mercy. Love, of course, is supposed to motivate men to treat their wives gently, but hardly anyone marries for love.'

'From what I hear, you've got scores of men who love you,' Ian baited her, hiding a smile. 'Why not marry one of them if that is your concern?'

'*Love* me?' She laughed. 'They don't even know me. They cannot see beyond my face and don't care enough to find out who I really am. Well – except for Adley, maybe. He's the only one who has the slightest inkling of what I'm all about. But I could never marry Adley, poor poppet. He is such a dear, hapless thing. No, one wants . . . a husband one can look up to.'

He studied her in guarded fascination, then shook his head. 'Your brothers were right. You are too picky.'

She turned to him in open-mouthed surprise. 'You three were gossiping about me behind my back?' She pursed her lips and gave him an indignant poke in the arm, only half jesting. 'How very rude!'

Ian laughed at her scolding. 'Your brothers want to see you married off. Surely this doesn't surprise you.'

'Well, it's none of their affair!'

'Of course it is. They are your brothers. It is their duty to see you safely settled in life.'

'On my own terms, thank you very much,' she retorted. 'I shan't be pushed into anything I don't want to do.'

'Yes, that much is obvious,' he answered dryly.

'It's not that I'm opposed to marriage in principle,' she attempted to explain in a more reasonable tone. 'If someone truly loved me and I him, that would be another story. *Then* I might consider giving up my independence. But until that chimera, that marvel, that weird, strange phenomenon should ever befall me—'

'Love?'

'Yes.' She nodded firmly. 'Until that day, I shall stick to my aunt's advice and flee the vicar's mousetrap. Wedlock is a padlock, you see. That's how Aunt Georgiana defined it in her book of essays.'

'Ah, the infamous book.' He looked at her shrewdly. 'Your father let you read it? A risky move on his part, I daresay.'

'My father raised me to think for myself.' She scanned his face with a guarded look. 'You disapprove.'

'Not of you, my dear, but the duchess . . . well, she hurt a lot of people in her day. Her husband and her children most of all.'

For a long moment, Georgiana fell into a contemplative silence, trailing her fingertip along the rim of her wineglass. She spoke again after a pause. 'What about you, then? Why aren't you married?'

'I was,' he said in a careful monotone. 'She died.'

Georgiana gasped. She covered her lips with her fingertips, sat up straight, and stared at him. 'Oh, God – I'm so sorry! I had no idea—'

'It's all right.' With a practiced smile, he felt himself withdrawing by degrees. An automatic reaction, like his automatic words. 'She is in a better place.'

Her eyes brimmed with compassion. 'I'm so sorry.'

He looked away.

'Was it long ago?' she asked him softly.

'Five years.'

Her hesitant pause brimmed with tenderness. 'Did . . . you love her very much?'

'She was my wife,' he said, not meeting her gaze.

If she noticed that this was in fact a cryptic answer, she did not pursue it, for at that moment, somebody called his name.

'Lord Griffith!'

Ian looked over. *Bloody hell*. He instantly donned his diplomatic mask once more. 'Yes, Your Highness?'

In the intimacy of their exchange, they both had forgotten about Prince Shahu, but the royal jackanapes had been watching Georgiana all the while with increasing frustration at his failure to lure her admiration.

Several glasses of Champagne had further bolstered his self-opinion but had not improved his manners, and his father, who was talking to some men on the other side of the banqueting hall, was no longer there to keep him in check.

'Didn't you hear my jest?' the prince demanded.

'I am sorry, Your Highness, no.'

'I said, "Throw *her* into the bargain and I shall get my father to sign that treaty for you!"'

Georgiana froze at his effrontery; the royal bodyguards uneasily laughed on cue, but Ian knew better than to rise to the bait. He also knew that in the East, women could be traded like cattle, and King Johar might well be persuaded that if his darling Meena wanted Miss Knight with her, then Miss Knight should stay.

'What you ask is quite impossible, Your Highness,' he replied smoothly.

'Why is that?' Prince Shahu demanded.

Ian reached over and put his hand on Georgiana's knee in a gesture that bespoke complete familiarity – and unquestioned possession. 'Because,' he said with an icy smile, 'she's mine.'

He held the prince's stare as a sudden burst of loud music, drums and drones, sitars and silvery bells hailed the rapid jingling arrival, in formation, of the maharajah's dancing girls. Prince Shahu glared at Ian, then turned away in a sulk, redirecting his attention toward them.

It took Ian a moment to remove his hand slowly from Georgiana's knee. His heart was pounding, a fierce agitation in his blood, as if his claim on her were real. He then noticed that the usually audacious Georgiana had turned three shades of scarlet, and he hid a narrow smile. Well, it seemed this time it had been *his* turn to shock *her*.

A crude move, maybe, but effective.

'I should go,' she forced out. 'I think I've pressed my luck quite far enough. Besides—' More hookah pipes were being passed around, and she nodded toward them with a small cough. 'The smoke is beginning to bother my lungs.'

'Of course.' Remembering her ailment, Ian rose and gave her a hand up from their nest of pillows. They had not yet put their gloves back on after the meal, and the shock of her bare hand in his did nothing to help dispel the tension between them.

They might still be a bit leery of each other, but the attraction was undeniable.

'Thank you.' Her delicate voice had gone a bit hoarse. The poor thing looked so shaken by his admittedly brazen touch that it seemed she could hardly bring herself to meet his glance.

How quaint, he thought in amusement, watching her look everywhere to avoid his gaze – the floor, the ceiling, the nautch girls. And here he had suspected her of being fast. He found her maiden reticence most unexpected and endearing.

'Shall I walk you back to your quarters?' he asked with tender gravity.

At last, she glanced up from beneath her lashes with a reluctant smile. 'Lord Griffith, they won't let you anywhere near the harem – but, thanks.'

He returned her smile and bent to murmur in her ear: 'Someday you'll have to tell me what goes on in there.'

'Actually, I've been wondering that myself,' she answered in a meaningful tone. She flicked a wary glance in Prince Shahu's direction, then looked at Ian again. 'I hope we'll have a chance to talk again soon – privately.' Her blues eyes flashed the message, *There is something I must tell you.*

He bowed to her with polished caution. 'I am at your disposal, Miss Knight. Send for me whenever you desire.' If she sensed any double meaning in his words, she kept her reaction to herself, merely giving him a small, nervous nod.

It seemed they understood each other.

'Until then, Lord Griffith.' Lowering her thick velvet lashes, Georgiana lifted the hem of her skirts just a bit and swept away without another word.

With heated intensity, Ian watched her cross the banqueting hall until she had disappeared through the gilded doorway.

CHAPTER 7

Whisking past the bald eunuch guards once more, Georgie escaped into the moonlit zenana. She paused a few steps inside and leaned against a fluted column, struggling to collect her wits after Lord Griffith's intoxicating touch. Good God! she thought closing her eyes. A feverish tremor ran through her. She could still practically feel that warm, strong hand upon her knee. Her heart pounded.

Of course, it had meant nothing. His shocking move on her had been a mere fiction, a ruse designed to scare the obnoxious prince away – and it had worked. But, oh, how real it had felt for that fleeting instant, she thought hungrily. And how naturally he had reached for her . . .

With a soft, steadying exhalation, she looked up at the domed ceiling, at a loss to explain how the Marquess of Griffith had come to dominate her thoughts since the first day of their acquaintance. His physical magnetism had snared her attention from the start, and she had only grown more attracted to him once she had realized he was a deeply ethical man. Now his latest revelation, that

161

he had lost his wife, tugged at her heartstrings, made her want to comfort him.

Dangerous longings. Especially when she knew firsthand what a very domineering male he could be.

Yet the memory of his touch tempted and tantalized her with a whisper that all the erotic secrets that had been forbidden to her for so long might finally be unlocked for her by this mysterious man, who clearly knew the answers.

Doing her best to shake off his potent effect on her, Georgie ordered her heated blood to cool down, put the enticing Londoner out of her mind with a will, squared her shoulders, and marched off to seek her friends.

She found Meena and Lakshmi sitting on the edge of the lotus pool in idle conversation, dangling their feet in the water and munching on sweets, a few candles burning around them, the little flames casting dancing reflections on the water.

Georgie kicked off her satin slippers, stripped away her silk stockings, hitched up her skirts, and joined them. The cool water helped to bring her temperature down, and soon she had nearly succeeded in getting Lord Griffith out of her mind.

She spent about two hours with her friends, catching up on their lives, though she had trouble getting used to seeing Lakshmi with hair chopped shorter than Gabriel's.

When Lakshmi decided to retire, worn out by the emotional strain of all she had been through,

Meena and Georgie were left alone. The lively and talkative princess spent most of the time extolling her husband's virtues, but Georgie didn't mind.

Earlier, she had thought of asking Meena some questions about the experience of carnal relations with one's husband, but now she couldn't bring herself to do it. She didn't really want to know what the Maharajah of Janpur was like as a lover. It was only that blasted Englishman who had captivated the naughtier side of her imagination, and on that subject, Meena couldn't help her.

At length, having talked herself out on the topic of her husband's innumerable charms, Meena finally decided to go to bed, too, but Georgie was still restless. She kissed Meena's cheek in farewell, said good night, and sat alone under the stars for a long while, trying not to contemplate Lord Griffith.

It really was sad that he had lost his wife. She wondered what sort of woman he had chosen for himself. A prim and proper London miss, no doubt. Some blue-blooded daughter of the aristocracy.

She sighed, growing restless again. She got up and slipped her shoes back on, leaving her stockings behind, then went wandering alone through the labyrinthine passages of the harem.

A person could get lost in here, she thought, unwilling to admit to herself that in reality, she was looking out all the various peepholes and listening grates in a covert effort to find Lord Griffith somewhere in the palace.

In one of the long, dark strolling galleries on an upper floor, she peered out through a narrow keyhole window and saw it overlooked the sprawling plaza through which she had first passed on her way into the palace, at the end of the processional road.

Flambeaux studded the darkness here and there, revealing pairs of guards on sentry duty. Some servants hurried about, as well, using the cooler air of night to see to their chores, sweeping up the cobbled ground and tending to the torches.

From her elevated position, she also had a good view of the king's torch-lit temple dominating the east side of the plaza. It was not very large but was heavily carved, tall and narrow, with a pyramidal roof. Not far from it was the ornate, wrought-iron tiger cage, as big as a cottage. It was full of leafy trees and impenetrable darkness. Most maharajahs kept menageries, but if Georgie recalled correctly, Johar had rampant tigers on his royal crest.

Movement in the middle of the plaza caught her eye.

An Englishman, hands in pockets, came strolling through the moonlight.

Georgie's eyes widened. A thrill rushed through her at the sight of him, so tall and elegant in the darkness, and at once, her heart began to race. For a moment, she bit her lip, debating with herself on whether she dared to go and see him alone, but then she remembered

164

she had a perfectly sound excuse for seeking him out. She had to tell him her suspicions regarding Queen Sujana.

With that, she was on her way, hurrying down to meet him.

She swore to herself that she meant no mischief. Had she not promised to help him if she could?

Realizing she would have to make haste before he either went back inside or was joined by others, she sped through the harem's maze until she found her way out and down to the plaza.

Within a few minutes, she was striding toward the towering cage, where she found the marquess in a staring contest with the maharajah's Bengal tiger. At her approach, the huge tiger vanished into the greenery, only to betray its position a moment later with gold-green eyes glowing high above them from its new perch on a sturdy branch.

'Poor beauty,' she murmured as she joined him at the railing that girded the cage. 'He should be running free in the forest.'

'Where he can eat people?' Lord Griffith drawled, flicking an intimate half smile of guarded amusement her way.

He looked not at all surprised to see her, yet his pleasure at her arrival was palpable in the balmy darkness. She suddenly wondered if he had rambled out here with the calculated purpose of giving her an opportunity to meet him in this clandestine rendezvous.

Leaving her to ponder the question, he looked

at the tiger again. 'Make no mistake, Miss Knight. He may look tame, confined in there, but this animal is wild. He'd tear you apart if he got the chance.' He eyed her in teasing, subtle menace. 'He's probably thinking right now how soft and juicy you would taste if only he could be allowed to sink his teeth into you.'

A tremor of response ran through her. 'Do tigers wait for permission, my lord?' she asked faintly.

'I suppose not. But . . . his cage is pretty strong. I think you're safe.'

She stared at him, wondering if they were really talking about tigers at all. As he turned to her, his smile faded to a more serious gaze.

'I apologize if I offended you earlier with my answer to Prince Shahu. It was the first thing that came to mind. I couldn't allow that notion of his to take root.'

'Of course – I wasn't offended.' She did not deign to tell him that the scandalous truth was quite the opposite. She suppressed a sensuous shudder at the memory of that strong, clever hand upon her knee. 'I – I understood what you were about.'

'I am glad.'

'Actually, the prince is part of the reason I needed to see you,' she said.

His face darkened. 'Has he insulted you again?'

'No, nothing like that.' She glanced around a tad nervously. There were guards and servants posted everywhere. 'Come. We must not be over-heard.'

'All right.'

'This way.'

She led him through the darkness toward the temple, thinking that they risked a lower chance of being seen and intruded upon there.

'Where are my brothers?' she inquired, trying to ward off the tension that had crept in as soon as she came within arm's length of him, close enough to touch.

'Guess.'

'Watching the dancing girls.'

He laughed quietly. 'Right-o.'

'The nautch girls couldn't hold your interest?'

'I have more . . . complicated tastes.'

She slanted him a fascinated glance. 'I see.'

As they rounded the corner and proceeded alongside the temple's carved wall, it was impossible to avoid the frank presence of the erotic sculptures that seemed to taunt them with their exuberant liberty. Paired stone lovers appeared to writhe together in the flickering torchlight. Every imaginable position was depicted in plain view across the temple walls, in all their voluptuous glory.

Georgie looked askance at Lord Griffith, wondering what his reaction might be to this 'native debauchery,' as one lady visiting from London had described a similar temple outside Calcutta.

He made no pretense of hiding his interest in the sculptures. His gaze trailed slowly over their lush couplings; then he looked at Georgie, as though curious about *her* reaction. 'Shall I fetch the smelling salts?'

She snorted, blushing a little. 'Hardly.'

He returned her nervous smile with a calmer, more knowing one. She found it strangely thrilling. They exchanged a searing gaze that lasted a little too long.

Lord, it could not be healthy for a heart to pound so hard! Georgie hoped she did not suddenly drop dead of the palpitations.

'If these carvings were in London, you know, you wouldn't be allowed to look at them,' he remarked, offering her his arm as he walked beside her through the darkness.

'Nonsense, it's art,' she said, accepting his escort, and savoring his nearness more than he knew. She curled her fingers admiringly against his big biceps.

'I have heard,' he continued, 'that certain people in London have even begun putting artificial fig leaves on the Greek and Roman statues their fathers brought back on Grand Tour.'

'How very respectable!' she exclaimed with a mild laugh. 'Well, it is a telling contrast, is it not? In our faith, the Almighty dwells alone in mystery above the clouds, but in Hinduism, nearly every god has a wife who is his equal – a goddess who's his opposite and whose powers serve as a complement to his own. And,' she added in a wry tone, 'as I'm afraid you can see quite plainly in these carvings, the deities express their devotion to each other in a triumphant celebration of . . .'

168

'Sacred sex,' he volunteered in a whisper when she lost her nerve.

'Yes.' Her voice sounded a bit strangled. She nodded, blushing.

'You should not know these things,' he chided softly as he watched her with a riveted smile.

'But I do,' she answered, looking into his eyes. 'Well, I know *of* them.' She turned away again and they continued walking. 'Not by personal experience, of course, but . . .'

'You'd like to learn,' he observed in a husky whisper, studying her askance.

'Why? Are you offering to teach me?'

'Hmm.' He considered it with fire in his eyes that pierced the night like jade-green lightning.

Georgie shivered with desire for him but had to turn away once more. Maybe she shouldn't be flirting with him so brazenly, for when he looked at her like that, as hungry as the tiger in his cage, she realized she might just get more than she bargained for.

With awareness throbbing between them in the darkness, they came to the temple's grandiose entrance, and Georgie noticed the light glowing from inside. She lowered her hand from his arm and peered into the temple, spotting the Brahmin priests tending their deities. At regular hours, the holy statues required various oblations and sacrifices, like the elaborate plates of food being laid before them with many prayers by the priests.

Georgie turned to Lord Griffith and shook her

head, warning him that they could not find privacy within; then she spotted the elaborate opening to Janpur's famous prayer cave and beckoned to him to come with her.

He followed, studying the rock-carved veranda that guarded the cave's mouth. A stone portico hewn from the mountain's native sandstone was supported by a pair of heavy columns and flanked by twin carvings of celestial maidens, who welcomed all devotees to the shrine from safe inside their hollowed alcoves.

'There are cave temples like this all over the Deccan Plateau,' she explained in a hushed tone as they approached. 'The fort is medieval, the shrine is older, but this cave temple is oldest of all. Some say it's been here for a thousand years. It was one of the reasons this mountain was chosen as the location for the fort. Something to do with fertility.'

'Why am I not surprised?' he murmured.

She gave him a wry smile and kicked off her shoes, leaving them by the wall, then she led the way past the shadowy veranda. Ian followed suit, but as they walked through the antechamber and peered ahead, down the rock-hewn stairs that descended into the belly of the mountain, the ever-gallant Lord Griffith moved ahead of her for safety's sake and took her hand. Still dressed in her dinner gown, Georgie used her free hand to lift the hem of her skirts.

Together they followed the trail of little candles

that the priests had left along the sandstone stairs. Their flames burned in the cave's deepening gloom like tiny stars.

The air turned cool and damp, and with every step they took descending into that tomblike space, the sense of the weight piled above them mounted. But Georgie was still agitated by their risqué exchange of a few moments ago and nervously cast about for a safer topic. 'I've been wondering something, Lord Griffith.'

'Ian, please. What have you been wondering?'

She paused on the stairs and smiled at him, warmed by his invitation to call him by his Christian name. 'I've been wondering why you came halfway 'round the world to take your holiday,' she said in an amiable tone as they continued down the long stone staircase. 'You said you visited Ceylon.'

'Yes.'

'But from England, it's a journey of some months, is it not?'

'It is,' he agreed. 'I needed someplace to relax.'

She sent him a skeptical glance. 'I take it you were called away before you succeeded in doing so?'

He laughed. 'Does it show?'

'Just a bit. Why come so far for a holiday?'

'I don't know,' he muttered as they reached the bottom of the cave. 'I suppose I just needed to get away. Far, far away.'

'From what?'

'Everything.' He avoided her gaze, waving off a fluttering moth. 'Work. Responsibility. The past.'

Georgie gazed at him in compassion. 'Memories of your wife?'

He scratched his cheek and glanced at her uneasily over his shoulder. 'Maybe a bit.' When he shrugged, his eyes were mirrors once more, shutting her out.

Georgie smiled at him very gently as they reached the temple floor. 'Life is for the living, Ian.'

'So they tell me.' He looked away, glancing around at the eerie, mystical cavern. 'Look at this place, it's fantastic! Come. Let's have a look.' He took her hand again and led her deeper into the temple.

Advancing into the giant nave carved out of the living rock, they beheld a soaring stone vault with massive octagonal pillars and a monolithic votive stupa in the apse.

Ancient as it was, the cave bore the contributions of many succeeding centuries, but everywhere the Tantric theme prevailed, the crowded stillness peopled with lovers both in sculpture and thousand-year-old murals, cracked and faded but still vibrant with life. Even the ceiling was painted.

Smoking incense and offerings of flowers graced the feet of the Bodhisattvas' likenesses on their arduous path toward enlightenment. Flickering votive candles cast strange shadows behind the friezelike layers of high-relief carvings, as if the little stone figures actually moved and danced.

Though the cave's dark, clammy, clandestine atmosphere summoned up the sense of being buried deep underground in a stone sarcophagus, the lusty images everywhere urged one to embrace life with fearless abandon so long as it lasted.

Carpe diem. At least that was Georgie's interpretation of what she saw.

Ian must have been following a similar line of musing, for he paused and turned to her all of a sudden. 'How did your mother die?'

'On holiday, actually,' she answered in surprise. 'It was a terrible accident.' Georgie paused. 'She drowned.'

A strange look – possibly shock – filled his green eyes; although it swiftly vanished, his chiseled face had tautened. 'I am very sorry.'

She shrugged, still ambivalent about the catastrophic loss. Grief had long done battle in her heart with anger at the arrogance of the mistake her mother had made that day. The sheer waste. 'She went out on an excursion with some of her lady friends, and they came to a river flooded by monsoon. The ladies were impatient and bade their driver cross it. He tried to tell them it wasn't safe, but they insisted, and they all were washed away.'

'That's terrible,' he said in a hollow tone. 'What about your wife?'

'Fever.' He looked away. 'What is it you wanted to tell me?' His stoic tone as he changed the subject tugged at her sympathy, but she didn't have the heart to push him. Besides, there wasn't much time.

'Has Prince Shahu been privy to your negotiations

173

with King Johar?' Georgie asked in a hushed tone, drawing him with her into the darker shadows beside one of the great columns.

'Yes. As the future ruler of Janpur, his father wanted him to get a lesson in diplomacy.'

'You mustn't trust him,' she whispered.

'I don't, especially after his behavior toward you tonight. But why do you say that?'

'When I was in the harem, I found out he comes every day to speak to his mother, and having met Queen Sujana for myself, I have a strong suspicion she's up to something.'

Searching her face, he folded his arms across his chest. 'What do you mean?'

'I think the prince is telling her everything that goes on in your meetings. Were you aware she is the sister of Baji Rao?'

He paused. 'Yes, I had heard that.'

'Well, what if she's using her son as a spy in your meetings? She could be passing on the information to her brother.'

He stared at her. 'I would think a man like Johar would have better control over his wife than that. She can't be that much of a factor, especially being in purdah. Besides, for the queen to pass information to Baji Rao would mean betraying her husband. Why would she do such a thing?'

'Revenge, of course.'

He furrowed his brow.

'Haven't you heard that King Johar is madly in love with Meena?' she asked softly.

174

He let out a sigh of great annoyance and rubbed his brow for a moment. 'The intricacies of the maharajah's love life were hardly included in my brief. Bloody hell, a woman scorned . . .'

'A *queen* scorned,' Georgie corrected him. 'Perhaps you could get the prince barred from the proceedings.'

He snorted. 'I don't see what possible explanation I could make for the request that would not give the maharajah a colossal insult. Telling Johar his son is a snake and his wife may be plotting against him? That's not going to get my treaty signed.'

'What if we had proof?' she ventured eagerly, but he eyed her in suspicion. 'There's a room in the zenana – a private audience chamber – where the maharani receives her visitors. No one else is ever allowed in there. If she's hiding something, that's the place to look. I'll bet you I could get inside there and have a peek about—'

'No,' he cut her off firmly, raising a finger before her face. 'I want you to stay out of it, Georgiana. It's much too dangerous. This is not a game.'

'Ian, with two brothers who cannot bear to miss out on a battle, I understand the stakes better than most. I would do anything in my power to help you stop this war from happening.'

'Well, that's very sweet, but I have no intention of meddling in the king's domestic squabbles. That would be the nadir of decorum and would only give offense. I'll simply have to work from the

175

other end of the equation – post a lookout for any possible spies the queen may be sending out from the fort.'

'Impossible. There are too many gates and too many people to watch, with an endless parade of comings and goings, what with all the merchants and such. Plus, you see how easy it is to carve away this sandstone?' She gestured to the sculptures all around them. 'Most of these old forts have secret tunnels burrowed under them for the royals' security. The queen would surely know about them. With my access to the harem, at least you've got a chance to find out what's really going on. She could be undermining everything you're working for!'

'Even so, she is too late. Our negotiations are almost concluded. I'm confident the king is going to sign the treaty. Georgiana, do you hear me? I don't want you involved. It's too dangerous.'

'I'm not afraid.'

'That is precisely the problem,' he retorted. 'You've put yourself enough at risk just by coming here, and God knows, you've already attracted too much attention. Aside from your brothers, every man in that banqueting hall was bewitched by your beauty. Even the prince.'

'Even you?' she blurted out before she could stop herself.

He stared at her for a long moment. 'I think you know the answer to that.'

'Ever the diplomat,' she taunted him in a

sensuous whisper. 'Don't you ever answer questions directly?'

He glanced at her lips, as though fighting temptation and debating with himself. He was so quiet and still for a moment that she wondered if she had been too bold. Then he lifted his gaze with a searing stare and moved closer, his massive shadow casting the Tantric carvings in gloom. He came to her like some elegant Lucifer in the fire-lit subterranean darkness, formidable and smooth, intent on his purpose.

Though she tingled with the thrill of his approach, her courage faltered slightly, for he radiated mesmerizing power. Then he touched her with intoxicating lightness, like a man biding his time. Skimming his fingertips upward over her cheekbone, his feather-light caress looped behind her ear and traveled forward slowly along the line of her jaw, until it came to her chin. This he lifted with two fingertips.

As he bent his head to taste her, Georgie trembled wildly.

She closed her eyes, waiting, her heart pounding.

His lips brushed hers in a silken caress, exploratory but still carefully restrained, teasing her like some tantalizing desert mirage conjuring an oasis. He stopped too soon. Her thirst for him was driving her mad. She knew he was working hard to hold himself back, keeping his passion under his total control, but it was strong. She could feel the fierce, hot need in him surging beneath the surface, just as she could feel the leashed strength in the large, elegant hands with which he touched her.

She lifted her lashes and found him staring at her.

'You are so beautiful,' he whispered.

She returned his gaze in wary invitation. *Take me, then. I am not afraid of you.*

He closed the space between their bodies, taking her firmly into his arms. He pressed his mouth to hers in heated yearning and brought one hand up to clasp her nape. The smooth, urgent stroke of tongue coaxed her lips apart, and his deeper kiss worked a lulling spell on her senses, luscious magic. The warm, glorious slide of their mouths enthralled her with its stroking motion, so erotic; the hypnotic rhythm made her knees go weak.

She clung to him for strength, lifting her arms around his neck, twining her fingers at his nape. At her embrace, his grip on her tightened. *You need this, don't you, Ian?* Whatever he needed she wanted to give. The way he held her, kissed her now, almost desperately, told her how hungry he was for this closeness. Heaven knew she hungered, too. His touch whispered secrets to her heart, tales of endless wanderings far from home, restless seeking for he-knew-not-what; it bespoke his loneliness, the coiled tension in him begging for release. She longed to soothe him, to hold and surround him, give him a home inside herself. To let him touch her as no one ever had.

Her hands tingled as she clutched and caressed

him, silently assuring him that he could have whatever he desired. She had tried to pretend for so long that she existed for justice, but deep down she knew that she really existed for love.

This truth at the core of her nature had frightened her for so long, men being what they were, but never before had she known a man worthy of all that she had to give. She wasn't frightened now. No, because she trusted him. And God knew their fit together was blissful.

As his hands glided down the contour of her back, pressing her harder against him, she felt the rigid thickness of his manhood pressed against her belly.

He pulled back, panting, and gave her a wicked, nearly insolent smile. 'Is that direct enough for you?' His eyes glittered hot, silver-green in the darkness.

She laughed breathlessly. 'You are bad.'

'Don't tell anyone,' he breathed in her ear. 'I've got the whole world fooled. Come here.' In the midst of many kisses, he lifted her and set her on a waist-high ledge carved into the stone, as if she were an offering for the gods. Hot and panting, still kissing her all the while, he ripped off his tailcoat impatiently, leaving it where it fell behind him on the ground.

Sitting on the ledge, Georgie wasted no time in exploring his magnificent body. She ran her hands along his sleek sides, down his broad chest, and across his taut stomach; she could feel his pulse pounding like the fast, steady beat of tabla drums. She caressed his arms as well, and then skimmed her fingers up to pluck at the gentlemanly knot of his cravat.

It had to go.

He helped her strip it off him, tugging it free, letting it fall to the ground as well. With his neck-cloth gone, the top bit of his white shirt parted easily for her further explorations.

She followed the proud lines of his neck with her fingertips, down to the little notch at the base of his throat and the top of his chest. He smiled at her, his eyes afire. She returned his smile with a gaze full of feverish joy and pulled him to her, curling her hand around his nape. Nothing could break the spell of kisses they had cast upon each other. In the candles' ruddy glow, Ian kissed her eyelids, her cheeks, her neck, her ears, her shoulders. She fairly squirmed with sheer delight at his attentions.

Then he went farther. The décolleté of her gown was admittedly low, with daring, off-the-shoulder sleeves. He slipped his finger inside her bodice and with a delicate motion, tugged it lower still. The next thing she knew, he had freed her breast and emitted a low, husky sound of male appreciation so acute it seemed almost painful. His well-groomed hand enclosed her breast in a velvet caress. But when he bent his head hungrily, Georgie shuddered and let out a groan as he swirled his tongue across her nipple again and again.

She leaned back, quivering, against pleasantly rough-textured stone, so cool against her burning skin. She petted Ian's head as he devoured her breast; sometimes she clutched his silky hair, intoxicated with his wanton giving. Dear God, if she had asked Meena a thousand questions, no words could have done these sublime pleasures justice.

Her nipples throbbed; her chest heaved with desire. Both his hands were on her, stroking, caressing her. The metal of the chunky signet ring that he wore on his pinky finger had grown warm with the heat of his touch. As the temperature between them climbed, she would not have been surprised if it was hot enough to brand her with the imprint of his family crest. Her skin felt as if it were on fire; she burned for him. She freed her other breast for him and, transfixed, watched his mouth descend. The darkened-pink tip of her swollen crest rose to graze his lips; she waited, aching, for his kiss. He teased her for a moment, but when he captured the whole of her nipple in his mouth, she groaned aloud, draping her arms around his neck.

The damp, rhythmic pull of his mouth at her breast both satisfied and inflamed her at the same time. He clearly relished it – sheer abandon and enjoyment were written all over his chiseled face. He reveled in her with a hidden decadence that nobody could have suspected of the strait-laced marquess. She was delighted to find him so wonderfully naughty behind all his supposed

181

propriety. She hugged his head to her chest, raking her fingers through his hair.

His lips were still moist when he had his fill of her breasts for now and kissed his way back up her neck, claiming her lips again gently. 'You really are, you know,' he murmured between kisses, '*ridiculously* beautiful.'

She laughed dazedly, only wondering what he'd do next.

'So?' she asked, giving him an impatient poke in the side. She must have hit a ticklish spot, for he winced and let out a laugh.

'So, what?' he retorted.

'So, Ian—' She took his face between her hands and stared at him in sultry anticipation. 'What are you going to do to me now?'

Debauchery glinted in his eyes as he turned his face a bit and kissed her palm. 'What would you like me to do?'

'I don't know.' She began blushing. 'How could I know? I've never done this before.'

Her reminder of this fact seemed to take him off guard. He stared at her for a second; his playful look vanished and he lowered his gaze. 'We should stop,' he whispered half-heartedly.

She let out a sound of dismay. 'No – please! I don't care what the rules of honor say. No one has to know.'

'My darling, you are so . . . deliciously misguided.'

'Kiss me.' She captured his hand and kissed his fingers, closing her eyes. 'Ian, I want you.'

She heard his shaky exhalation, then felt his other hand caress her thigh through her skirts.

She dragged her eyes open with a thrill of excitement, eager to be rid of her useless virginity now that she had finally found a man who could be entrusted with the task.

He gazed at her for a moment in stormy tenderness. 'I'll give you what you want,' he whispered. Kissing her once more, slowly, deeply, Ian slipped his hands under her skirts.

She shivered at the smooth expertise with which his palms glided up her naked thighs. With an incoherent murmur in Bengali, she closed her eyes. Then her failing voice dissolved like stars in the morning light as he touched her softly.

She was embarrassingly wet for him. She realized it by the slippery-warm ease with which his two fingers pressed inside her. She could tell by the pebble-hard resistance of her center under his thumb, the pressure he applied. Pleasure flashed like lightning; she sucked in a heady gasp for air.

'I know what you need,' he assured her in a raw whisper by her earlobe; his hot, panting breath stirred the tendrils of her hair by her neck, tickling her.

She groaned his name.

'Is that good, sweeting? More?'

'Yes – please.'

Any further questions would have been much too complex. Her mind was fading into the most primal awareness. They had become the lovers on the temple walls, worshiping each other, seeking their earthly Nirvana in the bliss of blind desire. Time lost all meaning as he stroked and pleasured her, not deflowering her, but showing her with his clever hands what that might be like.

Her yearning gradually turned to desperation. 'Oh, Ian, please—' She was not sure what she was asking for, but Ian knew.

He always knew.

He gave.

His kiss was fierce, his touch as rapid and precise as a master silk-weaver's hands on the loom, turning and turning her senses in a frenzy of delight until her mind dripped with impossible pleasure, and her moans echoed into the dark recesses of the sacred cave.

There was only time to wonder what she'd have to do, what price she'd have to pay, to win the privilege of doing this with him for the rest of her life, when suddenly, the whole world lurched. She clutched his big shoulders with a helpless gasp and went rigid with release, brilliant splendor erupting within her. Shudders racked her body, every nerve-ending exploding in a celebration like the wildest Holi festival she had ever attended, the ancient springtime rites, with colorful clouds of powder paints thrown in the air. Time, the inexorable goddess, paused in her sword dance as though frozen, and all the wanton joy Georgie found in that instant smelled of Ian and tasted of

Ian; she finished, gasping, dazzled by this man all over again.

Truly, she was in awe of him. He pulled back and looked at her with eyes that glowed in the cave's twilight, dark tenderness etched across his face. She reached for him with a strange threat of tears in her eyes, as though her heart chakra, which her guru had told her about many years ago, had just burst open like a dam in the monsoon, unable to hold back all the wonder that she felt.

She threw her arms around the Marquess of Griffith and kissed his cheek lingeringly. She would have thanked him but she couldn't even speak, so deep was her relief.

After a moment, he pried her back gently and let her lean against the stone wall behind her. He gave her a wistful smile, taking in her look of satisfaction.

'Well,' he said after a moment, making a still-heavy-breathing attempt at levity. 'That was worth traveling halfway around the world for.'

Georgie laughed, an idle, breathless sound. She rallied her strength to lift her hand, and gave his cheek a doting caress. 'You really are good at that sort of thing, aren't you?'

'A gentleman never brags,' he said softly, then flashed a devilish grin.

She laughed at him. 'You are too much.'

'Me?' he murmured innocently as he lifted his right hand that had pleasured her so deeply and, giving her a satyric look, licked the taste of her off his middle finger.

Georgie stared at him, wide-eyed.

'I think I'm beginning to figure you out,' she declared abruptly.

'Damn,' he drawled with a wicked smile.

At that moment, they heard the distant sound of Derek calling his name. Ian mouthed an epithet. They both tensed, her attempt to embrace him again curtailed.

'Ah, this is the part where I get murdered by your brothers,' Ian said sardonically.

'My brothers aren't going to murder you.'

'They could, and I think they'd enjoy it.'

'Oh, stop.'

'Griffith!' Derek's voice echoed down from the top of the temple stairs. When Georgie looked at Ian in question, he was readying himself to go forth again from the cavern.

Obviously, there was no point in trying to re-create his valet's artful cravat, so he shoved the white neck cloth into his pocket, then reached down and, still frustrated, no doubt, adjusted his swollen member through his trousers.

Georgie also hurried to right her clothes.

When they both had taken a moment to collect themselves, Ian glanced at her with eyes full of flame and stoic resolve, fighting an inward battle to suppress his desire. Oh, dear, Georgie thought in belated understanding. It seemed she had left the poor man in quite a state.

But fortunately, Ian had already proved a master of self-discipline. Restored at least outwardly to his usual cool control, he took her hand and raised it to his lips, pressing a discreet kiss to her knuckles. 'Ready?'

Georgie nodded and took a deep breath.

Side by side, they went in answer to her brother's call. She wondered if Derek might have spotted their shoes abandoned near the threshold of the holy place, but when she and Ian arrived at the top of the steps he was no longer there. They saw that he had gone back out into the plaza, still trying to locate Ian.

When Georgie and their mission leader came walking out from the prayer cave's veranda, both of her brothers were near the tiger cage, heading back to the palace.

'Gentlemen!' Ian called after them, sounding as civilized as ever.

What a fascinating enigma he was, Georgie thought, witnessing the marked transformation from the sensual private man to the brisk, no-nonsense public one.

Her brothers turned around.

The moment Gabriel and Derek spotted them together, the brothers exchanged a glance that Georgie feared spelled trouble, at least for her. Then they began marching toward them. It was hard to tell in the moonlight, but her brothers did not look happy.

'Is it true?' Derek demanded. He sounded incensed.

'Gracious,' Georgie murmured, wondering if her

brothers could have somehow discovered that mere moments ago, the two of them had been clenched in each other's arms.

But that was impossible.

'No worries,' Ian murmured to her in a soothing tone. 'I'll handle this.' He raised his voice to reply to Derek's question: 'Is what true, Major?'

'Did that little strutting bantam cock insult our sister while our backs were turned?'

'Ah.'

'We just heard about Prince Shahu's remark about Georgie,' Gabriel reported. 'Is it true?'

'Er, no harm done,' she spoke up hastily. 'Th-that's what Lord Griffith and I were just discussing.'

Ian shot her a look that sufficed to repeat his assertion that he would handle this.

'What happened?' Gabriel demanded.

'Youthful impetuosity, the best that I can reckon. Add to that a bit of French Champagne. His Highness tried to provoke a reaction by making rude remarks.'

'What did he say?' they demanded nearly in unison.

'Only that he'd work on his father for us if we tossed *her* into the deal.'

Georgie laughed nervously as Ian nodded in her direction, both of them making a joke of it. It was never a good idea, after all, to get her brothers angry. Men who crossed the expert duelists tended to meet a swift and bloody end.

'So, what did you tell him?' Derek demanded, folding his arms across his chest.

Ian flashed a roguish smile in answer. 'I simply told the little bastard that she's mine.'

'Ha!' Derek's short bark of laughter rang out across the plaza.

Thank God, Ian's answer did not appear to have offended them.

'I wager that shut him up,' Derek said.

'Indeed, it did.'

'What are you doing out here, Georgie? We thought you had gone back to the harem.'

'I did. But I – I had to see Lord Griffith again—'

'Is that right?' Gabriel inquired, folding his arms slowly across his chest just like Derek had done. One eyebrow raised, he looked from Ian to Georgie and back again.

She faltered, but Ian rescued her once more. He was awfully good at that.

'Your sister brought me some rather worrisome information concerning Queen Sujana. You'd better get back before you're missed,' he added, turning to her. 'I'll fill them in.'

'Very well. I'll see you all – tomorrow.' She smiled at her brothers and allowed herself one last, hungry, but she hoped not-too-obvious glance at Ian, which he returned.

His stare tracked her as she walked back into the palace. She could feel it on her, all the way across the square.

Ian watched her go back into the palace, taking covert pleasure in her bouncy little walk, though he still was not quite sure what sort of adventure she had dragged him into this time.

Well, 'dragged' was not, perhaps, an honest word.

All he knew was when that hot-blooded ingenue had moaned in his ear that she wanted him, he had been utterly powerless to refuse. Perhaps it was true that what he'd done with her just now was devoid of honor; but considering he had refrained from filling her with his cock as she had asked him to, he rather thought his restraint had verged on the heroic. And besides, if she was so eager for carnal experience, wasn't it so much better that she should experiment with someone who would make it safe for her, who could be trusted not to hurt her or to ruin her reputation with juvenile bragging?

For his part, Ian could not recall ever having been with such a responsive and passionate female; this was a woman who threw herself whole-heartedly into her pleasures. It was glorious to behold. And perhaps it was vanity on his part, but he found it incredibly gratifying to know that although countless men wanted her, she had offered herself to him.

Ah, Georgiana Knight. Somehow he should have known she'd lure him into misbehaving with her. She had snared him with his rampant curiosity about her, this alluring siren who could have been his wife if generations of talk about an alliance between their families were to be heeded.

Ian, however, had no intention of heeding those dictums. He had only wanted a taste; they both had wanted it. Badly. He knew now it had been on both their minds from the very day they'd met. He might be well versed in the art of self-denial, but she was having none of it, and devil take her, she was too damned hard to resist. He might be a gentleman, but God knew he wasn't a saint.

One day soon, when he left India and returned to England, he would look back on this as naught but a private and very pleasant memory. Sweet Georgiana in the prayer cave.

When he saw she had made it safely back into the palace, Ian told her brothers of the concerns Georgiana had raised about Prince Shahu telling the maharani everything that happened in their audiences with King Johar, and the sharper worry of Queen Sujana, in turn, informing Baji Rao. They decided to go back inside and try to investigate this possibility.

As they walked toward the palace, Derek casually asked what had happened to his cravat.

'Too bloody hot. I can't get used to this climate. How can you stand it in battle?'

'You just do,' he said with a cheery shrug, but Gabriel eyed Ian with some degree of wariness.

He *knows*, Ian thought. Or at least suspected. *Damn.* He looked away, hoping his face betrayed no outward sign of his guilt. *Sorry old boy, couldn't help myself.*

191

'I've been meaning to ask you something, if you don't mind, Griff,' Derek continued.

'What is it?'

'Earlier today in the Hall of Arms, I noticed you declined to join the demonstration.' The major elbowed him in ribbing good humor. 'Doubt your skills?'

'Actually, no,' Ian said smoothly. He glanced at Gabriel, then at Derek again, with a cynical smile. 'No point in announcing it, though. If anyone attacks me, they'll soon discover the truth.'

'Smart man,' Derek agreed with a hearty smile.

'Too smart,' Gabriel murmured as Ian walked on ahead.

The brothers lingered a few paces behind.

'I think he just gave us a warning,' Gabriel said.

'What, not to call him out?'

The elder Knight nodded.

The younger glanced in Ian's direction, then grinned at his brother. 'He's bluffing.'

'Is he?'

Derek shrugged. 'At least he's on our side.'

Gabriel gave him a hard look. 'They were together.'

'I know.' Derek sighed. 'Well, she could do worse. He *is* a marquess.'

'He's not looking for a wife!'

'How do you know?'

Gabriel shrugged and huffed in protective displeasure.

'Don't worry,' Derek told him. 'Lord Virtue is not the sort of cad to seduce our sister under our noses.'

'It's not him I'm worried about,' Gabriel said pointedly.

'Well, you do have a point there,' Derek conceded, well aware of their sister's wild nature. But he shrugged it off. 'What are we supposed to do? Georgie's a grown woman. She's always going on about her freedom, and as much as it drives us mad, we have to try to respect that.'

'Yes, but—' Gabriel's words broke off, and then he merely scowled.

'Gabriel, we've been over this so many times. She's not a little girl anymore. You sound like Father. I know we all appreciate having her at home to look after us, but sooner or later, we've got to let her have her own life. It's past time she married, and if she's got a serious interest in Griff, I'm sure as hell not going to stand in the way. He might be exactly what she needs. He's clever enough to handle her and all her tricks – and I daresay she can handle him.'

Still scowling, Gabriel dropped his gaze and shook his head after a moment. 'I just don't want him carrying her off all the way to England, where we'll never see her again,' he admitted with a glum look. 'It might as well be to the bloody moon.'

'Don't you think you're getting a little ahead of yourself?'

'No.'

Derek laughed ruefully and clapped him on the back. 'Come on, brother. We've got a job to do. I shall never understand why you always go galloping straight for the worst possible conclusion,' he remarked as they marched back to the palace, falling easily in step with each other. 'You are a pessimist, you know.'

He snorted. 'I'm a soldier, and if you haven't noticed, I'm usually right.' Gabriel looked at him matter-of-factly and then they strode ahead of him into the palace.

Inside, scores of people still milled about the glittering banquet hall, socializing and enjoying the antics of the nautch girls and other performers.

Ian paused upon noticing a heavily veiled woman seated at King Johar's table. He hid his shock when one of the courtiers told him that it was Queen Sujana herself. As the king's head wife, she was sometimes granted the rare honor of appearing in public beside her husband, especially on state or ceremonial occasions. Of course, Her Majesty could only be viewed through various layers of veils, in observance of purdah.

Eager for the chance to study the woman and do his best to read her in spite of her veils, Ian resumed his place at the maharajah's table.

When the Knight brothers sat down with him a moment later, he was still puzzling over how to draw the queen into conversation, when it was forbidden for any man except her husband, and possibly her son, to speak to her.

Neither was present at the table. Johar had drifted off to another quarter of the grand hall and stood conversing with his advisers. Shahu was nowhere to be seen. Without them, the poor woman was merely to sit there, no more allowed to speak than the fan-waving servants.

Ian sensed her watching everything, taking it all in. As he leaned back on the cylindrical pillow behind him, wondering how to approach this, he lifted his goblet to his lips to take a drink. The acute stare that he felt emanating from beneath the maharani's veil suddenly made him wonder if he ought not to swallow the contents of his glass. Her avid intelligence, her raging curiosity – and her mistrust – all were palpable.

Now he knew why Georgiana was suspicious. This woman was a force to be reckoned with.

And so he reached for his favorite strategy when locked in the sights of a hostile party, and smoothly began engaging in disinformation.

A few well-chosen lies to the courtiers about British plans regarding Gwalior would give Her Majesty something to pass along to Baji Rao. If her brother took action based on these little fictions, they would soon know that Queen Sujana was a traitor to her husband.

If that was the case, Ian dearly wanted to catch her in the act – trap her in her lies. Not just for the sake of his treaty, but for personal satisfaction.

There were few things worse in this world than betrayal by one's wife.

He should know.

★　★　★

Only a few minutes prior to this, Georgie had gained entrance to the zenana. She passed the new pair of hulking bald-headed guards on duty, went down the golden corridor, and found the marble atrium quiet.

Beyond the open doors to the garden, moonlight played on the lilting fountain. The children had been put to bed and the last of the ladies had withdrawn to their chambers.

Her heart was pounding because she, too, had seen Queen Sujana at King Johar's table when she had passed by the banqueting hall on her way back to the harem. Knowing that Her Majesty was safely distracted, Georgie turned silently and looked at the closed door of the maharani's private audience room, under its pointed arch.

Dared she?

This was the perfect opportunity to snoop inside that mysterious chamber and try to figure out, if anything, what the woman was hiding.

Impinge on the privacy of a queen? her better sense exclaimed. *You must be mad!*

But if it would help Ian . . .

A delicious sensation passed through her entire body at the thought of him. Oh, at this moment, she felt she could do anything for him.

Of course, he had warned her not to meddle, but he was only being a typical male, overprotective. She knew the routine, thanks to Gabriel and Derek.

She also knew – because Ian had trusted her

enough to tell her – that this peace treaty was vitally important. People's lives were at risk. And besides, hadn't she promised Ian that she'd help him if she could?

Well, here was her chance to prove her usefulness.

Swearing to herself that she would be in and out of that secret room before anyone was the wiser, Georgie's pulse escalated as she tiptoed toward the door.

Locked.

Well, naturally.

But this proved no impediment, thanks to her cousin Jack. She reached up with a sly half smile and plucked a long hairpin out of her coiffure, then bent down and as quietly as possible, jiggled the pin about in the lock.

Snick.

Ah. *Thanks, Jack.*

With a wary glance behind her, she opened the door and peeked inside. Reassured that no one was in the room, she sneaked in and closed the door silently behind her. She locked it again, just to be safe.

The private audience chamber was spanned by an ornate wooden screen with a few feet of empty space on both sides. Through the intricate teakwood whorls of the screen's tracery, the visitors' door on the other side of the windowless room was propped ajar.

The only light came in feebly through the open doorway, reflecting in from somewhere down that long corridor, near where the eunuchs stood guard. As her eyes adjusted to the gloom, she scanned the chamber.

A cushioned throne atop a low platform was the chamber's focal point. The surrounding walls were richly decorated with paintings and mosaics with the usual retinue of statues in religious themes. Some were life-sized; others stood on pedestals.

She noticed a dainty, European-style writing desk in the corner where the queen's secretary, or perhaps Sujana herself, recorded the business carried out during her various audiences.

Georgie sped across the room to it, opened the slanted desk top with painstaking care, and began rifling through the stationery, well aware that this could probably get her beheaded. She lifted stacks of papers toward the light, and knew just enough of the Marathi dialect to make out the general nature of each document: petitions, judgments, endowments, deeds, and various schedules.

There was nothing suspicious here, just the tedious paperwork of a royal personage meticulously carrying out what few duties were granted to her.

For a moment, Georgie felt sorry for Sujana, for even in the course of their short meeting, she had been struck by the aura of fierce pride and intelligence around the woman, and yet she was caged here, like that tiger in its elaborate pen outside. It could make a woman of talent and drive absolutely mad, she thought as she glanced around the room, wondering where to search next.

She approached the empty white throne and felt about to see if anything had been concealed inside, sewn into the cushions.

Nothing.

Carefully, she put the cushions back exactly as she had found them.

She had to hurry.

Moving more swiftly, she tried the paintings, rugs, and tapestries next, moving them aside, trying to uncover any concealed compartments.

Again, nothing.

She looked around with a furrowed brow; all that remained were the statues. Some of them might be hollow, so she checked them all. Shiva, Ganesha, Indra, Parvati – they had no secrets to hide. But then she came to the Kali statue – as tall as Georgie herself, painted black as death – and she truly did not want to touch it.

It's only a statue, she thought, scoffing at her apprehension.

Wincing a bit, she poked at all the hideous adornments of the death goddess, when all of a sudden, her searching fingertips detected a barely perceptible seam around the severed head in Kali's ruthless grip. She grasped it harder, wiggling the head carefully. She let out a gasp as the face snapped open and swung outward like a little door.

Inside was a folded paper.

Glancing around guiltily, Georgie took the paper

out and unfolded it, her heart thumping. Holding the message up toward the low light streaming in from across the chamber, she was able to make out the hastily penned lines.

They had been written by the queen, all right. In her arrogance, Sujana had not even bothered using code, and as Georgie struggled to translate the the letter mentally, the evil that the words carried made her blood run cold.

This was even worse than she had suspected.

Queen Sujana was not only siding with Baji Rao, she was plotting to murder her husband and put Prince Shahu on the throne!

Patience, little brother, the damning letter concluded. *I will send word when the English party has left Janpur. Then we will act.*

Georgie was so intent on deciphering the letter that she failed to notice another presence approaching until the faintest jingle of jewelry tinkled on the air. Then it was too late.

A curse exploded at the other end of the room.

'What are you doing?' a deep voice demanded.

As she looked up, wide-eyed, the blood drained from her face.

Prince Shahu!

She was caught.

Red-handed.

At once, she thrust the paper behind her back. Trying to hide the proof of Queen Sujana's plot, she retreated as he stalked toward her in his curl-toed shoes.

'How dare you invade my mother's privacy?'

Shadows twisted the sneer on his face and turned his countenance sinister while Georgie struggled to think of an excuse. She kept hoping some clever explanation would pop into her head in time to reassure him that this really wasn't as bad as it looked.

But of course it was.

'I—' She glanced around in rising terror, trying to spot the best means of escape.

'Foolish woman!' The jewel in Shahu's turban gleamed, and his long golden earrings flashed in the low light, but the hollows of his eyes were in shadow below his brow ridge. 'I had hoped for a friendly visit with you, *apsara*, but now . . . what a waste.' There was a whispery metal hiss as the prince drew his dagger.

CHAPTER 8

Everyone at Johar's table in the banqueting hall froze at the distant sound of a piercing scream.

Ian instantly came to attention and sat up straight, setting down his glass. He could tell it was a woman, though the voice was muffled through the palace walls.

Gabriel and Derek also glanced toward the gilded doorway, the pair of battle-hardened warriors going at once on full alert.

A second scream filled the air, closer now.

'Help!'

Derek and Gabriel shot to their feet and were already tearing out of the banqueting hall as Ian rose in horrified recognition of her voice.

Georgiana . . .

He was only a few steps behind them, his stomach in knots. *What the hell had she gotten herself into now?*

Shahu clenched her in a murderous hold and very nearly succeeded in slitting her throat – indeed, he nicked the side of her neck with the edge of his blade – but flailing against him and fighting for all she was worth, Georgie reached up and ripped the big, dangling gold earring right out of his head.

The prince roared with pain, clutched his torn earlobe, and she broke free. She bolted past him, out the open visitors' doorway through which the prince had entered the maharani's chamber. With terror stamped across her face and blood seeping from the cut on her neck, Georgie raced out into the palace proper, screaming for help, and clutching Queen Sujana's traitorous letter in her hand.

She burst out of the harem, past the startled eunuch guards, Prince Shahu mere paces behind her, chasing her at full speed, his face contorted in a vicious snarl.

The next thing she knew, she saw her brothers sprinting toward her up the central corridor of the palace. She let out a sob of terrorized relief.

Their keen stares homed in instantly on the blood trickling down her neck and chest, and their wrath exploded. They let her run past them and drew their swords, then put themselves between her and the heir of Janpur.

In the blink of an eye they had cornered the prince, who was screaming curses at all of them in Marathi; in another heartbeat, his bodyguards swarmed the Knight brothers, in turn, and then all hell broke loose.

Georgie was knocked to her knees in the eye of

the storm, a furious whirlwind of hacking metal blades that spiraled around her within the narrow confines of the corridor. She was crying and trying to tell them all to stop.

Nobody listened.

Oh, what have I done?

Derek and Gabriel kept her between them, fighting with all their skill as more and more palace guards piled into the hallway that had become a battle-ground. *We're going to die*, she thought. They were too badly outnumbered.

The giant eunuch guards now joined the fray, and as one of the potted palm trees tipped over, Georgie could feel her lungs starting to clench. The sudden shortage of air tripled her terror. The room began to spin.

Gabriel's sudden bellow rushed at her like a thunderbolt: '*Get down!*'

She reacted without a second's hesitation, diving onto the floor. A piercing scream arose as a serrated chakra wheel fell to the floor a few feet from her, clattering harmlessly across the polished marble.

She looked up in shock to learn who had thrown it at her and saw Prince Shahu staggering back, a dagger sticking out of his chest.

Gabriel stood, chest heaving, and watched the prince's horror with a black look full of ferocious satisfaction.

The whole brawl dwindled as the stunned guards realized it was their prince who had screamed; Shahu had just received a mortal wound.

Quick-thinking as ever, Derek grabbed Georgie's arm and pulled her toward Gabriel, prepared to help defend both siblings.

One of Prince Shahu's guards, who had been so friendly to her brothers earlier, picked up a long Maratha spear and walked toward them slowly, pointing it at Gabriel's chest.

Others followed.

'Don't, please,' Georgie begged the man.

They found themselves hemmed in by a bristling phalanx of gleaming spearheads.

The spears outreached their swords.

'I'm afraid, dear brother and sis, that we're about to become shish kebabs,' Derek drawled under his breath as the three of them backed slowly toward the wall in a tight cluster.

Georgie swallowed hard. 'Maybe you should put down your weapons.'

'Trust in their mercy?' Gabriel growled. 'Are you out of your mind?'

Behind the guards, propped up against the opposite wall, Prince Shahu yanked the bloody knife out of his chest with a scream: *'Kill them!'*

The warrior Marathas answered with a collective holler, and with crazed fury in their eyes, closed in to skewer them.

At that moment, Ian came barging into their midst with a lordly roar: *'Stand down!'* He repeated the order several times as he shoved his way through the phalanx, jostling the guards out of formation. 'What is happening here? Get a hold of yourselves! Lower your weapons, men! Everybody, calm down!'

Taking up a position between the two embattled sides, Ian turned to face the guards and all those deadly spears, one unarmed man, his hands up in a calming gesture.

The Marathas immediately began yelling at him to get out of the way, not to get involved in this, but he fearlessly refused to budge, and Georgie knew in that moment that he had just saved their lives.

'Let's all just stop and think for a moment and get this sorted out. Somebody send for a doctor. The prince needs help and others are wounded. Derek, Gabriel, sheathe your swords.'

'Lord Griffith—'

'Do *it!*' he bellowed harshly just as King Johar came striding onto the scene with a look of outrage.

'Father,' Shahu croaked.

Johar looked down and saw his son leaning against the wall, his face ashen, blood seeping past the hand pressed to his chest as he tried to staunch the wound. 'My son!' the king shouted, rushing over to him.

'Be careful, Your Majesty! He is a traitor!' Georgie yelled, taking a step forward.

From the corner of her eye, she was aware of Ian's stare at the cut on her neck. His sweeping glance checked to see if she was all right, scanning her from her rumpled hair to her feet as she walked past him, bravely going toward the maharajah, and holding out the letter that was their only hope of survival now.

Especially Gabriel's.

Her hand trembled as she offered it to him with a lowly bow. 'My brothers only fought in my defense, Sire. His Highness tried to cut my throat to stop me from giving you this.'

Shocked murmurs rippled through the crowded hallway.

'She lies!' Shahu protested weakly, blood dripping from the corner of his mouth.

With a dark look, Johar straightened up from his crouched position beside his heir. He snatched the letter out of her grasp, opened it, and read.

He did not move for a long moment, but when he glanced over at Ian, he looked grimly unsurprised.

At that moment, Queen Sujana rushed in, saw her son, and let out a bloodcurdling scream. 'Shahu!' To their collective shock, the queen tore off her veil in front of everyone and flew to his side, using the cloth as a bandage to press to Shahu's chest.

The guards gasped and all tried to look away, but her husband was icily silent.

'Get him a doctor! What is the matter with you, why are you just standing there? *Hurry!*' she screamed at the men in Marathi.

The royal physicians had already been sent for and now came bustling in. They moved Shahu onto a litter and quickly sped him away to try to save his life. Sujana ran after them, staying with her son.

Johar shook his head at his men, who looked at him in question, awaiting orders.

Obviously the queen did not yet know her treachery had been found out, but Shahu might stay conscious long enough to warn her. Georgie scarcely dared wonder what might happen then.

'Your Majesty?' Ian murmured.

They all waited for his response, Georgie with her heart in her throat, for she knew perfectly well that for anyone who attacked a member of an Indian royal family, the customary punishment was beheading. She held on to both her brothers.

King Johar slowly turned and pointed a jeweled finger at Derek and Gabriel. 'Throw them in the dungeon,' he ground out.

Georgie let out a frightened cry, but Gabriel sent her a stoic look.

'You two.' The maharajah gestured at Ian and Georgie. 'Come with me.'

From a room in the harem's labyrinth, down the hallway from where the surgeons tended Shahu, Queen Sujana in a state of ice-cold rage watched the drama in her husband's private audience chamber unfold. Johar obviously had forgotten that the room contained a high peephole camouflaged amid the gilded frieze.

While her boy's breath turned to a death rattle

in his throat, she tried to glean whatever information she could from their exchange.

Hateful Meena had been summoned to comfort her cursed, meddling British friend, while the tall, sly diplomat argued for all he was worth to win back the forfeited lives of his two condemned men.

Murderers.

She had not dreamed the depths of betrayal her husband was capable of until she heard him finally give in to the diplomat's demands, agreeing to let the Knight brothers be released into their old colonel's custody until their execution, instead of remaining in the dungeon where they belonged.

How could he give their son's killers a chance to escape? Sujana swore she would be damned before she'd let the Knight brothers live.

Johar ordered their brazen sister to get out of Janpur, and then Sujana was forced to witness the disgusting sight of the oh-so-touching good-bye between the diplomat and that horrid girl as they embraced near the doorway.

Her husband used to hold her like that, ten or twenty wives ago. Bitterness curled her lip as she saw the tender kiss the tall Englishman pressed to the girl's ivory forehead.

By Kali's sword, I want them dead. All of them.

They could not be allowed to get away with this.

Sujana knew by now that she was caught, for Shahu had recovered hazy consciousness long enough to warn her that the Knight girl had broken into her chamber and had discovered one of her letters to Baji Rao. She swore to herself she'd have revenge. All of these scheming English would learn the meaning of a queen's wrath.

After the girl had gone, Sujana heard Johar order one of his servants to make ready the upper room in the old tower.

So. That was to be her fate, she thought cynically. But of course. Johar didn't dare kill her, or Baji Rao would retaliate by unleashing the Pindari Hordes on Janpur.

'Now you know who your real friends are,' Lord Griffith was saying to her husband in the room below, wasting no time in hammering away at him once more to get his damnable treaty signed.

'Your Majesty!' One of the doctors hurried over to Sujana and whispered to her in urgent alarm: 'You must come! It is time.'

'No,' she breathed. Closing the peephole's cover silently, she glided to her son's bedside and sobbed for the death of all her hopes as Shahu breathed his last. 'Leave me,' she ordered the doctors in a raw voice.

They retreated, bowing out backward.

She clutched her son's bloodied silk finery in both her hands and wept until one of her loyal ladies-in-waiting spoke up in distress.

'Oh, my queen, is there nothing I can do?'

Absorbing the question for a long moment, Sujana remembered the fate that loomed ahead of her and slowly summoned the strength to put her tears aside.

There would be time for weeping later.

Any moment now, her husband's men would come to throw her in the tower. She must act swiftly if she was indeed to have revenge. She forced herself to release Shahu's robes from her fists.

Taking a deep breath, she drew herself up and turned to her maid. 'If you would serve me, go to the bedchamber assigned to Lord Griffith and leave a gift for him. You know what to do,' she added in a sinister tone.

'Yes, madam.'

'Search his room while you are there. Bring me anything that might be of use to me in destroying him. Go.'

The woman bowed to her in *namaste* and then padded away silently to do her bidding.

Next, Sujana summoned the top three captains of the palace guard's regiment, who would no doubt be as eager as she to retaliate against the Knight brothers. Not only had they failed to protect their prince, but four of their own had been cut down in the fray.

'Johar is deliberately giving the English officers a chance to escape,' she informed the still-seething palace guards. 'The moment they are in the old colonel's custody they will surely flee. I do not know what route they'll take away from Janpur, but find them – kill them. Do this, and I promise you my brother Baji Rao will see that you are richly rewarded for your service.'

'Yes, my queen,' they murmured. They bowed low to her and then went to round up whatever number of their fellows would join them in their brash quest.

Lastly, she called for her most deadly and trusted servant, the assassin, Firoz.

Even Sujana was a little scared of him. She half believed that he could walk through walls. Like some macabre specter, he came at once, as though he had anticipated the summons.

Firoz stood motionless, silent as ever on the other side of the wooden screen. The light from behind him glimmered over his sinewy shoulders and the wild curls of his beard as he waited, head down. 'My queen, how may I serve you?'

He excited her. It was like having her very own, terrible jinni from out of the bottle.

The question was, how best to use him now?

She paced on her side of the screen, her gown flowing out behind her, swirling with every pivot inside her cage. 'If they put me in the tower, can you get me out?'

'Yes, my queen.'

'I want the Knights dead. The woman, too. The royal guards may fail. They did so once.'

'I understand.'

He started to turn away to join the soldiers, melting into the darkness as he often did, but she stopped him.

'Wait!' she ordered him, for just then, her lady-in-waiting returned from her clandestine assignment. 'What did you find?'

'This, my lady.' She handed Sujana a small round object.

'You bring me his watch?' she snapped with an impatient glance at the silver fob.

'No, Your Majesty – look inside!'

Noting the shrewd glint in her lady's eyes, Sujana opened the fob, and it was then that she discovered the portrait of a child.

A beautiful little boy with brown, serious eyes.

Tears immediately flooded her eyes as she recalled Shahu at that age. Such high hopes – all dashed.

She trembled, unable to stop staring at that round, cherubic face through the mist of her tears.

'It is Lord Griffith's son, Your Majesty,' her attendant told her. 'See the inscription?'

'Yes . . .'

Matthew Prescott, 16th Earl of Aylesworth.

'Well, well . . .'

Slowly, daringly, knowing that there was no need to go on pretending that she was a follower of rules, Sujana walked around the great wooden screen that divided her audience box and placed the little portrait in Firoz's palm.

He looked at her in awe as she closed his deadly fingers around it; he had served her since she was eighteen, but it was the first time they had ever touched.

'Never mind killing the others. Bring me this child,' she whispered to him intensely. 'Alive. I'll make the boy my slave.'

'My queen?' Firoz studied her uncertainly, but Sujana shook her head.

'I want you to journey to England, Firoz. Pluck this boy from his home and bring him here to me. You are the only one who can accomplish this. You speak the English tongue well. You have been to distant lands before. You know how to move amongst men of different nations. Will you serve me, as you served my father?'

'Always,' he whispered.

'Good.' Her eyes narrowed in cruel satisfaction. 'If I cannot have my son by my side, then neither can Lord Griffith.'

Georgie and her brothers were already on their way even before the gray half-light of dawn had broken, trekking on horseback through rugged tiger country, with her band of sepoys in attendance, as well as Major MacDonald and some of his braw Highlanders.

They were not going back to Calcutta to collect their things. Colonel Montrose had ordered her brothers to drizzly England on a special assignment to report to Parliament about the urgent need for more funds for the army in India ahead of the looming war.

England! Georgie was in shock.

When she had set out for Janpur a few days ago, she had had no intention of ever leaving her beloved India, but now she didn't have much choice.

By releasing Gabriel and Derek into Colonel

Montrose's custody, King Johar had spared their lives, deliberately giving them a head start in their escape; but technically, her brothers were now fugitives from Hindu law, and it wouldn't be long before the maharajah's forces would be on their trail. If they were recaptured, Johar wouldn't be able to help them again. He would be forced to order their execution. After all, no king worth his throne could randomly break his own laws just because it was convenient. The facts were stark: Gabriel had killed the crown prince; Derek had helped; and according to Maratha dictates, they both had to pay by suffering some sort of horrible death. Some criminals were killed by being squashed under an elephant's foot. Others were fed to the royal tigers. But the likeliest fate was beheading in front of a bloodthirsty mob.

Georgie would have given her life to save her brothers from this fate, especially since they had slain Shahu only to save her. She knew she couldn't stay behind in India because she, too, had just made too many enemies. She could not allow herself to be captured and used as a hostage to lure her brothers back to face so-called justice for Prince Shahu's death.

Nor did any of the siblings wish to be separated. So it seemed that all three would soon be boarding a ship bound for the land of their parents' birth.

In their final farewell, Ian had told Georgie to explain to her brothers that they must not try to stay and fight. Given the fact that Gabriel and Derek were wildly popular among the rank and file of the army, their unjust deaths for the sake of honor, protecting their sister from attack, would cause a riot among Lord Hastings' troops amassed at nearby Cawnpur.

A fresh source of hostility between the British and the Marathas was the last thing anyone needed in this already precarious situation, so it was agreed that the Knights should leave for England from the much closer port town of Bombay.

There, one of their cousin Jack's merchant ships could get them out of India. Unfortunately, there were many miles to traverse, much of it through none other than Baji Rao's territory; and, if their little band crossed paths with the Pindari Hordes, then clearly they were done for.

Nobody was happy about any of this. Georgie was sick over the fact that they had had to leave Ian behind to sort everything out. He had urged them to go, and quickly. He said he would fix the situation. In her view, he already had. He had saved their lives. But he still had to persuade King Johar to sign his treaty, and then he had to get out of there alive.

By mid-morning, they all were irritable with the heat and the incessant buzzing insects that were continually biting sweaty humans and horses alike. The mounting sun had turned the thick teakwood forest through which the road snaked into a steaming, sweltering greenhouse. Removing layers of clothing to escape the heat only left more skin bared for the flies and mosquitoes to chomp upon.

With a wide-brimmed straw hat shielding her face from the sun and a pelisse thrown about her shoulders since it would be chilly once they put out to sea, Georgie had donned Indian-style silk pyjama leggings underneath her English-style walking dress so that she could ride astride. The terrain was too rough to chance using a ladies' sidesaddle. Finishing off her costume with riding boots and kid gloves, she supposed she looked rather ridiculous, but after the events of the past twenty-four hours, she knew she had best be ready for anything. They weren't in the clear yet.

Riding along, trying to soothe her vexed horse, she faced a weary mental review of the highlights: she had uncovered an assassination plot against one of India's most important maharajahs; had nearly gotten skewered by Maratha spears; had found the possible man of her dreams to boot; and had probably ruined her brothers' glorious military careers and nearly wrecked his mission.

She still couldn't believe what Colonel Montrose had asked of Derek and Gabriel. Eavesdropping while she waited to leave, she had overheard the whole thing.

'But, Colonel, what about our men?'

'They'll be assigned to someone else. You should be glad I'm not demanding your resignations!'

'Sir, prince or not, that vermin tried to murder our sister!'

'Your sister shouldn't even be here! Now, you both listen up! You've got all those powerful cousins in the House of Lords, don't you? Well, go make use of 'em! Don't argue with me, boy, I've been fighting wars since you were born! You get your arses off to London and make them damned cheese-paring windbags at India House and the Parliament understand that war's expensive! If we're to give 'em the victories they clamor for, we must have the funds they've promised us. Our men need horses – better arms – ammunition! Damn it, we're all but bankrupt here – and you see the kind of wealth these maharajahs have! They can afford to fight indefinitely. They've even got French generals on the payroll helping train their troops. That's not going to make our job any easier.'

'But, sir, we're soldiers! We're not cut out to act as lobbyists,' Derek had practically groaned, sounding as though he would half prefer the dungeon.

'Don't you complain to me, you hotheaded blackguard!' the old war-horse had bellowed at him. 'Nobody ordered you to draw your weapons under the maharajah's roof! You brought this on yourselves, the pair o' you! Now, work on those high-and-mighty cousins o' yours and demand that Parliament release the funds they've promised to the army! I don't care what that slick-talking diplomat says. You kill an enemy with bullets, not damned empty words!'

'Yes, sir!'

Georgie felt just terrible. She wished she had never come to Janpur and been so blindly self-assured.

Her brothers were furious. Her heroes, wanted men! And as for Ian, by now he must think she was some kind of walking catastrophe.

Gabriel was silent as they rode along, but Derek had never been shy about letting his feelings be known. 'So, now we are to go money-begging in London,' he drawled. 'Thank you, Georgiana. You've gotten us reduced to bloody beggars. How long is this going to take, anyway?'

'Don't know,' Gabriel answered, his brooding stare fixed down the road. 'Takes as long as it takes.'

'I guess you're right. We can do this, eh? We've faced a hell of a lot worse than a bunch of scheming, overfed bureaucrats.'

'Exactly.'

'Very well, so we'll squeeze that bloody gold out of Parliament's coffers, then we'll come back here, head up our troops again, and everything will go back to normal. I hope we make it back in time for the war.'

'You say it like you're going to a ball,' she mumbled.

'It's a lot more important than a ball, Georgie,' he retorted, the heat and the tense situation tempting them all to fall back into childish sibling squabbles. 'But you wouldn't understand that, now, would you, with all your pretty Jain philosophies? Must be nice to spout nonviolence when others will do your dirty work for you.'

'Leave her alone, Derek.'

'She's not a baby! I don't know why you always treat her like one. She's got to see her views make her nothing but a hypocrite!'

'I'm sorry!' she cried.

'What are we going to tell Father, anyway?' he demanded. 'We got kicked out of India? He is not going to be happy about this.'

'I don't imagine he would be very happy if we let our sister get killed, either, now would he? For God's sake, stop talking,' Gabriel muttered. 'You never shut up!'

'Fine!' Derek clamped his mouth shut, gave his horse a light kick, and galloped off ahead of them.

Georgie glanced at her eldest brother.

Gabriel still stared straight ahead.

She lowered her gaze and slowed her horse's pace slightly, letting him pull ahead of her, too. Gabriel might not be as vocal in his disgust with her as Derek was, but he was probably thinking the same things, just keeping them to himself.

Swatting a fat, ugly fly away from her horse, she turned her reflections to Meena's promise to make sure her servants and her hired elephant got back to Calcutta safely. Georgie couldn't even think about leaving her ayah behind or she would certainly break down in tears again. Purnima was too old and the path before them too uncertain and fraught with danger to have risked bringing her along for the simple sake of chaperonage. Georgie hadn't even had a chance to say good-bye to Lakshmi, but the person who most preoccupied her thoughts, of course, was Ian.

She kept thinking about how he had rushed into the fray to calm the situation. He had saved their lives, and she doubted any of them could ever repay him properly.

Unlike Derek, he had not said one word of reproach to her. Not a single 'I told you so.' In fact, he had been entirely kind, patient, and steady, his concern for her visible in his eyes.

When they had said good-bye, she had buried her face remorsefully against his chest, hating the knowledge that he would be left behind with much-reduced forces to help him if the situation turned ugly again after they had gone.

'Don't be afraid,' he had whispered, lifting her chin with his warm fingertips until her gaze had met his. He had stared soberly into her eyes. 'I will see you in England, all right?'

Georgie had stared at him, longing to kiss him good-bye, but with King Johar and Meena both in the room, it would have been unseemly. Instead, she had nodded.

'Good. Run along now. Chin up, my girl,' he had ordered her softly. 'And, mind you, save a dance for me at Almack's.'

He had sent her on her way with a knowing smile and a discreet wink, but tears had flooded her eyes at the thought of leaving him behind without allies.

'I'll be fine,' he had whispered. 'Go.' He had nodded toward the door with a tender look of reassurance that she knew she would remember for the rest of her days.

'A husband, that's what you need,' Derek informed her, dropping back to ride alongside her, apparently eager to resume his browbeating.

She gave him a warning look.

'I'm only thinking about what's best for you, Georgiana. If you were married off properly the way you *should* be by now, at your age, then this sort of thing wouldn't always be happening. With the responsibilities of a wife and mother, you could not go about doing whatever you please—'

'Derek, if you say another word, I'm going to take this riding crop and shove it down your throat—'

'Enough, you two! Derek, leave her alone! This isn't the time.'

'Oh, I think it's the perfect time, considering she nearly just started a war.'

'Let's take a break,' Gabriel ordered everyone, lifting his hand to signal a halt. 'We'll rest here for fifteen minutes and let the horses drink.'

'We should get off the road,' Derek asserted.

Gabriel nodded, and dismounting, they led their animals several yards deep into the woods, where one of Janpur's many crystal streams flowed parallel to the road.

As the horses drank greedily, Georgie looked at her eldest brother. His opinion had always carried great weight with her.

'What do you think, Gabriel? Is Derek right? Do you think I ought to take a husband?'

Stroking his horse's neck, he spoke slowly and chose his words with care. 'Not just any husband would do for you, Georgiana. It would have to be someone who'd make you happy. Someone you'd respect and trust.' He paused, slanting her a piercing glance. 'What do you make o' Lord Griffith?'

Her eyes widened and, at once, a telltale blush crept into her cheeks. Gabriel ducked his head, following her movement as she tried to turn away; he smiled knowingly at her embarrassment.

'Out with it.'

'Gabriel, he's a marquess.' She shook her head. 'He's too highborn for me. Besides, after what happened, he's probably going to run as fast as he possibly can in the opposite direction the next time he sees me coming toward him.'

'I wouldn't be too sure if I were you. On either point.'

'Why do you say that?'

'Well, for one, he *is* very highborn, and you may be merely the niece of a duke, but there is that old alliance between our families. Second, I have to say, it certainly looked like the two of you were getting along famously.'

'Yes, well, the man's not a glutton for punishment,' Derek opined, butting in on their conversation as he loosened his horse's saddle. 'Nobody wants a wife that runs around causing trouble.'

'Derek!' Gabriel exclaimed as tears leaped into Georgie's eyes.

Because she knew it was true.

Her eldest brother turned to her and saw her welling eyes. 'Oh, sweeting, don't cry—'

'I didn't mean it!' Derek practically shouted, for neither of her brothers had ever been able to stand seeing tears in her eyes.

'No,' she told them, her lower lip trembling.

'You're probably right. He's not going to want me now – I don't blame him! Oh, never mind!'

Georgie quickly walked away to hide her womanish sensitivity from the men, but she could hear her brothers arguing in hushed tones back by the horses.

'You idiot! What's the matter with you?'

'I didn't know she was going to cry—'

Georgie blocked them out. It was hard to hold on to Ian's gentle assurances amid her desolate certainty that she had made a complete fool of herself in front of him. She was quite sure he had made such kind comments only because he was a gentleman, and too chivalrous to tell her what a blockhead she was, especially when he could see that she was already distraught.

It was true. She was badly shaken up, robbed of her usual sturdy self-confidence. Maybe it was time to stop acting so bold, before she ended up like Aunt Georgiana – ruined, and causing her loved ones pain. Look at what had nearly happened. She could have gotten all of them killed. What a fool she was, meddling in important affairs in the realm of men! Maybe she *should* be in purdah, where she couldn't cause any disasters, or at the very least have a husband to tell her what to do.

Leaning against a big old teakwood tree, she wiped her nose on the edge of her sleeve in a most undignified fashion, since she had no handkerchief. She couldn't help thinking of Lakshmi with her shaved head. *Duty*.

Maybe Derek was on to something.

Never once had she conceived of marriage as her duty. She knew it was that way for other girls, but Papa had never made it seem so in her case, had never put that onus on her.

'Ach, lass, don't ye cry.'

Georgie looked over to find big, red-headed Major MacDonald offering her his handkerchief.

She accepted it tearfully. 'Thanks, Mac.'

'Aye, keep it. And if ye're wantin' me ta marry ye, why, only say the word,' he teased.

She mustered up a rueful smile of thanks.

All of a sudden, she heard a nasty whizzing sound followed by a loud, wooden *thunk*.

'Bloody hell!' the major cursed. Staring at the tree trunk right above the spot where Georgie leaned, he shoved her toward the ground. '*Get down!*'

'What's the matter?' she started, then heard that strange sound again.

Thunk.

She looked up and saw two arrows sticking out of the tree trunk, inches above the place where she had been standing.

'To arms, lads!' Major MacDonald bellowed, shielding Georgie with his fearless bulk. 'We've got company!'

Finally, Ian had gotten his treaty signed.

They were fortunate that Johar had suspected the maharani for some time, a fact he had admitted to Ian. But although he had suspected Sujana, he had not wanted to believe it. Now, thanks to Georgiana's meddling, the truth had come to light.

It was no exaggeration to say that the girl had saved King Johar's life; therefore, he had spared her brothers' lives in return.

As Ian strode back to his guest chamber to pack his traveling trunks, eager to be gone, he mused on the efficacy of her direct approach. Subtlety might be cleaner, but her way had certainly brought about faster results. There was something to be said for speed.

Though she had acted in direct defiance of his orders, Ian had to admit, ruefully, that if Georgiana hadn't interfered, then Johar's signature on the treaty would have been moot, for the king soon would have been a dead man. Queen Sujana simply would have waited until the English delegation had gone and then ordered her husband's killing. No doubt the maharani would have promptly thrown out his neutrality agreement to join forces with her brother, Baji Rao.

Now things would turn out the way they were supposed to, and Ian couldn't help but feel a certain degree of satisfaction in that.

Then he opened the door to his chamber, and his fleeting sense of triumph evaporated.

A pair of bare brown feet were sticking out across the floor from the narrow aisle behind his bed. Ian closed the door behind him and rushed around the bed, cursing to find his trusty servant Ravi lying unconscious on the carpet, his arms sprawled. No, not unconscious, he realized as he felt in vain for a pulse.

Dead.

Jesus.

His shocked gaze traveled over his interpreter's stark, wide-open eyes and rigid form. Foamy spittle mixed with vomit trailed from Ravi's mouth onto the carpet under his cheek.

Ian could hardly believe his eyes. He looked at Ravi's outflung arms and then spotted a mango on the floor with several bites taken out of it. It appeared to have rolled out of his hand when he had fallen.

On his guard, Ian's glance swept the room. Fury filled his eyes when his gaze homed in on the enticing fruit bowl that he was sure had not been there earlier.

Poison.

Oh, Ravi, I'm so sorry.

He sat back on his heels and wiped his hand across his mouth as he debated whether to tell Johar about this insidious attack. Poison was the favorite weapon of women, and there was not a doubt in his mind that this was the work of Queen Sujana, taking her revenge for Shahu's death.

With a grimace of remorse for Ravi's murder, he reached down and closed the dead man's blankly staring eyes. Obviously, that poison had been meant for *him*.

I've got to get out of here, he thought, his worry for Georgiana and her brothers suddenly renewed.

They were in danger. He had to warn them. If the maharani had sent poison up for him, God only knew what she might have sent out after the Knights.

Since there was nothing left that he could do for Ravi, he made haste to leave the palace, for the rest of them were not yet out of harm's way. Aside from his urgency to catch up to his friends, he still had to dispatch his riders to bring the signed treaty to Lord Hastings.

Throwing his belongings into his traveling trunk with none of his usual orderliness, Ian suddenly realized his picture of Matthew was missing.

Where the hell had it gone to? He looked all over the place, threw aside the bed covers, and pulled the dresser away from the wall, wondering if the picture had fallen behind it; he even looked under poor Ravi's corpse, but it was nowhere to be found.

Bloody hell, had he left it in Calcutta?

There was no time to keep hunting for it. *Leave it. You'll see the boy in person soon enough.*

Still, as he pulled his portmanteaux out into the corridor and called for a few palace coolies to bring his luggage down to his waiting retinue of soldiers, the picture's loss made him uneasy, a bad omen.

The sooner he got out of here, the better.

Within a few days, the smell of sea salt on the humid breeze heralded Ian's arrival at Bombay. Cantering past the outlying marshes, he entered the town with his few remaining soldiers and found his way to Jack Knight's shipyard.

'Good God,' he murmured as he pulled his weary horse to a halt and stared into the shipyard at the aftermath of a battle. There were scorch marks on the wooden fence, the smell of smoke and black powder still wafting on the air. Here and there were gruesome puddles of blood.

It appeared his luckless servant hadn't been the only casualty.

Ian quickly asked one of the battered Highlanders where the Knights had gone. The man pointed to a handsome brick house down the street. Ian turned his horse and rode down to it, realizing this must be the Knight family's Bombay residence. The Calcutta house was a glorious folly, but this one was all business.

Straw had been scattered on the street outside

the house to dampen the sound from carriages rolling by. That was an ominous sign, for normally this practice was followed when someone inside was ill. As Ian dismounted and tied his horse to the fence in the shade, his worry climbed.

Letting himself in the gate and then striding up the short front path, he knocked on the door. When a moment passed and still no one answered, he opened the door and poked his head inside. 'Hallo? Anybody here?'

An Indian servant came padding toward him on bare feet, her face etched with alarm. 'Sahib?'

'Don't be alarmed, I am Lord Griffith.' He stepped inside. 'I am looking for the majors and Miss Knight.'

'Oh, sahib! Thank heavens you've come! The masters are upstairs, sir. Go, go! They are expecting you!' She gestured to the polished teakwood staircase, looking relieved that someone had come along prepared to take charge.

'What of the lady?'

'She is gone,' the woman said, tears rushing into her eyes.

'Gone?' The blood drained from Ian's face. He did not wait for her explanation, but ran up the stairs with dread forming a knot in the pit of his stomach.

'We're in here,' a flat voice called.

Ian followed it into a neat, plain bedchamber. 'Derek?'

With a grim glance devoid of his usual jovial

irreverence, Derek looked up from the letter he had been writing.

He was sitting beside the bed where Gabriel lay, his chest bandaged, his face ashen.

Ian took a deep breath when he saw him.

Gabriel was not entirely conscious, but his glazed blue eyes were filled with suffering. He did not stir when Ian entered.

'Did Johar sign the treaty?' Derek asked in a deadened monotone.

Ian nodded.

'Well, then. At least there's that.'

'How bad is he?' he whispered, lowering himself for a closer look at Gabriel.

'He's been better,' Derek said, staring at his brother. 'Fought like a lion, he did. Never seen anything like it.' He paused. 'It was an arrow got him, Griff. It was meant for me, but he pushed me aside and took it instead.'

'Oh, God.'

'He saved my life. Just like he saved Georgie's.'

Ian turned to him, almost not brave enough to ask if she had been killed. Somehow he managed to form the words: 'Where is she?'

'We were attacked. We sent her on ahead. Safer that way. We had no choice. Queen Sujana sent her forces after us.'

'After me, as well,' he murmured, offering up a silent prayer in his relief to hear the news confirmed, that Georgiana was alive.

'They struck first on the road out of Janpur,' Derek

murmured. 'We fought them off and escaped, but they were relentless. They kept coming after us. The hottest fight was over at the shipyard. Didn't look like any of us were gettin' out of there alive, but we managed to hold them off long enough for Georgie to escape on one of Jack's ships.'

'Thank God,' Ian breathed, feeling a little shaky. All of this struck much too close to home.

'Yes,' he agreed, 'but she's alone, and, I warrant, scared to death.'

'Was she hurt?'

'No. We lost a lot of men. Major MacDonald is dead, along with half our sepoys.'

Ian bowed his head. 'God keep them.'

'Griff, my brother – cannot travel like this. The voyage will be long and grueling. It may be weeks until he's strong enough to chance it. I must stay with him.'

'Of course. Don't worry. I've brought you reinforcements. The rest of your men from the diplomatic detail are just down the street. They will help keep watch in case those bastards come back.'

'I think we got them all,' Derek answered with a nod. The hollowness of his tone sent a chill down Ian's spine.

'Lord Griffith, I – I realize we already owe you our lives as it is, but I have no choice; I must ask another favor of you.'

'Of course, man. Name it.'

'Look after our sister for us when you reach

England? She's never been out of India before. She's got none of her servants with her, no money, nothing. Jack's crew will get her to London safely, God willing, but she's not going to know a soul there except for you. She trusts you.'

'What is the name of the vessel on which she is sailing?'

'The *Andromeda*. It's a twenty-gun frigate in Jack's merchant fleet, so it'll probably be delayed by stops at numerous ports. You may be able to catch up to her.'

Ian nodded without hesitation. 'Have no fear for your sister. Just take care of him.' He glanced at Gabriel. 'I'll look after Georgiana as if she were my own.'

Gratitude filled Derek's light blue eyes. 'Yes, well, actually, now that you mention it, we really wouldn't mind it if she were.'

Ian's eyes widened. 'Pardon?'

'You have a way with her. I know she can be wild, but she – she's got a good heart. She listens to you. And after all that has happened, I think you may find her much more malleable.'

Ian stared at him uncertainly. 'What exactly are you saying, Derek?'

'I'm saying if you want to marry her, you have our blessing. Gabriel's and mine.'

For all his silver-tongued savoir-faire, Ian could not summon up a single word in response. His heart skipped a beat. He dropped his gaze and tried to think of something to say.

'Ah, never mind me,' Derek said with a weary sigh. 'I don't mean to put you on the spot, old boy. Haven't slept in days. Talking nonsense. Sorry.'

'You needn't apologize, it's just—' Ian found himself half confounded. 'I had no plans ever to remarry.'

'Of course. Then again, plans sometimes take the most unexpected turns, don't they?' He glanced at his wounded brother and then looked at Ian again. 'The voyage to England is long. If a change in course is due, you'll have plenty of time to discover your own mind on this matter. Certainly the choice is yours.'

With that, Derek dropped the subject, and Ian rose to go seek a ship at once that would take him to England.

'Give this to my father if you see him, would you?' Derek handed him the letter he had been writing. 'I've been making copies to send out on Jack's ships, so no matter where our old man is, he'll hear from us eventually. I've asked Father to meet us in London.'

'Anything else I can do?' Ian asked as he tucked the letter for Lord Arthur into the breast pocket of his waistcoat.

Derek shook his head. 'Probably best not to tell Georgie how serious Gabriel's wound is. She blames herself enough for all this as it is. Part of that is my fault. I . . . gave her a bit of a hard time about things when we were leaving Janpur.' He hesitated. 'Would you – tell her I'm sorry for all that I said and not to pay me any mind?'

'Of course. Derek, I'm sure your sister knows you love her, no matter what was said.' Ian gave the weary soldier a kindly squeeze on his shoulder. 'Try not to worry too much. Your brother's as strong as a horse. He'll pull through. You should get some rest,' he added.

'Right,' Derek said with a resolute nod, but the inhalation he drew in through his nostrils sounded a little unsteady. 'Safe journey, old boy. Give Georgiana our love.'

CHAPTER 9

London loomed before her, an eerie and alien new world shrouded in darkness and swirling fog.

As the frigate *Andromeda* sailed up the onyx River Thames, Georgie stood at the rails, staring at the city, a brown wool cloak wrapped tightly around her. The damp night's deep gloom was punctuated by little glowing lights that sketched the shapes of hulking buildings, great bridges, church spires, innumerable ships in the distance. The streetlamps cast a hazy glow into the mist. Somewhere in the dark, a cathedral's deep, bonging bells tolled the hour.

Two A.M.

She had spent Christmas at sea, and Easter, too, and now the new year, 1818, was well underway. The last time she had stood on dry land, she had fled a scene of terror. She closed her eyes against the still-vivid memory of the vicious battle at the Bombay docks, sickened by her unending questions every time they sliced through her mind. Were her brothers dead or alive? Had they survived their ordeal?

Now she was thousands of miles from home

without a penny in her pocket and nothing but the clothes upon her back. She wasn't even certain the authorities would let her come ashore, for she had no passport, no traveling papers to prove to the customs officers who she was. There hadn't been time for such things. She had barely escaped with her life.

The *Andromeda*'s dear old captain had told her not to worry, that when they got upriver to the Knight Shipping warehouses, her cousin, Lord Jack, might be there, and he would deal with the harbor master. She gathered this was a polite way of saying that Jack would simply bribe the customs officers to make sure she was allowed into the country. Georgie didn't doubt that he could do it – her cousin, the ruthless business tycoon, had a way of getting things done – but she had no reason to believe that Jack even was in England.

Fear continued whispering in her blood, reminding her that she knew no one in this city and that, in bluntest terms, she had nowhere to go. Her highborn cousins were her only hope, but she had never actually met them and had no idea where they lived. The city hugged the river bends for miles; she did not know how she would ever find them. But even if she did by some miracle locate Knight House, it would surely seem incredulous and rude in the extreme if she simply showed up on their doorstep in the middle of the night, claiming to be their long-lost cousin from India. They would probably call the constable!

Her anxiety climbed as she faced this foreign shore, all cloaked in darkness. Both sides of the river were crowded with buildings shoved together cheek by jowl, with an endless range of docks and markets. Shivering in the chilly northern climate, she clung to her courage as the boat glided onward, past a thronged pleasure garden on the south shore of the Thames.

Gaily colored lanterns illuminated gaudy pavilions filled with people having fun. Noisy, romping music played along with the chatty drone of hundreds of revelers. One of the sailors informed her the lively place was called Vauxhall. Despite the late hour, watermen were still ferrying people back and forth across the river to the pleasure grounds.

She borrowed the first mate's spyglass and saw a fanciful display of topiary sculptures, and then a performance that made her shudder, it looked so dangerous: costumed performers illumined by limelights were juggling various objects as they walked across a tightrope high above the ground.

She handed the spyglass back to the first mate, unable to watch, for she was certain they would all fall down . . . *just like her.* To be sure, she had learned her lesson about taking too-great risks and showing off.

Farther up the river, they floated past Lambeth Palace, the home of the bishop. She even got to see Whitehall, where Parliament met. Ian had a seat in Parliament, she knew, the House of Lords.

At the thought of him, her heart ached with her need to see him again. *Was he safe? Had he made it out of Janpur alive?*

It could be weeks before she'd know, but she had good reason to fear for his safety. If Queen Sujana had been so effective in sending her minions after her and her brothers, in how much more danger must Ian have been when they had been forced to leave him behind, all alone?

She could hardly bear to think about it, for in truth, her feelings toward the marquess had also undergone a change. For all those long, lonely months at sea, reliving the memory of every word they had exchanged and every kiss and touch they had stolen in the prayer cave, her admiration for him had deepened into something more insistent.

Unfortunately, after her recklessness at Janpur, she was quite sure Derek was right. Ian was never going to want her now. She might as well whistle down the moon.

How she wished he were here, she thought with an ache of longing. She felt so lost at the moment, and he always knew exactly what to say.

Upriver, a sprawling warehouse came into view with 'Knight Shipping' painted in huge block letters on the side. Her heart sank as she noticed the offices above were pitch dark.

Nobody home.

It seemed she really was on her own in this strange country.

The frigate dropped anchor not far from the shore, striking sail in the middle of the river.

The harbor master in his riverboat shuttled up alongside the ship, and soon the *Andromeda*'s captain was engaged in answering queries about their cargo.

Before long, however, the captain left off their conversation and came clomping over to where Georgie still stood by the rails. 'Would ye like to go ashore at once, Miss?'

What for? she thought glumly. *What should I do? Wander the streets of London until dawn?*

'Harbor master says you've already got permission,' the captain added with a twinkle in his eyes.

'What?' She turned to him. 'How is that possible? Did you tell him I don't have any papers?'

'Aye, and he says 'twas handled by a gentleman days ago in anticipation of your arrival.'

'A gentleman? Who?'

'Him, I reckon.' The captain hooked his thumb toward the sprawling warehouse shrouded in gloom.

She followed his glance in amazement. 'Lord Jack?'

'No, Miss, the one that's come to fetch you.'

She drew in her breath at these tidings and squinted into the inky darkness by the river's edge. 'Didn't you get the man's name?'

'Harbor master didn't say. Just called him "His Lordship." Shall I send one of my men ahead to find out?'

'N-no, I'll go at once!' Anything to get off this boat after so many months! A sudden notion took hold that the man waiting for her on shore might be her father. Derek had said he would be writing letters to Lord Arthur, telling him to meet them in London. Perhaps, somewhere out on the oceans, one of Jack's ships had taken the message to her beloved father in time.

Yes, why shouldn't it be Papa? She was quite convinced her father could do anything, and he had always been there for her whenever she needed him most.

If not he, then at the very least it must surely be one of her titled Knight cousins. She couldn't figure out how any of her as-yet unknown kinsmen could have heard she was coming, but she did not intend to make a poor first impression by keeping them waiting. She scrambled to disembark. Hope at last!

'If it don't smell right, you come right back, you hear?' the captain warned in a lower tone. 'These docks is no place for a pretty young lady, especially at night.'

'I understand. Thank you so much, Captain. You've been most wonderfully kind and, believe me, I intend to make sure Lord Jack hears of how well you and your crew looked after me—'

'Ah, go on!' His rugged face cracked into a grin. 'You run along, my lass. Good luck to you.' The old captain barked at his men to lower a boat to take her ashore, then trudged back to continue his business with the harbor master.

Before long, a few of the sailors were rowing her toward the docks, struggling against the strong current while she held on tightly to the edges of the skiff. She could hardly wait to find out if she would be greeted by a helpful stranger or someone she loved. The sailors thrust their oars into the oily current, angling the skiff closer to the docks.

When at last the bobbing boat was secured with two ropes slung around the mossy posts, the bosun's mate helped her climb up the wooden ladder onto the pier. Lanterns fixed to the posts every few yards apart cast a dim glow over the damp-slicked planks. Georgie ventured forward, placing each step carefully, lest she slip and fall into the river. It had taken her weeks to gain her sea legs, but now her knees felt wobbly again coming onto dry land.

At that moment, a tall, cloaked figure emerged from the swirling mist at the head of the docks.

Her cautious steps faltered.

At first, she could only make out a black, massive silhouette – then a flash of red as he threw his ebony opera cape back over one shoulder, exposing the silk scarlet lining. As he came striding toward her from out of the raven shadows, his gait graceful, his green eyes fierce, the lanterns' glow slid over the chiseled planes and angles of a familiar face.

Her jaw dropped; she stared at him in shock.

Ian!

But how—? She had left India ahead of him! She blinked hard. Was this an apparition?

'Georgiana!' he called sharply, the loud, terse tone of his voice very real. His driving stride to reach her was relentless.

Her heart lurched. A cry of amazed recognition tore from her lips; then she ran to him, forgetting her fears. Her mind briefly registered his brooding expression, but it did not slow her. His jaw was taut, his eyes as hard as polished green marble.

His grim stare traveled over her with a swift, assessing gaze as her footsteps pounded over the wooden planks, carrying her to him, and in the next second, Georgie flung herself into his open arms.

He caught her up in an embrace rough with emotion, holding her hard, as though he forgot his own strength. His hand cupped her head to his chest, his fingers tangling in her hair. 'I've got you,' he murmured gruffly. 'You're safe now, darling. I'm here.'

She clutched him to her, unable to speak or barely to believe her senses, overwhelmed with shock and anguished joy. With welling tears of stormy emotion, she closed her eyes and wrapped her arms around his waist.

She could feel his heart pounding beneath her cheek. Above her, Ian bent his head and pressed a few firm kisses to her brow with an air of almost desperate relief, comforting her, claiming her. Her mind was in a whirl. She had no idea how he could be standing here on this London dock, holding her, but as she clung to him, she scarcely dared question it.

He was alive. He was safe. He was in her arms, and that was all that mattered. She dug her fingers into his muscled back, holding onto him more tightly still. The bond between them came flooding back at once, the sense of it even stronger now after all they had gone through together, and after their long and painful separation.

Trembling it seemed with the violence of his feelings, Ian placed another soft kiss on her head and draped his cloak around her, letting the heat of his body warm her against the night's chill.

After a moment or two, he moved back just a bit, capturing her face between his hands. He searched her eyes with a fierce stare full of stern intensity. 'Are you all right?'

Georgie smiled at him through her tears. 'Much better now.'

At her answer, Ian nodded slowly, his tense demeanor easing by a fraction, but she could no longer contain her joy at this most unexpected reunion.

'What are you doing here?' she exclaimed, clutching his lapels. 'How can this be? How did you get here before me? I cannot believe you were here waiting, Ian! This is a miracle!'

He laughed softly and covered her hands with his own on his chest. 'Ah, never mind all that. I have my ways.' He lifted her hands to his lips and kissed each one in turn.

Georgie gazed at him in dreamy disbelief, then cupped his jaw against her palm. 'Oh, Ian, I've been so frightened for you. I didn't know if you were dead or alive! They came after you, too, didn't they? Did they hurt you? Are you all right?'

'So sweet,' he whispered, shaking his head as he studied her. 'Of course I'm all right. I'm always all right, Georgiana. You need never fear for me. Come. My carriage is waiting.'

'Honestly, Ian, how did you get here before me?' she persisted as he curved his arm around her shoulders and gently led her away from the Knight Shipping complex.

'Your ship stopped at so many ports for trade that we ended up passing you somehow,' he said. 'I had wanted to join you at sea, but then we lost you again in a gale off the coast of Africa. Since that proved so unfruitful, I decided to press on ahead of you and get to England first so I could make suitable arrangements for you.'

'Really?' She was sure that his casual nod and smile belied what must have been a superhuman effort on his part, not to mention a great sum spent.

'Fortunately, Jack's company has a reputation for keeping a reliable schedule of deliveries,' Ian continued. 'I got hold of a list of arrivals and departures, set a servant to watch, and that's how I knew when to expect you aboard the *Andromeda*. I only got in a few days ago, myself,' he added.

She stopped and turned to him in wonder. 'You are so good!' Petting his chest with a small caress, she shook her head. 'I don't know how I can ever thank you. Not just for this – you saved our lives. Mine – first by Balaram's funeral pyre – and then my brothers', too, at Janpur.'

'Any of you would have done the same for me,' he replied in a husky tone.

She stared into his eyes. 'I'm so sorry for everything that happened, Ian.'

'Nonsense.'

'Nonsense? I nearly got all of us killed!' she burst out; then the long pent-up words began tumbling from her lips. 'Why couldn't I listen to you? You told me not to meddle, but I went ahead and did it anyway – and the worst part is, I didn't even stop to consider the possibility of failure, or how my getting caught in that room could have impacted the whole war. I'm such a fool, Ian, such a blind, headstrong fool! Sometimes I wonder how all of you put up with me. But I *am* sorry, from the bottom of my heart.' She faltered. 'Do you think you can ever forgive me?'

He gazed at her for a long moment, tenderly.

'Georgiana,' he whispered her name, taking her firmly by her shoulders. 'Listen to me.'

She searched his eyes anxiously, hanging on his every word.

His green eyes glimmered with fond amusement. 'There is nothing to forgive. The truth is you saved the day. No, I mean it,' he insisted when she started to protest. 'I had no other way of getting hold of that information, about the queen's plot.

You listened to your intuition and you knew something was wrong. You had the pluck to act on your instincts, and to me, that's called courage.'

'You're only being kind.'

'You saved the life of a king,' he reminded her. 'Johar agreed to the terms of neutrality after you left.'

'Oh, that's wonderful! Well done, Ian.'

'Yes, but if you had not uncovered the queen's plot to assassinate him, that treaty would not have been worth the paper it was written on. What you did was rash,' he agreed, 'but if you hadn't done it, then Queen Sujana would have slain her husband after we left, ruled through her son, and joined forces with Baji Rao. And if that had happened, then Lord Hastings would have had a much larger and bloodier war on his hands. Instead, the conflict will be much more limited. With any luck, it should be over soon. So, you see, my dear, in the end, your disobedience helped save the lives of thousands.'

She gazed at him, not knowing what to say.

'You know, I lectured you when you arrived at Janpur—' He paused. 'But if anything, I'm the one who owes you the apology.'

'What?'

'In the end, I couldn't have done it without you. Frankly,' he said, 'I daresay we made a rather smart team.'

As she held his stare, her heart lifted with amazement at his words.

'What is it?' he murmured.

She shook her head. 'I was sure you would have despised me by now for all the trouble I've been.'

'Of course not. But I will tell you one thing.' His expression turned fierce as he gripped her shoulders once more, leaning closer. 'Don't you *ever* scare me like that again! We were lucky it all turned out for the best this time, but I won't stand for you ever putting yourself at risk like that again.'

Won't stand for it? she thought, wondering why he was speaking so possessively.

'My God, when I saw you come running down that hallway with blood streaming down your neck – I don't know how I kept my wits about me.' Ian paused, shaking his head at the memory of her brush with death. 'How is it, anyway? The wound, I mean.'

'Long gone. See? Just a little scar.' Eager to assure him she was fine, she leaned her head to the side and showed it to him by the dim glow of the lanterns on his waiting carriage nearby.

He brushed her hair back gently and gazed at her neck, touching the healed cut with one black-gauntleted fingertip.

Ian's heart pounded as he traced the inch-long line of her scar, entranced by the curve of her smooth white neck. Did she have any idea of her effect on him? he wondered.

Leaning closer to inspect the pale remainder of the wound that could have taken her away from him forever, he detected the scent of sea salt lingering in her night-dark hair, mingled with the alluring warmth of her own natural woman-smell. His breath caught with longing for her as her enticing scent stole over his senses. He breathed it in, instinctual hunger rising. His helpless desire for her came whispering back like a spice-laden breeze.

He had been stroking her neck with his fingertip, his glazed stare following the motion, but the lure was too overpowering. Unable to resist the impulse, he bent his head and caressed the pale slash with his lips.

She closed her eyes and dropped her head back, offering her neck. She breathed his name. Ian shuddered, wrapping one arm around her slim waist, the other hand gliding over her hair. He kissed her neck until she quivered in response and let out a soft moan.

'My lovely Georgiana.' He tried to stop himself, well aware that he was probably the only person in this city right now that she felt she could trust. The last thing she needed was her protector in this strange place making advances, taking advantage when she was most vulnerable. He hated himself for it, but he couldn't seem to stop. His hunger for her had only deepened over the months of their separation.

He was still chiding himself uselessly for his craven lust for her when Georgiana turned her face slowly toward his, bringing her lips nearer, so hesitant and shy, as though fearful he would reject her demure but unmistakable invitation.

Near blind with his need for her, he cupped her cheek against his leather-gloved palm; for a second, his mouth hovered above hers as he savored the exquisite torment of this sweet anticipation. God, how he had dreamed of tasting her again.

The soft puffs of her warm, rapid breath tickled his lips as she waited in virginal yearning for his kiss. Tangled up in her need for him, in turn, he claimed her mouth in a wild and burning kiss. She moaned again as he drove her lips apart and invaded the silken pleasure of her mouth with each deep stroke of his tongue.

She clutched at his shoulders as though to steady herself, and the fire between them came roaring back with every feverish degree of blazing heat that he remembered from the prayer cave. If anything, it had intensified from having been so long starved.

As he clasped her to him, his mouth slanting over hers with a desire that bordered on desperation, he was acutely aware of her hands on him. Warm beneath the luxurious folds of his cape, her arms around him, Georgiana pressed her palms against the curve of his back, stroking his sides and his chest, and sliding her arms up around his neck to hang on for dear life as he ravished her with his kiss.

He reveled in her yielding softness, and as she

melted against him with another gentle moan, he was besieged by the need to lay her down and make her his completely. To renew and reaffirm the bond that had formed between them – and to deepen it.

He had to have her, and he had to have her *now*.

For God's sake, man, get yourself under control. She had only just stepped off the boat moments ago and was probably becoming overwhelmed. As much as he yearned for her, he really ought to try to be a gentleman. If he didn't quit now, he was going to make her uneasy.

When he ended the kiss with great reluctance, Georgiana was panting and trembling. She swayed dizzily on her feet, so he quickly reached out and steadied her again.

'Oh, Ian,' she blurted out, dragging her heavy-lidded eyes open. They glowed with longing. 'What's going to happen between us now?'

The artless naiveté of her question moved him.

With a fond half smile, he brushed her hair gently behind her shoulder. 'Haven't you figured that out yet?' he whispered. 'Do you think I'd be standing out here waiting around in the middle of the night for just anyone?'

She returned his smile uncertainly, her cheeks pink.

He lifted her chin with his knuckle and pinned her in a forceful stare. 'What's going to happen, Georgiana, is that you are going to marry me.'

Her eyes widened; she went motionless with shock.

'Any questions?' he asked crisply.

It took her a long moment to absorb the news. Then she shook her head at him in lingering amazement. 'Only one.'

He arched a brow inquiringly.

'When?' she whispered.

A slow smile of dark, delicious satisfaction spread across his face. 'My, my. No arguments?'

Her eyes were huge and blue, full of trust and youthful desire as she shook her head.

'Good girl,' he whispered in lavish approval; then he leaned down and kissed her gently for a long moment. 'Come, sweet,' he ordered in a husky murmur, wrapping a protective arm around shoulders. 'Let's get you inside where it's warm.'

Now I *know* I'm dreaming, Georgie thought, floating along by Ian's side as he shepherded her over to the sleek black town coach waiting in the cobbled yard.

Four black horses stood in the traces. Clouds of steam puffed from their nostrils and were illumined by the carriage lanterns.

Ian acknowledged the waiting coachman with a nod and opened the carriage door for Georgie, then handed her in. She stepped up and took a seat.

The town coach resembled a little drawing room on wheels, dimly lit by a pair of tiny candles burning inside miniature sconces of etched glass.

The interior walls and ceiling were upholstered in luxurious pale damask to help muffle the sounds from the road. Georgie sat down on the ivory kid-leather squabs and then glanced at him, wide-eyed, as he joined her.

To be sure, she was in Ian's world now – and how perfectly he fit into his surroundings, a millionaire marquess eminently at home in the sophisticated setting of the Empire's capital. *Would this magnificent paragon really be her husband?*

She felt so ragged by comparison after her long journey. Her dress was clean enough but had been washed so many times that it was threadbare from constant wearing.

He, meanwhile, was so elegantly dressed: pristine waistcoat, beautiful cravat. He looked as though he had come from a night at the theater. She could just imagine how he turned heads among Society's fashionable ladies. *But he'll be all mine*, she thought, unable to stop staring at him in sheer astonishment.

He sent her a worldly little smile. As the coach rolled into motion, he opened a small satinwood panel that revealed a hidden compartment with a selection of crystal decanters. 'Drink?'

She managed a tight nod. 'Please.'

While he proceeded to pour, Georgie couldn't get enough of simply gazing at him, soaking up his presence. How handsome he was, she thought, suppressing a sigh. The bronzed tan he had picked up under the Indian sun had faded, and he had grown in a neat pair of short, fashionable sideburns.

He noticed her study and lifted an eyebrow.

'Sorry – I don't mean to stare,' she said with a blush. 'It's just – so good to see you. You've made me very happy. I-I fear that I'm in shock.'

He laughed softly and handed her a small glass with a generous splash of brandy in it. 'This should help.'

She nodded her thanks, accepting it.

He poured a second brandy for himself and then lifted his glass in a toast. 'To India.'

'To London,' she countered in a wistful tone.

'No,' he murmured, watching her intently. 'To us.'

This brought a smile to her lips. Her hand trembled at the fruition of her wildest dreams as she lifted her glass in answer. 'To us – my dear Lord Griffith.'

They stared at each other for a moment longer, then drank.

Georgie's first cautious sip of the fiery spirits made her eyes water; Ian sat back in the squabs across from her and draped his arm across the back of the seat, watching her with a soft glow in his eyes.

'Lord!' she exclaimed with a slight cough, laughing a little. 'That's strong.'

'It will warm the belly on a cold night.'

'I'll say!' She took a second sip, hoping it would help her wrap her mind around the notion that this wonderful, strong, brilliant, incredibly handsome man was going to marry her. She would be Ian's wife – a marchioness! Blazes, she thought, looking back on all those months at sea tormenting herself about whether or not he despised her or if he would ever speak to her again! She'd had no idea that this plan had come into his mind.

'I noticed you haven't asked me about your brothers,' he remarked, watching the play of emotions on her face as she tried to come to grips with her new reality.

His choice of subjects jerked her head up. 'You saw them?' She leaned forward anxiously in her seat. 'Oh, what news, my lord? We were separated at Bombay. The last I saw my brothers, they were fighting off a bloodthirsty horde of Marathas! Did they – survive?'

'Yes,' he said with a firm nod. 'Both of your brothers survived. Gabriel sustained a wound that could be rather serious,' he warned, 'but as strong and fit as he is, we must have faith, and expect his full recovery.'

'What happened?'

'I'm not sure,' he said vaguely. 'Derek was unscathed, though, and was taking care of Gabriel. I spoke with him before I left. It was he who told me the name of the ship on which you were sailing. Above all, your brothers' main concern was for you, Georgiana. They send their love and they want you to know they'll be joining us as soon as they can. Till then, they've asked me to look after you.' He gave her a smile like an intimate caress. 'I promised them I would.'

She returned his stare with her hand pressed to her heart in sheer relief to hear the news that her brothers were alive. She closed her eyes with a fleeting prayer of thanks.

'More brandy, darling? I daresay you look like you could use it.'

Opening her eyes again, she smiled ruefully at him. 'No, thanks.' The talk of her brothers had made her homesick. Ian studied her for a long moment.

'I have a particular message for you from Derek.'

She perked up. 'Yes?'

'He wanted me to tell you that he's sorry for what he said to you on the road leaving Janpur. He did not relate the details of your quarrel, but he wanted me to tell you that he didn't mean a word.'

'He said that?' she echoed.

He nodded.

She smiled wryly at him and raked her hand through her hair. 'Actually, Ian, what we fought about was you.'

'Me?'

'I was telling Gabriel that I was interested in you—'

'Oh, really?' he purred interrupting.

She chuckled at his pleased grin. 'Yes. But then Derek came along and opined that you'd have to be *mad* to involve yourself with me, after seeing the sort of trouble I get into. Isn't that mean?'

'Well, there might be a hint of truth to it.'

'Hey!' she protested as his green eyes danced.

'Come here,' he teased, grasping her wrist and tugging her onto the opposite seat beside him. He draped his arm around her shoulders and pulled her near, kissing her temple as he let her snuggle up close beside him. 'At least life with you, Georgiana, will never be dull.'

She snorted, but it was so wonderful to be close to him, and all her future prospects suddenly seemed so much brighter, that she couldn't hold her scowl, and joined him in laughter.

'Where are your little ankle bells?' he asked all of a sudden, noticing their absence as he tugged her partly onto his lap.

'I threw them away.'

'*What?*'

'I tossed them in the ocean.'

He looked askance at her. 'What did you do that for?'

She sighed rather unhappily. 'Because I mean to change, Ian.'

'Change, how?' he asked with a frown.

'Be more careful, more circumspect. More like Meena and Lakshmi.'

He arched a brow. 'Shall I keep you in a harem?'

'No! Don't jest, you rogue, this is very serious. I mean to be more dutiful, more co-operative. More as I should.'

'I see,' he murmured with a grave nod, not making much effort to hide his amusement.

'What?' she exclaimed.

He shrugged. 'I liked your bells. Your wearing them expressed a part of who you are. A part I liked,' he added, slanting her a knowing look. 'Ah, well, I suppose it's too late now.'

Startled, she furrowed her brow and mulled his words.

'At any rate,' Ian continued, 'let us move along to the practicalities, shall we?' His arm rested comfortably around her shoulders. 'You'll be happy to hear that I brought along several traveling trunks full of your gowns and things from your family's home in Bombay.'

'You did?' She twisted around to face him with a quizzical look.

He nodded. 'Your housekeeper packed them while I was off making the arrangements for the voyage.'

'Oh, Ian, you think of everything!'

'Yes, well, life is in the details,' he said dryly.

She threw her arms around his neck and merrily covered his cheek with pecking kisses. 'Thank you, thank you, thank you! My own gowns, my shoes! I shall be human again!'

'Everything is ready and waiting for you over at Knight House, which is where we're headed now,' he continued with a chuckle at her exuberance. 'We'll be there in a trice. It's just around the block.'

'Oh, but must we go there now?' she protested,

easing back a bit, but keeping her arms linked loosely around his neck. 'Please, can't we be alone together – just for a little while longer, please? I've missed you so.'

'Sweetheart,' he murmured as he grazed her cheek with one knuckle. 'It's already two in the morning.'

'I'm not tired. Are you?'

Not anymore, Ian thought as he stared into her eyes. He was acutely aware of her delicate fingers at his nape, toying with the back of his hair. Her light touch made him shiver. He did not think he had ever experienced such overt affection before.

'Please, Ian?' she cajoled him with a pretty little pout. 'It's not that I don't *want* to meet my relatives, but this is a special night for us, isn't it?' As she gazed at him so sweetly, the elated glow in her eyes made all his weeks of agonizing over the decision so gloriously worthwhile. 'Can't you take me to their house tomorrow?'

He touched her face with a gentle caress, but his heart was pounding. 'You want to stay with me tonight?' he whispered, and he quivered as she nodded slowly.

'*Yes.*'

He hesitated, debating with himself. Of course, it was not proper, and he had a duty to shield her reputation, but he fully intended to marry her, and besides, he had never wanted any woman like this. She had no idea of how he had been dreaming of this – literally dreaming.

Night after night, making love to her in sweat-drenched realms of fantasy.

It was so much better than the nightmares surrounding Catherine's death.

'Are you sure about this?' he murmured with a smoldering gaze that let her know exactly what would happen if she came home with him tonight.

'I'm very sure,' she whispered with a fever in her eyes that matched his own.

God, how she intoxicated him. How could he deny her, especially when it was what he wanted, too? It was impossible to say no to Georgiana, so fair, so soft and willing, with her arms wrapped around him. The sensual young beauty robbed him of any will to resist.

Just like she had in the prayer cave.

'Very well.' He bent his head and pressed a soft but urgent kiss to her lips. At once, she cupped his jaw in heated response, returning his kiss with all the ripe willingness of a hot-blooded virgin eager to please and so ready for her initiation.

He shivered with longing, marveling at her power to drive him mad. All of a sudden, he could hardly wait to get her to his bed. He couldn't wait to show her everything that a man and a woman could share – couldn't wait to find out what she'd be like under him, sampling it all for the very first time. He had his suspicions, of course. If he was any judge, the little hellion would prove to be a tigress in the sack.

He couldn't wait to find out.

Ending the kiss with a glittering stare, Ian rapped on the side of his carriage and informed his driver of their change of plans.

CHAPTER 10

Instead of going to Knight House, they drove around to the other side of Green Park to Ian's residence.

When the coach glided to a halt before his tall, stately townhouse, he alighted first and glanced around at the gracious avenues, making sure no one was watching. They were in the heart of fashionable London now, where gossip could spread like a fire out of control. A young lady could not afford to be careless, especially if she was the Hawkscliffe Harlot's niece. Pending nuptials or otherwise, it would not do for Georgiana to be seen coming home with him in the dead of night.

Given the hour, however, the streets were as empty as they were dark. There was no moon, and the corner streetlamps glowed but feebly. Determining that the coast was clear, Ian helped her down from the carriage, exchanging a smoky glance with her like a delicious secret just between the two of them. He pointed out Knight House on the far end of the park, and then hurried her up to the front entrance of his townhouse, faced in Portland stone, and let her in the burgundy-painted door.

The dimly lit entrance hall welcomed them with all its empty grandeur, from the large round Roman-style mosaic in the middle of the floor to the Corinthian marble columns standing sentry all around. In the center of the cavernous space, the spectacular double staircase with its fanciful iron banister swept up to the first floor, the *piano nobile*. On the wall behind the stairs stretched a glittering glass triptych of three magnificent arched windows. In the morning, the grand windows filled the space with light; up and up the ceiling soared, two stories tall, a full fifty feet above the staircase and the hall.

'Oh, Ian, your home is beautiful,' Georgiana murmured, glancing around shyly.

He locked the door behind them and then joined her, clasping his hands behind his back as he admired it with her. 'Our home,' he reminded her softly.

A beaming smile lit up her face, as though he had surprised her all over again.

He gave her a wink. 'Come.'

Just then, his butler, Mr Tooke, came bustling in to take their cloaks. A kindly old fellow of short and portly proportions, he had a mostly bald pate, a neat white mustache, and twinkly blue eyes. Tooke's face was always wreathed in smiles, but never more so than when Ian informed him who Georgiana was.

Having already hinted to his longtime, trusted servant that there might be a Particular Significance in Miss Knight's arrival in London insofar as his household was concerned, Tooke had grasped his meaning at once in astonishment – their long-solitary master meant to take a wife! – and now the man effused over Georgiana like some sort of mother hen.

'Oh, my dear, dear, *dear* young lady, is there nothing that I can get for you, nothing at all? Are you hungry, my lady? Have you supped? A cozy cup of chocolate, perhaps?'

She laughed with delight at his outpouring of warmth and thanked him, but declined.

Accepting her answer with a bow worthy of a courtier, Tooke whisked her ragged cloak away with Ian's fine one, then sped out of the entrance hall to leave the two of them alone, too discreet a captain of this sophisticated household to raise an eyebrow at the impropriety of their unchaperoned, late-night visit. He knew his master to be a man of the world.

Tooke did not fail, however, to send Ian a discreet nod of lavish approval on his choice of brides.

Ian, in turn, cleared his throat, picked up the candelabra that Tooke had left for them, and escorted Georgiana up to the main floor.

Though a bit more restrained in its ostentation than Knight House, Ian's home reflected his lofty rank as well as his worldly tastes. The staterooms throughout the first two floors had been carefully laid out to accommodate his function as a diplomat, and the size and scope of the home were easily up to the task of entertaining foreign dignitaries in style.

In everyday life, though, he had to admit, its grandeur somehow emphasized its hollowness. It was equipped for large receptions, but hardly anyone besides the staff was ever here.

As a child, when it had been his father who was the marquess, he had innocently assumed that everyone lived the way he and his best friend Robert did, in eight-story mansions with walled sculpted gardens, gilded ceilings thirty feet tall, and marble busts unearthed from the Hellenistic age on display.

By now he knew better than that, thank God. He had long since learned how blessed he was in life, and he took seriously all the responsibility that came with so much privilege.

After he'd led Georgiana past all the pomp of the public regions, they ascended to the third floor and walked through the intimate private gallery. The long, narrow room ran along the back wall of the house, overlooking the garden.

The front portion of the floor had been divided in half, creating two large and sumptuous private apartments, one for himself, the other designed for the lady of the house. The latter had long stood empty.

Each suite contained a spacious bedchamber, a sitting room, an enormous closet and dressing room, as well as a bathing alcove and water closet with all the most modern accoutrements.

The two apartments adjoined, of course, for the usual marital visits, while the common sitting room along the back of the house had always been intended as a private family space.

As he escorted Georgiana across the long, narrow, family parlor, he could remember his mother sitting in here with his sister Maura, teaching her fancy sewing. He remembered himself as a boy, lying on his stomach on the blue carpet, playing with his pet cat's whiskers and trying to memorize his Latin passages from the Stoic philosophers that his father had raised him on, half-listening all the while to his mother's gossip disparaging the latest escapades of 'that woman,' their neighbor, the scandalous Duchess of Hawkscliffe.

The first Georgiana.

Mother would not have approved of this match, he mused sardonically. Mother had believed in cold and dignified marriages, preferably unhappy.

No wonder it was Mother who had campaigned so hard with him for Catherine.

Taking both of Georgiana's hands, he backed into his bedchamber, drawing her slowly into the room with a reassuring smile. Then he closed the door on all those old memories, and locked it.

Georgie was beginning to wonder if the blush that had invaded her cheeks half an hour ago was becoming a permanent feature, for it showed no signs of going away. If anything, her face glowed even more hotly as she dwelled upon the knowledge of what Ian and she had come here to do.

It seemed strange to her that she had zero misgivings about letting him seduce her. Then again, she had total trust in the man. He had always made her feel safe – not surprising, since he had saved her life in the very first moments of their acquaintance. To that lovely safety she now added a truly warm affection and a comforting sense of belonging. She knew that she belonged with him, and it made what they were doing feel very natural.

Still, though, that didn't mean she wasn't nervous. Her heart was racing with anticipation, and she slipped him a self-conscious little smile as he locked the bedroom door.

'Come in,' he murmured with a suave gesture toward the room. 'Make yourself at home.' Then he turned away, crossing the cavernous space to set the candelabra on the distant lowboy.

Georgie scanned her surroundings by the low lights burning in the vast room. The space was conceived on a grand scale with gravity and dignity, pomp and splendor, as if deliberately to remind her that she was about to be bedded by A Lord. The colors were soothing dark blue and reserved brown, a bit of sophisticated black, with touches of gilding and splashes of red. Creamy walls stretched between oak floors cushioned by dark Persian rugs and a coved ceiling with painted medallions.

Off to her left, a cheerful blaze crackled in the fireplace beneath a pristine mantel of snow-white limestone. Around it, elegantly strewn, sat a sleek grouping of gilded ebony furniture in the Roman style, as though this were the retiring room of Caesar himself.

To her right, however, Ian's giant bed loomed in the shadows. Georgie gulped silently as her stare traveled over it.

Four towering Corinthian columns served as bed-posts, holding up a crown of heavy velvet drapery. The coverlet was lustrous chocolate satin and the sheets, thoughtfully turned down by a servant, were of creamy cotton. A mound of tasseled pillows were piled against the ebony headboard. In all, they presented a prospect both intimidating and deliciously inviting.

Across the room, her darkly charming host slipped off his black evening coat and hung it on the doorknob to a closet.

As he headed back toward her, the firelight cast a ruddy halo over his dark hair and glimmered all along his powerful V-shaped silhouette. Her heart skipped a beat. A part of her wanted to lose her nerve and run, but she had waited and wanted and wondered about The Act for too long to back out now. Tonight her only desire was to let the man of her dreams satisfy all her sensual curiosity. Tonight she resolved to follow her heart, explore her instincts, find the secret to this mystery she had puzzled over for so long, and follow Ian's lead.

After all, she thought as she slowly began peeling off her gloves, the man would soon be her husband. The thought of it brought a nervous, giddy, and yet joyful laugh bubbling up to her lips while Ian approached in his white shirt-sleeves and gray pinstriped waistcoat.

'What are you giggling at?' he demanded in a velvet murmur as he gently took hold of her elbows and stroked her arms in a soothing fashion.

'Sorry, I just can't believe this is really happening!'

'Too sudden for you?' he murmured.

'No.' She moved closer to him, tilting her head back. 'I'm happy.'

He slipped his arms around her waist and smiled at her. 'Me, too.' Then he leaned down and pressed a soft kiss to her lips.

If she had any underlying doubts, they vanished when his lips brushed hers with silken care. Georgie couldn't stop smiling as she returned the kiss, caressing his iron-hard arms through the crisp lawn of his shirt.

All of a sudden, he lifted her off her feet without warning; she laughed aloud as he carried her toward the fire.

'Um, Ian?'

'Yes, my darling?'

'You're going the wrong way,' she pointed out,

clasping her hands behind his neck in girlish delight.

'Mm?'

'The bed's that way,' she whispered in his ear.

'So impatient,' he chided her with a smoldering glance of pure wickedness.

'Ah, you have a plan?'

'Always.' Arriving near the fireplace, he set her gently on her feet again. 'Now you won't get cold when I undress you.'

'Oh.' Her eyes widened, but she recovered her usual daring rather quickly. 'Or – when I undress you,' she countered, reaching up to pluck at his impeccable cravat.

He bent to kiss her again, so smooth and sure of himself that she barely noticed that when his arms encircled her, he was in fact unbuttoning the back of her gown. He distracted her from his true intent with a nuzzling kiss on her cheek. 'You're not scared, are you?'

'No.'

'Good. I'll be gentle.'

When she realized what his clever fingers were doing behind her back, she decided that turnabout was fair play, and she reached for the buttons of his waistcoat. She was nowhere near as deft as he, fumbling her way through the job, but he completed his task and glanced down fondly, enjoying her eagerness if not her lack of expertise.

At last, she parted the silk halves of his waistcoat and pushed it down off his big, wide shoulders. He loosened her bodice with a casual air, sending wild thrills crashing through her body. How hard it had been to get him to kiss her back in the prayer cave! she mused. Now that he'd made up his mind about her, it seemed there was no stopping him.

Nevertheless, he maintained a slow, leisurely air to avoid upsetting her with too much passion, kissing her shoulder as his efforts now bared it, kissing his way up one side of her neck. He threaded little tickling kisses across her hairline and then down the other side of her cheek, her earlobe, her neck, down low to the other shoulder, delighting and relaxing her with his lover's play. Georgie was throbbing all over.

He captured her face between his warm, wondrously skilled hands, and as he kissed her slowly, deeply, he tugged the tortoiseshell combs out of her hair and brought her tresses tumbling down. This was a man who knew exactly what he was about.

When he ended the kiss, she wove a little on her feet in blissful unsteadiness. Ian, meanwhile, gathered her skirts in his knowing hands and slipped her dress off over her head with a practiced skill that would have impressed her lady's maid.

Across the tall ceiling, the fire cast huge shadows of the two of them stealing more kisses and continuing to undress each other. Her senses were so sharply heightened she noticed the subtlest current of air moving against her bare arms as Ian gently unlaced her light stays. Discarding them behind him, his glazed stare fixed upon her now freed breasts.

He seemed to forget what he was doing as he stood there admiring the shameless jut of her swollen nipples against the paper-thin cotton of her chemise. He brought his hand up slowly from his side, ran one knuckle up her stomach through her chemise, and then diverted the center line of his caress, rubbing his knuckle across the hardened peak of her left breast.

Georgie sighed, but she wanted to see more of him, too. Reaching up to unfasten the single button that closed the front V of his shirt, she parted the smooth lawn fabric, revealing an expanse of his sculpted male chest so enticing that it made her moan a little. 'Your turn,' she whispered, trailing her fingertips hungrily down the expanse of smooth skin that had been revealed.

Ian shook himself out of his daze and obeyed her, loosening his silver cuff links and then lifting his shirt off over his head. Tossing it aside at once, he moved toward her again to rid her of her petticoat, but Georgie stopped him in sheer awe, planting her hand on his splendid chest to keep him at arm's length, just so she could admire.

'Oh, Ian,' she breathed in stunned awe. 'You are magnificent.'

He smiled at her and dropped his gaze with almost boyish modesty, but it was true.

He was breathtaking, tall and powerful and beautifully proportioned from head to toe. His chest was at her eye level, so Georgie could not help but gape at the flowing swells of his pectoral muscles, the adorable flat circles of the masculine nipples, the slight dip in the center, running up to the beguiling notch at the base of his throat. His collarbones spanned outward like flying buttresses to reinforce the might of his wide, iron shoulders. Meanwhile, just below his lovely chest, all the compact rippling muscles of his abdomen and trim waist invited her exploration. She could see by the firelight that his skin there was velvety smooth, but she was almost too much in awe to dare touch him.

Looking lower, she admired his lean hips and strong, sweeping thighs. The size of the bulge between them, however, chased her frank scrutiny away in sudden recollection of what lay ahead.

How would it be possible for him to lie on her? she wondered. The man had to be more than two hundred pounds of pure muscle. Surely he would crush her.

She lifted her chin to ask him about it, but forgot the question as her stare traveled up over his wonderful torso. The beauty of his powerful arms lured her gaze now, and her touch.

Lifting her hands to his shoulders, she slowly traced her fingertips down his thick biceps, over his lightly furred forearms, to his warm, strong, gentlemanly hands. Her touch ended at the signet ring that he wore on his pinky finger, when Ian suddenly captured her venturesome hands. When she looked up in surprise, she found him watching her with rising fire in his eyes.

'Looked your fill?' he asked in a husky murmur, but Georgie couldn't find her voice to answer, still caught up in staring.

She gazed at the strong, enticing column of his neck, the forthright angle of his Adam's apple. She understood now why men kept their necks covered under restrictive cravats – to keep ladies from day-dreaming all day about kissing those beguiling lines, tasting that sensitive skin. She admired his steely jaw, the narrow planes of his smoothly shaved cheeks, his generous, sensual mouth.

She had barely noticed the subtle gold streaks in his dark brown hair before, but now the gold in it sparkled in the firelight. His forelock had fallen forward over his brow, and beneath its tumbled shadow, his eyes smoldered with bright jade intensity. She reached up and tenderly brushed his hair out of his eyes, revealing the thick, feathery lines of his eyebrows once more.

Impossibly handsome, and there was an end to it.

Somehow finding her wits again, she wondered if she should apologize for staring, but then, all of a sudden, she noticed the cheval mirror in the corner and caught a glimpse of his broad, bare back in the reflection. *God.* She shuddered violently in a fresh wave of fiery yearning.

What struck her most about that strong, beautiful back, however, was his proud, erect carriage. Posture that fine couldn't be taught. A man was either born to stand like a leader or simply couldn't do it. In the solidity, the sheer predatory grace of his posture, she could see his Norman warlord ancestors in him. It made her smile. Oh, yes, every line of this princely man proclaimed his innate nobility.

She met his gaze again and couldn't speak, a lump in her throat to think that he would truly be hers, always. She may have looked her fill, but if he was really hers and this wasn't a dream, then she wanted to touch him.

She wanted to claim him for her own.

Every inch.

Georgiana reached out and touched his stomach; then she began caressing him, and Ian melted against her hands. He closed his eyes and dropped his head back slightly as an eager sigh escaped him.

The way she touched him made him tremble. She stroked him with reverent delight, like some fair archeological lady who had unearthed a precious find that she alone knew how to decipher, she alone could understand.

It didn't matter at all in that moment that she was a member of the grand Knight clan. If she had been the lowliest dairymaid and yet touched him with so much love, he would have married the chit. The value to him of being touched like this was greater than she could ever understand. What he mostly remembered of marriage, after all, was being pushed away.

But Georgiana's heartfelt caresses traveled up his chest and over his shoulders, making him feel almost as though it were the first time for him, too. Maybe in some strange way, it was. For behind all his practical reasons for marrying Georgiana, so logically thought out, and quite apart from their crazed physical desire for each other, an indescribable something *else* had sparked itself into existence between them, a promise and a possibility, like some magical seed that with proper tending might flower into something beautiful.

She gave him hope that a closeness he had long given up on might still be possible for him. That maybe he could be truly known by a woman, and maybe even . . . truly loved. Not until finding her had he realized how much he needed this. She made him aware, too, of how much he had to give. Perhaps her native daring inspired him, for, at last, despite the nightmare of his first marriage, she made him willing to try again. To give again. To risk opening himself anew. Then her touch curled around his nape, pulling him down to kiss her.

He obliged, still frankly amazed at how easily

she had agreed to the match after all her brave words at the maharajah's feast, flaunting her independence. He hadn't forgotten her silly quote from her aunt's ridiculous book: 'Wedlock is a padlock.'

Well, there was a time not very long ago that he would have agreed, but the events at Janpur and their brush with death had forced them both to consider life a bit more seriously. For his part, Ian had realized during all those long months at sea spent wrestling with Derek's request that he didn't really want to spend the rest of his life alone.

The truth was, it hurt every time he went to Knight House. All his friends were paired, and all his friends were happy. It wasn't as though he hadn't had plenty of chances to remarry. After the official year of mourning for Catherine had passed, his secretary had shown him a list of the town's top thirty debutantes whose parents had already begun making discreet inquiries about his future plans.

He had never had any illusions about their motives. It all boiled down to his title, his obscene fortune, and his worldly position. Having had his fill of being used, he had shied away from all their simpering daughters. But with Georgiana, everything was totally different. She had become his second chance at the one, secret thing he had always wanted most, the one thing that fate, despite all the gifts that it had showered on him, had not seen fit to give: a family.

A real family of his own, and a home filled with happiness and love.

He had expected to have it years ago, but the whole thing had turned into a cruel joke.

Fearless Georgiana made him brave enough to try again. If there was one thing he was sure of, it was that this passionate beauty would never betray him.

Thrusting the past out of his mind in favor of his much rosier future, he continued kissing her, reaching down to untie the tapes of her single petticoat. All he wanted this night was to make her feel as treasured and beloved as she did him. When her loosened petticoat crumpled to her feet, he glanced down to help her step out of it and noticed that she was still wearing her shoes. For that matter, so was he.

Realizing it simultaneously, they exchanged a smile, then both of them kicked off their shoes. Ian gazed at his soon-to-be bride for a long moment, relishing the sight of her stripped down to her chemise.

Helen of Troy was no match for Georgiana. She truly was the most ravishing woman in all of the world, he thought, admiring her midnight tresses, her creamy skin, her rosy lips with a blush to match. Her cobalt eyes.

'Excuse me, you're staring,' she said sardonically, the pot calling the kettle black.

But he only smiled. 'Can't help it. I feel like a king.'

'You look like a god,' she whispered fervently.

He lowered her head, abashed by her too-lavish praise. 'And you look like an angel.'

'But I'm not,' she reminded him with a saucy little smile, drawing him closer.

'No, you're not,' he agreed with gusto, and when he tugged the charming vixen into his arms, she laughed aloud. 'It's your best quality.' He kissed her soundly, then released her from his snug embrace and offered her his hand, casting a nod of discreet invitation toward the bed. 'My lady?' he murmured.

Cautiously, Georgiana placed her fingers atop his offered palm and let him lead her there, to her seduction.

As she climbed up onto his bed, he stole a peek under her chemise at her bare bottom. She gave a small shriek at his roguery and laughed, coming up onto her knees to hook her arm around his neck, and pulling him down with her as they kissed each other madly.

'You taste so good, Ian,' she whimpered when he finally let her up for air. 'Are you going to do what you did to me before?'

'Oh, that, and much more besides,' he purred.

'There's *more*?'

He lifted an eyebrow and gave her a slightly sinister smile.

'Ah, of course there is,' she whispered in a knowing tone. 'How silly of me! I've seen those carvings on the temple walls.'

'Mmm,' he agreed, nodding.

'What will it be like for me?' she asked him almost shyly.

He tucked a lock of her dark hair behind her ear with a tender motion. 'Would you like a little precursor, my darling? An introduction, as it were?'

'Yes.'

'Lie back,' he whispered, and the trust with which she obeyed him shook Ian to the core. 'Now spread your legs,' he instructed in a husky murmur as he eased into position atop her.

Still safely trousered as he settled between her slim thighs, his senses reeled with bliss at the feel of her soft, warm body beneath him.

'Ian, you're heavy!'

'Sorry.' Roused from his daze by her protest, he immediately shifted more of his weight onto his elbows, then paused to glance down at her, making sure that she was comfortable. 'Better?'

'Yes – much.' She gazed at him with such sincerity, such sweet wonder, that Ian couldn't break the spell of her wide, violet-blue eyes. He could not look away.

He had never made love to a virgin before.

He was supposed to have done so on his wedding night, but things were never what they seemed.

On some level, in fact, being a man of the world, he had prepared himself for the possibility that Georgiana wasn't a virgin.

She was, after all, an extremely sensual young woman with an avid interest in the erotic. He had braced himself already not to be shocked if he learned in taking her that she had given way before at some point in her past, to some other man.

He wouldn't be happy about it, God knew, but at least this time he wouldn't be taken off guard. If he did still choose to go ahead with the marriage, then at least this time he would know what he was getting into. Last time, he hadn't been granted that courtesy, and he had lived to regret it ever since.

But now, as Georgiana lay in his arms, he knew with every fiber of his being that she was pure, niece of the Hawkscliffe Harlot or no. It was written all over her lovely face. For her, this night was an earth-shattering event, and to be the man she had chosen to gift with her virginity made it just as profound for him.

No, indeed, he thought as he traced the line of her cheek and petted the delicate curve of her eyebrow with his fingertip, this was a new experience for him, too. To be sure, this was not how it usually went when he brought a woman to his bed.

The acts he performed with his carefully selected lovers were mere empty performances of cold virtuosity beside this. A necessity for a healthy grown male, like water or food.

But this, she, nourished him so much more deeply. Her sweetness pierced into the very soul of him and loosed a floodgate of emotion. He leaned down and kissed her softly. She cupped his face and returned his kiss with all the nubile eagerness that he had come to know from her. Her responsiveness made him want to protect her all the more from other males who might think they could take advantage. They wouldn't dare touch her once they knew that she was his. And she wouldn't dare let them once he had schooled her lush young body in the arts of ecstasy. When she wanted pleasure, she must always come to him.

'Now,' he continued, resuming the lesson in a voice gone gravelly with desire. 'You'll push with your hips against me as much as you please. The stimulation will heighten your pleasure.' He swallowed hard, trying to contain himself. 'Try it,' he whispered.

She did.

Georgie did as he told her, delighting herself and him with her first, slow, exploratory efforts. Ian smiled and closed his eyes with a low *'Ahh,'* while she shuddered in wild thrill at the dazzling sensations that that small motion sent coursing through her body. She was acutely aware of every place that his bare chest and arms pressed against her skin. He was warm and pleasantly heavy atop her and smooth to the touch everywhere, and so wonderfully hard, muscle and bone, strength so skillfully restrained.

She lifted her hips again, caressing him with her

whole body, and he met her movement, raking himself against her. Georgie groaned aloud. 'I think I'm going to enjoy this, Ian,' she panted.

His low laughter tickled her earlobe. 'I fully intend to make sure that you do.' He hooked his finger under one strap of her chemise and dragged it down off her shoulder, freeing her breast while she continued rubbing against him. She could feel him there between her legs, big and throbbing, gaining in size, as hard as steel.

He cupped her bare breast for a moment, fondling her, and then did away with the other strap, peeling the top part of her chemise down about her waist. Again, he stroked her gently, and then paused to cover her chest in kisses. As he sucked on her nipples, she ran her fingers through his hair and then down to his shoulders, dragging her nails in light, taunting play across his splendid back.

He moaned and came back up to claim her mouth again. Her whole body eased against the mattress as she found her rhythm, her legs dropping open wider to cradle him between her thighs. She wrapped her arms around him. Her temperature rose another few degrees when he reached down and tugged the hem of her chemise up her leg and slipped his warm, smooth hand beneath the light cloth, apparently to pleasure her as he had that night in the prayer cave. For a long moment, she savored his touch, emitting a needy sigh as he penetrated her with his fingers.

This time, however, unlike in the prayer cave, she was determined to reciprocate. Shoring up her courage, she reached for the placket of his trousers.

Ian paused.

It seemed she had His Lordship's full attention! He barely breathed as she unfastened his trousers and pulled out the prize. 'Oh, my,' she breathed, taking hold of him, her fingers wrapping around his weighty girth. She explored the kingly length of it and could not believe its size. 'Ian, it's so *huge.*'

He laughed breathlessly and winced a bit, closing his eyes. 'Don't worry, I told you I'd be gentle. *God.*'

'Am I doing this right?'

He never did answer the question. His closed eyes and rapt expression gave her all the information she required.

He appeared completely absorbed in the hand that she had wrapped around his rock-hard member. How curious, the way it throbbed against her firm grasp.

'God – your touch,' he whispered abruptly, his fingers curving around her shoulder. 'I could spend in your hand. Stroke me. Stroke me, Georgiana. It feels so good.'

His silken plea set her on fire. She did as he asked, letting him show her how he wished it to be done. Once she got the hang of it, she pulled back and murmured to him to turn. He obeyed, moving onto his back. He reclined on one elbow; Georgie slung her leg across his thighs and straddled him on her knees. She leaned down and kissed him for all she was worth as she gave him the hard caresses he said he liked best.

As he accepted her ministrations in lavish pleasure, his sleek hips riding against her touch with every stroke, she had never seen him so close to letting go. After several minutes of this, his chest heaving, he tried to stop her, but Georgie refused to stop, not when she wanted so badly for him to let go.

And when it finally happened, she couldn't take her eyes off him, devouring the look of anguished rapture that fled across his gorgeous face. His groans intoxicated her while his massive pulsations burst against her hand, hot and thick, spurting halfway up his chest. She was drunk on his soul-deep groans, mesmerized by the rippling power of his abdomen as another spasm racked him. Instinct alone was her guide at this point, but the wave of release that crashed through him was nearly contagious, shaking her, too.

Her heart slamming, she leaned down and kissed him as the height of pleasure left him adrift some seconds later. In the meantime, though, she wasn't quite sure what to do with her hand, coated in his seed and turning sticky.

'I cannot believe,' he said at length, 'that you just did that.'

'Did what?' she asked innocently, smiling to herself as she nuzzled his cheek.

He snorted, his low laugh husky and dazed. 'Made me lose my mind. Could you get us a towel, love?' he added wryly.

'Where?'

He nodded toward the distant washstand. She gave him a mischievous smile and went to do his bidding.

In all, she was so thrilled with her success that she wanted to do it again right away. But, she supposed as she rinsed her hands at the washstand, he'd probably need at least a moment or two. Then she dried her hands and brought him the towel.

By the time he had cleaned himself up a bit, he looked like a different person, or perhaps a younger, happier version of himself, almost as if he were drunk. His lips looked fuller, plump and seductive. His heavy-lidded eyes shone with a lustrous golden glow. All the taut angles of his chiseled face – square jaw, sharp cheekbones – these were softened by deep, sensuous relaxation.

As she climbed into this new, cuddly Ian's arms, she wouldn't have thought it possible, but he looked even more handsome than before.

'You know,' he drawled, 'I think I needed that.'

'You think?' she exclaimed in jaunty irreverence.

'Don't get cheeky with me,' he retorted as he tumbled her onto the pile of pillows behind her.

He came up onto all fours and crawled toward her slowly, like a big, hungry tiger. Wickedness glinted in his green eyes. 'Don't think I'm done with you yet, my girl,' he purred.

'No?' she asked with a gulp, her blush rising again.

He held her gaze with a smoldering stare as he kissed her knee – and licked it. 'You're delicious,' he told her as he pressed apart her knees, moving lower.

'What are you doing?'

'Oh, nothing,' he murmured as he strewed a primrose path of light, little, nibbling kisses up the inside of her thigh. He hiked her chemise higher with one hand until it was little more than a belt of loose fabric hanging around hips.

'Ian?'

'Georgiana,' he panted, his mouth hovering an inch above her mound. She could feel his hot breath against her most delicate flesh. He dropped his head lower as his tongue came out and explored at the juncture of her thighs. He clasped her hip possessively with his left hand, stroking her deeply with his right. All the while, his lush, uninhibited kisses adored her womanhood.

Good God. He built bliss in her body like a man would build a fire. She melted back against the mound of pillows by the headboard, petting him, and watching him through hazy, glittering eyes. He lay on his stomach between her legs, enjoying himself immensely, it seemed, as he gave himself over to this diversion, teasing and tasting her, playing with her and turning her into an utter wanton.

Never in her life had she felt so completely worshiped. His endless kisses celebrated her body, each cunning stroke of his tongue exalting her to new heights. Its warm tip sported and circled about her hardened center, and more deeply, he lapped up her nectar, still greedy for it even as it dripped down his chin. She filled his vast room with her moans and writhed against his warm, wet mouth in total abandon.

But soon, she needed more. All teasing fell away as she clutched at his shoulders, bidding him without a word to rise. She wanted him on top of her. Inside of her. She wanted him to make this impossible craving go away. She was so aroused that she bit his chest in hungry love-play as he came up to oblige her, freeing his fully erect phallus from his trousers once again.

'I want you so much,' she said in a shaky whisper, watching it spring free. She started to caress his hard length, but he captured her hand and pressed her down onto the mattress, linking his fingers through hers as he moved atop her. She wrapped her arms around his waist, spreading her legs wider to enfold him.

'It might hurt a bit,' he said gruffly.

'I don't even care,' she panted, his for the taking.

She could feel Ian shaking with lust as his mouth swooped down on hers in a rough, ravishing kiss.

She took it gladly, parting her lips and her legs for his most welcome invasion. As his stiff rod angled into the damp curls enshrouding her core, she clutched him to her, pressing her fingers into the supple flesh of his muscled back, urgently drawing him closer still.

She wanted to be filled with him. Her body arched beneath him as he glided up to her dew-drenched brink.

'Dear God,' she gasped out, her chest heaving against his.

'Georgie,' he whispered.

'What is it?'

'Look at me. I want to gaze into your eyes when I take you.'

'Oh, Ian.' She did as he asked, holding his stare in desperate adoration. She saw the fierce, stark need in his eyes, but more than that, she saw the tender reassurance. After all, he had promised to be gentle with her and she could not even imagine him breaking his word.

Wonderful man.

Somehow she summoned up the self-control to lift her hand and caress his cheek in a wordless affirmation that there was so much more than lust between them. Still, it was heaven to know that he was in control and he would get her through this fevered madness, satisfy her wildest hungers, and bring her out safely on the other side.

With an intensity in his stare that told her it was

time, he began inching deeper into her aching passage.

Unfortunately, that was the same moment that they were interrupted, and the sheer fantasy of this night came crashing down.

From the long, narrow parlor adjoining his bedroom came the sound of bickering voices.

Jarred by the noise, both of them paused.

As the intruders came closer, Georgie recognized the butler's voice, his tone full of pleading agitation.

The other voice – a woman's voice – was breezy and sophisticated. 'No worries, my dear Tooke, Lord Griffith is expecting me, I'm very sure. What has gotten into you? Would you please stand aside?'

'No,' Ian whispered in an agonized tone, going motionless. 'God, no. Bloody *hell!*'

'Ian, who is that?' Georgie demanded.

He didn't answer. He just looked at her in pain.

'Lady Faulconer, you don't understand!' Mr Tooke berated her. 'His Lordship isn't at home!'

'Then why is the light burning in his window? Silly old man, of course he is.'

'But he isn't feeling well!'

'Oh? I saw him at the theater earlier, and he looked perfectly healthy to me,' she declared while Georgie stared at her near-seducer in shock.

'Madam, I really must insist, you cannot go in there!'

Georgie gasped as the doorknob jiggled, but her

jaw dropped when the haughty intruder rapped impatiently on the door.

'Griffith? I am here to visit you. Would you please tell your butler to stop nipping at my heels like a dashed terrier?'

'I'll get rid of her,' he whispered, 'I swear. Don't move.'

'What is going on?' both women demanded nearly in unison.

But while outrage filled Georgie's face, the woman on the other side of the door let out a sudden peal of worldly laughter.

'Ian Prescott, you wicked beast, do you have somebody in there with you?'

'Tess – you really must leave,' he ground out in a strangled tone over his shoulder. 'This isn't a – good time!'

'Sorry, darling, am I ruining your fun?' she retorted, sounding a little less elegant. 'Oh, I see. You're with Baroness Watson again, aren't you? Hallo, Emily!' she called sarcastically. 'I do hope you're enjoying yourself, for you have quite ruined my night.'

'Who is Emily?' Georgie demanded.

'It doesn't matter!' Ian said hotly.

'Yes, it does!' With a furious huff, she planted her hands on his shoulders. 'Get off of me!'

He lifted away from her with an exasperated growl.

Freed of his weight, she sat up at once. 'Who is that woman outside of your door?' she whispered, trying to keep her voice low as she pointed angrily toward it.

'That's Tess. Lady Faulconer.'

'And?'

'We've been – friends. For a number of years.'

'Friends! I see.'

'Damn it, Georgiana, she means nothing to me,' he whispered furiously as he fastened his trousers again with a rough, hurried motion. 'I went to the opera earlier tonight to see her so that I could tell her that it was over. When I got there, she was with some other fellow. She looked quite content enough, so I assumed with my long absence to India that she had moved on.'

'Well, it seems you were wrong!'

'I don't know what she's doing here. We had a small conversation – considering she was with somebody new, I didn't think it necessary to come out and specifically give her the jilt! I assumed it was understood!'

'Didn't you ever hear you should never assume?'

'Georgie—'

'Go! Get her out of here, for heaven's sake. I can't believe you have a mistress!'

'*Former* mistress. Georgie, it was long before I ever met you.'

'I'm *waaait-ing*,' Tess called in singsong impatience, unaware of their whispered exchange. She was drumming her fingernails on the door, as if she found all of this very amusing.

Georgie bit back an unladylike reply, disgusted

with the way the woman had paraded through his house as if she owned it, straight up to his bedroom. If the door weren't locked, she'd have walked right in!

She narrowed her eyes at him. 'You've had her in this bed, haven't you?'

Ian just looked at her. 'Lock the door behind me. I don't want her seeing you or she'll spread word of this all over Town.'

'What are you going to tell her?'

'I'm going to lie,' he clipped out.

'Right. You're fairly good at that when you choose!'

'Well, darling, I do work for the government,' he drawled. He got up from the bed and walked, bare-chested, to the door.

Georgie nearly protested about him going to face the woman in his half-naked state, but then she realized with rising fury that if they had been lovers for years before she came along, it wasn't as though 'Tess' hadn't seen him in the buff already.

No wonder the hussy wouldn't go away. What woman in her right mind would give a specimen like Ian Prescott up without a fight?

He waited at the door for Georgie to come over and lock it behind him. No doubt Lady Faulconer would not have any qualms about coming into his bed chamber if she were able.

Georgie punched a pillow out of her way with a low expletive as she got up and marched over to the door to let him out.

He waved her off to the side so she wouldn't be seen, and then he went out, pulling the door shut behind him.

'Well, aren't you a naughty boy,' Tess chided as he joined her.

'Come on,' he muttered through gritted teeth. 'Let me show you to the door.'

'Ow! I'll thank you not to break my arm.'

Georgie turned the lock, but she remained beside the door, eavesdropping in bone-deep indignation. Still wanting to wring his neck and Lady Faulconer's, too, she unlocked the door and opened it a crack, peeping out as she heard their voices receding.

Though she was vexed enough to spit nails, she was keen to see what sort of female he was in the habit of choosing for companionship.

'Tess' had arrived with an impressive hat that she had taken off and discarded on the console table, but Ian swiped it up and carried it for her as he grabbed her elbow none too gently and steered her toward the exit. The woman let out a short, indignant 'Oh!' as Ian shepherded her out into the hallway beyond the long, narrow parlor. Mr Tooke followed them all the while, apologizing profusely to his master.

'It's all right, Tooke. We all know dear Lady Faulconer can be a great deal more stubborn than the average female,' he said in a taut monotone, then kicked the parlor door shut behind them.

Georgie closed the bedroom door again, locked it just to be cautious, and leaned back against it. Folding her arms across her waist, she glared into the room and shook her head in lingering disbelief.

She'd had no idea he had a mistress. Or were there several such women in his life? And who the deuce was Emily?

This was all very disturbing. It begged the obvious question that if she hadn't known this about Ian, what else didn't she know? She dropped her head with a low sigh, rubbing her brow and trying to contain her bewilderment at how close she had come mere moments ago to being deflowered.

If that had happened, then she wouldn't have had any choice but to marry him – a man that, perhaps, she didn't know quite as well as she'd thought.

Oh, God, what am I doing? she wondered as the terms of his proposal flooded back into her mind. *'You're marrying me. Any questions?'*

Any questions! She lifted her head again with a scoff of renewed indignation. The more fool, she, falling right in line with His Lordship's will like some vapid little simp! It was as if he'd put a spell on her, an aphrodisiac spell of craven lust, that made her eager to become his slave. Had the events of Janpur changed her so much that she was suddenly happy to let a man walk all over her, make her decisions for her, tell her what to do?

Wedlock is a padlock . . .

Don't forget, she reminded herself with a keen look, narrowing her eyes. *This was the man who put you under house arrest.*

Yes, he had saved her life and her brothers' lives, and he might have his wonderful moments, but Ian Prescott could be very controlling at times, and she might as well just face the fact head-on that marrying him would mean willingly putting herself under his full legal power.

For the rest of her life.

As Aunt Georgiana had often warned in her essays, in the eyes of the law, marriage formed a couple into one person – and the man was that person.

She had never met her aunt in life, but in the silence, she could almost hear the duchess lecturing her. *You'd better think about this, my girl. Be sure, be so very sure, before you make a move that cannot be undone. Don't make my same mistake and sign your will away to an autocratic lord . . .*

Georgie heaved a sigh, staring bleakly at nothing. Why couldn't things ever be easy?

Yet as Ian himself had admitted earlier, this was awfully sudden, his offer of marriage. It was true, she had dreamed of being with him, but she had disembarked from the boat tonight thinking he despised her, and now, an hour later, they were engaged.

This was certainly not the time to be impulsive. Maybe she had better think this through a bit more carefully, not go flinging herself blindly into some reckless adventure the way she would have done before. This was marriage they were talking about. This meant the rest of her life. If Ian really cared for her, he would at least give her some time to be sure of her decision.

Resolving herself to this course of action, she marched back over toward the fireplace to find her clothes.

Matthew Prescott, the sixteenth Earl of Aylesworth, heard the arguing below, sat up in his comfy cot in the nursery at the top of the stairs, and rubbed his eyes drowsily.

He didn't know what they were talking about, but at the sound of his magnificent Papa's voice, sleepiness fell away like his favorite blue blanket, which he now kicked off excitedly. Papa was awake!

Climbing down from his bed, the boy padded barefoot to the door. He went up on tiptoe, reaching high to turn the doorknob, and then he snuck out quietly to avoid waking the nursery maids.

The stairs led down to the long, narrow family parlor, but Papa wasn't in there. Matthew had heard the door shut angrily, so he realized that his sire was in the hall.

As he started down the darkened stairs to the long, narrow family parlor, taking one step at a time, holding on to the banister, he figured out by the tone of his Papa's voice that the person he was talking to was the Hat Lady.

Matthew made a face.

The Hat Lady had often come to visit, but she wasn't very nice. Matthew had always thought she had hard eyes that gleamed like little polished river stones. She did not feel children should ever eat at table and she looked at Matthew coldly whenever Papa turned away.

He heard her whining at Papa now in a manner that would have gotten him scolded by his nurse, were he to do it. He could hear their words through the wall as he approached, though he didn't understand them.

'Tess, don't play wounded with me,' Papa chided. 'I saw you at the theater with your new friend.'

'Oh, him! Come, darling, were you jealous? Is that what drove you into another woman's arms tonight?'

'No.'

'Blast it, Griffith, I have waited months for you to come back from that horrid continent, and now you're completely ignoring me!'

'I'm not ignoring you. Tess, you're not listening – it's over.'

Out in the hall, the Hat Lady launched into a shrill tirade, but Matthew stopped paying attention as the door to his Papa's bedchamber opened below and another girl came out.

She shut the door quietly again and walked over

toward the fireplace. She paced back and forth with delicate clenched fists, the dingy skirts of her walking dress swirling about her ankles. Without warning, she suddenly sat herself down on the couch.

She leaned forward, rested her elbows on her knees, hung her head in her hands for a moment, and then she clapped her hands over her ears as if she couldn't stand to hear Papa arguing with that other lady.

What a curious person!

Hesitant in his uncertainty about the newcomer, Matthew lingered in the shadows, but he was filled with great curiosity about this odd, pretty lady on his couch. Her long hair was black like soot, and her dress was plain and blue.

He could see that she looked upset, and he had half a mind to go to her and ask her what was wrong. But if she was anything like the Hat Lady, she would only frown at him and call for his nurse, and then he would be scolded for getting out of bed.

When she lifted her head and squared her shoulders, he saw that she was much prettier than the Hat Lady.

Then she sniffled and wiped her nose with the back of her sleeve, at which Matthew's giggle nearly betrayed his position in the stairwell. He didn't know much, but he knew that wasn't good manners, and this stranger's private lapse in etiquette made him like her right away.

Out in the hallway, he heard the Hat Lady go storming out at last, with old Mr Tooke trying to be helpful as he showed her out. Their hurrying footsteps faded, then Papa came back into the parlor.

Unseen in the shadows, Matthew watched Papa and this new lady intently. He wanted with all his heart to run to his father, but something told him he should not.

Papa's face looked grim and serious as he closed the door quietly behind him and walked past the bottom of the stairwell, near the place where Matthew was spying. He heard his father let out a low sigh, and saw him rest his hands wearily on his waist. After a moment, Papa walked over to the rumpled lady.

She rose from the couch as he approached and folded her hands before her waist. Her cheeks were pink and her hair was mussed, but Matthew didn't mind, for he was never neat enough for anyone, himself.

'Would you please take me to Knight House now?' she asked his father.

Matthew perked up. Knight House?

His best friend, Morley, lived there. Knight House was his favorite place in all the world, much better than his own gloomy, too-quiet home, where everyone had to be on their best behavior. Knight House was a good deal easier, in all, and he went there every day, across the park. Aunt Bel was the closest thing to a mother that he had ever known.

'Georgiana—'

'Please, Ian.' The messy lady's voice was soft like wind chimes.

Matthew couldn't take his eyes off her.

'Georgiana, I'm sorry,' Papa said.

'You have nothing to be sorry for.' She dragged her hand through her rumpled hair. 'I realize you did not invite her here.'

'But what about us?' He glanced meaningfully toward his bedroom door.

'No! Please, Ian. I'm very tired. I think – really think I'm going to need some time.'

'Time?'

'This is all happening so fast! It's confusing – please, won't you take me over to my cousins' house? I'm so tired I can't even think straight.'

Papa let out another sigh that seemed to say a hundred things, but he did not explain them. He just stared at the wall. 'Of course.' He went into his room and came back out a moment later with a shirt and jacket on. He gestured toward the parlor door and the dark-haired lady walked ahead of him.

As she came closer, Matthew saw a glimmer of tears in her eyes. Papa didn't seem to have noticed.

Of course, Papa failed to notice many things.

Like Matthew, for example.

From his perch in the shadows, he watched the adults pass, filled with awe as always at how huge and mighty and important his father was. Sally the nursery maid had told him that marquesses didn't have time for little boys. Nevertheless, Matthew wished he could go to Knight House with the two of them, though it was the middle of the night, and Morley was probably sleeping.

But then he recalled that he was going to Knight House himself tomorrow. If Papa was taking the messy lady there, he could get a closer look at her in the morning.

CHAPTER 11

Delicate English sunshine filtered through her lashes the next morning as Georgie opened her eyes, slowly awakening to the easy luxury of Knight House and the cream-colored bedchamber she had been assigned. The first thing her gaze fixed upon was the vase of muted purple hydrangeas basking before the window.

She sighed and closed her eyes again, contentment rippling through her. She stretched on the wonderfully comfortable bed, but did not hurry to rise. She lay on her side, listening to the birds chirping in the park outside her window.

It was a new day, and things no longer looked so dire. Her brothers were alive. The cousins she had feared would look down on her had turned out to be lovely people and had welcomed her with open arms. Their kindness had humbled her, given her earlier prejudices about Londoners. Now she knew better. She was in a safe place, and Ian had asked her to marry him.

Remembering the lascivious things they had done to each other the night before, only to be

303

interrupted by a late-night visit from his former paramour – what a debacle! – she let out a groan of frustration and pulled the pillow over her head.

Today she would have to figure out what to say to him in response to his offer of marriage. Unless, of course, it had all been a dream!

Casting the pillow aside again, she sat up, still clad in the battered chemise in which he had nearly ravished her. She climbed out of the canopied bed and went over to the curtained window, peeking out. Across the park, she could see his stately home – the one with the door painted burgundy. It was even grander in the light. She stared past the swaying trees of Green Park hoping to catch a glimpse of him, but this was an idle fancy.

He did not appear.

Above, the yellow sun was high. Below, all sorts of people strolled along the park's graveled lanes. She folded her arms across her chest and leaned against the waist-high chest of drawers that held the vase of ball-like flowers, musing on the prospect of seeing him again today. He had promised he would come and visit her.

A light knock at the door just then drew her from her thoughts. 'Are ye up now, Miss?' a soft Cockney voice inquired. 'It's Daisy. I've been assigned as your maid.'

'Come in,' she called, glad of the interruption. She turned away from the window and went to meet the girl.

As the staff hurried to serve her, Georgie was touched by their solicitude. Daisy worked on getting a bath drawn for her, while two more maids brought her breakfast.

'Lord Griffith told the kitchens not to fix ye any meats, is that correct, Miss?'

'Oh – yes,' she said, startled that he had remembered she was a vegetarian. Of course, he was thoughtful like that.

'Is eggs all right?'

She nodded as the maid lifted the silver lid off her plate and revealed an English breakfast revised of the customary bacon and sausage. She helped herself to the fruit, pastries, a scrambled egg, and some of the breakfast beans.

'Would you like us to open your trunks for ye, Miss?' the girls offered while she ate.

She nodded, eager to be reunited with her personal effects after all these months.

The scent of sandalwood and incense wafted out of her traveling trunks as each was opened. Georgie reviewed the contents between bites. The maids were ooh'ing and ahh'ing over her brilliant-hued saris and other exotic items, especially the scarves of pure Kanchipuram silk in her wardrobe, when Camille arrived, the duchess's own lady's maid.

The resident beauty expert of Knight House presented herself to help Georgie dress and fix her hair. Noting how the sea voyage had taken its toll on her complexion and hair, Camille briskly brought out an array of beauty potions to help restore her looks. It proved to be a formidable task. Avocado was smashed into her hair while lemons were rubbed all over her face and hands and the top of her chest to fade her light tan from the ocean's blaring sun. Milk and rose water followed, while a thick concoction of cocoa butter soaked into her hands. An oatmeal mixture was used in the bath to refresh all of her skin. Lastly, she washed it away with a lavender soap.

When she emerged from her luxurious bath wrapped in a large dressing gown, Camille snipped the ragged ends off her hair, bringing it back to life, and finished her off with a brisk manicure. At last, Georgie gazed into the mirror at a very English-looking girl, neatly dressed in a long-sleeved, high-waisted gown of sprigged muslin, her hair arranged in a top-knot with soft tendrils framing her face.

Well, she thought, a sari was more comfortable, but she certainly looked a good deal more like someone who might have received a spectacular offer of marriage from a wealthy and powerful marquess.

She stared into the mirror, wondering, given her unconventional ways, if she was equal to the demands of such a highly visible public role, for that was what being Ian's marchioness would mean.

For the moment, however, it was time to face the world. Brushing her doubts aside. She thanked the maids and left her room to present herself in her much improved state to her cousins.

As she walked down the hallway, not altogether sure where she was going, she found herself once more contemplating some of the astonishing news she had received last night when Ian had brought her here, to the opulent residence of her cousins, the glamorous Duke and Duchess of Hawkscliffe, who had insisted on her calling them Robert and Bel.

They had revealed that Jack had been in London and just left, but if this were not surprising enough in itself, considering how much he claimed he hated the place, they told her he had brought along – his wife!

Georgie could hardly believe that any woman had succeeded in taming wild Jack. She could hardly wait to meet this extraordinary lady, but the pair had already sailed away again due to Jack's pressing business in South America.

To Georgie's added surprise, her cousins had told her that Papa had also been in Town. Unfortunately, Jack had needed her father's help in his dangerous scheme, and so Lord Arthur had been obliged to set sail at once – in spite of having received an urgent note from Derek about their trouble with the maharajah while he had been out at sea.

At first it had been hard for Georgie to accept that her father would put Jack's business before the welfare of his own offspring, but then her eldest cousin, Robert, the duke, under whose roof she now sojourned, had explained that Jack and her father were involved in nothing less than the liberation of the Spanish colonies in South America. Jack had filled several of his ships with soldiers, guns, and supplies to keep the revolution alive, and he needed her father to help him blast his way through the Spanish blockade.

Georgie hated knowing that her father, in his sixties, was in every bit as much danger as her beloved brothers were back in Asia. He really was too old for this!

Lord Arthur did not know how soon he could return, but until then, he had asked Robert and Bel to watch out for her. And so, left behind – as always – she could do nothing but wait and pray and try not to go mad until her adventuresome family was back safely together again under one roof.

As Georgie proceeded down the hallway trying to wrap her mind around all the changes that were happening, she was unaware that the biggest shock of all still lay in store.

Then she saw the little boy.

He was sitting on a chair by the wall with a remarkable air of patience, but when he saw her, his eyes widened, and he climbed down at once and walked toward her calmly.

Dressed up as a tiny gentleman, the child was only about as high as the chair rail or the top of the wainscoting. He had brown hair, fair skin with a smattering of freckles, and enormous dark eyes.

She regarded the boy in surprise as he stopped in front of her, tilted his head back to meet her gaze, and gave her a cheerful 'Hallo.'

'Well, hallo to you, sir.' Tickled by the greeting, she folded her hands behind her back and bent down a little. 'You must be Morley. I am looking for your mother.'

He shook his head. 'I am Matthew and I don't have a mother.'

'What?' Georgie asked softly, her eyes widening, altogether taken aback by the heart-tugging response. She crouched down in wonder to meet Matthew at his eye level.

The boy studied her with a serious stare. 'Why do you sleep in the daytime?'

'I don't usually, but today I was awfully tired.'

'Oh.' He studied her hair and her earrings with a fascinated look. 'I like dogs. Do you?'

'Some.'

'Aunt Bel said your name is Miss Knight.'

'That is true, but you can call me Georgie.'

He laughed all of a sudden, an infectious giggle. 'Georgie! Like the king!'

'Yes,' she said, laughing with him. 'Just like the king.'

'Papa says King George is cwazy!'

'Who is your papa, Matthew?' She recalled hearing that the fourth Knight brother had inherited a son by marriage. 'Is it Lord Lucien?'

'No, ma'am, my papa is Lord Griffith. And when I grow up, I'm going to be just like him.'

A feather could have bowled her over at this news. She stared at the child with the breath half knocked out of her.

'Lord Griffith?' she echoed. So that's why this child seemed so familiar!

Matthew edged closer to her and nodded, but he seemed to be growing bored of this topic, now examining the sprigged flower pattern on her gown with great interest, as though he had never seen a lady before. Growing bolder, he reached out an exploratory finger and poked at one of her sparkling earrings, making the pearl bob swing.

Georgie let him look while she did her best to absorb this shocking revelation.

Ian had a son!

Obviously, Matthew was the product of his first marriage. She looked at the boy more closely and thought, *Of course.* Who else's child could this be? He had his father's serious air, his intelligent gaze, his good-natured sobriety. His quiet intensity. And like the father, there was something sad about the son.

How could he not tell me that he had a child? Reeling, Georgie looked at the adorable little boy and knew that this changed everything.

'Matthew, do you know where the duchess is?' she asked at length, barely managing to locate her voice. 'I should like very much to see her.'

He perked up. 'Aunt Bel? She's in the morning room with Baby Kate!'

'Where is the morning room, please? I'm afraid I do not know the way.'

'Come on, I'll show you!' He latched onto her hand and escorted her down the hallway.

She noticed that the boy continually kept glancing at her, again and again, watchfully, as if he feared that at any second she might disappear.

Hours later, after a select committee meeting followed by a typically unproductive haranguing session with a few members of the Cabinet, Ian and Hawk returned to Knight House.

The silence informed them at once that it was the children's nap time. Practically tiptoeing, the butler, Mr Walsh, appeared and relieved them of their hats and things. He also informed them that luncheon would be served in half an hour on the terrace, per Her Grace's wishes.

That sounded to Ian like a pleasant suggestion, for it was a balmy June day. They proceeded upstairs to see the ladies, keeping their voices low as they exchanged a few ideas and observations on the morning's political business.

Ian felt his heartbeat quicken as they ascended. He'd had some difficulty concentrating all morning due to his distraction over Georgiana.

Obviously, last night had not gone according to plan. What today might hold – well, with her, it was anyone's guess. He wasn't sure if she would still be angry about Tess or if a good night's sleep might have inspired her to wipe the slate clean.

Hawk's duchess, Belinda, a graceful blond, came out quietly into the corridor and greeted both men, Ian with a smile, her black-haired husband with a kiss on the cheek.

'Robert, may I speak with you for a moment?' She plucked at her lord's sleeve, drawing him closer, while she pointed Ian toward the music room. 'Go and look in there,' she whispered to him.

Ian smiled uncertainly at his best friend's wife and went to investigate, while Bel whisked Hawk into the drawing room across the hall. The door closed.

He heard a soft voice murmuring as he approached the music room. When he stepped into the open doorway, he stopped, arrested at the sight of his little son half asleep on Georgiana's lap.

The future marquess was sucking his thumb, a babyish habit that still carried over into nap time, and holding onto the demure lace ruffle of her sleeve as if had claimed her for his very own. Georgiana was reading to him softly from a book of children's verses.

Ian stared, totally taken off guard.

The sight of her there, cuddling his motherless son, a wholesome portrait of maternal tenderness, filled him with a sudden, exquisite blend of sweetness and pain, pointing once more to the gaping hole in his life. But now, he realized, he could be looking at the start of a real family. A real home.

His house had never quite become a home because it had always lacked a heart, just as his son had always lacked a mother's nurturing love.

Georgiana looked so soft and kind and inviting, so capable and so very gentle, that Ian's throat tightened as he gazed at her. He leaned against the door frame, unable to take his eyes off her. *You have to marry me*, he thought. *I won't have it any other way.*

Again, he thought of the past. He wanted better for his son than the upbringing he had known, and it was his sharpest regret that he knew he was doing even worse than his parents had done.

The aristocratic household he had grown up in had been cold and strict, substituting rank, pride, and dignity for love. Though messier and far more chaotic, the Knight clan he had attached himself to had been much more closely knit due to the strong bonds between Hawk and all his brothers. It had been easy for Ian to tag along at the edges of their tribe, but it wasn't the same. Especially now, when all of them were married, with wives and children of their own. How many years had passed?

And he was still alone.

Until the moment she looked over and saw Ian leaning in the doorway, Georgie was still angry at him for not telling her about Matthew. Failing to mention his former lovers who might come bursting in the door at any moment was one thing, but keeping his child a secret from her was a far more serious offense.

But then she sensed his presence, glanced over, and saw him there, watching her with his child in the drowsy hush of afternoon, and the expression on his face drew her up short.

His green eyes were deep and haunted; the stark planes and angles of his face had tensed. He stood there, mute, the rugged line of his mouth pressed shut, every inch of his big, solid frame limned with an indescribable loneliness.

Georgie stared at him.

She had sensed the hidden pain beneath his polished surface from their first meeting in Calcutta, and had glimpsed it again in the prayer cave when she had asked about his wife. Usually he hid it well, but now, for the first time, as he watched her with his son, it had emerged in plain view, showing on his face, written in his soulful gaze.

This man was hurting. And one long, searching look into his eyes was enough to transmute her earlier anger at him into compassion. How could she stay angry when he looked so bleak, so obviously in need of tenderness?

It dawned on her that there might be some greater purpose in her being sent to London. A hint of destiny. Ian Prescott had saved her life and that of her brothers. Maybe now it was her turn to save him.

She returned his stare in silence, careful not to disturb his sleeping child. He pushed away from the doorway and sauntered into the room.

His boy sensed his presence, though half asleep, and stirred in her arms. She hushed Matthew with a kiss to his warm brow.

'Papa.' Matthew wiggled his stockinged feet but was too content to climb off Georgie's lap.

Ian smiled at the tot with a glow of pride in his eyes. 'Son.' He bent down and gently captured one of the child's happily dancing feet. 'I see you made a friend.'

Georgie's heart quaked as Ian lifted his guarded gaze to hers. 'Hallo.'

She smiled ruefully at him, recalling that she had received the exact same greeting from his son.

'Lunch will be served on the terrace in a bit,' he murmured. 'I'll go find one of the nursery maids to watch him.' Ian gently cupped his child's sleepy head for a moment. 'Were you good while I was gone?'

'He was an angel,' she replied stoutly on Matthew's behalf. 'He hasn't got a bad bone in his body.' She kissed the child's tousled head and hugged him a little more tightly. 'I'm keeping him.'

'Are you?' He glanced at her in subdued surprise. 'I'm envious.'

'We need to talk,' she whispered, giving him a firm look.

He read her eyes and a fleeting shadow of uneasiness passed across his chiseled features. Then he

315

nodded to her and withdrew to find one of the children's caretakers.

When Matthew was safely handed off into the maid's care a few minutes later, Ian closed the door quietly and turned to her, unaware that her womanly protective instincts had been roused and that she was feeling a trifle belligerent on his child's behalf.

A part of her wanted to throttle the man, but his armored demeanor betrayed the raw vulnerability just under the surface. This warned her she had better tread carefully, for it seemed she might have stumbled onto his Achilles' heel. She wanted answers, but she didn't want to hurt him.

Wondering for a moment how to proceed, she concluded with a shrug that she usually fared best with the direct approach. 'Why didn't you tell me that you have a son?'

He shrugged, eyeing her from a cautious distance as he sauntered past the pianoforte. 'It didn't come up.'

'You could have brought it up!' she exclaimed. 'Were you trying on purpose to hide him from me, or did you just forget that he exists?'

'Neither!' He frowned at her as he turned and set his hands on his waist. 'Good day to you, too,' he muttered.

'I am sorry if my greeting doesn't suit you, Ian, but I'm afraid my day started off with quite a shock. Generally, when one proposes marriage, one ought to mention if children are involved. Any others I should know about?'

'No!' His cheeks flushed at the question. He turned away and paced, beginning to look a trifle caged.

Georgie exhaled slowly, but the faint pain in her lungs reminded her afresh that her fierce and immediate connection to little Matthew Prescott had a lot to do with her own childhood and the grief she had so often felt at being left behind, left alone. It was important not to take that out on Ian. At the same time, who better than she could help him understand his child's needs?

She leaned against the scrolled arm of a fauteuil. 'He is a beautiful child.'

'I know. Thank you,' Ian growled.

'He's sweet and clever and very well behaved. And—' Her words broke off.

He paused and sent her a dark look over his shoulder. 'And what?'

'Starved for your notice,' she said softly.

He stared at her.

'Why didn't you ever mention him to me?'

He looked at her for a long moment, at a loss, then turned away, dragging a hand through his hair. 'I don't know.'

'You don't know? That is no answer! The poor little thing, he might as well be wearing a sign around his neck that says, "Please, somebody, love me!" Surely you see that he craves your attention.

Does he not interest you? Surely you are not ashamed of him somehow?'

'Of course not.' Ian gave her a painted look, then fell silent for a long moment. He looked away again, staring blankly at the wall.

'Talk to me,' Georgie urged him. 'Don't turn away. Help me understand.'

He rubbed his mouth in agitation and then shook his head as studied the floor. 'When I am away from home, I try not to think about Matthew. I have to put him out of my mind. It is the only way that I can do my job. My work, you see, requires a cool temper and a lucid mind. Detachment. Objectivity. And nothing, Georgiana, is objective for me about that boy.' He swallowed hard as he sent her an anguished glance. 'He is my child. He is never far from my mind.' He faltered. 'I don't talk about him when I'm on a mission because I know he's left at home wondering why I'm not there. It hurts to be away from him. And . . . it hurts to be near him, too.'

'Oh, Ian.' She rose from her perch on the chair's arm and went over to him, laying a comforting hand on his shoulder.

She did not need to ask why it was painful for him to be near his son. The answer was obvious: grief over Matthew's mother. The child must have reminded Ian of his dead wife. He must have loved her very much, she thought wistfully.

'Come and sit with me,' she whispered, taking his hand between both of hers.

Avoiding her tender gaze, he let her lead him over to the sofa. They sat. She let out a long sigh, but neither of them spoke. She could almost feel his first wife with him in the room like some pale ghost.

He studied his loosely clasped hands for a long moment. When he broke the silence, his tone was once again controlled and carefully sardonic. 'He is part of the reason why I need you, you see.'

'I've realized that.' She paused. 'I'm honored by your trust, that you think I would make a good mother.'

He cast her a wry shadow of a smile. 'Of course you would. You have a way of . . . sprinkling joy everywhere you go.'

His words brought a fresh mist of tears to her eyes. 'Thanks.'

'It's true.'

'But, you know, it doesn't serve Matthew unless you and I are sure that marriage is what we both want.'

'I'm sure,' he answered without hesitation.

'You've thought the matter through, then?'

'Of course. I wouldn't have asked if I still had doubts.'

'Perhaps, if you're willing, you would explain to me some of the reasons that helped you arrive at this conclusion.'

He shrugged. 'Well, there's Matthew. And the family alliance that has long been sought. It does seem to be inevitable. I've already told you I think

319

we make a good team. We hold many of the same values, and of course you're very beautiful. And, lastly, someday I would like to have another child. Perhaps a few.'

'Really?'

'Yes.' His nod was full of conviction, but then he hesitated. 'And, er, after what happened in the prayer cave – and last night, too – marrying you is the only right and decent thing to do.'

Oh, Ian, she thought in a poignant mix of longing and sudden sorrow.

His reasons all made sense, but it was not lost on her that he hadn't mentioned love. She knew this was no accidental oversight. He was a man who always said exactly what he meant. A pang of disappointment clenched her innards, but she voiced no protest. At least he did not insult her by telling her merely what she wanted to hear. Honesty was part of love. At least it was a start.

'It does sound as though you're very sure,' she offered in a measured tone.

'Yes. After your brothers suggested the match, I had the whole voyage to make the decision, and I can assure you, I thought of little else.'

'Hold on!' she exclaimed. 'My brothers suggested you marry me?'

'Mm.' He nodded to her in idle amusement, but Georgie paled.

'Did they pressure you into this, Ian? I know how forceful they can be with their opinions—'

'No, of course not. Don't be vexed at them. They

only want what's best for you – and that's me,' he said matter-of-factly.

She gave him a wry smile and took his hand again. 'Ian – I'm going to need a little time.'

'What for?'

'Frankly, you can be very domineering, and if I am to put myself in your power, I need to be sure.'

'I'm not domineering, I'm decisive!' he retorted. 'Isn't that a virtue, anyway? You said one wanted a husband one could look up to.'

Georgie stared at him and thought, *I want to know if you can fall in love with me.*

He scowled at the floor, then slanted her a piercing glance. 'You seemed very sure last night.'

'Yes, but then *she* showed up, and I realized there's so much I don't even know about you.' She searched his face, willing him to be co-operative. 'Why do we have to rush? Can't we take it step by step and get to know each other better until we both are absolutely certain this is right? For Matthew's sake?'

'Step by step? I think we've already skipped a few,' he said with a glint of innuendo in his eyes.

She blushed. She dropped her gaze, twining her fingers in her lap. 'I did enjoy last night.'

'You would have enjoyed it more if Tess had not interrupted,' he murmured.

She flashed him a smile, but as he touched her face, his gaze turned serious. 'I want you to know that she is not going to be a problem for us. I made sure she understands now that our affair is a thing of the past.'

321

'I'm glad to hear it.'

A light knock on the door interrupted just then.

'Lunch is ready!' Bel called through the closed door, not having abandoned her duties as chaperon, after all.

Georgie wasn't surprised that she had been allowed some time alone with Ian. Her cousins seemed determined to play matchmaker between them. 'Thank you, we'll be right there!' she answered.

'So, what do you want to do, Georgiana?' Ian asked bluntly.

She captured his hand in a light grasp. 'I just want to take things a bit more slowly. It seems to me that all three of us – you, Matthew, and I need a chance to get to know each other better before we make a definite commitment.'

'How much time do you want?'

'You don't look very happy about my answer.'

'I'm not going to wait around forever,' he said irritably. 'I don't play those kinds of games.'

'It's not a game! I've just explained how I feel.'

He leaned over and planted a firm kiss on her cheek. 'Two weeks,' he murmured. 'Then I'll want an answer.'

'Ian!'

'Shall we?' He rose and gestured toward the door.

Through her exasperation, Georgie recalled that her relatives were waiting. She heaved a sigh and followed, nodding her permission to him to escort her down to lunch.

They left the music room in silence, falling into step with each other naturally as they strolled through Knight House, arm in arm. Georgie's mind churned, meanwhile, with her efforts to understand why he was so hard to reach.

'Tell me a story about you when you were a child,' she said abruptly, slipping her hands in a more snug hold around his arm.

'Why?'

'I'm trying to picture you at Matthew's age. You must have been adorable.'

'Of course I was,' he drawled. 'But I don't have any stories.'

'You must have one.'

'I was born grown up, don't you know?'

'Oh, Ian, please, just one little anecdote? I told you I want to know more about you. Details, man!'

'Oh, very well,' he mumbled. 'Matthew's age, eh? Well, when I was about Matthew's age, I decided to give my mother a huge bouquet of flowers.' They proceeded from the wide marble corridor to the curving marble staircase. 'I was so pleased with myself. I picked them all and carried them into the house, certain that this would make her happy – she was never very cheerful for some reason. But instead, to my astonishment, she took one look at my gift and fainted dead away, and I was sent up to the nursery with no supper. There was quite a row.'

'But, why?' Georgie exclaimed.

'Unfortunately, all the flowers I picked were

from Mother's prize-winning garden. Alas, in my enthusiasm, I had unwittingly destroyed it, at least for that season.'

With a tender wince mingled with laughter, Georgie gave his arm an affectionate squeeze. 'Poor boy.'

He let out a low, worldly laugh. 'Ah, my dear, it was not exactly a 'Gather ye rosebuds while ye may' sort of home that I grew up in.'

'No, it doesn't sound like it. But you know, these things can be corrected,' she informed him.

'How's that?'

'Well, you have to start small. At lunch, for example.' She waved to her cousins as they walked toward the pleasant shady terrace. 'I say we start our meal with the sweet course.'

He looked at her in feigned shock. 'You can *do* that?'

She paused, pulling him a wee bit closer to murmur, 'You certainly did it with me.'

His left eyebrow shot up.

She bit her lip and sent him a frisky look askance, then tugged on his arm again, drawing him toward the summery abundance of the table.

She's good for you. There was no getting around it. *Ah, Georgiana,* he thought. What was to be done with such a creature?

Admittedly, her request for more time so they could get to know each other better had resonated with Ian. He had hardly known Catherine at all

324

before assenting to that match. If he had insisted on more than a few cursory meetings without the usual crowd of family and chaperons present, then maybe he would have sensed that the prim heiress wasn't what she seemed.

On the other hand, he held firm on the point of having her answer within a fortnight, because in negotiations, it was always a bad sign if the other party tarried too much over making a decision. It nearly always heralded some sort of refusal.

He wanted this alliance made, the merger sealed, the treaty signed; but if she had to drag her feet too much over the decision, then that was a valid cue that she really didn't want this marriage, which in turn meant he'd be wise to call the whole thing off. He and his son didn't need another woman in their lives who didn't really want to be there.

They had already been through that.

In the meantime, as the days unfolded, he made an effort not to be what she called domineering. For Matthew's sake, and hers, he showed her that he, too, could bend. She left him little choice.

Plainly, the woman had her own ideas about how things should go between them, and he was intrigued enough to follow along to see where she might lead.

He was aware that she was taking him toward dangerous territory, near to the desolate border-lands of things he had no desire to confront. But he wanted to find out what lay ahead, lured toward something he had always secretly longed for but had never known how to find. As the days passed with her, he was like a man who had lived years underground, slowly groping his way out toward the light.

Freed of his duties for the Foreign Office at the moment, he made it his mission to win this woman for his wife.

They took the boy on a picnic with a bevy of servants and friends. He taught Matthew how to fly a kite. They rode horses and went boating on the Serpentine. They attempted a balloon ascension one day, but Matthew was too scared to fly, so instead they took the boy to a puppet theater.

Neither he nor his son had ever known anyone like Georgiana before. He had never known such warmth and simple joy.

She had a talent for relishing every moment, and she shared this gift with them both. Being with Georgie, he was learning, was like a walk through the spice market, full of strange treasures, exotic adventures, slightly dangerous enticements, and sharp new flavors that had a tonic effect on the soul. She danced her way through life with a sensual exuberance that mesmerized him.

As subtle changes shifted deep inside him, sometimes uneasiness arose and tried to unseat all his progress with whispered reminders of the coal-black secrets he had to hide. But for once in his life, he refused to think too much. The blot on his soul had held him back for too many years, keeping him separate from the world. Even those dearest to him didn't know the truth, and by God, they never would. Beyond that, he strove to erase the haunted past from intruding upon the present.

Georgiana made him happy. She made his child happy. She was their future, and he willed himself with all his considerable discipline to focus only on that.

Soon, the night of the ball came, when she was to be introduced to Society.

Ian's heart and his step were light as he strolled through the milling throng in keen enjoyment of the occasion, much to his own surprise. Usually these things bored him insufferably, and he ended up talking politics for hours in the corner with the old, dry gents.

Not tonight.

He popped a meringue into his mouth as he ambled along and let out an enthusiastic '*Mmm*' as it melted on his tongue in a sugary burst of delicate flavors. Almond? Lemon? A hint of vanilla? Whatever it was, it was good.

Humming along absently with the music, which indeed sounded extraordinarily melodic this night, he did not think he had ever tasted a meringue as delicious as that before. In a short bit, perhaps he'd have another.

Passing under the colonnade, he overheard a portly, red-nosed, ungracefully aging rake telling his cronies a ribald joke. But for reasons unknown, Ian discovered that this evening, not even their crude humor could annoy him. He was usually quite stern in the opinion that such talk was better left at the club or the racing track, certainly not in the company of ladies, but tonight, his whole being was flush with a newfound noblesse toward the countless foibles of the human race. Even the brilliant glow from the chandeliers seemed more forgiving as it shone on the pinched, careworn faces of all Society's most discontented matrons.

God only knew what was happening to him. So heightened were his senses that he was even aware of the texture of the clothes against his body, the crisp linen of his shirt, the smooth merino wool of his black trousers. His cravat was looser than he usually wore it, his collar not so starched.

Yes, he reflected. There was a sweetness in his veins that had infected him like some wonderful disease that instead of making men sick, made them well.

He felt a full-blooded heartiness this eve, as though he had newly awakened from a winter's-long sleep. It all was due to Georgiana's enlivening effect on him, of course. He wondered if this meant that in fact he was falling in love. He felt sharper, more gregarious, easier in general. He smiled more and laughed louder as an acquaintance passed him with a grin and a jest.

Ian moved on until *she* came in sight.

And there she was, across the room, a gorgeous

bit of magnificence in a lustrous satin gown like summer roses.

He leaned slowly against one of the ballroom's towering Corinthian columns and indulged himself in simply watching her with all the spell-bound fascination with which those dreamy Lakeland poets watched the sun rise. From his discreet angle, it looked like she was doing well.

They had agreed yesterday to keep a polite distance from each other at the ball as she went about establishing herself in Society. Their own delicious little secret joke. Well, plucky thing that she was, she did not wish to ride in on his coat-tails, forcing Society to bow down to her for his sake. Georgiana wanted to stand on her own two feet, to make people see and know her as an individual before word got out about their future match.

Possible match, he reminded himself wryly. At least in *her* mind. In his mind, it was as good as certainty, and only a matter of time.

At any rate, he could acknowledge that her way of handling this night had been a wise decision. As soon as word got out that the two of them were romantically connected, she would become the target of choice for all the jealous females who had set their caps at him since Catherine's death.

He saw now, as he watched her, admiring the graceful drapery of her India shawl flowing through the angle of her elbows, looping down below her lovely backside, that he really needn't have worried about how she'd do in Society. Nevertheless, he had given her some advice on how to handle the town and was pleased to see that she had taken it to heart.

Georgiana employed all those amusing Queen of Sheba airs that she had used to such effect in her arrival on her painted elephant at Janpur, outdoing the bluest-blooded aristocrats in London as she played it exceedingly lofty, thoroughly cool, blasé in her greetings to dukes and princes, as though it were their privilege to meet her and not the other way around.

Damn, she was good.

No, indeed, the niece and namesake of the Hawkscliffe Harlot was making it clear from the start that, provincial or no, she was not about to let London Society push her around. Her great beauty combined with her regal bearing and her deliciously scandalous bloodlines set the town on its ear. Tilting his head a little to listen for the gossip, he heard the buzz of wonder-struck whispers flying around the room. Her triumph only made him want her more.

Within a few hours, the first Georgiana and all her errant ways had been eclipsed, half-forgotten in the shining glory of the new one.

At last, midnight struck, the agreed-upon hour of their rendezvous. Ian was glad of it, for in truth he was beginning to feel a little jealous. It was not easy to see her dance with other men.

Every young lady was supposed to have a talent

with which to make her company more pleasurable and interesting. Some sang, others played the pianoforte, while others still were known for their watercolor paintings. Georgiana, however, was undeniably a dancer. It was a joy to watch her move. Perhaps it was her yoga practice that gave her such limber grace, but everyone noticed how divinely she carried herself, her exquisite balance, a sort of innate awareness of where each lithe limb was situated in space. Even so, he had a feeling that she was holding back. Those bells she used to wear around her ankle, after all, were the favorite baubles of India's temple dancers.

He had a very strong suspicion that she could keep pace with any maharajah's troupe of nautch girls. Perhaps one day she would dance for him.

For now, however, it was time to collect on that dance that she had promised to save for him all the way back at Janpur. He pushed away from the column and sauntered toward her.

She looked over as though she had felt his stare, or as if she had been discreetly keeping track of him, too, all night long. Her glance was potent from across the room.

He gave her a subtle *namaste*, which made her smile.

Blushing, she glanced at the large clock on the wall and saw that it was midnight. *Good.* He was absurdly pleased that she had not forgotten their appointed hour. She sent him a secretive smile and artfully disengaged herself from her crowd of admirers.

His heart beat faster, but he kept his pace slow and measured as he strode across the ballroom to claim her for the dance.

Upon reaching her, Ian offered up a gentlemanly bow, the hint of sandalwood in her perfume intoxicating him when he leaned closer. 'Miss Knight.'

'Lord Griffith.' She responded with an exquisite curtsy.

He put out his hand. She laid her fingers on his palm without a word.

'I'm impressed,' he murmured as he led her to the dance floor.

'I'm glad that you approve.' She adjusted one high white glove a bit as the orchestra played the first introductory bars. 'Did I never mention that the little enclave of British ladies in Calcutta society are known for being even stricter than your London dames?'

'No,' he said in surprise as they stepped into a gliding waltz.

She smiled at him. 'It is their way of making up for being mere provincials.'

'Aha.'

'Since all those ladies were my mother's bosom friends, they made sure that I knew how to behave myself when the occasion calls.'

He laughed softly. 'And to think that I was worried.'

'Haven't I told you you worry too much, my lord?'

'Indeed, you have, my dear.'

Then they danced, smiling and gazing into each other's eyes like two smitten fools as they swept through the daring steps of the waltz in effortless unison. He tightened his hold on her waist. Georgiana's palm seemed to caress his shoulder. He savored the dance, though he couldn't help wondering if she was recalling her little visit to his bed and that night in the prayer cave, too.

'Did I mention that I have a present for you, my pretty friend?' he asked at length.

'For me? Oh, how divine! What is it?'

'A surprise,' he chided. 'But you won't have long to wait. It should be ready by tomorrow. Shall I deliver it in person?'

'Please do! Oh, please, at least give me a little hint,' she cajoled him. 'I hate surprises.'

'That's odd, considering you're full of them.'

'If I don't know what it is, then how can I tell whether or not it would be proper for me to accept this gift from a gentleman?'

He snorted.

'Oh, please, please!'

He laughed. 'Very well. It's jewelry, and you may think me improper and overly familiar with the gift, but I don't care. You must have it.'

'Ian!'

'Shh,' he warned.

'I mean – Lord Griffith,' she corrected herself hastily, lowering her voice lest they were heard. 'Lord Griffith, my dear, I thought I still had five days left.'

'It's not a ring, if that's your worry,' he drawled as he whirled her smoothly through the turn at the far corner of the dance floor while a crowd of smiling guests looked on. 'I assure you, it's quite something . . . else.'

'Well, aren't you mysterious,' she said with a toss of her head.

He smiled.

When the music ended, she laughed, her cheeks flushed, and pressed her hand to her chest to catch her breath. He offered to get her a drink, and she accepted with an appreciative nod.

'I'll be right back,' he whispered. It was difficult to leave her, but he could feel her watching him as he walked away.

As he pushed his way politely through the crowd, heading for the smaller parlor where refreshments were being served – and those superb meringues – he was apprehended by dear old Lord Applecroft, one of the elder diplomats, along with a young courier from the Foreign Office.

'Griffith! Ah, there you are! This lad has just arrived in search of you.' Lord Applecroft latched onto Ian's sleeve to halt him, then turned to the uniformed courier. 'Here, here he is, my boy. What news? You may tell us both! Is it word from India?'

'Yes, sir.' The young man glanced at Ian. 'But I've only got orders to tell it to Lord Griffith.'

'It's all right, young man,' Ian said. 'I'm the one who gave you the orders.' He had left instructions at the Foreign Office that he should be alerted as soon as any ships from India arrived with tidings of the war. 'Lord Applecroft has long been a friend. You may speak freely. The two officers I inquired about, have they come?'

'No, sir, but there's news on the general situation. The Maharajah of Gwalior signed the same treaty of neutrality that you were able to accomplish at Janpur.'

'Excellent!'

'The war's begun, and the reports have it that, so far, Baji Rao has put up a significant defense. But the largest development of all since your departure is that Amir Khan, the leader of the Pindari Horde, has already surrendered!'

'What?'

'The Pindari Horde has decided not to fight!' the courier related with great excitement. 'There was a short skirmish, they were quickly routed by Lord Hastings, and driven into disarray. Our forces gave pursuit and now they have surrendered. Many will be hanged; the rest have been disbanded.'

Ian stared at him. 'That's incredible,' he murmured, marveling. So much for the Pindaris' reputation for ferocity!

In hindsight, it seemed clear that they had merely been emboldened by the lack of any serious challenge to their marauding practices up until Lord Hastings had vowed to bring them to justice. Then their essential cowardice showed through.

'They put up no resistance?' he asked.

'Only a few of their captains tried to make a stand, but these, too, were crushed. Word has it one of their top leaders tried to escape into the forest and was eaten by a tiger!'

'Dash my wig!' old Lord Applecroft murmured, wide-eyed.

'A tiger? Ha!' Ian abruptly laughed aloud. 'Well, I cannot think of a better fate for him,' he declared with an edge of bloodthirsty relish in his voice. 'If you ask me, the bleeder got what he deserved.'

'I say!' Lord Applecroft answered, then he eyed Ian shrewdly. 'Never heard you talk like that before. Perhaps you picked up a bit of Eastern savagery in your travels, Griffith?'

'Ah, my old friend.' Ian clapped him on the shoulder. 'If I had not been born with a savage streak myself, I should never have attempted to negotiate with the wild maharajahs in the first place.' He winked at the old earl, laughed at the courier's astonished look, and then moved on alone to fetch the promised punch for his lady.

'You danced very prettily with Lord Griffith.'

Georgie turned in surprise to see who had addressed her. The woman, in her middle thirties, had flawless skin and champagne-blond hair swept up in an artful arrangement. Her columnar gown of shellpink satin had a high vandyked collar around the back of her neck, though the front plunged to reveal a generous bosom. Smiling benevolently at her, the graceful creature sauntered closer, waving her fan by her neck with a slow, idle, decidedly calculating motion.

For some reason, everything about her put Georgie on her guard. 'Thank you, madam,' she replied, greeting the woman with an amiable nod. 'I don't believe we have met.'

'Lady Faulconer, my dear. You, of course, need no introduction. The whole ballroom is abuzz with you,' she said lightly, her voice breathy and smooth. 'And after such lovely dancing, I predict that by tomorrow you shall have conquered all of London.'

'Lady Faulconer?' Georgie did her best to hide her astonishment and managed to smile coolly at her supposed praise, but she couldn't help wondering why this woman was complimenting her. To be sure, 'Tess' was up to something. 'You're very kind. However, the credit must go to Lord Griffith. He is such an excellent dancer that he could make . . . nearly any partner look good.'

Tess eyed her sharply at her smooth parry, taken aback, it seemed, that she could give as good as she got.

Georgie bestowed a serene smile on the woman.

'Yes, well, my dear, you're not just *any* partner, are you?' the woman tried again, countering with a knowing smile.

'Hm?' Georgie looked at her inquiringly.

'You are a Knight and he is a Prescott,' his former lover explained. 'Your two clans have always been very much – in step.' Lady Faulconer glanced at the dance floor as the couples now separated into two lines for a country dance. Then she let out a worldly sigh. 'Ah, well, you certainly have a better chance of snaring him than anyone.'

Georgie managed an uneasy laugh. 'I am not trying to snare him,' she informed her.

'Well, maybe not. He is rather old for you.'

Georgie started to frown at the woman, but realized that she was merely being baited.

'Nevertheless, you will be instructed to marry him, mark my words,' Lady Faulconer said in a breezy tone. 'I warrant he and Hawkscliffe are drawing up the settlement already.'

Georgie was growing annoyed by the woman's presumptuousness, but she refused to show it, meeting her words with an idle laugh. 'My dear Lady Faulconer, I'm afraid you take me quite aback with your predictions. You must know something I don't,' she added dryly.

'I do,' she replied, staring intensely at the dancers. 'And that, my dear, is why I am talking to you now.'

'Ma'am?'

She looked at Georgie and her gray eyes gleamed. 'I can hardly be accused of doing many good deeds in my day, but somebody really ought to warn you about – that man.'

Georgie blinked. '*Warn* me?'

'I don't envy you, being put in this position. All the pressure the families will put on you to become his marchioness. And him! Ah, he is so cunning and smooth . . . I daresay you'll never know what hit you.'

'My lady, I don't understand,' she said with an uneasy laugh. 'Lord Griffith is a model of chivalry.'

'Do you think so? Well, you are young,' Lady Faulconer said indulgently. 'And you don't really know him yet. Not like I do.'

Georgie stared at her incredulously even as she cursed herself for letting this woman's lies draw her in by one iota.

'Far be it from me to criticize such a fine man,' she continued, 'but you see, my dear, Lord Griffith and I – oh, how shall I put it? We have, you might say, a history together.'

'What sort of history?' Georgie demanded bluntly.

'We have been . . . close for a number of years,' she admitted with a look of satisfaction. A look that told Georgie this woman had no intention of letting him go without a fight.

'How many years?' Georgie tested her, annoyed at the jealousy that had sprung up inside her like cactus needles.

'Four, I think,' she answered with another sideward glance that seemed to relish Georgie's discomfort. 'Long enough for me to know beyond all doubt that no matter what lucky lady stands by Griffith's side, the only woman he will ever truly love . . . is Catherine.'

Georgie paled as she stared at her.

Lady Faulconer looked bitterly toward the dance floor once again. 'His precious Catherine. Save yourself the heartache, sweeting,' she murmured, keeping her gleaming stare pinned on the dancers. 'Marry him if they insist on it, but you are too young and vibrant to throw your heart away on a man incapable of returning your love. Take it from one who knows.'

'What do you mean?' Georgie forced out, barely able to find her voice.

Lady Faulconer looked at her at last. 'For four years I tried to make him love me, to no avail, and I can't see why you should have any better success. We are both beautiful, intelligent, well-bred women, are we not? Of course we are. We are both worthy of him. But neither of us is *she*, and that is the problem.' Lady Faulconer paused. 'Haven't you noticed how he's always so cool and unfeeling? Why does nothing ever anger him? Why does he never quite – care? I'll tell you why. Because our dear Lord Griffith laid his heart inside the tomb with his dead wife, and he will never love again.'

Georgie felt a sharp pain in her lungs as if she suddenly couldn't get enough air.

'If you're wise, you will save yourself the misery of trying to love him. His wife was taken from him with the birth of their son, and all his deeds since then have made it very clear that no one else will ever come close to equaling her in his affections. I daresay he's in love with her still – a ghost! Well, there you have it.' Lady Faulconer snapped her fan shut. 'Now you can't say you were never warned.'

She sauntered away, while Georgie was left reeling.

CHAPTER 12

In dire need of a moment alone to sort out her crashing thoughts, Georgie walked out onto the flagstone terrace overlooking the garden. A few lanterns glowed atop wrought-iron poles, while billows of flowers fountained up from mossy urns here and there. A breeze rustled through the leaves of the surrounding trees, and above their boughs, stars glittered against a plum-dark sky, with a thin sliver-moon skimming over a wispy bank of clouds idling westward.

But despite the beauty of the June night, her mind was awash in confusion, her stomach in knots after Lady Faulconer's shocking claims. Shrugging her silk shawl higher around her shoulders to ward off the night's chill, she drifted over to stand by the low stone balustrade, then dropped her chin with a low exhalation.

Any fool could see that Lady Faulconer had an ulterior motive for saying those things, and she was not about to fall into that jealous harpy's cunning trap.

Still.

One simple fact was staring her straight in the

face. That day in the music room at Knight House, when she had asked Ian to explain his reasons for offering marriage, he had not mentioned *love*.

He had spoken of family and duty, desire and propriety, but had said not a word about being in love with her. And that, she knew now, was what her heart had so been longing to hear.

Was Lady Faulconer right, then? Did Ian love his late wife still? He never talked about the woman. Georgie had not even known her name was Catherine, let alone the fact that she had died giving birth to Matthew. Ian had said it was fever that took her.

Of course, puerperal fever killed thousands of women who never recovered from giving birth. Perhaps he blamed himself, for making her pregnant. She hated to think of him tormenting himself over that.

All she knew was that on the only two occasions he had mentioned his late wife, back in Janpur, his tone had turned clipped and remote and, Georgie recalled, he had quickly changed the subject. She knew he was not in the habit of discussing the things that mattered most – affairs of the heart. She had already discovered that on the topic of Matthew. The closer it cut to his emotions, the more closemouthed he was.

So, did that explain why he never spoke of Catherine? Had he loved her so much that, five years later, the wound was still too raw for him to stand the torment of speaking of his loss? And did he love her still, as Lady Faulconer had claimed? Maybe she should just come out and ask him, she thought. But she might just get an answer that she wasn't ready to hear.

Georgie was willing to fight for him, yes, but not if her efforts were doomed from the start. Of one thing only she was very sure. Unlike her friend Princess Meena – or her enemy Queen Sujana, for that matter – she could never submit to the notion of sharing her husband. She was no more willing to share Ian with a ghost than she'd have shared him with the likes of Lady Faulconer.

True love, in her view, was all or nothing. She wanted him entirely – the same way she would give herself – or not at all.

Just then, a cheerful male voice intruded on her thoughts.

'There you are! I've found her, chaps! She's out here!'

She turned around as one of the young gentlemen she had been introduced to earlier appeared in the open doorway with an eager grin. Alas, his name had slipped her mind.

'Oh, my dear Miss Knight! Have you forgotten? You promised me a dance!'

'He's found her! She's on the terrace!' other male voices called to each other from just inside the ballroom as the first young buck came rushing toward her.

In a moment she was surrounded by four young

fribbles with dandyish winker collars and slicked-back hair. All gleaming smiles and clean-shaven rosy cheeks, they reminded her for all the world of Adley, her lovable foppish suitor back in Calcutta.

'My dear young lady, are you quite all right? Egads, you look distressed!'

'Don't crowd her, you villain!'

'Do you need something to drink?' the third asked.

'I'm fine, truly,' she said, wondering if she might have to settle for one of them, in the end.

'What a relief! I thought you might no longer wish to dance with me!'

She turned to the first fellow, swallowing an impatient answer as the second one elbowed him aside. 'It's my turn, anyway, she promised me!'

'You're quite mistaken.' The first planted his fists on his waist. 'Miss Knight distinctly said that the next quadrille she would stand up with me. Don't you remember, Miss Knight? Tell him so, won't you please? He is the rudest fellow.'

'Me, rude? You're the one bothering her!'

'Don't listen to either of them,' another intervened with an oily smile, cutting between the first pair and stealing her hand. 'You're too beautiful to waste your time with them. Dance with *me*.'

'Oh, he's penniless! You know, you really are the most interesting girl to arrive in Town in ages—'

'*Gentlemen!*' a deep, furious voice boomed from over by the door.

Everyone stopped.

Georgie looked over, startled by the roar.

Ian loomed across the terrace, the brooding glower on his face sculpted by the lantern's glow.

Her new friends seemed to shrink like gregarious pups before a large, bristling lion.

'*What* . . . is the meaning of this?' he growled, glaring at the dandies one by one, for they really had been growing much too forward.

They stammered out a few haphazard excuses, then, blanching, fled in a herd, stampeding toward the door.

Ian turned his head, the fire-glow shimmering along his wide, tensed shoulders and patrician profile as he watched them scramble back inside. But when he eyed her again with a brooding look, Georgie took umbrage.

For heaven's sake, what was he scowling at *her* for? If anyone had cause to be upset about their rivals at the moment, it was she – first his horrid mistress, and then his sainted wife!

The sight of Georgiana surrounded by lusting suitors had raised the hackles on his nape and brought a wave of dark impulses surging up from the depths of a place inside him that Ian had never cared to experience again.

Though she stood alone at the balustrade now, he could not get the brazen image out of his mind, nor halt the rapid series of associations that it set off in the darkest recesses of his heart.

Never again would he let a woman trifle with him.

Humiliate him. Betray him. Break his trust.

Never.

And if this was how she was going to behave, holding court over a horde of panting men, then he wanted out. Before he was drawn in any deeper.

He could not go through it all again.

Don't forget, she's the niece of the Hawkscliffe Harlot.

Across the terrace, Georgiana set her hand on her hip and shot him a feisty look. 'Why are you scowling at me?'

Her frank question and insolent tone jarred him out of the past's dark hold over him and back to the shaky present.

Georgie, he reminded himself.

This was Georgie. His spicy little chili-pepper girl.

Not his lying wife.

He scrutinized her and was content after a moment that Georgie hadn't done anything wrong.

Yet.

'Hm?' Her chin came up a notch as she waited for his answer, her eyebrow raised.

If he was not mistaken, she looked like she was itching for a fight.

Well, that was odd. Of course, it might have something to do with the wrathful glower that he had fixed on her. Very well, he would force himself to stop scowling. This was Georgie, after all, not Catherine, and all things considered, his harsh, knee-jerk reaction to seeing her surrounded by men might be a tad out of proportion.

Reining in his very rare but very black temper, Ian drew a deep breath and willed his fury back down to mere displeasure, with a healthy dose of watchful suspicion thrown in for his health. He squared his shoulders, eased the anger out of his face, and brought his lady her drink. 'Forgive me,' he clipped out, offering her the goblet of Champagne punch. 'I was detained.'

'Something wrong?'

He knew he should not answer the question, so he evaded it. 'Yes, actually,' he murmured, frowning as he held up his glass to the light. 'There is a damned fly in my drink.'

A little winged insect that had fallen into his punch and was thrashing about among the floating bits of fruit, drowning in the sweet liquid.

'Ian,' she said.

He glanced at her, on his guard.

'You know that isn't what I meant.'

He knew he should just shut up, find a smile, deny all – he was an expert at that – but after brief consideration, silence proved beyond his power. He set the cup aside. 'It really is not wise for you to wander off alone without your chaperon,' he informed her in a seething tone, though highly controlled. 'You must be more observant, Georgiana. As I'm sure you are aware, you cannot enjoy the company of strange men without damage to your reputation. And your family's. And mine.'

'I came out here to get some air, for your information! I was standing here minding my own business when they joined me.'

'And what do you think they wanted?' he bit out in a lower, harder tone.

Her eyes flared, but she looked away from his intense stare and focused on the garden, refusing to meet his gaze. 'They said they wanted to dance with me.'

'Right.' He scoffed, but then a new thought struck him, and ice promptly formed in his core. 'Did they offend you?' he asked, poised to rip someone's head off if that was the case.

'No,' she replied with a snort.

'Frighten you?'

'Of course not,' she retorted, but the glance she sent him suggested that *he* might be doing so now.

Ian dropped his gaze, taken aback. A moment's clarity beamed into the dark chaos of his churning emotions like a ray of sun breaking out from amongst the thunderheads. Good God, what was happening to him? He clamped his jaw shut.

Georgiana glanced at him again, her bright-blue gaze wary and much too shrewd as she scanned his face.

Ian slowly picked up his glass, poured its contents, bug and all, over the railing, letting it water a flower bed, and then, with a highly civilized motion, set the empty goblet atop of the wide balustrade. 'We should return to the ballroom.'

'Yes,' she murmured, eyeing him with a guarded look. 'Let's.' Lifting the hem of her skirts, she whooshed around in a rustle of rose-colored satin and strode back across the terrace ahead of him, returning to the ball.

His brow furrowed, Ian followed a step behind her, but he was mystified as to how this night had suddenly gone so wrong.

The picture matched.

In the darkness, Firoz squinted at the locket in his hand, then peered in the window at the child. Cloaked in the shadows of the trees in the park opposite, he could see right into the diplomat's house.

The small boy, tousle-headed, barefoot, draped in a long white nightshirt, was being shepherded up to the nursery by the household servants. Firoz noted the portly old butler, two maids, and a sturdy footman. They did not worry him.

He had been doing this sort of thing for too long – though, in truth, the political abductions he had carried out for the royal family of Baji Rao did not normally involve a child. He did not like to sully his hands in dealings with youngsters, but for *her*, for his dark queen, he was willing to make an exception.

Closing the locket with the miniature portrait of Matthew Prescott, Firoz slipped it back into the pocket of the plain English-style clothes he had adopted to draw less attention to himself.

The ship on which he had crossed the seas had arrived from India only today. On the journey, he had attached himself to a wealthy traveler, following the usual Thuggee procedures – a florid English nabob who liked to hear himself talk.

Firoz was itching to kill him just to be relieved of having to hear him drone on about fox hunting, but somehow, he refrained. Sir Bertram was useful. No subject was dearer to the bloated Englishman's heart than the country house he meant to build in one of the Home Counties with his Indian fortune.

On the ship, Firoz had begged humbly for the privilege of serving such a wise and noble sahib, winning Sir Bertram's trust through the usual flattery. When he cooked for him his finest curry, playing the slavish role, eager to please, Sir Bertram had fallen right into his hands, declaring that it was the best curry he had ever tasted and Firoz must become his man.

Of course, Sir Bertram's other Indian servants suspected him immediately. They were afraid of Firoz, but the nabob would not listen to them.

One of the Bengalis had even tried to whisper to the old drunkard that Firoz had a dangerous look, but Sir Bertram had scoffed at him, eager to show off his human menagerie of exotics to all the English gentlemen back at his club in St James's.

Upon their arrival at the London docks, Firoz had stayed close to Sir Bertram's party, marveling at the cosmopolitan mix of men and women from every corner of the world. He must have heard a dozen languages merely in crossing from the ship's gangplank to the wagon that had come to pick them up, following along behind the baronet's fine coach.

For the edification of his favorite nautch girl, whom he had brought with him, Sir Bertram pointed out all the different sorts of people on the quay, with their odd costumes and strange practices. Silvery-blond Swedes, rugged Poles, and bearded Russians, intense-looking Germans, bickering Scots, and whistling Irish. Italians, Spaniards, and Portuguese arguing loudly. There were even dark-skinned Africans, a race of men Firoz had never seen before.

What a strange, chaotic world these English came from! he had thought. He was eager to return to the quiet of the desert mountains north of Janpur.

Once he had managed to orient himself a bit in his new surroundings, he had waited until nightfall and then had sneaked away from Sir Bertram's town-house, stealing out of the stables above which he had been housed. In the stables, he had discovered the coachman's map of London. Firoz had studied it closely, tracing his finger along the route to Lord Griffith's street address. He had already been given the location of the residence before leaving Janpur. Queen Sujana's maid-servant had procured it for him when she had delivered the poisoned fruit to the diplomat's room and paused to snoop among his things. Firoz knew exactly where he was going and had little trouble finding the place.

Now he took a good, long look at the park, which would offer ample cover for his escape when he made off with the child. Getting his bearings, it was only a matter of waiting for the proper time.

He made a mental note to arrange in advance for transport back to India. Queen Sujana had given him plenty of gold to pay for the voyage. Deciding to make his way back to Sir Bertram's before he was missed, he glided out of the shadows of a large elm tree, when suddenly a carriage came barreling down the darkened street and clattered to a halt in front of Lord Griffith's house.

Firoz leaned back into the shadows, staring as the marquess himself jumped down from the coach and slammed the door with an irritated air. Not pausing, Lord Griffith jogged briskly up the few front stairs and let himself in, waving off his butler.

A sinister smile curved Firoz's lips, but by now he had seen enough. He withdrew from his hiding place and headed back to Sir Bertram's stable.

Along the way, he mused on the probability of a violent clash with the marquess.

His original assignment from Queen Sujana had been to tail the British negotiator all along the road to Janpur, and then to spy on him once he had arrived at the palace. Thus, Firoz had had a fair chance to study Lord Griffith in depth.

Not once had he seen the man allow himself to be drawn into a fight, and though some of the royal guards at Janpur had privately, among themselves, taken this to mean that the silver-tongued diplomat was despicably unskilled in defending himself – indeed, they had laughed about it – Firoz was shrewder than that.

Experienced as he was in the ways of death, he knew a fellow killer when he saw one. For the sake of efficiency and ease of escape, he decided not to chance a clash with Lord Griffith if it could be avoided. He had no doubt that he could kill the man, but he might well come away injured, and that would slow him down.

Eager to be rid of this infidel country, Firoz only wanted to complete his mission and go home, back to Queen Sujana.

He worried for her in that tower.

Yes, he mused as he jogged lightly, tirelessly, through the darkness of this strange city. He must snatch the cub while avoiding the tiger. He would watch for his chance, and take the boy when the father wasn't there.

Radiant sunlight beamed through the high arched windows of the morning room the next day as Georgie sat at the breakfast table, poking morosely at the heavy fare of buttered eggs and cheese on the plate before her. Setting her fork down with a low sigh, she picked up her butter knife and jellied a piece of toast instead. But then, unsure if she could eat even that, given the tumult of her emotions, she tossed it to the edge of her plate and took a sip of tea. At once, she winced at its bitterness.

Propping her elbow on the table, she rested her cheek in her hand – bad manners, true, but she was alone except for the portrait of Aunt Georgiana, watching her from above the mantel with a frozen smile. Her cousins were right – they did look alike – Aunt Georgiana and she. Only Georgie had blue eyes, while those of the scandalous duchess were brown. Somehow the similarities between them brought her no pleasure today. Those boys last night believed or at least hoped that she was like Aunt Georgiana in the naughtiest sense, and as a result, Ian had been annoyed.

But I didn't even do anything!

Feeling wronged, she reached wearily for the dainty silver tongs and plopped another lump of sugar into her tea. Then she stirred idly with her spoon until the contents of her cup swirled like the thoughts in her mind.

What a dismal turn the ball last night had taken.

After Lady Faulconer's interference, everything had gone downhill. Ian and she had not quarreled outright, but somehow the night that had started with such happy enchantment had turned tense and cool, and ended disagreeably.

'More flowers, Miss!'

She perked up as a uniformed maid came sailing in, her rosy-cheeked face beaming under her white lace cap as she brought over another large bouquet for Georgie to inspect. 'Who's it from, Martha?' she asked eagerly.

'I haven't looked, Miss. Would you like to see the card?'

'Oh, yes, please!' She waved her over in a rush, her heart racing with sudden hope. Could they be from Ian?

Martha set the brightly colored bouquet on the table, fished the little linen card out from among the ravishing and fragrant blooms and sprigs of baby's breath, and handed it to Georgie.

Holding her breath, she accepted it and read.

A second later, however, her shoulders dropped and she handed the card back to Martha with a look of impatience. 'Who do you suppose "D" is?'

The maid grinned. 'Somebody you danced with at the ball, I should think?'

She just sighed and shook her head. 'I suppose.'

Martha eyed her in wonder, marveling at her lack of enthusiasm after her social triumph. 'Shall I put it with the others, then?' she asked uncertainly.

Georgie nodded with a vague wave of her hand. 'Thank you.'

When the maid had gone, Georgie sat for another moment staring at nothing, brooding on the question of whether or not Ian was angry at her.

Well, how the devil should it be that *he* was the one angry at *her*, when *she* was the one who had far greater reason to be cross?

He was the one who might be in love with a ghost!

It was so hard to tell sometimes how he really felt, though, admittedly, she was learning to read him better every day. That was how she was certain that when he had first stepped out onto the terrace last night and had seen those witless rakes crowding around her, he had been perfectly enraged.

Not that he would admit to it.

Oh, no. Not him.

Not the paragon.

But just because he didn't discuss it didn't mean the anger wasn't there. No, she quite feared there was something worse going on under the surface with him, and she wished she knew what it was.

Sometimes she almost felt as if he were hiding something. But then she realized she could hardly complain about Ian not telling her what *he* was feeling if she was not willing to come out and do the same.

Ugh, this whole line of thought was beginning to give her a headache.

She turned her spoon slowly, tapping it on the table in her musings. Telling him about her little visit from Lady Faulconer, asking him flat-out if there was any truth to her claims – it all sounded like a dreadfully risky and embarrassing ordeal.

If she dared broach the subject and Ian confirmed Lady Faulconer's story, admitted that his dead Catherine would always be first in his heart, Georgie knew her own would break. On the other hand, this uncertainty was worse. Surely she had to take the risk and find out how he felt about her versus Catherine. She had to ask and get it over with. She had to talk to him.

Suddenly too restless to sit in her chair anymore, she downed the last swallow of her tea and headed to her chamber. There had to be something she could do to keep from going mad until she heard from him – *if* she heard from him. Perhaps she'd buff her nails, she thought dully. Her mind was too cluttered, her heart too riled up to work at anything much more productive than that.

As she climbed the staircase, however, she heard the angry sobs and incoherent protests of a child in the throes of a temper tantrum. Instinctively concerned, she furrowed her brow and ran the rest of the way up the steps, following the sound down the wide marble hallway. The child's cries led her to the music room.

Glancing in the open doorway, she found a beleaguered nursery maid, Sally, trying to soothe a red-faced, outraged Matthew.

'Come, Master Aylesworth, is this any way for a young gentleman to behave?'

'I don't gotta listen to you! You're not my mother!'

'But you can't sit on the doggy's back! He's

an old dog, you'll hurt him!' The long-suffering girl had Matthew by the hand and was trying gently to coax him out of the room, presumably to take him up to the nursery to see his best pal, Morley.

Today, however, it was clear that Ian's heir wanted no part of the usual routine. He was thoroughly fixated on the duke's favorite dog, Hyperion, a huge, floppy Newfoundland of advanced years. The duke's loyal pet was lying near the corner of the sofa, watching Matthew's show of rage in amiable canine indifference, merely panting.

'Hyperion's too old for you boys to sit on his back anymore,' the maid was explaining for the tenth time when Georgie walked in to see if she could help. 'What if he gets vexed and bites you?'

'I want to ride him! He'd never bite! *Leave me alone!*' Pulling against her hand, the little lordling let out a screech of fury so loud it was a wonder he didn't shatter all the windows.

'Oh, dear, oh, dear!' Georgie exclaimed fondly, hurrying over to them. 'Matthew, darling, what is this little storm in a teacup?'

When the boy looked up and saw her, his whole mien changed in a heartbeat from rage to abject sorrow. Lord Aylesworth burst into tears.

'Oh, there, there, poppet.' Georgie went down on one knee and encircled him in her arms. She did not know what was bothering him, but she doubted that, in reality, it had anything to do with the dog. 'What's the matter, sweeting?'

'She yelled at me!' he wrenched out.

'Oh, no, she's only trying to make sure that you don't accidentally hurt Hyperion, Matthew. He's a grandfather doggy now. You have to treat him gently or you'll break his old bones, and then Uncle Robert would be very sad. Why don't we go up to the nursery and play with Morley now?'

'*Nooooo!*' He pushed against her, but she wouldn't let him go.

'Hush. Did you eat your breakfast? There's cinnamon crumpets in the morning room,' she whispered, ignoring his halfhearted kick.

'I don't want it!'

'Matthew.'

'Leave me alone!' His inscrutable needs were clearly not being met, and he was getting furious again.

'I know, let's go play with Noah's Ark! You can show me all the animals, and I'll tell you a story about an elephant.'

'No!' He pulled away from her with an angry little growl. 'I don't care about an elephant!'

'All right,' she said. 'Why don't we go out to the stable and visit the ponies?'

'I don't want to!' he bellowed. 'Why won't you listen to me?'

With a patience that amazed even her, Georgie gazed at him softly. 'What do you want then, my dearest boy?'

And then the truth came out.

'I – want – my – *papa!*' Matthew wailed. 'He never comes home! He never wants to play with me!'

'Oh, sweetheart.' Georgie pulled him into her arms and gave him a long hug. The poor little prince's loneliness was enough to break her heart. He was crying again quite angrily, and from her own childhood days, she knew exactly how he felt.

She simply held Matthew and let him cry it all out.

After a time, his sobs dwindled and he laid his overheated head on her shoulder. He seemed calm enough to try reasoning with him at last. 'Matthew, I know it seems like your father is always busy, but I promise you, he loves you to bits. It's just, well, he's a very important man, and in the grown-up world, people need his help solving their problems. Your papa helps people get along better, so they won't fight. It isn't an easy job. You should be very proud of him.'

'He never stays home. Pretty soon I know he'll leave again.'

'Oh, poppet.' With the boy's tears wetting her shoulder, Georgie glanced up to meet the anxious gaze of the nursery maid. 'Could you please find out for me if Lord Griffith is at home this morning?'

'Oh, His Lordship went to Parliament, Miss,' the girl replied, then blushed to confess the staff's gossip. 'Scott, the footman, told me so.'

'I see.' Georgie nodded her thanks, then pried Matthew back a bit and smiled tenderly at him.

361

'I have just had the most splendid idea, Matthew. Would you like to hear it?'

He nodded, drying his eyes. But first, Georgie took out her handkerchief and put it to his nose. 'Blow.'

He obeyed, and she tidied him up.

'My idea is this – why don't we go to Parliament and see your papa at work?'

The maid gasped. 'Go to Parliament, Miss?'

Georgie glanced at her. 'Yes. I daresay it would be most educational. There's a gallery there for citizens to come and listen, is there not?'

'Yes, Miss, the Stranger's Gallery, but they hardly ever let ladies in, and a child—?'

Georgie smiled sympathetically at Matthew as she smoothed his dark forelock. 'Yes, well, don't forget, this particular child will have a prominent seat in the Lords one day, and control who-knows-how-many pocket boroughs in the Commons. We'll just pop in for a moment or two, won't we? Just long enough for my little Lord Aylesworth to see that his papa really is hard at work, not just leaving him alone for no reason.'

She was confident that this would help the boy realize that he really was not being abandoned, even if sometimes it felt that way.

'How does that plan sound to you, my lad?'

Matthew had lit up. His eyebrows were arched halfway up his forehead and his mouth had formed an O.

Georgie laughed. 'I'll take that for a yes! Come on,

you rascal. Would you accompany us to Whitehall and arrange for one of the footmen to join us, as well?' she asked the maid.

'Aye, Miss! I'll tell the coach house to ready the gig, too.'

She nodded in thanks, then rose, holding Matthew's hand firmly. Watching her, his big, brown eyes were wide.

Those dark eyes must have come from Catherine, she thought, for Ian's eyes were green. She felt a twinge of dismay at her exclusion from the original Prescott trio, but she dismissed it.

What did it matter whose child this was? He was hurting, and she could help.

'Come along, my dear, we have to find your shoes.' She bent down and gave him a wink. 'We're going to have an adventure!'

CHAPTER 13

Matthew's mood had improved considerably by the time he and Georgie rode down busy Whitehall in the open gig, making their way to Westminster Hall beside the Thames, where the Parliament was housed.

The sun was out, the June breeze playing with the ribbons that tied Georgie's bonnet. Before long, the squeaky one-horse gig rolled to a halt in the bustling New Palace Yard, just as the mighty bells of Westminster Abbey across the way bonged once to toll the half-hour.

The driver stayed with the carriage, while Scott the footman helped the boy and the two women down. Then the four of them – Georgie and Matthew, footman and maid – walked toward the hodgepodge of ancient buildings that remained the medieval palace complex. Georgie glanced up at weathered gray pinnacles and octagonal towers before Scott hurried them into the two-story building known as the old Court of Requests, where the Lords convened on the upper floor.

Outside the formidable entrance, however, Georgie paused, bent down, and straightened

Matthew's little jacket. She took his cap off his head and gave it to him to hold.

'Hats off. Shoes on,' she reminded him sternly.

He giggled.

'Now then, my cub,' she said, smoothing his tousled hair, 'you must promise to be quiet as a mouse when we go in. If you're very good, we will go to Gunther's for some ice cream when we're done.'

'With Papa?'

'Maybe. Come, let's go have a look.'

He latched onto her hand and they marched into the stuffy lobby with Sally and Scott in tow. The place was quiet, and no wonder, that, she thought. Few among the populace cared about dull politics on such a balmy spring day. The servants retreated to stand respectfully by the dark-paneled wall while Georgie took a few steps into the chamber, leading Matthew by the hand. In short order, the Gentleman Usher of the Black Rod approached in his old-fashioned uniform of somber ebony, and inquired about her business. Georgie promptly explained who she was, and who Matthew was.

The man seemed disinclined to grant her request for a peek into the House of Lords via the Stranger's Gallery. Ladies were not usually allowed to witness the proceedings, he told her. But Georgie charmed and cajoled him; pleaded and promised to stay for only two minutes, three at the most; swore on the grave of her mother that she would not cause a disruption; reminded him of her lofty family connections; boldly described herself as betrothed to the Marquess of Griffith, and generally browbeat the stalwart fellow for Matthew's sake until her will finally won out over his.

Then she and Matthew were whisking along gleefully behind old 'Black Rod' through the lobby to the stairs, past a dim-lit library and committee rooms shabby with age, up to the second floor. The Gentleman Usher took a pointed look at his fob watch, prepared to time them, while Georgie gave Matthew a final warning to be silent once they went in. Then their escort opened the door and let the two of them go tiptoeing into the otherwise empty Stranger's Gallery.

Hand in hand, Matthew and she crept to the railing of the slender balcony and peered down upon the dazzling House of Lords, and its session in progress.

Massive chandeliers of brass lit the oblong hall, the far end of which was dominated by the crimson velvet canopy of state above the sovereign's gilt throne – empty at present. Above the mellow oak paneling, old tapestries in dark wood frames depicted the great defeat of the Spanish Armada.

Only half listening to the speakers' remarks on dry economic matters, Georgie eagerly scanned the rows of red seats, looking for Ian. She spotted her cousin Damien, Lord Winterley. He sat toward the back, because he was the newest-made earl. Robert claimed a very different position by the formal order of precedence, as one of the dukes of longest standing. Within each rank of the peerage, the lords' precedence was determined mainly by whose title was the oldest.

All the while, different men had been rising from their seats to speak their piece in quick succession, the seeming chaos of the process all directed by the bewigged Lord High Chancellor from his place of honor on the Woolsack. The old man banged his gavel once again. 'The Marquess of Griffith is now recognized.'

When Ian stood, Georgie and Matthew exchanged an eager grin. The topic could not have been drier; he criticized excessive government spending of late and forcefully protested some new policy of taxation. Georgie watched and listened, unabashedly admiring. The man was as much at ease before the peers of the realm as he was in cultured conversation over dinner.

'My learned and noble lords . . .' As he took his turn to expound upon the question, Ian's gaze wandered over the crowded hall and up to the Stranger's Gallery.

Georgie's heart beat faster.

He suddenly paused mid-sentence, spotting them. Astonishment flashed across his handsome face, and then, all of a sudden, Matthew could no longer hold himself back.

The boy jumped up and waved at him excitedly. 'Papa! There's my papa!'

'Shh!' Georgie hushed him, aghast after all the usher's admonitions. But as the child's happy outburst echoed through the chamber, the lords laughed and turned to look, craning their stiff necks.

'Order! Gentlemen, the house will please come to order,' the Lord Chancellor chided, though he, too, fought a grandfatherly smile.

Her face scarlet, Georgie plucked the beaming Matthew back from the rail and tugged him toward the door before they embarrassed Ian any further by having to be officially ejected.

Still, she could not help stealing one last glance at him over her shoulder. For the barest instant, their eyes met. His expression softened as he held Georgie's gaze.

'Lord Griffith, anything further?' the Lord Chancellor inquired.

Ian turned toward the Woolsack as though dazed. 'Er, no, sir. I yield the floor.'

'As you wish. Next we shall hear from Lord Forrester. Sir, proceed.'

As the next speaker rose, Ian brushed his coat-tails gracefully aside and sat back down, sending Georgie a rueful smile.

When the Lords adjourned for a short recess, Ian beckoned them down. Georgie led Matthew by the hand to see his father, but as soon as they entered the august chamber, the boy broke away from her and went hurtling toward his sire.

To her relief, Ian bent down and welcomed his son with open arms. Rather than scolding Matthew for his interruption earlier, he picked the boy up and held him proudly as the elder statesmen came over to meet and jest with the wee lad.

Matthew clamped his hands around his father's neck with a fastness that seemed to say that now that he'd finally got hold him, he was never letting him go.

Georgie nodded self-consciously to the gentlemen, some of whom she had met at the ball the previous night. Ian set Matthew down at length, and while the elderly lords looked on with indulgent smiles, he led his little heir by the hand over to the seat that his ancestors had held for hundreds of years, and which Matthew would one day occupy, in turn. Matthew climbed onto it and grinned at him, delighted with all the attention, especially from his father.

Georgie watched them fondly from across the venerable hall. When she saw Ian help Matthew down from the seat, she approached the pair. Ian spotted her and led Matthew back toward her.

They met up in the middle of the aisle. There, some of the old gents engaged the boy anew while Ian turned to her, still looking a bit mystified by their visit.

'This is a most unexpected surprise,' he murmured, while a few feet away, a trio of kindly old earls quizzed Matthew on how old he was.

'You don't mind, I hope?' she asked. 'He was having a bit of temper tantrum and he really just – needed to see you.'

'No, I'm glad you came.' Ian scanned her face with probing intensity.

Georgie faltered, looking away with a blush. 'We're, um, going to Gunther's next. Perhaps you'll be able to join us?'

'There's a vote next hour. I can't,' he said.

'I see.' She dropped her gaze.

An awkward pause ensued.

Her heart pounded. 'Matthew wasn't the only one who missed you,' she blurted out all of a sudden, lifting her shoulders with a hapless smile. 'I did, too.'

'You did?'

'I – wanted to make sure everything was – all right between us,' she said haltingly. 'Last night sort of . . . went off track.'

'That it did.' He nodded cautiously.

'I'm sorry,' she confessed in earnest quiet. 'I was a – a little rude to you – and you were right, anyway. I really should be more careful about not wandering off without, um, my chaperon. I would hate to embarrass my cousins or, especially, you.'

He was shaking his head. 'I was too quick to criticize. Honestly. You didn't do anything wrong. You just needed air. The ballroom *was* rather close.

I didn't think about the asthma. Were your lungs bothering you, then?'

'No.' Staring into his eyes, she shook her head slowly. 'It was . . . something else.'

His eyes narrowed in question.

Georgie glanced about at the busy chamber. 'Maybe we could talk about it later?'

'Of course,' he said at once. 'Are you all right?'

'Oh, yes – I'm fine.'

'I was planning on dropping by this afternoon, anyway,' he said. 'To give you your present. Only I wasn't sure if you still wanted to see me.'

She smiled tenderly at him. 'Of course I do.'

He returned her smile with a hesitant one of his own, then dropped his gaze and paused. 'Sometimes, you know, I can be a pompous arse.'

'No, you're not,' she chided, her soft laughter easing some of the tension between them.

He shrugged, but she reached out and captured his hand, giving it an affectionate squeeze, not caring who saw. His fingers curled around hers, so strong and gentle. Just that small touch felt so good, so reassuring.

People noticed, but she didn't care.

'Are you sure you're all right?' he whispered, holding her gaze with great warmth.

'I am now.'

'Well, very good, then. And you promise you'll tell me what's on your mind when I come over?'

She nodded, bracing herself for a conversation that was sure to test her courage.

'Whatever it is,' he added softly, 'we'll figure it out.'

I love you, she thought all of a sudden, staring at him with a lump in her throat.

But she gave him another firm nod.

A burst of laughter arose from nearby as Matthew came scampering back to them and attached himself to Ian's leg. 'Papa, are you coming with us to eat ice cream?'

He laid his hand on the child's head. 'No, pup, these gentlemen need me here. You go with Miss Georgie and I shall see you in a bit – I promise.'

'Yes, Papa.'

'And you will behave yourself,' he added, giving his son a no-nonsense look. 'I don't want to hear about any more temper tantrums. That is no way for a Prescott to behave.'

Georgie stifled a smile as Matthew shuffled his feet remorsefully.

'Sorry, sir,' he mumbled.

'It's all right,' Ian said, chucking him under the chin in affection. 'Very well, then, you two had better run along before all the ice cream melts.'

'Come along, Lord Aylesworth,' Georgie said cheerfully. 'Let's go see what flavors they've made for us today.' She took the boy's hand and sent Ian an intimate smile, which he returned with a golden glow lighting the depths of his eyes.

Matthew waved farewell to the elderly lords he had befriended, and Georgie tugged him by the hand out of the halls of power. Ian remained where he stood, watching them until they both were out of sight.

It was another two hours before the session was ended, the vote taken, the count announced. Ian's side had carried the motion, but he wasted no time on his colleagues' congratulations. He left Westminster in a hurry, ordering his coachman to take him at once to Knight House.

When he arrived, Mr Walsh, Hawk's stately butler, informed him that Miss Knight was waiting for him in the music room. Thrusting his top hat and walking stick into the old fellow's waiting hands, Ian strode across the marble foyer to show himself up, but as he started toward the stairs, the entrance to the ante-room caught his eye.

Through the open doorway, he spotted a profusion of flowers, as though the adjoining room had been turned into some dashed florist's shop.

He turned abruptly to the butler. 'Egads, Walsh, did somebody die?'

'Er, no, sir. The flowers arrived today for Miss Knight. Admirers from the ball,' he added in a confidential whisper.

'What, all of them?' he exclaimed.

'You are welcome to inspect them for yourself if you desire, my lord.'

Ian frowned at him, then marched over to have a look. He nearly sneezed upon stalking into the ante-room, so thickly did the cloying floral perfumes hang upon the air.

With a faint scowl, he snatched the card off the nearest dozen roses and read it. His frown deepened. A survey of the various bouquets revealed a formidable tally of rivals for Georgiana's affections: one duke, eleven earls, and two viscounts.

Bloody hell.

In the doorway, Mr Walsh clasped his white-gloved hands behind his back and lifted his chin with unconcealed pride in the legions the newest member of the family had conquered.

Ian pursed his lips and looked at him without a word.

'It is fortunate that milord has always been a sporting man,' the imperious butler remarked with an impertinent lift of his bushy gray eyebrows.

Ian snorted, prepared to forgive the cheeky observation, since, after all, Mr Walsh had known him since he was Matthew's age. 'Damned lucky I didn't come empty-handed.'

'Indubitably, sir. Good luck,' he added, staring forward once more with a polite show of indifference.

Ian gave the savvy old fellow a resolute nod, then left the entrance hall and bounded up the stairs.

When he stepped into the music room above, he found his fair friend bathed in a pool of sunlight from the expanse of sparkling windows along the back wall.

She was on the floor, clad in strange clothes, her willowy limbs contorted in a bizarre position.

Ian tilted his head in perplexity as she unfolded her legs and pushed up into an upside-down pose.

What in blazes . . . ?

Her dainty feet pointed straight toward the ceiling. Her hands braced the curve of her back, snug and secure, and the slim column of her body was supported by her elbows, forming a sort of tripod.

As a man who woke up most days feeling like his joints were made of iron, he thought it looked like some cunning form of torture, but her expression appeared one of perfect repose. Her wispy, Indian-style shirt had fallen down just a bit, exposing a few inches of her flat, ivory belly. Likewise, the loose black leggings that hugged her trim figure had also descended, giving him a scandalous view of her darling ankles.

Her face was turning red from being upside-down as she managed to turn her head a little. 'Ian!' she greeted him in a cheerful burst of pleasure. 'Come in! Oh, and shut the door, would you? I don't want my cousins to think I'm eccentric.'

He laughed in spite of himself, fearing she might be a little late for that. Nevertheless, he obeyed; then he sauntered over to her with a growing smile, tilting his head again to meet her upside-down gaze.

'What in the devil are you doing, girl?'

'I'm playing the piano. What does it look like?'

'Torture, actually.'

'It's yoga, you silly-head. I told you it's my saving grace, remember?' She closed her eyes again with a look of great tranquility. 'You should try it sometime. It would help you not to be . . . so stiff.'

'I thought you liked me stiff,' he purred as he pulled off his morning coat and dropped into the armchair nearest her.

She laughed. 'You are wicked.'

'You have no idea,' he replied in a low murmur. If only she knew where his errant thoughts were wandering to now . . . He found himself inspired by her impressive flexibility. 'Isn't that painful?'

'It's wonderful,' she declared, then rolled slowly out of the shoulder stand and lay flat on her back.

Lying there, stretched out on the plush carpet, she looked so soft and inviting – temptation incarnate, with her skin aglow, her eyes as blue as the sky. Leaning forward in the chair, he let his gaze travel over her in rapt appreciation.

She reached a hand up to him; he linked his fingers through hers. Instead of helping her up, he joined her on the floor, lowering himself to his knees and smoothly straddling her. He lowered himself atop her and instantly claimed her mouth in a deep, unhesitating kiss, claiming her anew.

She moaned softly and wrapped her arms around him. Parting her lips, she returned his kisses with eager passion, her tongue swirled, mating with his. Her hands were warm and gentle as they cupped his face, stroked his hair. Ian slid his forearm under her, holding her in ardent hunger.

The nice part about fighting, he thought, was that then you got to make up. He splayed his palm beneath her long, luxurious tresses, cradling her head upon the floor. Georgiana kissed him again and again, intoxicating him with the warm, wet sweetness of her mouth and the sincerity of her welcome.

His heart was pounding, for her kisses told him more than any words could have expressed that he really had no reason to be jealous. Sending flowers was all very well, but those other chaps were wasting their time. Her every touch and kiss and sigh assured him she was his and his alone. He kissed her neck, then turned his head to kiss the lean, fine, womanly arms that held him.

All the while, she tormented him with her lithe body's supple undulations. His need for her climbed and his kiss deepened as she wrapped her legs around him. Then he groaned against her mouth as she raked her nails down his back.

The woman needed bedding, and how he longed to give it to her! This was not what he had come here to accomplish, but every time he touched her, it was nearly impossible to stop.

He forced himself, reining in their passion and resting his forehead against hers. If Hawk walked in on this, he wouldn't be pleased. Rolling around on the floor with his friend's luscious young cousin would not be looked upon as suitable behavior, considering she was under the duke's protection while she dwelled beneath his roof. Debauching her across the park at his own residence, well, that was easier to justify.

Georgiana kept kissing him, but Ian did his best to curb her exuberance. 'You are,' he vowed, panting, 'the most delicious angel.'

'*More.*' She grabbed the back of his head and pulled him down roughly again.

With a husky laugh at her fiery demand, he obliged, powerless to resist her. God, he must have died and gone to heaven. Nevertheless, he thought of one way to bring his passionate nymph back down to earth before their mischief was discovered by others in the household. 'Don't you want your present?' he whispered in her ear.

She paused, nibbling thoughtfully at his cheek. 'You brought it?'

'It's in my pocket.'

'What else is in your pocket, Ian?' She reached down with a wicked laugh and grasped his hard cock.

'Georgiana Louise!' he exclaimed with startled laughter. 'I meant in my coat pocket, you incorrigible minx.'

'I'd rather have this instead.'

She squeezed him and he groaned.

'You are . . . so very bad.'

'Don't you know it's in my blood?' she whispered.

'So it would seem.' With a wince of delight, he

let her hand wander, but only for a moment longer. Pulling himself away from her, he went up onto his knees and reached for his coat, thrusting a hand into the inside breast pocket.

She sat up, beaming at him.

'Close your eyes and put out your hand,' he ordered.

She obeyed, and he indulged in simply staring at her for a second, admiring those ridiculously long, coal-black lashes.

What a pretty thing she was, with such an innocent quality. It never failed to surprise him every time he noticed it.

'Are you still here?' she prompted impatiently.

'I'm here, princess.' He bent and pressed a kiss into her waiting palm, and then replaced his lips with his gift. The light silvery tinkling sound gave it away even before she opened her eyes. When he placed the silver anklet in her hand, her cobalt eyes flew open wide.

'Ian!' She looked at it joyously. 'You got me new bells!' All of a sudden, she pushed up onto her knees and flung her arms around his neck.

He held her in return, encircling her slim waist. 'I never thought you should change, Georgiana,' he told her in a husky whisper. 'You're perfect just the way you are.'

'Oh, Ian.' She clung to him, her arms twined around his neck in a long, heartfelt hug.

He did not think he had ever been hugged so thoroughly in his life. Her unbounded affection still abashed him sometimes, but he could get used to this, he thought as he smiled to himself. 'Here,' he murmured to her at length. 'Let me put them on you.'

Pressing a kiss to his cheek, she released him from her embrace only with reluctance, but then sat obediently on the floor again. When Ian sat back on his haunches, Georgiana stretched one dainty bare foot across his lap in the most provocative fashion.

He sent her a satyric grin, enticed by the flirty loveliness of her feet. He took hold of her heel gently and deliberately tickled her foot with a slow, light stroke of his fingertip along the arch of her sole, but she bit her lip, refusing to let herself laugh. He pinched her toe and then abandoned their little game for some other time, resting her foot on his thigh.

Taking from her hand the intricately wrought chain of tiny bells, fresh from the silversmith's shop, he draped the delicate chain around her extremely alluring ankle and fastened the clasp.

'*Voilà*,' he said, flicking it to make the bells jingle.

She swung her knee and gave her new bauble a try. 'Ah! It sounds even prettier than the original!' Giving him a beaming smile, she removed her foot from his lap and leaned back, planting her hands behind her as she gazed at him. 'What an utterly thoughtful gift, Ian. How kind you are to me.'

'You were being too hard on yourself.'

'I really can't tell you how much it means to me that you feel that way. That you truly accept me as I am. Let's face it, after all, I am a – bit odd; I'm perfectly well aware of it.'

He laughed.

'Maybe I am an acquired taste,' she said. 'I *try* to get along with everyone, but still . . . I never quite felt like I fit in anywhere until I met you.'

He laid his hand on her knee in a soft caress. 'Not everyone will understand you, but I do.'

Without warning, she leaned toward him, cupped his jaw, and pressed a firm but tender kiss to his lips.

His heart clenched, adoring her, but somehow he maintained his decorum. The way she left him dazzled, it took him a moment to recall the purpose of his visit.

She sat back slowly, stroking the side of his leg with her bare foot.

Pure temptress, even when she wasn't trying.

He cleared his throat a little. 'So, what did you, ah, want to talk to me about? I thought it was your asthma giving you trouble last night, but you said today that it was, er, something else that had been bothering you.'

'Right.' She lowered her gaze, nodding. 'Oh, this is rather difficult.'

He frowned. 'What is it?'

'Remember last night after we danced, when you went to get me some punch?'

He nodded.

'When you were gone, Lady Faulconer introduced herself to me.'

He froze. 'What did she say?'

Georgiana hesitated, looking intensely uncomfortable. She took a deep breath, and then visibly forced herself to reveal what had been gnawing at her. 'She claimed that even if we married, you would never love me because your heart died with Catherine.'

'I see.' Ian's eyebrows arched high as he absorbed this. 'How perfectly absurd. And you believed her?'

'I didn't know what to believe! That's why I went outside, to think. I was quite confounded by her revelations.'

'Not revelations, lies. What other lies did she tell you?'

'That's all. That's mainly it.' Her cheeks were a deep shade of rose, her blue eyes full of youthful vulnerability. 'Lady Faulconer said you never loved *her*, so that meant you would never love me, because of Catherine. But if you *can't* love me, Ian, I'm not sure I even want to know it. Perhaps you should not tell me, because I'm so in love with you, I don't think I could bear it—'

'Shh.' He stopped her lips with his fingertip and gazed at her in amazed, welling joy.

Her eyes were wide.

If he was not mistaken, she had just said she loved him.

He lowered his touch to her chin, capturing it gently between his finger and thumb. As he

382

stared at her, a wave of awed splendor rose from the deepest core of his being. 'My darling,' he said very softly, 'I never loved either of them the way I love you.'

He heard her soft intake of breath and watched her blue eyes fill with agonized hope.

'You – love me?' she whispered.

He couldn't take his eyes off her. The words flowed from his lips, straight from his heart. 'Georgiana, I loved you from the first moment I saw you go tearing through the spice market on that white horse. I had no idea who you were, except that you were the boldest, maddest, most beautiful creature I had ever seen. And now that I do know you, you're a thousand times more beautiful still.'

She let out a wonder-struck laugh, brilliant tears suddenly shining in her eyes like diamonds. Without warning, she launched herself into his arms, hugging him hard, while her frantic whispers spilled joyously into his ear. 'Marry me. Yes. I want to marry you, Ian. I want us to be together always.'

He grasped her shoulders and pushed her back to arm's length. 'You're saying yes? You'll be my wife, truly? You've come to your senses at last?'

'Yes!' She nodded zealously. 'Yes, I do want to marry you! I love you, Ian. I love you, and if you still want me, then nothing can keep us apart.'

He stared at her, imprinting on his memory exactly the way she looked right now, in this moment, so that he would never forget the love on her face, his future in her eyes.

'If?' he whispered. Then he drew her slim body into his arms and held her hard.

He could feel her trembling, and he kissed her cheek in choked silence. 'You are so dear to me,' he said brusquely, closing his eyes.

A long time ago, he had given up hope that real love could ever come into his life.

Now he had this beautiful, magical woman in his arms. Somehow she had become as precious to him as his own flesh and blood.

He kissed her head, trying to becalm the towering seas of emotion in his breast. The pitch and swell of it was still so unfamiliar. So much happiness made him feel odd.

She pulled back a small space and smiled at him, caressing his cheek.

She started to speak, but then a distracted look flicked over her face.

She furrowed her brow and turned toward the window. 'Do you hear that, Ian? That dog?'

As soon as she said it, he registered in vague annoyance the sound of a dog's vicious barking. It sounded as though it was coming from just outside Knight House.

He glanced toward the window, then looked at her again. 'Ah, never mind that,' he began with a smile, but then he stopped, listening more intently. He went very still. 'That sounds like Hyperion.'

God knew, Hawk had had that dog forever. It had been a pup with them when they were boys.

He suddenly frowned. 'That dog hasn't barked since King George was last in possession of his wits,' he murmured.

Something's wrong.

'Let me check on that.'

She released him without argument as he rose and crossed to the bank of windows. He scanned the courtyard below.

Sure enough, the big old dog, normally so placid, was racing back and forth along the tall, black wrought-iron fence that girded the grounds of Knight House. Good Lord, the Newfoundland was barking through the bars and snarling like a rabid wolf, trying to get at something.

Or someone.

Ian's eyes narrowed. *Intruder?*

At once, his stare swung to the leafy park, trying to spot the object of the dog's frenzy.

His gaze homed in on a dark-clad man, and then he froze.

Horror spiked through him.

Disbelief.

Matthew.

'Ian, what's wrong?' Georgie cried as he whirled away from the window, ashen-faced, rushing for the door with his heart in his throat. He barely heard the question.

'Ian!'

'He's got my son.'

'*What?* Who?'

He was already out the door, not wasting one second to explain.

Barreling into the hallway, he flew down the curving stairs and through the marble entrance hall, bursting out the front door.

'My lord?' Mr Walsh exclaimed, running out after him in alarm. 'What is amiss?'

'Send for the constable!' he shouted as he pounded toward the wrought-iron gate, Armageddon in his eyes.

CHAPTER 14

What in the world –? Someone had Matthew?

Throwing her Indian tunic on over her yoga clothes, Georgie stole the briefest of glances out the window bay but saw nothing strange except the frenzied dog. She was not sure what was going on, but she had never seen Ian react like that before.

Still barefoot, she rushed out of the music room mere seconds after him. When she arrived outside, she found the normally placid courtyard of Knight House in a state of frantic commotion. The servants had left their posts, Hyperion was still barking loud enough to wake the dead, and from inside the house she could hear Bel screaming for Robert to help them.

'It were a Gypsy, ma'am!' one of the maids nearby was shrieking. 'A Gypsy's tried to steal the little master! Sally and Scott were playin' hide-and-seek with him in the park and now they've vanished!'

'*What?*' Looking past the chaos to scan the park, Georgie suddenly spotted a wiry, dark-clad man in a low-brimmed hat as he came tearing out from behind a stand of trees that had obscured their view. Horror seized her as she saw that he had lifted Matthew off his feet and with one arm hooked roughly around the boy's waist, the other clamped over his mouth, the man was running with him, full speed, toward a waiting horse.

Matthew struggled, trying to kick his way free as his feet dangled well above the ground. Then Ian burst into view only a few steps behind them, and gaining. She was sure her heart had stopped as she watched him sprinting across the green in an explosive burst of speed.

He dove at them just a few yards away from the horse, tackling the man with the brute force of a runaway stagecoach. Marquess, boy, and would-be kidnapper all went crashing down to the soft green turf.

Ian grabbed Matthew, picked him up bodily by the back of his short coat, and tossed him out of the heap, shoving him toward Knight House. '*Run!*'

The boy went flying clear of the fight and sprawled on all fours in the grass, but bravely stumbled to his feet and obeyed his father's order. Sheer panic stamped across his face, Matthew went racing toward safety as fast as his little legs could carry him, but then he halted in childish uncertainty, turning back to look for his father.

Seeing his sire engaged in a brutal fight, the

five-year-old began crying as he stood alone in the park.

Georgie was already on her way. Jagged pebbles under her bare feet turned to soft grass as she raced toward him, her sights fixed on nothing else.

She didn't even hear the shouts, or look for Ian, or notice her cousin Robert tearing past her with a rifle, let alone his order to her to get back inside. Her instincts heeded nothing but the crying child, and nothing deterred her until she reached his side and had the small boy in her arms. Not even stopping to ask him if he was all right, she picked him up and ran back to Knight House with a strength she did not know she possessed.

Ignoring her straining lungs, Georgie did not stop until they were inside the gates again. Mr Walsh and the children's head nurse crowded around at once, the heavy-set woman taking the boy from her. Georgie's knees were wobbly, but when Mr Walsh urged her to come back into the house, she refused.

Gripping the fence, she stared through the wrought-iron bars at Ian in savage pursuit of the would-be kidnapper once again. The man had gotten to his feet and was trying to reach his horse, but Ian clearly had no intention of letting the blackguard get away. He was taller, with longer strides, and more than that, he was enraged.

As she watched their renewed chase, riveted, something deep inside Georgie suddenly prayed he would not catch the man. Ian had rushed out with no weapon, and what if that low criminal had a gun?

Robert, fortunately, had managed to grab a weapon before leaving the house and now rushed to Ian's aid. With an innate anticipation of each other's movements ingrained in them from the rugby fields of their boyhood, Robert took up a position to head the man off. Bringing the rifle up smoothly to his shoulder, the duke took aim at the criminal's chest, but with Ian hot on the man's heels, just a few steps behind, he held his fire.

Caught between the two, the criminal veered to the left trying to escape the pincers they had created for him, but this shift gave Ian the two-second gain he needed.

Once more, his relentless pursuit ended with them both slamming down onto the earth. But when the assailant whipped out a knife and slashed at Ian with it, Georgie's mind was taken right back to the horrific battles she had gone through with her brothers in fleeing Janpur.

The hair on the back of her neck stood on end. Dear God, Ian was a diplomat. A peacemaker. Unlike Derek and Gabriel, he had not spent the past few years in constant combat. Sheer dread paralyzed her. *Oh, please, don't take him away from me.* Dizzy with horror, she clutched the bars of the fence harder, neither able to watch nor to turn away.

Robert ran over and planted himself nearby as

Ian arced his body clear of another wild swing of the villain's dagger.

'Drop the knife, you bastard, or I'll shoot you where you stand!' the duke roared, taking aim again.

But Ian grabbed the man's wrist on his next swift lunge and pivoted smoothly, jerking him off balance. He banged the man's forearm over his knee with a shattering blow that made him release the dagger with a bellow of pain. He elbowed the man in the face, and a closer struggle ensued.

Though Robert stood at the ready, he dared not pull the trigger for fear of hitting his friend.

With both opponents now reduced to bare fists, their struggle devolved into the most brutal fight that she had ever seen.

Though Georgie had noticed the man's jet-black hair and swarthy countenance, she did not realize just what they were dealing with until she heard the would-be kidnapper let out a curse – in Marathi.

Her jaw dropped as it sank in now that Queen Sujana's hatred had followed them all the way across the sea. With awful memories of the battles that had left poor Major MacDonald dead and her brother wounded, Georgie grasped the fact that the man whom Ian was fighting was no Gypsy child-stealer, as the maid had naively claimed, but one of the maharani's trained assassins!

Just then, Mr Walsh appeared by her side and tried to pry her away from the fence before she saw something far more terrible. 'Miss, you must go back inside!'

'Leave me alone!' she cried, wrenching free of him just in time to see the Indian attacker curve his hand into a hooked claw and gouge at Ian's neck as if to tear his throat out.

But a change had come over her gentlemanly diplomat.

Savagery in him had come unleashed. His knees were muddy from the turf, his shirt was torn, his face streaked with a smear of blood, his hair wild. The angry flush in his cheeks made his green eyes burn with an unholy light.

He had jested in the past about the brutal Norman warlords in his ancestry, but now he proved their spirit in his blood as his vicious fight against the maharani's agent climbed toward a crescendo.

Kneeling on top of his kicking, thrashing quarry, pinning him down with his greater weight, Ian planted his knee across the assassin's neck as though to hold him immobile until the constables arrived. But then the Indian man wrapped his powerful hands around Ian's throat in a crushing stranglehold, striving to choke the life out of him. He tried to pry the hands away, but as the seconds ticked by, nothing could dislodge their ruthless grip.

He drew his elbow back and smashed his fist into the man's face half a dozen times in lightning-fast succession, but the massive blows with which he battered his opponent barely stunned the hard-ened killer.

As Ian gasped for air, his face turning redder, he must have realized that his time was running out. Georgie watched the scene unfold with horror, knowing all too well from her own battles with asthma that a person couldn't live for more than a few moments without air.

Then she saw Ian reach for the castoff knife that he had forced his foe to drop earlier. It lay on the ground nearby.

Still holding the man down and fighting for breath, his searching hand scrabbled around for the weapon, and when he found it, his fingers flicking around its hilt, he wielded it without a shred of mercy. Arcing the knife upward, he plunged the blade into the base of the assassin's throat.

He left it there, wrenching back to gasp for breath as the assassin's hands suddenly fell away from his neck.

The man stopped flailing; his body went limp. He hadn't even had time to scream, and in seconds, he was dead.

Georgie looked on in open-mouthed disbelief, relieved to the core of her soul, but scarcely able to comprehend that the diplomat Marquess of Griffith had just outfought a trained assassin and had slain him in broad daylight, there in the middle of Green Park.

Still more about him that I didn't know . . .

Ian moved off his dead attacker, and the lifeless body rolled a bit to be rid of his weight. Still kneeling on the ground, he sat back on his haunches and rested his hands on his thighs; he dropped his head back, his chest heaving.

Hawkscliffe walked over to them slowly and nudged the prone man with the muzzle of his rifle.

The two lords looked at each other in grim silence, remaining like that, frozen in a fearsome tableau, as the stout-hearted constables came rushing onto the scene with Mr Walsh hurriedly pointing the way.

Georgie stayed where she was, ashen-faced, both hands pressed against her mouth.

Throughout the park, frightened onlookers were staring from a safe distance.

Mr Walsh finally got a leash on Hyperion and made one of the footmen drag the still-agitated dog back inside. In a sharp tone, the butler ordered the rest of the staff back to their posts as well.

Meanwhile, Bel hurried over to Georgie and curved a comforting arm around her waist. 'Come, dear. Let's go inside.'

'He killed him,' Georgie told her.

'I know. It's all right. It's over now.'

'Captain! Two bodies here!' one of the constables called from over by the thicket around the stand of trees.

Georgie let out a sob at the grim discovery, but Bel tried more firmly to bring her inside. 'Come, now. We've seen enough.'

'No, I have to talk to Ian. Just let me see if he's all right.' She did not wait for Bel's response, but slipped back out through the wrought-iron gate and ran into the park, toward the knot of men loitering near the body – Ian, Robert, and a few constables.

As she approached, her gaze swept over Ian's big, powerful form, scanning for wounds. He was a bit bloodied and bruised, and still trembling slightly in the aftermath of violence, but he appeared for the most part unscathed.

'I know his face from Janpur,' he was saying to the others as she joined them.

'What's left of it, y'mean,' one of the constables muttered as they covered up the body and then carried it off without ceremony to be loaded into their wagon.

'Don't worry, Griff, we're going to get to the bottom of this,' Robert said, the rifle now resting across his shoulder.

'You've got to get Georgiana and Matthew out of London,' he answered forcefully. 'Queen Sujana tried to have me poisoned before I left Janpur. Her agents raided my room and stole this locket to help them locate Matthew. Don't you see what this means? We killed her son and now she's come after mine. Who knows how many more of her men she's sent after us? Her agents nearly killed Gabriel. I thought it had ended there, but I see now I was wrong. My son's in danger, Hawk. So's your cousin. I want them far away from here, under guard. You have to take them someplace safe.'

'Damien's estate ought to be remote enough. It's only a few hours from here. You know how to get there?'

'Yes.'

'I'll send Lucien to you, as well. He's always useful in these situations.'

Ian gave him a grim nod, then coughed and rubbed his throat, still recovering from his near-strangulation. 'Frankly, I'd welcome the help.'

'My lord, would you please come with us now, sir?' the brawny captain of the constables spoke up. 'You're going to have to come with us and answer a few questions.'

Ian nodded at the man, but then noticed Georgie's presence. 'One moment, please.'

'Aye, sir.' The captain allowed this, but still eyed him suspiciously.

Her cousin Robert gave her a taut smile of re-assurance as she passed him. Georgie suddenly remembered she was wearing Indian garb, not exactly decent by London standards. That would explain the odd looks from the constables.

Ian and she walked a few paces away from the others.

'Are you all right?' she whispered.

'I'm fine.'

'Your lip's bleeding.'

He wiped the blood away, glanced at the trace of it on his hand, and then eyed her uncertainly.

'Hawk's going to take you to Winterhaven. Damien's estate. I've, er, I've got to stay in Town for a while longer until all this has been straightened out.'

'Are you under arrest?'

'I don't know.'

She glanced around and saw that the constables were already taking down the names of the onlookers who had been strolling in the park when the whole thing had happened. Another of the officers was going through the saddlebag strapped to the horse that the assassin had tried to use for his escape.

Ian followed her glance, but when she looked at him again, he stared into her eyes, his expression fierce but tormented. 'I'm sorry – for this,' he forced out in a raw voice.

'No – it's all right.' She reached out and started to touch him, but something stopped her. A newfound uncertainty about him.

He saw her hesitate and closed his eyes with a stunned look, as though she had slapped him. He lowered his head. 'Go,' he whispered.

'Ian, I didn't mean—' She reached for him again, more bravely, but he pulled away.

'Look after my son, will you?'

'Of course,' she whispered with a fervent nod. 'We'll be waiting for you. Both of us.'

His nod was brooding and remote. She knew he had already shut her out as he turned away. 'I'll see you when I can.'

★ ★ ★

Short of harm befalling someone he loved, the worst thing Ian could have possibly imagined happening to him had just occurred.

He had snapped, his dark side on display for all the world to see. He felt exposed . . . as a monster, capable of all the same bestial, warlike impulses in mankind that he struggled to curb and channel to positive ends through his diplomatic efforts.

But what choice had he had?

The threat to Georgiana and his son had ruptured all the stiff restraints with which he had so conscientiously controlled his own nature for so long. When would he ever learn that emotions could never be trusted? Every time they came pouring out, it seemed as if something bad happened.

Well, it was done, he thought in disgust, and it couldn't be called back now, could it? The cat was out of the bag – the tiger out of his cage.

In a way, he was almost relieved not to have to hide anymore. Finally, he could breathe, as if he'd been freed from a too-starched cravat. He rubbed his throat again, still jarred by how close he had come to death. Indeed, if he had not loosed the beast inside himself to destroy the maharani's agent, his son would have been stolen from him for God-only-knew what purpose, and Georgiana would probably have been the next to have been killed, since it was she who had exposed Sujana's treachery.

But in his rage, Ian had prevented that from

happening. This gave him a certain dark satisfaction. Now if Queen Sujana's agents came after his family again, he'd be fully prepared to meet death with death.

He only hoped that his victory against the assassin had not cost him what mattered most: Matthew's trust. And Georgiana's love.

He was willing to do anything to hold on to these two. Whatever it took. What good was anything if they didn't feel safe around him?

But he had seen the way she shrank from him, and he was well aware of her non-violent views. He could not bear for her to look at him with the same horror and fear in her eyes that he had seen on Catherine's face in those last few seconds before her death.

The constable summoned him then, and they left Green Park. Ian was taken into the magistrate's closed chambers, where he spent the rest of the afternoon answering the same questions over and over again for a parade of officials from Bow Street and the Home Office.

Meanwhile, the Knight brothers' close-knit unit clicked into action. Hawk and their good friend Viscount Strathmore used their rank to get in to see various Eastern ambassadors around London, trying to find out whether they knew anything about this plot, or Queen Sujana or her brother Baji Rao, or if Firoz had contacted them.

Lucien, meanwhile, came to look after Ian's interests during the interrogation. A fellow agent of the Foreign Office whose specialty had been intelligence gathering, Lucien had gone on inactive status as an operative ever since his marriage, but in the meantime, he had made many friends at Bow Street. He liked to keep his spy skills honed by helping the Bow Street Runners solve the occasional baffling mystery. He was the right sort of friend to have on hand at a time like this.

As for Lucien's twin brother, Damien, Colonel Lord Winterley, it was to his Berkshire country house that Georgie and Matthew had been taken. Bestowed on him by a grateful nation after his extraordinary service in the war against Napoleon, his beautiful estate of Winterhaven was ideally located, not too close and not too far from London. What made Winterhaven especially safe for a woman and child in danger was that the war hero Damien had established a racing stable there, which he preferred to man with battle-hardened veterans from his regiment, his own soldiers who had served under him in the war.

Lord Alec, the youngest of the Knight brothers, had gone with them for added protection along the road. Alec was also extremely handy with a sword, thanks to the constant duels he had fought in his days as the wickedest rakehell in London. A perfect foil for all of Damien's stern, disciplined command, Alec was sharp and daring, with the soul of a gambler, although since his marriage, he no longer touched the cards or dice.

With all this help while he was detained, Ian

could enjoy at least some peace of mind that Georgie and Matthew would be quite safe until he was able to join them.

When that might be was difficult to say.

The interrogation dragged on. Finally, Lucien got hold of his colleagues from the Foreign Office, who verified the link between the dead foreigner and Ian's last diplomatic mission. His claim that the man had been Queen Sujana's agent was backed up by the fact that his miniature portrait of Matthew, which had been missing since he left Janpur, had turned up in the dead man's pocket. It also helped that several eyewitnesses in the park had seen the whole thing, and their testimony corroborated everything Ian had said.

Then the London map the officers found in the horse's saddlebag provided more information when it led them to an address of one Sir Bertram Driscoll. Newly arrived from India, the nabob and his Indian servants gave the investigators a full account of how Firoz had joined them in their travels. The rest of the staff reported their fear and suspicion of him from the start.

Though Sir Bertram swore to the Bow Street Runners that Firoz had been traveling alone, Ian was not about to rest assured that Queen Sujana had not sent additional assassins to carry out her revenge.

In truth, he was shocked that she would go so far as to try to take his son in exchange for Prince Shahu's death. Twisted woman! Ah, well. Perhaps

401

it had been only a matter of time before one of the temperamental foreign powers that he dealt with decided to punish him personally for his role in negotiating arrangements that were not always to everybody's liking.

Finally, Ian was informed, much to his relief, that no charges were to be brought against him.

This, the officials concluded, was a clear case of natural justice and, indeed, of self-defense, since the man had been trying to strangle him to death. Ian assured them that if they had further need of him, he would continue to co-operate, and he told them where he could be reached, either at Winterhaven or at his own Cumberland estate.

He planned to stay out of London until the sensational storm of gossip died down a bit. He had no doubt that it would be all over Town by tonight that the mild-mannered Marquess of Griffith had slaughtered a man in broad daylight for trying to kidnap his son. He did not think people would blame him, generally, but he knew for sure that they would be flabbergasted to learn that he was capable of such ferocity. He had no desire to linger here and answer *their* questions, in turn. He could almost hear them now. Where had he learned those skills? Had he ever killed anyone before? Private man that he was, he shuddered with aversion at the thought of all their prying, which was sure to come.

No, the most pressing matter at hand was to get

to his son and his fiancée and make sure they both were safe and not too badly traumatized by their ordeal – and by what they had seen him do.

Finally walking out of the magistrate's sweltering chambers around sunset, he and Lucien got some food and soon were on the road, riding their horses through the cool night air. Neither of them had spoken for miles, all talked out from the grueling day, each immersed in his own thoughts.

The westward road away from London stretched like a silver ribbon ahead, and Ian kept thinking about Georgiana. The way she had looked at him after the fight. The way she had reached out to touch him and then stopped herself – had actually been afraid to touch him. Ian knew he could not have that. He was used to a Georgiana who could hardly keep her hands off him. She had gotten him addicted to her boundless affection and he'd die if she took it away from him now. He'd never had love like this before.

It tormented him to contemplate Georgie rejecting him, but Lucien's words of a few hours ago had helped. When asked if he thought what he had done was wrong, his friend had answered, 'All I can tell you is I would have done the same thing, and so would all my brothers. *And*, I wager, so would Georgiana's brothers, too.'

He knew Lucien was right, and that bolstered his determination to hold onto her esteem, even if he had to take drastic measures. His work and training had made him a master of manipulation; he knew just how to seduce people by giving them their heart's desire. By God, he was not going to lose her love now that he had finally won it, nor Matthew's, for that matter. He felt exposed, but could not bear for them to see him as a monster, and so he had come prepared, with a special gift for his son and potent plans in mind for winning back Georgiana.

At last, Lucien signaled him to the turn ahead, leaving the road for the gated drive up to Winterhaven. Ian was pleased to find the iron gates locked, just as they should be, the gatehouse being guarded by four armed sentries. As Ian and Lucien paused to let their horses breathe, the guards told them that Damien had posted lookouts all around the boundaries of the property, and so far, all was quiet.

Welcome news, indeed.

'They're waiting for you up at the house, my lords.'

'Thank you very much,' Lucien replied, nodding to them as the men shut and locked the gates again.

From there, it was an easy canter up the avenue of young plane trees that led up to the house. The drive meandered through the sprawling park, past the fine gardens with their ornamental lake, and of course, past the elaborate stable block. Ahead, the pale limestone mansion took on a pearly glow in the moonlight.

They dismounted wearily and dusted themselves off a bit as grooms and footmen came out to attend the horses and men alike.

Ian took a swig of wine from the flask in his jacket and paused to stretch his back a bit. He looked up to scan the skies for signs of rain, but it was clear. The waxing crescent moon gave off little light. The sky was very black, the stars garish in their brilliance.

He put his flask away and followed Lucien into the house. Damien greeted them in the drawing room. Ian shook his hand and thanked the elder twin for his help, also thanking Alec when he sauntered in with his air of effortless ease. Ian told them briefly what had transpired; then Damien's wife, Miranda, came bustling in, gave him a sisterly kiss on his cheek, and informed him that he had the room next to Alec's for the duration of his visit and that he could stay for as long as he liked. He smiled at her take-charge warmth, remembering the days when Damien had actually tried to foist her off on him before the fierce colonel had come to his senses and realized the woman had been made for him.

'Oh, and by the way,' Miranda added, twirling around to face him on her way out of the drawing room, 'Georgiana put your son to bed half an hour ago. Third floor. Turn left at the top of the stairs. He's probably still awake if you want to see him.'

'How is he?' he asked uneasily, but he trusted

Miranda's female judgment on this, since Damien's countess was raising twin sons of her own.

She sighed. 'Georgie was able to calm him down a lot – she's so good with him! Still, you're his papa and I think a visit from you would make him feel much better. He was worried about you. So was Georgie, for that matter.'

'We all were,' Alec interjected.

Ian cast him a look of gratitude. 'Where is your cousin?' he asked quietly.

'She went out walking in the gardens. It's such a beautiful night.'

He nodded. 'Thanks,' he said to all of them, then sketched a bow and went up to check on his son, the canvas knapsack containing Matthew's present slung over his shoulder.

He found his way up to the third floor as Miranda had instructed. He peeked in a few of the nursery room doors, all of which had been left a few inches ajar so the wee ones could have a little light shining into their rooms.

At last he spotted his son, and for a moment he stayed where he was, just staring at the boy, so little in his bed.

But when a strange sound came from inside Ian's knapsack, it summoned Matthew back from the outer reaches of dreamland. His long-lashed eyes flicked open. Noticing Ian in the doorway, he sat up all of a sudden. 'Papa!'

Ian slipped into the room with a smile, set the knapsack down carefully by the wall, and crossed to take his son into his arms. Matthew hugged him, and for once, Ian really allowed himself to hug him back.

'I'm so proud of you, Matthew. You were so brave today!' he whispered.

'As brave as you, Papa?'

'Braver than me. As brave as Uncle Damien fighting against Napoleon.'

'Really?'

Ian nodded, pressing his lips together against the tug of emotion that clouded his eyes. 'I'll never let anyone hurt you, son. Do you hear?' he whispered. 'I'll always keep you safe, no matter what I have to do.'

'I know, Papa. That bad man's not coming back anymore 'cos Uncle Alec said you kicked his arse!'

Ian laughed, squeezing his eyes shut and tightening his embrace around his child's little frame. God bless Alec. He always knew what to say to the kids. Probably because the rogue still was one himself, at heart, and always would be.

'I know I'm not allowed to say those words, Papa, but Uncle Alec told me this time it's all right and Aunt Miranda said so, too.'

'Yes, this time I would have to agree. So, what do you think, Matt? Are we going to be all right, then?'

He nodded, resting his small hands on Ian's shoulders. 'I'm all right, Papa, but you should have a word with Miss Georgie. She was crying, but she didn't want me to know.'

'I'll do that, son. Now, then.' Changing position, he set Matthew on his knee. 'That reminds me about something very important that I want to tell you.'

Matthew tilted his head back and looked up at him attentively.

'When I thought about what a good job old Hyperion did today in letting us know you were in trouble, something occurred to me,' Ian said in a musing tone. 'I thought to myself, you know, there's one thing every boy needs.'

'What's that?' Matthew piped up.

'Go take a look in my bag over there, and you'll see,' he replied with a mysterious smile.

Matthew gave him a curious frown, then slipped down off his lap and crossed the room to investigate the canvas knapsack Ian had left by the wall.

'Careful!' he warned softly.

Kneeling down to open the bag, Matthew suddenly let out an exclamation of wordless astonishment. He reached into the knapsack and carefully lifted out his present.

'It's a puppy! Papa, can I keep him?'

'Of course you can. That's why I gave him to you.'

Matthew carried the small speckled pup over to the bed, where it bounced around a bit, not quite awake. It climbed on Matthew, tail wagging. The boy laughed in delight, and Ian couldn't stop smiling.

During his endless interviews with the authorities today, he had sent a message to Tooke asking him to track down a suitable dog for Matthew. A blend of spaniel and some sort of terrier, the fuzzy little creature was white with a few black blotches.

'He won't grow up to be enormous like Hyperion – I mean, you won't be able to ride on him. But Mr Tooke said these dogs are very smart. His spaniel side makes him extra loyal and his terrier side makes him brave.'

'He's the best puppy in the world, Papa!'

'Well, he's yours. What are you going to name him?'

'Robin!' Matthew answered without hesitation.

'Robin?' Ian repeated in quizzical amusement, but he would not have dreamed of protesting. 'Very well. Robin it is.' He would have expected the child to go for the obvious, Spot, but his son was proving to be quite a complicated little fellow.

Chip off the old block.

'Well, my lad, you and Robin need to get some sleep.' He held up the covers for Matthew, who scooted back into bed. The puppy continued prancing around him until it, too, found a comfortable position, snuggling up close to the boy. Matthew looked at his new pet and giggled again in pure delight.

'Matthew,' he started in a musing tone as he smoothed the covers over his son's chest. 'Would it be all right with you if I asked Miss Georgie to marry me?'

'*What?*' He tore his gaze away from the puppy and stared at Ian, wide-eyed.

'Well, you see, that way she could come and live with us, and look after us.'

'And play with us?'

'Yes.'

'Like a real mother?'

'Yes, son. Just like a real mother.'

'Yes, do, Papa! Please! Miss Georgie's all the kick!'

Ian laughed softly as his heart clenched. He bent to give his son a kiss on his head. 'Another of Uncle Alec's expressions, I take it?' he murmured knowingly.

'Huh?'

'Nothing. Good night, son. Good night, dog, er, Robin.' He straightened up and headed for the door to go and find Georgiana.

'Papa?'

Ian paused at the door and looked over his shoulder one more time in question.

'I hope she says yes.'

'Don't you worry, Matt. She will.'

I'll make sure of it.

Tranquil gardens rolled on before her, silvered by starlight. Night-blooming flowers shyly opened to release their delicate perfumes into the silken summer air. Constellations shone among the water lilies in the glassy reflection of the ornamental pond. An unseen nightingale warbled its lonely song.

As the breeze whispered through the trees and

bushes, Georgie wandered restlessly along the grassy banks of the pond until she came across the blanket covering the ground, left behind from their earlier picnic with the children.

Matthew had been clingy and unsure after the kidnapping attempt, but Georgie had already begun to see improvement in the resilient child. When she thought about how close they had come to losing him, it made her physically ill.

She had only learned afterward how it had all unfolded. One of the other maids had come forward and revealed that Sally and Scott had suggested a game of hide-and-seek with Matthew in the park, but when the girl admitted that the two murdered servants had been secretly courting, the true picture emerged.

The couple had suggested the game because 'hiding' together had afforded them a perfect excuse to sneak away and steal a few kisses – and that was all the opportunity Firoz had needed.

The violence that followed had summoned up frightening memories of Janpur for Georgie, and made her wonder when her brothers were ever going to arrive. After all, Colonel Montrose had given them a mission to complete.

She was unsure, too, about Ian's angry words to Robert today, that Gabriel had nearly been killed in fighting against Queen Sujana's henchmen. Had he minimized her brother's injury to avoid scaring her? And where was Papa, for that matter? She hated being parted from her family almost as much as she despised being parted from Ian.

Ian . . .

Oh, what was she to do about him?

When he had gone after Firoz, she had seen a side of him that she had never dreamed existed. Not that she felt Firoz deserved any particular mercy, but the savagery that had emerged from her oh-so-civilized diplomat struck a jarring and discordant note against the calmly rational, justice-minded man she knew.

At the level of instinct, the strength and virile power of this new, savage side of Ian thrilled her. She had lost most of her nonviolent Jainist principles inside Janpur Palace, after all, when she had nearly caused her brothers' deaths. It was naive delusion to deny that sometimes violence was necessary to protect the innocent.

But at the same time, she had never guessed that Ian had that sort of fury bottled up inside him. It made her uneasy to wonder what else lurked beneath his polished surface. And it made her wonder once again how well she really knew this man she had promised to marry.

Every time she thought she finally understood him, some new side of Ian emerged. It was disturbing. Would she ever really know him at all?

But yet, whoever he was, he for his part had accepted her completely, flaws and eccentricities and all. He had made that sentiment clear when he had presented her with her new ankle bells.

Now she was learning that her champion of humanity had a dark and dangerous wild streak. So, did that mean that she, in turn, would run away?

At this point, she doubted it would do her any good even to try, for in truth, she already knew she belonged to this man, body and soul.

Standing at the water's edge, lost in her thoughts, she became aware of someone watching her. She turned, searching the shadows, and saw that it was he.

At first she saw only his ebony silhouette, tall and commanding against the deep blue darkness of the garden. But then, when he knew she had spotted him, he prowled slowly out of the gloom, silver-dappled by starlight and shadow.

Georgie could not move, mesmerized by the silent potency in his stare. His green eyes were luminous in the dark as he moved toward her with the rangy grace of a big, predatory cat. Her heartbeat quickened, and all her skin began to tingle at his nearness. There was something altogether new in this night, anticipation, a surge of electrifying awareness.

He must have gotten off his horse only a short while ago, she thought as he neared, for his black coat still held the dust from the road. He looked so different – gruff and rugged, in need of a shave. There was a grim set about his mouth tonight, narrow and unsmiling, a fierce intensity in his burning eyes. Seeing him like this and remembering anew what he was capable of was both intimidating and unsettling . . . and yet, strangely arousing.

He greeted her with a hand pressed gently into the small of her back as he bent down and kissed the corner of her mouth.

She turned to him and pulled him into her embrace, trembling with relief that he was here, and safe. 'Oh, thank God you're free,' she whispered. 'I feared it would be days before they'd let you go.'

'No, I'm cleared,' he murmured. 'There'll be no charges pressed.'

'What other news?'

'Nothing you need to worry about right now, my sweet.' He brushed her hair back gently behind her shoulder. 'I'm here now. Everything's going to be all right.'

She pulled back and gazed at him somberly. 'I didn't know you could do that sort of thing, Ian.'

He nodded, avoiding her gaze.

'You frightened me,' she said.

He turned to her with a piercing stare. 'Are you frightened now?' he whispered.

She didn't answer.

'Don't quit on me, Georgiana. I want you too much to let you go. I need you,' he breathed.

'But you've hidden from me so carefully. I see that now. I want to *know* you, Ian.' She clasped his lapels with anguished insistence. 'How can I love you properly if you won't even let me know you?'

'Know me now. Know me tonight.' His hot whisper at her ear sent a delicious rush of pleasure cascading all the way down to her toes.

Standing behind her, he gripped her hips and held her, nuzzling her neck and luring out her wantonness with his smooth kisses. She recalled his words before the tiger cage at Janpur.

Make no mistake, Miss Knight. He may look tame, confined in that cage, but this animal is wild. He's probably wondering right now how soft and juicy you would taste if only he could be allowed to sink his teeth into you . . .

The cage was open now, and Ian bit her neck gently in teasing love play, the hunger in his masterful caresses too deep tonight to be denied – as if he no longer had the will to keep it under control. What was the point, now that she knew what he really was?

As his fingers kneaded her hips, holding onto her with a captor's touch, she knew with breathless certainty what he wanted, needed, tonight. She had a feeling, too, that he wasn't going to give her much choice. Overwhelming pleasure, that he would supply, but tonight His Lordship seemed disinclined to heed her hesitation.

Standing behind her, he brushed her hair to the side and deepened his arrogant kisses on her nape. Georgie moaned softly, swiftly becoming swept away by his beguilement. His every touch spelled her seduction. Oh, yes, she knew what he wanted. She could feel it in his touch tonight that he was not taking no for an answer – as if she had the power to deny him!

When she turned around in his arms, he sank down onto his knees on the soft, grassy turf before her, encircling her waist with his strong arms. He descended slowly, kissing her body everywhere as he went down, warming her skin through the ethereal white gauze of her gown. On his knees before her, he worshiped her body, kissing her breasts and stroking her center until she was on fire.

Time had lost all meaning, but all she knew was that she couldn't stand to have her dress on anymore. She wanted the silken air against her skin, his sweet weight atop her, and nothing more. She didn't care in this moment what the consequences brought. She had to have him, now.

He pulled his coat off, his vest, too, as if he were too hot for clothing on this summer night.

Georgie was quivering, enthralled by the smell of him and the hardness of the thick corded musculature over which her hands glided so lovingly. As he heightened her pleasure with endless caresses, her knees became too weak to hold her.

A moment later, she was naked, lying back slowly on the blanket under the stars. Ian finished undressing and came down into her arms, his bare chest warm against hers, his kisses utterly luscious. From the corner of her eye, she was aware of the starlight that spangled the pond's smooth surface beside the place where they lay.

The sparkling light danced across her eyes like magic as Ian entered her; she was panting as she caressed his chest, his arms, reveling in every inch he gave her.

He was trembling with passion, raw and fierce yet tender, taking everything as he possessed her, giving all to her in return, giving her his full self, with all its shadows and mysteries. Rising up onto his hands above her, he gazed down at her in dark devotion as he claimed her in a deep, slow, and total taking. There was pain, and, she believed, a small amount of blood, but not to have joined herself with him here and now, forever, would have been more painful by far.

Bliss was born as the act of love intensified, their ardent kisses soul-deep, their breath mingled, his maleness gloved inside her core. She held onto him in exquisite passion, surrendering to him, body and soul, as they achieved orgasm together. He came hard inside of her, one massive pulsation after another; his low groans faded down to exquisite whispers.

'*My love.*' Running her fingers through his hair, she kissed his brow. 'My dearest Ian. Never believe that I could give up on you. I never could.' Her words were still breathless, but her whispers overflowed with love. Georgie slid her arms around his neck. 'You'll never lose me, my darling. No matter what.'

'Beloved,' he breathed. Closing his eyes, he bowed his head and kissed her gently, their bodies still joined as one.

They remained like that as the nightingale warbled, and the breeze rippled the stars' reflection in the lake.

CHAPTER 15

They were married a few days later in the drawing room at Winterhaven – a small, private ceremony by special license, with family only, children included.

It was all rather spontaneous in how it came about – no fancy dress, no grand feast, just a lovely wedding cake for good luck. There was none of the pomp that might have been expected of this grand alliance that had been in the making for centuries.

The ring was a simple gold band, the flowers came from the garden, as many pink and white roses as could be plundered from the bushes, and some pretty purple flowers, too, whose name Georgie did not know.

The joyful day helped erase some of the darkness that had intruded in their lives in the form of Queen Sujana's henchman.

But . . . as they joined their hands in matrimony, both attentively heeding the preacher's words, Georgie was aware that in some ways, the man to whom she had given herself, and was now pledging herself for the rest of her days, was still an enigma to her.

His face was stern and serious, intently focused, as the preacher recited the age-old words. Handsomely clad in a dark blue morning coat, Ian was nothing short of beautiful. The white-gold daylight softened the hard lines of his high cheekbones and square jaw. His dark hair was neatly combed, his face freshly shaved and oh-so-kissable.

In all, she thought, as she sneaked another sideways glance at him, he looked neither as crisp and sleekly polished as when she had first met him, nor as dark and wild and gruff as he had been on the night of her seduction, but somewhere in between, as though the extreme ends of his inward pendulum were finally beginning to find a balance.

Balance and breath. Yoga had taught her these things.

He still seemed a tiny bit distant, perhaps having trouble accepting the fact that she had seen his barbarous side that day in the park. In truth, she was relieved to have visual proof of it at last, for she supposed that despite her initial surprise, she had always rather known it was there, sensed it, deep down.

Eastern philosophy maintained that darkness always lived in equal measure with the light. Only in trying to deny the dark's existence did it become truly dangerous, and besides, she did not wish to live in an illusion, believing him to be perfect. Who could relate to perfection? She was far from perfect herself, and yet he had accepted her.

She vowed to accept him with an equally open heart.

Her only real worry on this good day was that maybe his distant air sprang from reminiscences of Catherine, his first wife, perhaps from some lingering uncertainty about his decision at last to move on past her memory. To come back fully into the land of the living.

Georgie linked her fingers through his and gave his hand a gentle squeeze, prepared to anchor him to the here and now.

He glanced at her with a soft little smile, and her heart danced. Yes, she thought, she had full faith in love to light the way as she traveled into her new life ahead, shadowed as it was by the secrets that he kept.

Bravery, fortunately, had never been a trait she lacked. As her new husband slowly opened to her in time, then she would see what she would see. Until then, she must be patient; but one day, she vowed, when he was ready, he would trust her completely.

If she had planned to make her answer to his offer of marriage contingent upon first finding out what he had to hide, then she wouldn't have made love with him. But this was Ian, and she knew down in the marrow of her bones that nothing he had inside of him could ever negate her love.

They said their vows, and it was done.

She was a married woman – Ian's wife, and

surrogate mother to Matthew, who had served as their ring-bearer.

Society might have gasped at the apparent suddenness of the match, but then again, Society still had Ian's battle in the park to chew over. That should keep the gossips busy for a while.

For now, there was much to celebrate, and so they did.

Eventually, though, as the day of their wedding waned, their new little family and bevy of attendants, servants, and armed guards borrowed from Damien's employ finally set out for Ian's ancestral pile in the north.

Ian had ordered his fine traveling chariot to be brought from London to Winterhaven, and from thence they set out in the most luxurious style, with no less than six horses speeding them homeward.

After a few hours' travel, they stopped at a pretty inn along the road and took their finest rooms for the night.

A night that they spent feverishly indulging in all the things from the *Kama Sutra* that Georgie had studied with such avid curiosity. Things from the temple carvings. Things they had longed to do before but hadn't dared.

Now that they were married, it couldn't be sin, but as they reveled together in wanton abandon, she was sure at the very least that it was delicious decadence. Ian took her from behind, and then later, invited her to ride astride him, and by diverse delightful methods, furthered her education in pleasure with consummate skill.

After hours of exertion, they lay in spent silence and quivering, boneless satiety, gazing at each other, caressing idly, exchanging lazy smiles.

'Ian,' she spoke up shyly after a time, 'there's something I've been wanting to say to you.'

'Mm?' He drew a weary fingertip along the line of her arm.

'I want you to know that I'll never try to replace Catherine in your life. She was your first wife, and Matthew's mother, and I just wanted you to know I will honor her memory along with you, and do my best to raise her son in a way she would have approved.'

He stared at her for long moment, and then leaned near and pressed a soulful kiss to her swollen lips. 'Thank you. Darling, what a generous thing to say.'

Georgie paused, petting his chest. 'What was she like?'

'Sweeting, I don't want to talk about another woman on my wedding night with you.'

'You never talk about her. I confess, I've sometimes wondered why that is.'

He frowned, furrowing his brow as he studied her. 'Georgie? What's wrong?'

She shrugged a little, sulkily. 'Maybe it's a part of your life you don't feel you can share at all with me.'

'It's not that. It's just – that chapter of my life is closed. It's not something I like to revisit.'

She lowered her gaze.

'What?' Ian demanded patiently.

'I just want to make extra sure that Lady Faulconer was wrong, and that there's not some little part of you that's still in love with Catherine. I can't help it. Yes, I'm a little jealous of a dead woman. I know you'll think it's silly, but I just – I want you to love me best!'

'Georgiana.' He sighed and rolled onto his back, resting his hands on his middle. 'Dearest, did you know that my marriage to Catherine was essentially arranged by my parents?'

'No. How could I know when you'll never speak of it?' She could feel her cheeks heating with a blush. She hoped he didn't think her a possessive fool.

'Well, there you are,' he said. 'She was my son's mother, and for that, I will always honor her memory, but I was never in love in my life until I met you.' He rose onto one elbow and gave her a wicked look. 'Shall I prove it to you?'

'Oh, *Ian*. No! Stay away from me, you insatiable beast,' she purred not-too-convincingly. But it wasn't long before she surrendered with a giggle to his silken efforts, and soon, the master of persuasion made love to her again . . . and again.

And again.

The summer sky was cobalt blue, with stacks of puffy clouds drifting over the neat quilt-work of Cumberland's rolling hills and sheep-dotted meadows. After nearly a week of traveling, the day had come that they were to arrive at Ian's country house, called Aylesworth Park, after the old earldom that his family had long held before being raised to the marquisate. Aylesworth, likewise, gave Matthew his courtesy title as Ian's heir.

Georgie brimmed with cheer and excitement as she snuggled the boy on her lap, both of them gawking out the carriage windows at everything.

Meanwhile, Ian sat across from them, watching their enthusiasms with a faint smile, yet growing strangely quiet as they drew close to his ancestral home.

'Look, Mama, it's Hawkscliffe Hall!' Matthew exclaimed as he pointed to a distant hilltop. He seemed to enjoy using her new title. He turned to her in excitement. 'Morley's house! It's a real castle!'

'My goodness. Hawkscliffe Hall? Well, that sounds familiar.'

'That's where your cousins grew up – and your father,' Ian reminded her. Then he told her about his boyhood jaunts, traipsing across a mile or so of peaceful countryside to go and play with Robert and Jack and Damien and Lucien and Alec.

She listened, thoroughly charmed by his recollections of roaming these green valleys with his band of trusty mates, chasing the herd of wild ponies that lived in the fells, and playing around the crumbling ruins of a far more ancient keep nearby, rumored to have belonged once to Uther Pendragon, the father of King Arthur himself.

'Oh, I'll want to see that!'

'Then you shall. Maybe we'll have a picnic there,' he suggested.

'Hooray!' Matthew cried. 'Can Robin come?'

'What, you without your shadow? Of course he can,' Georgie said, giving him a doting rumple of his hair, and they continued on their merry way.

The carriage stormed down the road that ran alongside the River Griffith for a time. Ian said the river that had inspired the name for his family's latest title poured out of the Scottish Highlands and disappeared somewhere in East Anglia.

'Oh, the bridge is out,' Georgie murmured, pointing to the broken remnants of wood that she could see had once spanned the wooded ravine through which the River Griffith plunged more fiercely.

'Yes,' Ian said, seeming to withdraw before her eyes. 'A storm destroyed it years ago.'

'And you never had it fixed?' she remarked. 'Mustn't that make it all the more difficult to get to the house?'

'Yes, well, actually, I enjoy the seclusion,' he said sardonically. 'It keeps unwanted guests away.'

'Hm.' She found it quite unusual that a man normally so scrupulous about his responsibilities could have tolerated leaving an important job like that undone.

He seemed to read her thoughts. 'Bridges are

very expensive to build. Anyway, I'd rather wait and have an iron one than simply throw a wood bridge up and have it be destroyed again. The weather in spring,' he said, choosing his words with care, 'can be very wild in these parts. The water rises steeply when the Pennine snows begin to melt.'

'I see.'

'Matthew, can you tell Mama what do we do around the river?'

'Be careful! Stay back!' he chimed in.

'Very good,' he congratulated his child, who promptly beamed.

'Look!' Matthew suddenly cried.

Georgie peered out the window, following the direction of his pointing finger. 'Oh, it's one of your neighbors. A tenant, perhaps?' she inquired, spotting an old woman on foot ahead, walking alone by the side of the road. 'Don't point, Matthew. It isn't polite.' She pulled his hand down.

As their traveling chariot barreled on down the road, Georgie offered the old woman a small, friendly wave – but got only a piercing stare in return. Her fleeting glimpse of the elderly woman before they passed by revealed a hunched and bony frame draped in a hooded cloak, her gnarled hands gripping a basket of apples.

'What a strange old lady.'

'The old midwife. She's known as Mother Absalom,' he murmured. 'My mother was always in awe of her. Nowadays, I'm afraid, she's quite mad.'

'Really?'

'Yes, she lives in one of the cottages that I provide for the elderly staff who have served my family.' He shrugged. 'If you hear her talking to herself, don't be alarmed.'

'Why should I be? I talk to myself all the time.'

He cast her a fond smile.

'Poor old thing,' Georgie said in compassion, glancing out the window, though Mother Absalom was no longer in sight. She couldn't help wondering if the cool look in Ian's eyes suggested the possibility that Mother Absalom might have helped deliver Matthew – and failed to save Catherine from the childbirth fever. 'Maybe we should stop to say good morrow. She's very old. Perhaps she needs a ride.'

'Don't let her frail look fool you,' he countered. 'She's a sly old piece of leather, I assure you, full of vinegar. When your cousins and I were small, we were scared to death of her.'

Georgie chuckled. 'Really? You and all my mighty Knight cousins, terrified of an old woman?'

He nodded sagely. 'We were sure she was a witch.'

'Maybe she is,' she shot back, but Matthew's wide-eyed blanch at this possibility roused a laugh from her. 'Oh, poppet, I'm only jesting.'

'You see?' Ian said in a reasonable tone. 'Wherever she's going, she can fly on her broom.'

'You are bad.'

'No,' he murmured, giving her a smoky glance, 'I'm merely in a hurry. I'm eager to get to my bed.'

'Are you tired, Papa?'

'Mm,' he answered, staring at Georgie.

Her cheeks heated even as she sent him a pointed smile that chided archly, *Not in front of the boy, my wicked husband.*

The carriage slowed as they arrived at the towering wrought-iron gates of Ian's property, monogrammed with an ornate letter G that matched the one emblazoned on the carriage door. A ruddy-cheeked fellow manning the little gate-house came forth to admit them, and offered a cheerful tip of his hat as they drove by.

Matthew waved to him excitedly.

'Oh, the grounds are beautiful beyond compare!' Georgie exclaimed, staring out at the picturesque clusters of bushes and shady stands of trees.

'Capability Brown,' Ian said.

'What's that?'

He smiled. 'Never mind. Just enjoy them.'

'Look at the huge weeping willow tree, it's magnificent! That is a willow, isn't it?'

'Yes.'

'We don't have them in India, but I've always heard about them. Oh, and what's that? That white thing beyond the trees. A garden folly?'

'No, that is Catherine's monument,' he answered in an even tone.

Georgie looked over at him in surprise.

'Mother's gone to heaven with the angels,' Matthew informed her in a sage tone.

Georgie turned to the boy with a startled glance, then smoothed his hair tenderly out of his eyes. She could feel Ian staring at her, and when she looked at him again, some dark shadow lurking in the depths of his green eyes warned her that this wasn't going to be easy.

But it was too late to turn back now, nor would she.

The carriage progressed down a hill, then up a gentle rise, and as the trotting horses bore them around the graceful stone fountain in a cloud of dust, the house came into view ahead.

Georgie's heart beat faster as she peered out the window at her new home. Large and white and imposing, the house had sharp, clean lines carved with pristine symmetry and neoclassical precision. It was built on a grand scale, the lofty, columned entrance looming at the top of a wide flight of stairs.

She glimpsed the uniformed staff hurrying into their places to greet them. The servants formed a neat row near the porte-cochere, where their chariot presently glided to a halt.

Georgie was used to managing a household. In India, indeed, she had run two for Papa, and had overseen a number of charitable homes, as well. But she could admit to a trace of nervousness at the prospect of meeting all her new domestics.

Ian might love her more deeply than he had his first wife, but that didn't mean the staff might not resent her out of loyalty to their dead mistress. No matter, Georgie thought. She was determined to win them over for the sake of creating a harmonious home environment.

Ian handed her out of the coach and soon began the introductions, starting with the tall, gaunt butler, Townsend. Housekeeper, cook, footmen and maids, grooms and groundskeepers, all greeted her with humble courtesy.

When Ian presented her to them, in turn, Georgie gave them a small speech she had prepared for her new household, giving them her thanks for their welcome and expressing her confidence that they would all get on quite happily.

Afterward, she went down the row meeting them individually, smiling at their bows and curtsies as each one stated what posts they kept in the house. While she conversed with this one and that in brief measure, Ian went over to stare with an appalled look at the huge mound of climbing yellow roses that were flourishing so richly by the wall.

'My God!' he said, looking up to survey how their thick blooms and thorny vines had surmounted their trellis, had grown up around the first-floor window, and seemed to be trying to swallow the house.

At his low utterance, Georgie looked over. 'Gracious, what are you feeding those roses?' she cheerfully asked the head gardener. 'You must give me your secret. They're stunning.'

'They're ghastly,' Ian muttered.

She looked at him in surprise. 'Why on earth do you say that? They're roses, my lord. They're beautiful.'

'They're horrid. Eh, the smell is choking, they're covered in thorns, and drawing swarms of bees. They're a damned hazard!'

'Oh, they're not so bad. Come on, you.' Laughing, she slipped her gloved hand through the crook of his arm and tugged him affection-ately toward the door, resting her head on his arm.

The way she touched him was not lost on the silent servants, though Georgie did not notice the tacit glances they exchanged.

'Mama! Papa! Wait for me!' Matthew came running after them with Robin scampering at his heels.

Ian followed with his hands politely clasped behind his back as his butler gave her a thorough tour of her new home. Georgie eyed her husband now and then in suspicion as Townsend led them from room to room.

What was wrong with him? she wondered. He really was acting a wee bit strange. She still did not understand his quarrel with the roses. Perhaps he just didn't like being here, plain and simple. Perhaps old memories assailed him here in the home he had shared with Catherine.

Well, it had been his idea to come here, Georgie

reminded herself. The remote location would help to keep her and Matthew safe in case any more of Queen Sujana's men tried to hunt them down. Come to think of it, even that broken bridge could help protect them, as it made Aylesworth Park all the more difficult to reach. They had had to come by a roundabout way themselves. Only people familiar with the place would know how to get here. So, in that regard, she felt quite safe.

She wondered if Catherine had felt safe here, too.

Continuing on with their tour, she kept an eye out for a wifely portrait of her predecessor displayed in some prominent place; her curiosity about Catherine was becoming acute, but there was none to be found. If pictures of her had existed, they had been taken down.

Georgie was beginning to find the whole thing very strange.

When she expressed polite admiration for a handsome sideboard in the dining room, Townsend looked pleased and informed her that the previous Lady Griffith had chosen it herself.

'Ah,' Georgie replied, but as their tour moved on, it was difficult to glean much about Catherine's personality from studying the decor of the house. Each room was tastefully appointed with rich fabrics, safe colors, elegant but wholly predictable choices. Everything was in the best taste, but whose taste? she wondered. That was the question, for there was nothing individual or distinctive about one square foot of the Prescott showplace. Perhaps the architect's firm had also designed the furnishings, for it could have been anyone's home – or nobody's.

'Darling, were you and Catherine married long before her death?'

'Less than a year,' Ian answered.

'I see. So, all these lovely rooms were done by—?'

'Mother.'

'Ah, of course.' This was the home Ian had grown up in, after all.

'Now that you mention it, I think we're due for some changes,' he whispered diplomatically in her ear.

She grinned.

But when they went upstairs and approached the lord and lady's adjoining bedchambers, she detected an icy turn in his demeanor. 'Ghastly,' he said again under his breath, glancing around at the gold and scarlet bedroom in distaste.

She turned to him, losing patience with his gloomy attitude. 'Are you quite all right?'

He blinked, as though drawn back abruptly to the present by her tart tone. 'Of course. Forgive me. The long journey seems to have taken a toll on my agreeable nature.'

'I daresay. You're ruining my fun! Maybe you should go and take a nap.'

He snorted.

'Please do, if it'll improve your humor.'

'My dear, I shall leave you to settle in. I have a few matters to attend to, anyway. Damien's fellows will want their instructions.'

'Right.'

He bowed to her. 'I will see you at dinner.'

'Ahem!' she said pertly as he started to turn away.

He glanced back and raised a brow at her in question.

She tilted her head, angling her cheek toward him and tapping it with an expectant smile.

Some of the tension eased from his taut countenance. 'Ah, how could I ever forget?' Looking very much the besotted husband, he returned to her, bent, and gave her offered cheek a tender kiss.

The butler coughed in astonishment and studied the curtains.

'You must always kiss me, coming or going,' she reminded him with a flirtatious smile.

'Especially coming,' he murmured with a potent gaze into her eyes.

'Wicked man.' She hoped old Townsend didn't hear.

'I will see you at supper, my love,' Ian said softly. He bowed again. She caressed his arm as he pulled away.

'I love you,' she called after him as he went out the door.

He sent her a rueful smile over his shoulder, but he didn't say it back. He didn't have to.

She could see it in his eyes.

★   ★   ★

Over the next three or four days, Georgie observed that Ian's mood grew increasingly distant. He did his best to try to hide it, and when the night came, he still made love to her with all of his usual, passionate vigor. But every now and then, she felt that moody isolation creeping over him, taking him away from her in some vague way she could not quite define.

As the days passed, his brooding aura deepened, and he became ever more withdrawn. She asked him if he wanted to talk, but of course he said no. She saw him on more than one occasion standing by the river, staring down the ravine at its churning flow.

The most bizarre behavior that she witnessed in him, however, was when she stepped outside and found him with a pickax, tearing out the yellow roses that climbed up the side of the house. She stared in astonishment to find the marquess mud-flecked in his shirt-sleeves, covered in sweat.

'What on earth are you doing?'

'Uh – um – they were in need of a trim. Actually, I'm thinking of tearing the house down. Would you like a new one?' His chest heaved as he paused, squinting against the sun. 'It's old, you know. Out of fashion. I was thinking, maybe, something neo-Gothic?'

She stared at him in disbelief.

He rested the pickax over his shoulder and paused to gulp a swig of water. 'Was there, er, something you wanted?'

'N-no.' Even if her mind had not been rendered blank by his odd behavior, she wasn't sure she would have dared protest, let alone remind the famed peer that he had gardeners for that sort of thing. Instead, she just shook her head and went back inside.

When he had finished tearing down the roses, he discarded the whole pile by throwing it in the river. She stared out the window in alarm as Ian watched the yellow clumps disappearing downstream. He seemed to be in his own world, and clearly, it was not a happy place.

She turned to ask the servants discreetly if they had any notion of what ailed their master, but they fled when they saw her coming, as though they anticipated her bewilderment. Instead of offering answers, they rushed back to their tasks in conspiratorial silence.

Something very strange was going on around here, and Georgie had no idea what it was. She wondered if even Robert, Ian's closest friend, could have explained this to her.

But whatever demon haunted her husband, the destruction of the roses seemed to appease it for a few days. Once more, her amiable mate became his gentlemanly self again.

Eager to reclaim a sense of normalcy, Georgie suggested a picnic the next day. Whatever was bothering Ian seemed to have begun when they had arrived, so, she reasoned, perhaps it would help to get him away from the house for an afternoon.

To that end, she let him and Matthew choose the spot.

They did not go as far as the ruins of Uther Pendragon's castle. Ian did not want her to leave the grounds – for safety's sake, he claimed, though somehow she wondered if there was more to it than that. Grateful merely that he was human again today and not some shadowy beast, Georgie did not care to argue.

Before long, a large blanket was spread out on the grass in the shade of a huge oak tree, along with a low folding table and a few large pillows for them to lounge on.

The servants helped set up their simple luncheon, then withdrew to a respectful distance. Meanwhile, Ian indulged in kicking a ball around with his son. The spotted pup raced around them, yipping gleefully and occasionally disappearing in the tall grass.

Georgie was profoundly relieved to see Ian enjoying himself, carefree for once. Matthew was as delighted as ever by the attention, protesting with gusto when Georgie called to the pair to come and eat. They lingered at their game while she applied a bit of muscle to the corkscrew, struggling to open a bottle of chilled white wine to share with her handsome lord.

She gazed at him in unstinting admiration as he strode toward her in bone-colored trousers, loose white shirt-sleeves, a dark brown neckcloth casually knotted, and a single-breasted waistcoat of sky-blue and tan pinstripes. He looked beautiful, she thought, and thankfully, sane again.

'Need some help with that?'

She handed the stubborn wine bottle over to him with a smile.

'Papa! Come back!'

'Time for lunch, Matt,' he replied as he uncorked the wine bottle with ease.

'But I'm not hungry! I want to play!'

Ian sent her a twinkling glance. 'I think it's your turn to entertain him.'

'I'm not half bad at the old kick-to-kick, I'll have you know. I did grow up with brothers, after all.'

'I don't doubt it, my love, though you may be the first marchioness ever to possess that skill.'

She laughed, and he leaned down to give her a kiss.

'Papa, somebody, play with me!' Matthew insisted.

'That boy needs a little brother or sister,' Ian said softly.

'In due time,' Georgie murmured with a smile. 'Matthew, Papa is going to eat now!' she called. 'Why don't you try kicking the ball against the tree and let it bounce back to you? We'll watch.'

'All right.' He heaved a long-suffering sigh.

'There,' Georgie said to Ian in a low tone. 'Now perhaps you can have a nice glass of wine with your wife, and a little peace.'

'Hope springs eternal,' he said sardonically.

She laughed and lifted her empty glass, and Ian

poured for them both. He sat down across from her and they both began helping themselves to the simple luncheon fare, cold meats that she would not touch, cucumber sandwiches, potato salad, some cheeses and fruits, and soft rye bread.

Georgie was glad she had come up with this idea. A relaxed afternoon together on a balmy summer's day was just the thing. More important, it provided her with the perfect chance to try to find out what was bothering him.

Slanting a probing glance his way, she noticed him rubbing his shoulder. 'Sore?'

'Bit of a twinge. Can't say I'm used to swinging a pickax.'

'No, I should hope not. Here. Let me help you.' She set her plate aside, got up, and knelt behind him, massaging his sore shoulder.

'Mmm, that feels good.'

'You know, darling, yesterday – that attack of yours on the roses was a little strange.'

'Eh, I couldn't stand looking at them anymore.'

'Why?'

'They were ghastly. Honestly, aren't you glad they're gone?'

She lowered her gaze. 'If it makes you feel better, then of course I am.'

'They were hers, you know.'

'Your mother's?' she inquired, recalling his childhood anecdote of gathering a bouquet for his mother and being punished for it, but Ian shook his head.

'Catherine's.'

'Oh!' she murmured, pausing.

'For such a well-bred girl, she really had some low and vulgar tastes.'

'Hey! Did you see how good I kicked it?' Matthew exclaimed, holding the ball triumphantly over his head.

All this time, he had been running back and forth, kicking the ball against the tree trunk, frequently missing altogether and having to chase it, and carrying on a chirpy monologue that he presumed they had been heeding. Now, however, little Lord Aylesworth realized in all his aristocratic hauteur that their attention had strayed from him. 'Watch me!' he ordered them. 'Papa, you're not watching me!'

'I'm watching you,' Ian called back wearily.

'No, you're *not*!' In a defiant show of temper, the heir to the marquisate drop-kicked the ball into the air. It flew up with impressive velocity, ricocheted off the underside of a thick gnarled oak branch, and careened down, meteor-like, onto Ian's plate. It knocked his food all over him, splattering him with potato salad and spilling his glass of wine across his lap.

Georgie gasped. Ian jumped to his feet with a curse, and Matthew's jaw dropped, his brown eyes growing perfectly round.

'Young man!' he bellowed. 'Get over here, sit down, and eat your lunch, as you were told!'

Georgie rose and sought to intervene with the

441

utmost delicacy as Matthew and his puppy both visibly cowered. 'Darling, he didn't mean to do it. I'm sure it was an accident—'

'Don't defend his actions. That was a thoroughly obnoxious stunt and he knows it! Get over here, Matthew, *Now!*' he thundered.

Matthew sidled over to the blanket and dropped into position, as ordered, suddenly making himself look quite tiny and pitiful, his shivering puppy huddled beside him.

'Matthew, I think you had better apologize to your father,' Georgie advised in an even tone.

'Sorry, sir.'

Ian leaned down slowly. 'You cannot throw a fit of temper every time you don't get exactly what you want. That is no way for a Prescott to behave! So help me, you will not grow up to be spoiled like your mother was! If I want to have a conversation with my wife, you will wait until it is your turn to speak.'

'Ian, that's enough!' Georgie exclaimed. 'The boy's been through a lot of late! You're scaring him – and you're scaring me.'

Her words caused Ian's jaw to clamp shut. He turned pale, staring at her for a second. Without another word, he reached down for a large table napkin, then straightened up again, pivoted, and began marching away, angrily brushing himself off with the cloth as he stormed off.

'You're leaving?'

No answer.

Georgie watched him in disbelief. All of a sudden, she felt her lungs seize up in response to his abandonment, and her temper frayed. 'Ian, tell me what is wrong!' she cried.

'Trust me, Georgiana,' he bit out, pausing only for a moment, 'you don't want to know!' Then he turned around again and kept walking, and he didn't come back.

Scared her, did he? No doubt of that. No doubt he scared his son. God, maybe he really was a monster. Just like Catherine had said. What kind of foolish monster ever hoped he could be loved?

Ian stood above the swirling river a short while later, his heart pounding. The broken bridge looked terrible, unmended as a gaping wound.

He closed his eyes, struggling for control with a slow, lengthy breath. The sound of the rushing river below filled his ears, and the scent of it teased his nostrils. If only he could make her understand!

He had been raised from the cradle with a lofty role to live up to, a gleaming family image to fulfill. He had worn this bright and polished steel armor for so long that it had fused into his skin. How could he rip himself open just to show Georgiana what he truly was?

Leave her her illusions. She did not really want to know.

Nobody did.

Yet he could not escape the feeling that the writing was already on the wall. She was going to leave him. It was only a matter of time. She was getting too close to the truth, just like she had with Queen Sujana. There could be no secrets with Georgiana Knight.

She'd find out, and then the only way to keep her would be to make her his prisoner, just like the beast he knew he was.

Only, Ian could not bear to make his bride unhappy.

When he flicked his eyes open again, the swirling waters of the River Griffith swiftly mesmerized him, always gliding by, catching against strewn branches and twigs, spinning leaves in the current. Spiraling miniature vortexes turned where the water seemed calm. Foamy rills, deadly rocks. One particularly jagged stone whose sharp edge matched the scar on his shoulder.

'Catherine!' His roar had echoed down the gorge.

'Let go of the horses, you brute! I'm leaving you, I hate you, you monster! Brute! I hate the very sight of you!'

'Hate me all you like, but I will not permit you to abandon your newborn son.'

'Oh, really? Watch me.'

He shut his eyes again, trying to ward off the memory. The past was behind him now, the future ahead, with Georgiana. *Please don't make me tell her.*

It was the first time in his life he'd had anything close to real love, and if he told her what had happened that night, she would run from him, and he might never get her back.

Honestly, he did not know how much more of this he could take. He was on the verge of going mad, consumed by guilt, never-ending dread that she might find out some other way.

But then again, surely he was aware that Georgiana had given him another chance after his display of violence in Green Park. He refused to squander it by informing her that he was capable of even worse than what she had seen. He didn't want her to know. He didn't even like to acknowledge it to himself.

No, he could keep this awful secret bottled up tightly inside him. He knew that he could. Keeping secrets, hiding his feelings, these were his forte, were they not?

She loved her humanitarian diplomat, her noble justice-maker, her man of reason. *Oh, Jesus, he was such a goddamned fraud.*

When he had taken it into his head to marry Georgiana, he had been thinking logically, not realizing that things would ever become so . . . *sticky*. He'd had no way of knowing how it would be when they had grown so truly close.

Intimate.

But how could their love go any farther with this terrible secret in his soul forming a chasm between them? And yet he was sure if he told her, she would be gone.

It was not lost on him that in a sense, he was doing the same thing to Georgie that Catherine had done to him, coming into the marriage representing himself as something other than what he really was. But he couldn't help it. He loved her so much. He would have done anything, been anything, to win her.

Somehow, he would fight this secret back into its cage and carry on in the hypocritically proper Prescott way, just as he had since that unspeakable night.

Henceforth, he would simply have to try harder to be the man she wanted, loved, needed him to be.

At the very base of it all, though, as deep as the dark silt and cold black river rocks, he knew that he did not regret a thing. He had told Georgiana a lie, true – he had told the whole world a lie – and now he had to live with it. But although it hurt, he would do so happily.

For Matthew's sake.

Matthew went down for his nap later that afternoon. After the boy had dozed off, safe in his bed back at the house, Georgie decided to walk for a bit through the grounds.

Her husband's brooding lately must have turned contagious, for she found herself still hurt and troubled by his abrupt exit from their picnic. Things had started out so well today, but now she saw that the trouble was still there, only hidden, just beneath the surface.

Lord, what had she gotten herself into? Married scarcely a week, and already her husband had barked at her, clearly wishing her to leave him alone.

Well, if that's what he wanted, that's exactly what he would get, she thought stubbornly. She wasn't going anywhere near the man until he apologized.

Wandering across the green meadows, Georgie took solace in the company of pale yellow butterflies that zigzagged across her path. Now and again, she could swear she sensed somebody watching her, possibly following her, but when she glanced back, peering over her shoulder, no one was there.

July had come. Her English-born husband thought this weather too hot, but Georgie was still used to India. She was comfortable, strolling through the sun-splashed parklands. Birds flitted about in the lilting fountain, and here and there, a rabbit nibbled the taller grasses in the shade.

She walked on. But when she spotted the top of the white marble obelisk beyond some robust saplings, she decided to go and have a look at Ian's monument to her dead predecessor. Maybe it would hold some answers about the mysterious man whose life she and the late Catherine both shared.

A meditative silence reigned in the gentle hollow from which the white marble needle rose to rake the azure sky. A tall square column that tapered to a pyramid at the top, the obelisk's setting was a perfect circle of crushed gravel, surrounded, in turn, by low boxwood parterres and a wreath of flower beds planted with violets and forget-me-nots, with burgeoning white azaleas here and there.

There were two curved benches where those who came to pay their respects could sit and remember Catherine in solemn serenity. Georgie wondered if Ian came here during those lonely hours when he wandered off away from the house.

She chose not to sit, but walked across the crunchy gravel to study the portrait of her predecessor inside an oval medallion set into the front of the monument. The picture showed an unsmiling, pale-skinned blond with brown eyes like Matthew's.

There was a Latin inscription scrolled around the portrait, but Georgie had never learned Latin and could only wonder what sort of lofty platitude it communicated.

She was studying it pensively when a thin, quavery voice behind her broke the silence. 'You've married the devil, my girl.'

Georgie nearly jumped out of her skin. She whirled around, clutching her chest. 'Oh, my word! Mother Absalom, is it?' She laughed in relief, recognizing the old midwife whom they had seen hobbling along the side of the road on the day of their arrival. 'Goodness, you gave me a start!'

'You *should* be frightened, dearie. I'd be, if I were you.'

'Ah,' Georgie answered with a bemused but

patient smile. She was glad that Ian had warned her the old woman was senile. Even so, her words were a little disturbing under the circumstances. 'No apples today?' she asked in a friendly tone.

The old midwife carried no basket now, but instead leaned upon a gnarled walking staff to support her wizened frame. She cupped her ear. 'What's that, dearie?'

'No apples,' Georgie repeated, smiling. 'I saw you on the road when we arrived. You had a basket of apples that day.'

'I've got leave to pick from that orchard!'

'Oh! No – I didn't mean that at all! I was only, er, making conversation.'

Mother Absalom's lined mouth worked belligerently.

Goodness, all told, she could see why her cousins suspected she might be a witch! The woman presented quite an ominous aspect, with her thick dark cloak, piercing eyes, and stringy gray hair falling free of its bun.

She swung closer, leaning heavily on her staff. 'So, how does it feel to know that you've married the devil?'

Georgie's eyebrows shot up. 'Lord Griffith?'

She cackled. 'The devil, I say! The Father of Lies!'

Georgie blinked in pure astonishment. 'He's not so bad, I'm sure.'

'Aye! He did this, didn't he?' Mother Absalom nodded toward the obelisk. 'Put the poor young harlot in her grave.'

'Georgie blinked. Good Mother, you mustn't blame my husband for the lady Catherine's death. It is only natural for a man and wife to want to have a child. Sometimes things go wrong. But that doesn't mean it's anyone's fault. Not his. And not yours. Sometimes, it's just – fate.'

'Fate? Bah! It wasn't fate that threw her in the river the night the bridge gave way!'

Georgie stared at her, paling. 'W-what are you talking about? The first Lady Griffith died of fever.'

'Foolish girl, you had better be smarter than that if you mean to survive this place. Fever? That's just the tale he told everyone to hide his wicked-ness. He is dark and wild and cunning, I tell you! But you are young and sweet, like this,' she said, pulling a ripened apple out of her voluminous cloak.

She offered it to Georgie, who took it, in a daze.

'*They* know what he did,' Mother Absalom said with a sly glance toward the mansion. 'Every one of them was there that night. They don't dare speak up, for fear he'll kill them, too!'

'I don't believe you,' she declared, hurling the apple away with a defiant throw. She turned back to Mother Absalom, who eyed her keenly. 'Foolish old woman! How dare you tell such ugly and terrible lies about m-my beautiful husband? He houses you on his property, no less!'

The ungrateful hag laughed at her. 'Pretty young marchioness. Blind girl! Watch your step

450

with him. There's room in these gardens for another monument. To you.'

She shuddered. 'Go away!'

'Ask old Townsend if you don't believe Mother Absalom,' she added as she began hobbling away. 'The master killed Lady Catherine with his own hands, and he'll kill you if you cross him, too. Beware, child, beware!'

Georgie stared after her in stricken silence. She didn't believe one poisoned word of the old woman's madness!

So, why, then, was she shaking?

CHAPTER 16

Confident that he had himself well in hand once more, Ian visited Matthew and re-established amity there. The most blessed virtue of children, he thought, was how quickly they forgave and forgot their parents' errors.

Wives, now, they were another story. Resolved to take his lashes like a man, he went in search of Georgiana.

A few hours had gone by since their quarrel and he still hadn't seen her. He knew this couldn't go on any longer. He despised fighting with her.

As the offending party, he knew it was his place to go to her rather than the other way around, and to tell her he was sorry for losing his temper and ruining their picnic.

He glanced in different rooms searching for her, determined to make things better between them, for without her, he was empty. He knew he had been difficult of late, but having had some time to think and will away his darker impulses, he was better now. All he really wanted was for things to go back to normal between them.

He was rather wishing they had never come here,

a sentiment that intensified when he finally located her in the ghastly red-gold bedroom fashioned for the lady of the house.

She was alone, sitting on the edge of her bed, her back to him. She was very still, gazing out the window, her dark hair falling in soft, loose ringlets down her back. Maybe she was waiting for her maid, he thought. It was nearly time to dress for supper, but she was still clad in the same pale, pretty walking gown that she had worn this afternoon.

'My love?' He hesitated in the doorway when he saw how her spine stiffened in response to his soft greeting.

Oh, dear. He knew Georgiana didn't hold grudges, but he had reason to fear that today she might not be so quick to forgive.

Vexing her was one thing, but his upsetting Matthew tended to drive the girl to rage. It touched him, how protective she was of his son.

'May I come in?'

'You may do as you please, I'm sure. It is your house.' She didn't turn around.

He bit his lip, her low, clipped words enough to warn him he was in for a row. He closed the door behind him, going in. 'I acted badly today. I'd like to make it up to you.' He paused to lean against the bedpost, keeping a wary distance.

When she turned her head and looked up at him slowly, his heart sank to find her blue eyes red and swollen. Obviously, she had been crying.

He gazed at her in tender remorse. 'I'm sorry, darling.' He moved closer, but when he laid his hand on her shoulder, hoping to take her into his arms, she jerked away.

He stopped.

She froze, keeping her head down.

He stared at her, bewildered by the fear in her sudden movement.

At a loss, his gaze fell, and he cast about for something to say in response, but it was then that he saw her traveling trunk, open, by the bed.

A week ago, it had been emptied and put away in storage. Now it was out again; there were clothes in it, and they looked hastily packed.

His stomach plummeted with sickening speed.

'Are you . . . going somewhere?' he asked, summoning up every ounce of his self-discipline to maintain an even tone.

'I haven't decided,' she said barely audibly. Then she turned her eyes to him again.

He furrowed his brow in hurt confusion. 'Georgiana?'

'Sit down, Ian.'

He obeyed, lowering himself to the space next to her on the bedside. She stared at him, her great, blue eyes filled with solemn intensity. 'I need you to tell me exactly what happened to your wife Catherine, or I'm leaving.'

As quietly as she had uttered the words, they still knocked the breath out of him. She studied his reaction, though he did his best to absorb

454

her ultimatum with at least an outward show of equanimity.

'I have been hearing . . . terrible rumors. If you don't tell me the truth, then I'm taking Matthew and I'm going to Hawkscliffe Hall, and back to my cousins to wait for Papa.'

He stared at the hardwood floor, his mind reeling, his pulse a slamming drumbeat in his arteries. He rubbed his mouth for a second in thought, and then looked at her guardedly.

She met his glance with piercing force in her eyes, her delicate jaw clenched with all the resolve that reflected the blood of the warrior clan that flowed in her veins. '*Don't* lie to me,' she whispered.

He dropped his gaze again and swallowed hard. *My God, I'm damned if I do and damned if I don't.* He stood and walked over to the window. He leaned against it and stared out at the still-sunny, peaceful evening. 'I don't want to lose you, Georgiana,' he said, staring blindly out the window.

'Then you'd better tell me what happened. Now. Can it be true, Ian? Are you everything I loathe?'

It would have hurt less if she had picked up a rapier and run him through. Struggling to absorb the blow that only she could deliver, he turned to her with pain in his eyes.

Her plump lips trembled as she held his stare from several feet away. 'Did you kill her?'

He shut his eyes. He squeezed them tightly, and then he lowered his head. 'It was an accident.'

'Oh, my God.'

He dragged his eyes open and stared at her in anguished pleading. She had risen to her feet, and one look at her shocked, white face assured him he had two choices: come clean or kiss her good-bye. World-class diplomat or not, it was too late now even for him to dance around the situation. And, in truth, he found he didn't want to.

This was the very thing he had dreaded most, but now that it had happened, he realized how very tired he was of carrying his secret alone.

He didn't bother asking who had told her. It scarcely mattered now. Probably one of the servants. Surely he had known that, sooner or later, one of them was bound to crack. Their little household conspiracy had lasted intact for five years.

'Promise me at least you'll listen,' he said heavily.

'Talk,' she ordered in a shaky whisper. 'Tell me if you loved her. Tell me how she died.'

'Loved her?' he echoed with a bitterness that rose up from his very core. 'I hated her, Georgiana. We hated each other.'

'You hated her, so you took her life, is that it? I've already seen that you can kill.'

He stared at her, stunned by the accusation. 'It was nothing like that. I was responsible for her death. But I didn't *murder* her, if that's what you're thinking!'

'Then, what happened?'

He looked away with an agitated exhalation.

456

'So help me, Ian Prescott, if you tell me one single lie with all your silver-tongued—'

'I will give you the truth,' he interrupted. 'Just please promise me you'll listen. Georgie, without you, I – have nothing.'

Tears rushed into her eyes. 'Nor I, without you. I don't want to lose you, either. But I don't even know who you are!'

'Do you really want to know?'

'Yes! Yes. More than anything,' she uttered quietly.

He dropped his chin to his chest, resting his hands on his waist. He studied the floor for a long moment. 'Within a fortnight of our wedding,' he said at length, 'it all went wrong. Disastrously so. But I never meant to harm her. I swear it on my father's grave. Ours was . . . an arranged marriage.'

She sat back down on the bed, moving a little unsteadily. 'Yes, you already told me that.'

'I only met her twice before we married. My parents chose her. I trusted them. And the truth was, I didn't really care. I wasn't the type to marry for love. Marriage was merely part of my duty.' He shrugged. 'There was something about her I pitied. Tried to protect.' He went back to lean by the window and stared unseeingly into the distance. 'The grand wedding took place in London. A line of carriages. Royal guests. Heads of state. Feast for a thousand. Nothing like ours.'

At his mention of their joyous wedding day, one crystal tear spilled from her eye and ran down her cheek. Ian watched it fall, longing to catch it for her, but he doubted she would permit his touch right now.

'Afterwards – well, she was so pure, so delicate, with such fine sensibilities,' he resumed in a bitter tone, 'that she could not face the . . . vulgarities of the marriage bed, as she put it. Can you imagine that?' He cast a dark glance out the window, leaning his shoulder against its frame. 'Women all over the world had gone out of their way to entice me. But my own wife couldn't bring herself to sleep with me.'

Georgiana looked away, not appreciating this information, no doubt. 'And?'

'I was patient with her, of course,' he replied. 'I began to sense that she was troubled. But when a fortnight passed and she still showed no interest in consummating the match, I began to take offense.'

She scanned his face suspiciously.

'I could have wed nearly any girl in England,' he explained. 'It did not sit well with my pride to be rejected by the one on whom I had bestowed the privilege of my title and my name. I was in my rights to claim her. Being continually pushed away—' He shook his head. 'It infuriated me. It *insulted* me. So, one night, I plied her with wine to ease her fears and help her relax. And then I seduced her.'

Staring at the floor, Georgiana folded her arms across her waist.

He knew this could not be easy for her to hear, but then again, it wasn't easy for him to tell. 'And she gave herself to me at last. Unfortunately, I soon realized the truth about why she had been refusing.'

She looked up at him from under her lashes with a glare. 'Why?'

'Catherine wasn't a virgin. A fact that she was desperate to keep me from discovering. But I'm afraid that I, ah, turned out to be a little smarter than she anticipated. You see, she asked me to get her more wine after we had made love. A fool's errand, naturally. It was the middle of the night by that time, and all the servants were a bed. I had no wish to wake them. We keep the wine cellars locked, of course, and I realized I had forgotten the key. I keep it in my writing table in the bedchamber, and when I walked back in to fetch it, that's when I caught her. Sprinkling a little vial of pig's blood on the sheets in order to deceive me,' he said in disgust.

Georgiana's lip had curled in revulsion. 'Pig's blood?'

'I would not have believed it either if I hadn't seen it with my own two eyes. I had heard about that trick, but I never thought . . .' He shook his head in lingering bewilderment, then gave another shrug. 'That was the moment I realized I had been betrayed from the very start.'

'Betrayed,' she echoed. 'Yet you said the match was arranged. Who else knew? Her parents? Yours?'

'I cannot say for certain. All I know is that both families pushed the match. Well, it wasn't as though she could simply come out and admit to her parents that she had allowed one of their stable grooms to succeed with her.'

'A stable groom!'

'Just so. Catherine had no wish to be disgraced, haughty as she was. She thought that if she played her cards right, she could have her cake and eat it, too. And I, well, I was the perfect target, wasn't I? Too straitlaced and bloody honor-bound even to let it cross my mind that I could have possibly married a budding harlot. My God, it was the one thing I swore I'd never do. Not after I'd seen all the pain and havoc that your wanton aunt, the duchess, put her children through.'

'Aunt Georgiana?'

'The same.' He nodded and sat down beside her again, falling silent for a long moment. 'Catherine was worse,' he finally admitted. 'At least the Hawkscliffe Harlot made no secret of her amours, but faced up to the consequences of her actions with some spine. My wife, no, she was a coward as well as a liar. I tried, you know. I entered into our marriage with every intention of being an honest, decent husband. In those first two weeks, before the truth came out, I did my very best. I treated her gently and with as much consideration as I knew how. I intended to love her . . . in time. And I had presumed, rather naively, that one day she might love me.' He looked at the floor again with a bitter smile. 'Unfortunately, she was infatuated with her stable groom.'

'So, what did you do?'

'Well, after I found her dispensing the pig's blood, the rest of the night involved a great deal of screaming on my part and crying on hers.'

'Did you strike her?'

He turned to her impatiently. 'Georgiana, do you really think I'd ever hit a woman?'

She flicked a chastened glance over his face. 'No. Sorry.'

He shrugged. 'Well, I'm glad you can at least see that. All I could do was browbeat her into making a full confession. Threats of social exposure worked better on her than anything else,' he added dryly. 'I made her tell me everything, though I loathed hearing it. How it had begun, how many times she had met with him, which of her servants had helped facilitate their liaisons. By morning, I had a clear picture of their involvement.'

'You must have wasted no time in dealing with it.'

'Correct. The next day, I dismissed her servants, ordered mine not to let her out of their sight, confined her to the house, then rode to her father's stables to put an end to this affair.'

461

'You mean you put her under house arrest. Just like you did me, back in Calcutta.'

He glanced at her uneasily, startled by the comparison, but he had no answer and continued with his tale. 'When I arrived at her father's stables, I found the man, and privately confronted him.'

'Did he challenge you?'

'On the contrary, he tried to blackmail me. My wife may have been in love with him, but he didn't care about her in the slightest. Amoral blackguard. Aside from pure sex, his interest in her had been rooted in gold from the start. He wanted a hundred pounds in exchange for his silence.'

'Not that great a sum, considering. Did you pay?'

'Hell, no. I would never allow myself to be black-mailed. I told him he had twenty-four hours to get out of England or he was a dead man, and that if he ever opened his mouth and said one word about my wife, I would hunt him down wher-ever he was, and kill him like a dog.'

'I see.'

'He fled.'

'I would,' she said dryly.

'He went to Calais. That rogues' haven.' He heaved a large sigh, musing for a moment. 'I was so relieved to be rid of the threat that he posed, that I'm afraid I then did something I am not proud of. It was, in hindsight, my main mistake – second only to marrying her in the first place.'

'What did you do?'

'I lied to her. Told her he was dead. That I had killed him. Most men would have, you know. But I tried to be better than that. I knew that my false words would make her hate me all the more, but I wanted him out of our lives for good, out of her head. I didn't want her entertaining any remote possibility that he might be coming back again, that she could find a way to be with him at some future time. I wanted her to know that it was over. And I told her this . . . because I wanted to hurt her.' He looked away. 'As I said, I am not proud of it.'

Georgiana gazed at him.

'Things got quiet after that. I knew I'd succeeded in hurting her, because she withdrew into herself. I continued to use my staff to monitor her every move. And then, nine months later, a child was born. But was he my child, the true heir to my ancient lineage and all my fortune? Or was he the lowborn by-blow of a stable groom? There was no way to know for certain.'

'Matthew,' she whispered, her eyes widening.

He nodded slowly. 'Matthew.'

Georgie gazed at Ian, mystified and upset by his unfolding tale, aching for him, for the pain and betrayal this woman had put him through. For his disappointment and humiliation.

Now the strained and distant relationship that she had found between Ian and his son when she had first arrived in England made sense. But she shook her head. 'You doubted Matthew's paternity?'

'For a long time, yes.'

'Not anymore, I hope? Surely you can see he is the spitting image of you. He's got your dark hair, your few little freckles, the shape of his nose,' she said softly as her stare trailed over his beloved face. 'He's you all over again. Even your nature. Calm and serious, clever and curious about everything.'

'And willful?' he suggested with a wry smile that reminded her of Matthew's flash of temper earlier today.

His own temper had already proved very dangerous, indeed.

She smiled back warily. 'Oh, yes, he's your son, all right. An aristocrat, through and through.'

'Which is why he will need discipline in life. Men in my position have too much power and gold and influence to be allowed to run amuck.'

'I do not disagree.'

For a moment, they gazed at each other in silence. Ian reached for her hand and she allowed him to take it. But although everything in her longed to wrap her arms around him, she held herself back.

'You still haven't told me how Catherine died.'

He nodded and released her hand, drawing a deep breath. 'As the months of her pregnancy passed by, I began to notice a change in her.'

'What sort of change?'

'For the better. She quit hating me quite so much. She became almost pleasant now and then. I deemed this a good sign and sought to encourage it. I thought, perhaps, she was beginning to forget her stable groom. I decided not to hire a wet-nurse for when the child came. I thought this would force Catherine to be truly responsible for the first time in her life. I knew she disliked me, and I was afraid she would reject the babe because of it. I thought if she were forced to feed the child from her own breast, this would strengthen the bond between her and the baby. Then the day came when she went into labor. Matthew was born in the afternoon, and the accoucheur informed me it was a boy, and that they both were well.'

'No fever?'

'No,' he whispered, lowering his gaze. He shook his head. 'I am sorry for that lie.'

She reached over and touched his arm. 'What happened, darling?'

He looked at her for a long moment, and something in his stare made her take back her hand. She twined her fingers on her lap in rising tension.

'Two weeks later, Catherine ran away.'

'*What?*'

'If I thought that woman had betrayed *me*, it was nothing compared to her betrayal of Matthew.'

Georgie stared at him, appalled.

'She just – left him,' he said. 'A newborn child. Barely two weeks old.'

'But, how could she? Why?'

'Remember her servants that I told you I had sacked? Well, through her former maid, the stable groom had secretly managed to get a letter to Catherine from Calais. He told her where he was, and urged her to flee me when she could, and come to him. So, for all those months that her behavior had improved, it was only because she was biding her time, knowing she was going to escape once she had given birth.'

'She planned on leaving Matthew even before he was born?' It was unthinkable.

'Just so. As for the man, I have no doubt he was still bent on extracting funds either out of me or from her family, in hopes that we would eventually pay to avoid the scandal. Anyway, that night – the night of the storm – I had gone over to Hawkscliffe Hall for supper and drinking and a bit of billiards with your then-bachelor cousins. They wanted to congratulate me on the birth of my son. They had no idea of all the trouble I'd been having since my marriage.'

'You never told them?'

'No. Not even my closest friends.' He shook his head. 'It was all so sordid. I didn't want them to know how I had been cuckolded. I feared they'd lose respect for me.'

Male pride, she thought, though she supposed she couldn't blame him.

'At any rate, when I returned from Hawkscliffe Hall, I found my household in an uproar and learned from my servants that Catherine had run away. Townsend said a carriage had arrived for her – the same maid and footman I had dismissed months ago from her service had remained loyal to their mistress, and had come to help her to effect her flight to France.'

'Oh, Ian,' she whispered in shock.

'I tell you, I was tempted to simply let her go and never have to see her face again, but I had a newborn infant in the nursery, and with no wet-nurse on hand, we had no other way of feeding him.'

'You're telling me she would have left her child to starve?'

'That is exactly what she did.'

Georgie's jaw dropped. She quite believed she hated this woman by now. Abandoning Matthew? And Ian, too?

'Under the circumstances, I had little choice. I was immediately back up on my horse and riding hard through the storm to catch up to her. By this time, I assure you, I had no feelings for the woman other than scorn, but I was not about to let the baby starve to death under my roof, whether he was really mine or not. I caught up to their carriage at the bridge.'

Anguish brimmed beneath his quiet tone, as though the words themselves were each a heavy weight. 'The footman was driving. He kept striking at me with the whip, but then I aimed a pistol at him and he realized I was not going to let this happen. He floundered, and I managed to grab the leader's bridle. I brought the carriage to a halt in the middle of the bridge. I got off my horse and went to pull her out. She and her maid were both inside, hysterical. Catherine somehow pulled herself together. She ordered her servants to stay with the coach while she got out and came at me – with a pistol.'

'A pistol!'

'Oh, yes. Charming, no? She said she hated me and that she'd kill me if I didn't let her go. She said, "You've got your heir. That's all you needed me for. Now let us be rid of each other for once and for all." I told her that notion would have suited me quite well, but I couldn't let an infant die from her neglect. So I grabbed her.'

'What about the gun?'

'Misfired. The powder got wet.'

'Thank God!'

'The fact that she had actually pulled the trigger, though, that enraged me. I threw the gun over the bridge into the river, and that's when I noticed how high the water level was. I looked around and noticed it was already sloshing across the bridge in places, weakening the joists. You could feel the whole thing swaying. The wind . . . was fierce. And the lightning was driving the horses to madness. It was all her footman could do to keep the team under control. Then all of a sudden, I heard a loud crack and the bridge lurched – Catherine screamed, but I still wouldn't let go of her. That was when the horses bolted, taking the whole carriage and both of her servants with them. In seconds, they were tearing off down the road and out of sight.

'That left only the two of us on the bridge. My horse was still nearby. I picked Catherine up and slung her over my shoulder to carry her back bodily to the house, since she refused to come of her volition. The way she fought, you'd have thought I was a marauding Hun carrying her off rather than her husband. When she elbowed me in the eye, I set her down fearing I would drop her – I didn't want to hurt her. She *was* still recovering from childbirth, after all. She tried to run—'

'What, after the carriage?'

'Yes. She was in such a screaming, violent rage by that point that I swear she barely knew what she was doing. Again, I caught her by her arm. I yelled at her. I said we had to get out of the storm. But she pulled away from me sharply, with a violent motion – and that was the same moment that the bridge cracked open. Right before my eyes, she slipped over the railing and fell into the river, and was washed away.'

Georgie stared at him with her fingers pressed to her lips.

'I ran to the edge and spotted her in the water below. It was all white, churned to foam. I couldn't see where the rocks were, but I threw off my coat and jumped in to save her.'

'Ian!'

'The current was raging. The water was frigid

and full of debris. God only knows how, but I managed to get an arm around her. I started to pull her to safety, but she continued to rage against me, though she was half drowned. She was like a crazed animal, like a cat, clawing me. I was so intent on dragging her out of the water that I didn't see the rocks that we were about to be driven into. I just felt the edge of them slam into my shoulder and the back of my head. I was knocked nearly senseless. I lost my hold on her.' He paused with a grim look. 'And that was the last time I saw her alive.'

Georgie gazed at him in somber silence.

'We found her body the next morning, less than two hundred yards downstream. We brought her back to the house, and that was when the lies began. I pledged my staff to secrecy about the circumstances surrounding her death. There was no need to embarrass the families. Hers. Mine. No need to spill her shame to all the papers. And above all, I would not allow the world to begin questioning my son's legitimacy.' He shook his head with a formidable gleam in his eyes. 'Not after watching what your cousins went through all their lives, thanks to their mother's indiscretions. I had to protect my son's future and his reputation. And my own,' he admitted as an afterthought. 'I could not stomach the thought of becoming an object of ridicule and scorn.'

He swallowed hard. 'So we dreamed up an honorable death for Catherine. Puerperal fever was an apt excuse, considering. I never told her family the truth. I never told my own. I never even told your cousins, my dearest friends. I didn't want anyone else involved in our private ugliness.' He paused for a long moment. 'Anyway, I was brought up to make a good show of things, wasn't I? We had the funeral and it was all as respectable as the wedding had been. It was the first time in our acquaintance that I could recall her looking genuinely peaceful,' he added in a sardonic tone.

'My servants made her up carefully with white powder, her bridal veil covering her face. With my son in my arms, I never breathed a word about the stable groom. I built her monument and mourned her with every proper sign of grief. Society proclaimed me some sort of tragic hero.' He sighed with a cynical shake of his head. 'But she wasn't all that had died that night.'

'What else died, Ian?' Georgie whispered.

'Any hope in me that I would ever know real love.' He looked at her sadly. 'That same hopelessness drove me to bury myself in work. Perhaps I was trying in some way to pay for my sins by helping others make peace, though I myself knew none.'

'Perhaps that made you understand its value all the more.'

'Perhaps. All I know for sure is that working full-force for five straight years without halt, especially during such difficult times for our country – Napoleon and the war and all – I wound up in some strange sort of dark fugue, spiritually, I suppose you might say. Desolate somehow. Your cousin Bel suggested that I might be exhausted. But it was not a physical exhaustion. It was . . . something else. Deeper. An emptiness. And that, Georgiana, was what sent me wandering off to Ceylon, where I was trying at last to make peace with my own private demons – without much success, I'm afraid. And then Governor Lord Hastings caught wind of my presence in the region, and asked for my help in dealing with the Maharajah of Janpur. I answered the summons,' he whispered, reaching over and gently cupping her face, 'and then, there, on the far side of the world, I saw you. Like the promise of love I'd always dreamed of, but never thought I'd know. I'd given up on hoping.'

'Oh, Ian.' She moved closer to him.

'You saved my mission in Janpur with your meddling, and now, once again, I find my fate in your hands, my sweet Georgiana.' He looked into her eyes in stark longing. 'Can you still love me, even though you know now what a fraud I've been?'

'You're not a fraud,' she whispered, pausing for a long moment as she tried to absorb all that he had told her. 'I think you're a man who tried to hold his family together with dignity, despite a huge and terrible betrayal. And you're a father who'd sacrifice what he holds most dear out of love for his son.'

'My honor,' he agreed barely audibly.

'But it isn't lost, my darling. It's right here.' She touched his chest, laying her hand over his heart. 'And to answer your question, yes. Of course, I *do* still love you. I'll always love you. Never doubt that.' She gazed into his eyes. 'Thank you for trusting me at last with your secrets. Now I can see why it took you so long to confide in me. If someone had done such things to me, I don't know if I could ever trust again. I love you, Ian. And I promise I will never betray you.'

'Does that mean you'll stay?' he whispered.

Georgie summoned up a tender smile. 'What, leave you? And that darling son of yours? That would make me an even bigger fool than she was. I'm not going anywhere, sweeting. This is where I belong now. With you.'

He shook his head, looking stunned.

'What is it?'

'I was so terrified that if I told you all this, I would lose you.'

'No. Not telling me, now, that would have been worse.'

He nodded solemnly. 'I understand.'

She leaned closer and kissed his cheek, draping her arms loosely around his wide shoulders. 'You know,' she whispered, 'I don't expect perfection from you – even though, for some reason, you seem to demand it of yourself.'

He covered her hand with his own against his chest and leaned his head against hers. 'Georgiana,' he whispered. 'Tell me one more time that you'll never leave me.'

'I won't ever leave you, darling. I could never bring myself to go.'

He turned his head and kissed her face. She lifted her chin as he sought her mouth. Her blood caught fire as he gently caressed her lips with his own and took hold of her hip. She wrapped her arms around him, parting her lips to invite his deeper kiss. He thrust his tongue into her mouth and moaned softly as he pressed her back onto the bed with a smooth motion.

She knew his intent by the way that he kissed her – and she assented to it heartily.

'Never leave me,' he whispered again as his clever hands began deftly unfastening her bodice. 'I love you.'

'I adore you, Ian,' she breathed, melting under his touch. She caressed his face and hair. 'No one should ever have hurt you that way. But I'm going to spend the rest of my life giving you all the love you need.'

'I do need it. I need you.'

'Then take me,' she whispered, looking into his eyes. 'I'm all yours.'

His groan was barely audible as his mouth swooped down on hers again in burning hunger, his fingers tangling roughly in her hair. He dragged her neckline down while she freed him from his cravat, in turn, and tore away his waistcoat.

'Hurry,' she panted.

'Wrap your legs around me.'

She obeyed eagerly as he lifted her skirts, then he mounted her in a fierce, needy, and passionate coupling. The whole bed rocked as they made love hungrily. She kissed him as he took her, certain she would never get enough of this man.

'Oh, God, Ian!' she fairly sobbed with pleasure, her heart brimming.

'I want to start over,' he whispered fiercely. 'I want a whole new life with you. Let's have a child.'

'Whatever you want, I will do it.'

'Sweeting.' He slowed, paused, stroked her flushed, perspiring face for a second, and looked into her eyes, a misty sheen of tears creeping into his for a fleeting instant. 'I'm so sorry I hid so much from you. I won't ever do it again.'

'I forgive you, love.'

'I just thank God you believe me.'

'Of course I do.' She captured his hand and linked her fingers through his. 'Just don't keep secrets from me anymore.'

He shook his head, the coltish forelock of his hair falling into his eyes. 'I won't. You have my word.'

'The word of a gentleman,' she answered with an unabashedly doting caress.

But the little smile he sent her from under his dark forclock filled her with that particular brand of thrill that only Ian Prescott could inspire in her. 'Not always,' he whispered.

'Thank goodness for that!' she declared. Then she laughed in luxurious pleasure as he proceeded to show her what a very bad boy he could be.

EPILOGUE

In the quayside hubbub of the Thames docks at London, smells from the fish market hung on the close summer air, while swirling seagulls cawed for scraps. The summer sun glinted in bright flashes on the deep olive river as innumerable small skiffs and fishing boats scuttled among the great square-rigged ships. From the nearby docks, where Georgie and Ian stood with Matthew, each holding a hand, they could hear the rhythmic cries of sailors throwing more muscle into their tasks.

They had left Aylesworth Park only a few days ago, hastening to Town after receiving word that her brothers' arrival was imminent. Her father, Lord Arthur Knight, was expected to appear with Derek and Gabriel. According to his letter, Papa had managed to join her brothers when their ship had docked at Portugal to unload some Indian cargoes.

Now the three Prescotts watched the ships eagerly, Ian pointing out noteworthy sights to his son. In all, they made a very proper English family, Georgie mused, holding a parasol over her bonneted head to ward off the midday sun.

They had arrived at the pier with two carriages: Ian's large town coach for the family to travel in, and a wagon to transport the new arrivals' luggage.

'There!' Ian said suddenly, pointing as yet another longboat full of disembarking passengers approached the pier.

Georgie drew in her breath, a smile breaking across her face. She looked on in breathless delight as her brothers and her sire soon climbed the ladder onto the docks. Derek sprang up easily, then turned to see if Gabriel required help; Papa remained below to steady their wounded warrior. Gabriel moved slowly, gingerly up the ladder. Georgie could only imagine how much the proud commander must hate his weakened condition, but for her part, she could only thank God he was alive.

'Why don't you go ahead and see them first?' Ian suggested softly, meeting her glance.

'You don't mind?'

''Course not. Go.'

She gazed at him in loving gratitude – then grinned, unable to contain her exuberance. Handing off her parasol to one of their servants who stood in attendance, Georgie picked up the hem of her skirts and rushed to the pier to greet her family.

Papa was the first to spot her as he climbed up the ladder after Gabriel. Tall and hale, still handsome and robust in his sixties, Lord Arthur swept off his bicorn hat and waved it to her with a grin from ear to ear, the sunlight gleamed on his thick white curls that had once been as black as her brothers' hair was.

'Papa!' Georgie pounded down the planks toward them, dodging tattooed sailors and fish-wives carrying crates of herrings on their heads, and in the next moment, she was in their arms, all of them hugging each other in joyous reunion. Georgie could barely speak, choked up with the knowledge that they had nearly been parted *permanently*.

She turned to Gabriel, wrapping her arms around him in a gentle embrace. 'I don't think I've ever been so happy to see you,' she whispered. 'How are you?' When she pulled back a small distance to study him, her stern eldest brother only nodded, his lips pressed into a taut line. She cupped his jaw, noting that he was thinner than before, and a trifle pale.

The traces of pain had been stamped into his rugged face, but his dark blue eyes were as deter-mined as ever.

Tears filled her own. 'My hero-brother. You saved our lives and nearly lost your own. But now you're finally here, and I'm going to take care of you until you're strong again.'

'Good, 'cause I'm a little sick of Derek,' he muttered dryly.

'Hey!' their middle brother retorted in mock indignation as the others laughed. 'Ungrateful bastard. He's had me waiting on him hand and foot!'

Gabriel cast him a sly grin.

'How now, where's my little girl?' Papa boomed.

When he opened his arms to her, Georgie lit up and flew into his embrace. 'You old rascal!' She hugged her father hard and then pulled back to stare sternly at him. 'No more adventures for you, sir! My nerves can't take it! Jack is going to have to find a new volunteer, because I'm not letting you go anymore. Do you understand?'

'Tut, tut, my dear.' With a fond chuckle, Lord Arthur pried her back and held her by her shoulders, giving her a once-over glance of distinct pride. 'Well, look at you: Mrs Married Lady!'

'Thanks to me,' Derek interjected.

Georgie turned, beaming at him. '*Derek.* Come here, you brilliant matchmaker!' She captured him next, and he returned her embrace with a roguish bear hug. 'Sometimes, you know, you are the very best brother in the world.'

'Aren't I, though?'

She rolled her eyes. 'Very well. Go on, say it.'

He flashed a charming smile. 'I told you so.'

She laughed at him, shook her head, and hugged him again. He returned her embrace for a moment longer, neither needing any words to ensure they both understood there were no hard feelings left over from their quarrel upon leaving Janpur.

'How's the war going?' she asked, pulling back.

He shrugged. 'It's going. Haven't heard anything since we left India months ago.'

'Are you still under orders from Colonel Montrose to lobby Parliament for more army funds?'

'Yes, God help me,' he drawled. 'I told Gabriel I'd handle this one myself. That way, he can concentrate all his efforts on getting well. By the way,' he added, glancing over as Ian approached, bringing Matthew down the pier to meet his new kin. 'King Johar found out about Queen Sujana's attempts to have us all butchered, and well, let's just say he took care of the problem in the Eastern fashion.'

'Oh, dear,' Georgie said, wincing at the amount of bloodshed that his words implied, but nevertheless, she was wholeheartedly relieved to hear it. If King Johar had ordered all of Queen Sujana's loyal henchmen beheaded or thrown to the tigers, or otherwise done in by some imaginative Eastern device, that meant there was nobody left to come after *them*. Now each night when she put Matthew to bed, she'd be able to assure the boy more convincingly that he truly was safe.

Ian was accepting handshakes and congratulations on their nuptials from Papa and Gabriel.

'Oh, look,' Georgie suddenly murmured to Derek, nodding toward their father, who had just been introduced to his new grandson. 'Remember that old trick?'

Derek rolled his eyes and laughed.

'Right here, m'boy,' Lord Arthur ordered Matthew, holding up his palm and pointing to it. 'Give me your best punch! Let's see what you've got!'

Matthew looked up at Ian with a puzzled glance.

'Go on, son,' her husband murmured, his amused look suggesting that he, too, remembered Lord Arthur's hallmark challenge from when he and all her Knight cousins were boys.

'Come on, lad! Have at you!' Lord Arthur urged. Matthew knotted up his brow, drew back, and punched his new grandfather's open palm as hard as he could, at which, predictably, the old man let out a bellow of pain. 'Oh, blast! I think it's broken! My, my, this boy's got a fist on 'im! I say!'

This, of course, was all part of the charade. Matthew looked around uncertainly at the adults and, slowly catching on, joined them in their laughter.

'Come on, Dad,' Gabriel muttered, clapping him on the shoulder. 'That trick is thirty years old.'

'It's new to him. Isn't it, lad?' Lord Arthur gave Matthew a cheery wink and rumpled his hair.

Matthew decided on the spot that a real grandpa of one's own was an excellent thing to have, and latched onto Lord Arthur immediately. The old nabob, in turn, looked completely tickled by his plucky young grandson-by-marriage, and took the boy's hand protectively.

For a moment Georgie watched them together, her darling father and her small adopted son, as they headed off down the pier hand in hand; then her gaze traveled over her brothers' dear faces. They both looked glad to be done with their long and difficult journey. Gabriel still had a lot of healing to do, and as for Derek, though his manner seemed as wry and carefree as ever, she sensed a grim seriousness beneath his outward show of breezy charm. It seemed that nearly losing Gabriel had affected him more deeply than he cared to admit.

'Come on, everybody,' she forced out past the sentimental lump in her throat. 'Let's go home.'

'Don't know if I'd call it home,' Derek said under his breath as he scanned the unfamiliar vista of London Town.

Georgie turned to him in surprise, lingering behind as Ian showed Gabriel up the pier toward the waiting carriages. 'You plan on going back to India?'

'When my mission is complete, yes. Ah, don't fret, sis. We younger sons have to make our fortunes somehow.'

'Maybe you'll meet an English lady and end up getting married here, too.'

Derek snorted. 'Why on earth would I do a foolish thing like that when the East abounds with dancing girls? Besides, I have to get back to my men. There's a battle on, you know. I should be with them.'

She gazed at him wistfully, and then he swept a gentlemanly gesture toward the pier, inviting her to go ahead of him. She did, hastening forward to direct everyone into the appropriate carriages.

'Are we all going to fit in there?' Lord Arthur inquired, glancing into the stately town coach.

'We're family, we can squeeze!' she answered brightly.

'Maybe not the best thing for Gabriel's wound,' Derek murmured.

'You all sit in the back. I'll drive,' Ian volunteered.

'What an excellent son-in-law!' Lord Arthur exclaimed, giving Ian an affectionate slap on the back as he strode past him toward the driver's box.

'Why, thank you, sir.' He flashed her father a charming half smile and waved his coachman off to ride in the servants' wagon.

'But, er, won't the town be shocked to see the Marquess of Griffith driving his own carriage?' her father baited him with a knowing twinkle in his bright blue eyes.

Ian sent Lord Arthur a devilish glance. 'Who gives a damn what the town thinks?'

'I say, Lord Griffith! Such shocking sentiments from a proper Prescott.'

'I know,' Ian answered dryly. 'It's all your daughter's doing. She's run amuck with all of our stately Prescott traditions.'

'Perhaps that is a boon,' her father said with a sage look as he lifted Matthew into the coach.

484

'Indubitably so,' Ian agreed. 'Come, then. All aboard!'

'I'll ride up here with you, husband!' Georgie said brightly, bounding up onto the driver's box ahead of him. 'If you're going to shock Society, I want to help!'

'Which is just as it should be – my loyal help-mate,' he replied, shooting her a smile of sardonic affection.

Then he helped her up onto the driver's box.

A moment later, as the four passengers all settled into the coach with a cheerful air – her father and Matthew and both of her brothers – they all plainly overheard the newlyweds' curious exchange from up on the driver's box.

'Give me the reins, darling.'

'But Ian, I want to drive this time—'

'Georgiana. Give me the reins.'

There was a long, stubborn pause.

Listening in, Lord Arthur furrowed his brow with the barest shadow of paternal worry.

But then the sound of a smitten feminine sigh floated down to them. 'Oh, *very well*, husband. Take them, if you must. They're all yours – as am I.'

'There now, princess.' Suppressed laughter softened his deep voice. 'That wasn't so difficult, was it?'

'No, not when you know full well that you're wrapped around my finger.'

'Oh, am I? I shall kiss that saucy grin off your lips if you're not careful,' the marquess purred.

'I dare you to try!'

Lord Arthur raised an eyebrow as a besotted giggle echoed down to them from the region of the driver's box, and indeed, it was some moments before the coach finally jolted into motion.

But at last they were underway, merrily rolling homeward.